THE BOOK OF JOBE

A TALE OF
VICTORIAN LIVERPOOL

A catalogue record for this book is available from the British Library

ISBN: 978-1-7395285-0-8

Cover Photograph

John Thompson

To an Angel, a Monk, A Frog and a Queen

I love you All

Chapter I

1886

The dockers paused periodically to catch their breaths and wipe away beads of sweat that ran down their foreheads and stung their eyes. Those that had them used crusted and filthy handkerchiefs to stem and dab at the rivulets. Those that didn't used forearms and fingers that left a smear of soot and dust across their brows. They looked at the crowd of idlers that had gathered around George's Basin and muttered their resentment toward them before once again losing themselves among the barrels and sacks being unloaded from the three-masted barque.

A young boy emerged from the shadow of Our Lady and Saint Nicholas, and, like an insect leaving the safety of a skirting board, froze, blinking in the sunshine that bathed him. A sudden itch freed him from his inertia and after satisfying it with a soothing scratch he moved past the yards and warehouses that were crammed into every available space and on to the margins of the crowd. All the time careful to protect his bare feet from those in the throng, who, eyes fixed firmly on the balloon in the sky, took a step backwards every so often in order to reset their balance.

Silky didn't know what all the fuss was about. To him it was just an over-inflated pig's bladder bobbing above the Mersey. He'd heard it was there to allow some nancy a bird's eye view to make sketches of the city, from which a painting would eventually be produced. He trudged on threading his way through the spellbound crowd with ease, his professional eye resting on half a dozen well-to-do targets in as many yards. Easy pickings were galore.

Albert Warburton's gaze, unlike those around him, wasn't turned to the sky. He scanned the crowd. It was comprised of people from every conceivable colour, constituency and walk of life the city had to offer. Rich and poor, old and young they all shared the same single-mindedness as necks craned they looked to the heavens. Albert was, as always, fascinated by the diverse melting pot that somehow managed to coexist and create the unique pool of life. He tightened his grip around the woolen-clad shins of his young son who sat astride his shoulders and risked a look upward at the cause of the mobs awe. He had to admit that the hot air balloon floating high above the Mersey was indeed a marvel.

A grimace replaced his look of wonder and he instinctively thrust a hand into his trouser pocket and, with a vice-like grip, held on to the small hand he found already in there. His son, sitting astride his broad shoulders was jolted forward as Albert craned his neck to peer down at the imp who the hand in his pocket belonged to. The urchin, snared and with no chance of escape, flapped and writhed with the shock of a hooked fish. On realising he was hurting the lad Albert immediately relaxed his grip, relieving the bone-crushing pressure while retaining his hold on the boy. He looked into the youngster's face with a stare that he hoped was, if not friendly, was at least benign. He wasn't shocked at the features that looked impudently back at him. They were, like so many of the city's children, sharpened and chiselled by hunger. "Your hands would be better employed helping the stevedores over there or perhaps scavenging cotton from under a scutching machine, my lad, wouldn't you agree?"

Silky stopped jerking at the mention of a cotton mill and looked mutely up at his captor, an anxious defiance etched across his prematurely wizened face. The fear that there could be Mill Men skulking in the crowd consumed him. The thought of the Lancashire cotton mills and the enforcers who paced the factory floors on behalf of their paymasters, the mill owners, filled him with dread. Their 'straight back' in hand they would silently stalk in between the grinding machines and bring the two short pieces of venomous rope, bound together with wax, down on the backs of anyone they found not bent double at their work.

He knew some of the men also doubled as hunters. Charged with returning those who had the temerity to flee the mills. Silky had lived the few months since escaping the mill in constant fear of them. He knew what was in store for him on being caught. Had witnessed what happened to those who had escaped and been captured. He'd be forced to walk to and from the factory floor, to work in and sleep in, rusted shackles that would rub raw to the bone. Causing him to leave bloody footprints wherever he went until the passage of time toughened his skin. The punishment diet of black bread and gruel would leave him relying on the kindness of others to share their meager rations with him. If that were not forthcoming he would be forced to creep out at night, his chains silenced by rags, to steal any food that the mill owners' pigs had left over. His heart thumped with the realisation that he had risked everything by ill-fatedly dipping the giant whose huge hand enveloped his own.

Albert looked away from the boy, ostensibly to scan the crowd and vendors surrounding it, but in reality, because he was unable to maintain contact with the boy's piercing blue eyes. As he looked first left and then right, his son who sat astride his wide shoulders, was involuntarily twisted and turned at the mercy of his father's every movement.

Finding what he was looking for Albert addressed the boy. "Do you have a name?"

Silky, presuming his captor had spotted a copper, remained mute. And would remain so on finding himself in the Bridewell or in front of a judge. He would rather be sent to Kirkdale Gaol or even onto one of the reform ships than be returned to the mill.

"On the other side of the crowd," said Albert, fishing around in his pocket with his free hand. "There's a woman selling penny pies," he held out a coin. "Here go and fetch three." On the boy taking the threepenny piece Albert released his hold completely. "Attempt to cheat me again and there'll be a consequence, do you understand?"

Silky, slack-jawed, could only nod in disbelief as he took the offered threepenny piece. He remained where he stood unconsciously rubbing his liberated hand.

"Off you go, then! Three penny pies!" stated Albert. "And make sure they're hot," he added, shooing the boy away.

Silky didn't need telling twice and he melted into the crowd in a dream-like-daze. There had been a twinkle in the unusually green eyes of the giant, a twitching of his neatly trimmed moustache, as if he were trying to stifle a smile and Silky became certain that he was the victim of some cruel jest. He spun around once or twice, positive he could feel the giant's breath on his neck, his fingers tightening on the threadbare collar of his shirt. But on looking back over his shoulder he could see that the boy on the giant's shoulders was still stationary. And still had the best view on the dock.

Jobe shifted slightly. Momentarily relieving the pressure on his thighs and unconsciously allowing the blood to circulate through his femoral artery and feed down to his lower limbs before settling back onto his perch and re-impeding the flow. Like the exchange that had just taken place below him he remained blissfully unaware of the paraesthesia that was building to a tingling buzz in his already numb legs. He was usually an avid student of the bustling docks. Happy to sit on an old copingstone, often for hours, while his father worked on an article. Observing and absorbing every detail of what went on before him. He was able to identify a clipper from a ketch, a schooner from a cutter, could tell the difference between a stevedore, docker or porter simply by looking at the chaff and scuff marks on their boots. If intelligence could be measured by attention span, then he was a genius.

But today Jobe had no time for the hustle and confusion around the dock. No interest in the myriad of cargoes being unloaded, their origins or their final destination. Today his usually insatiable thirst for information had been sated by the majesty of the hot air balloon floating serenely over the Mersey. It was tethered to a ketch anchored deep into the river, and, Jobe assumed from the stillness of its two masts, that a bilge keel had been fitted to either side of the boat to help with stability.

Jobe, through living on the high hills of Everton and his own father being a giant, was no stranger to spectacular views but he could only wonder at the view the artist aboard the balloon had, having never been so high as to share the sky with the seagulls and the clouds. It wasn't the voice of the man that shook him from his reverie but rather the tone and the realisation that it was being directed at his father.

Although Albert hadn't considered his small show of compassion anything than just that, a witness to the exchange deemed it as a threat to the very fabric of society itself. He approached Albert and addressed him with a well-practised air of superiority. "Do my own eyes deceive me?" he asked, his breath fetid with whisky and tobacco. "Am I to believe that you have just released that pick-pocketing scoundrel to go and prey on some other poor unfortunate?" The man was squat and well heeled, his pate shining through the greasy strands of his carefully combed-over hair.

Albert looked down at him "Actually I've released him on an errand. He's under strict orders to fetch myself and my son a penny pie," he replied blithely.

"Have you taken leave of your senses, man? I must say, I find it an outrage, nothing less than an outrage, for you to have released such a fiend back into the crowd—and with a tuppence reward to boot," whined the man, his high-pitched voice corresponding perfectly with his small stature.

Albert remained unperturbed. "I assure you he'll return with my pastry and it was thruppence, actually. I intend to make him a gift of a hot pie."

The man became exasperated, confusing Albert's light attitude with some hidden weakness of the mind. He began to wave his hands at the taller man, revelling in the spectacle he was creating. "Return! Oh, I'm sure he will, sir, and with a multitude of his High-Rip brethren. Why, once they hear that there's a fool at the dock who rewards attempted robbery and impertinence with thrupenny bits, I'm sure there will be a veritable horde. You, sirrah, ought to be dragged in front of a magistrate on the charge of incitement."

Albert remained a picture of composure under the verbal assault and, for the second time in as many minutes, fished around in his pocket until he felt the familiar shape of a threepenny piece. "Well, congratulations, my good man, although I could not accuse you of attempted robbery, your impertinence has certainly earned this!" he said flicking the coin at the man, its impact causing him to yelp. "Now good day, sir," he said drawing himself to his full height and looking down at the man.

Sensing he had made a grave error of judgement the man stamped his heel against the ground before disappearing into the crowd with as much dignity as he could muster.

Although Silky had experienced a moment of terror on being apprehended his brush with capture hadn't slaked his appetite for dipping. He'd made a mistake that was all and again rebuked himself; why on earth had he attempted to dip the giant? He'd been on his tiptoes just to reach his pocket! He'd had a lucky escape, there was no denying. One that he had already learned from, regardless of the leniency he had been shown.

He had never planned to be a pickpocket. Didn't belong to one of the many gangs that roamed around the town, usually under the direction of an adult accomplice. But he needed a way of feeding himself and he seemed to have a natural talent for dipping. Besides, he reckoned his years of forced labour in the mill, sixteen hour a day for what amounted to bed and board, gave him special dispensation. He only ever dipped the well-to-do, those who looked like they were, if not an actual mill owner, at least had some sort of financial stake in one.

He risked a glance up at the balloon and imagined the rich toffs marvelling at the finished article as they hung it on a wall in some fine gallery. Slapping each other on the back and congratulating themselves on constructing such a fine town, most of which they failed to notice, chose to ignore or were careful to avoid every day of their lives. But he wasn't arguing. He'd heard it was going to take the nancy another two days to finish his drawing, and if the balloon attracted crowds like this one, he wouldn't be going hungry for a while.

Unsure who the giant had spotted on his perusal of the vendors, but in no doubt that there was no better purveyor of penny pies than Maggie McGhee, Silky made his way to where she sat in the shadow cast by the Goree Warehouse, a tray of mutton pies spread before her. Spontaneously he spread his arms and sang the words. "How about four for three, Missus McGhee?"

"Penny a pie," came the stock reply from the dour faced barrel of a woman.

His talents wasted Silky shook his head and placed the threepenny piece into an outstretched palm, the lines of which were ingrained with flour. He cradled the pastries like newborn babies and carefully reentered the crowd, edging his way back to the giant who had liberated him, and, Silky assumed, his son.

The aroma that rose from the hot pastry both tormented and gratified him and he licked his lips as he looked down at the golden crust, enjoying both their sight and the feeling of their warmth against his body. His mind momentarily blurred by something approaching bliss Silky was, for once, oblivious to his surroundings. Specifically the fat man, who, the girth of his neck making it difficult for him to crane it and view the balloon to his liking, took a step back, transferring all his formidable weight to the heel of the riding boot that landed plum on the big toe of the bare-footed-pie-bearing-boy.

The shock was absolute. The pain extreme. The scream in keeping with both. Eyes screwed shut, mouth stretched wide he tried in vain to stop himself from hopping on one foot as he fought every sinew and natural reaction to keep his arms pinned to his side.

Two of the pies remained safely cradled into his chest but he could only watch in helpless horror as the third and topmost pie somersaulted in mid-air before descending and falling onto the ground in front of him. The pain in his toe forgotten Silky looked from the pie to the owner of the heavy foot in anger. He was incensed. "Look what you've gone and done!"

The man, tall but vastly rotund with a crimson complexion caused by a fondness for claret looked down at Silky, the bulbous, vein-ridden nose, that dominated his face twitching in revulsion as he realised it was the boy's bare flesh he had stepped on.

"Why, if you didn't have so many chins, maybe you'd be able to look up at the sky like everybody else."

The sphere that was the tip of the man's nose almost vibrated on hearing the laughter that greeted Silky's barb from one or two of the surrounding crowd. He stepped forward, planting his foot firmly into the fallen pie and ruining its pathetic contents, his turkey neck trembling with rage and effort.

"Ahh, that must've hurt you, trampling on good food," fumed Silky. He turned his attention to those who had dragged their gaze from the spectacle in the sky. "Keep an eye on this gent! I'll give you a silver shilling each if he's not on his hands and knees snaffling that pastry down his big fat gullet the instant you next look up at that pox-ridden balloon." His words were greeted by more laughter, those whose employment depended on them treating such a gentleman with well-measured deference, ensuring they added an extra element of derision.

Silky escaped into the crowd as the man, hand raised, took a step toward him. This is your reward for being honest he admonished himself, crestfallen. He considered eating the remaining two pies and getting back to dipping. Maybe he'd go back and have a go at the fat toff with the big foot. But something about the giant with the boy on his shoulders drew him back, and he knew it was neither the promise of a penny pie or the threat of consequences.

* * *

Try as he might Albert couldn't shake the interaction that had taken place on the dock from his mind. Images of the pickpocket's sharp angular face pervaded each step of the three miles it took to get home from the waterfront. The air became clearer as he reached the higher slopes of the Everton hills where his house was comfortably nestled and he sighed deeply, his focus still on the boy.

Although of similar size and stature to his own son, Albert imagined the pickpocket had a couple of years on Jobe. But where his son had the healthy glow of an eight-year-old, the boy was stunted and starving. Jobe's expressions still retained the inquisitive innocence of infancy something that, in all likelihood, the other had never experienced. The poverty and hardship of his young life plain to see in the bare feet and tattered rags that hung from, rather than covered, his body.

Despite all of this Albert couldn't help wondering whether the irate stump of a man who had confronted him had been right. He had to concede that the fellow certainly had a point. Had he done the right thing? He'd not only released the little street Arab, but also rewarded him with a pie and sixpence? Was the boy one of the High-Rip who were spreading so much fear throughout the north-end of the city? He thought it unlikely. The broken, bleeding nail of his dirty big toe certainly proved testament to the unfortunate fate of the third pie.

With another sigh, a little less strained than the first, Albert decided that he was indeed correct to afford the boy his liberty. It would do little harm to those in the crowd wealthy enough to own pocket watches and silk handkerchiefs to be relieved of them in order to help fill an empty stomach. He had been right to split the two pies between the urchin and his son and give the boy the tanner with a warning for him to get home before his good fortune was spent.

Thoughts of the pie brought his mind back to the present and he realised that the slurping sound that had followed him up the hill was the noise of his son sucking remnants of the unfamiliar grease from his fingers. "Jobe, there can't possibly be anything left of that pie?" he said, raising his eyes to the boy on his shoulders. "And remember, no mention of it to your mother." His last statement caused his moustache to twitch in thought and he reached up to take Jobe from his shoulders. Swinging him to the ground Albert brushed the pastry crumbs from the baggy pants of his velvet knicker-bocker suit and grey woolen socks.

The blood began to flow into Jobe's legs. The sensation of pins and needles making his legs felt like they were on fire. Following his father's advice he began to stamp up and down. While his father massaged his legs, his huge hands gently rubbing the meatless muscles, all the time explaining that the pain was only caused by the blood rushing to where it was needed. Although his legs still hurt the explanation made Jobe feel better.

Once back on his father's shoulders Jobe continued the exploration of his fingers and palms with his tongue in a futile attempt to discover any remaining vestiges of the pie. Now high on the rolling hills of Everton he turned to look back at the balloon lingering above the Mersey. The view he was met with nothing short of astounding. The roofs of Great Homer Street, Scotland Road and Vauxhall stretched all the way to the docks in a black confusion, punctuated here and there by church spires and chimneys and ending with the radiance of the Mersey that sparkled like a jewelled ribbon as the sun reflected from it.

The river was crammed from north to south with shipping that transported goods from all over the world. And looking down on it all was the magical balloon. But even its presence couldn't stop his eyes from wondering to the mouth of the river where the Mersey became the Irish Sea. The estuary held an almost mystical appeal to him and he closed his eyes, imagining the point where the sea joined the mighty Atlantic that stretched onto America, the place of his birth.

Jobe fancied he could remember parts of the journey aboard the Catalonia, the Cunard liner that had brought him from Boston to Liverpool. His mother would smile when he raised such ideas. 'Ach but you were just two, my love. It's your father's tales that you remember.' But then her smooth porcelain forehead would wrinkle as she listened to him describe his memories of porpoises swimming next to the ship or the haunting lament of the foghorn stirring him from his slumber when he would be carried to the deck to fall back asleep under a blanket of stars.

Jobe turned his attention back to the hot air balloon. He wondered if the artist could see him and his father. His father being a giant, Jobe thought it likely and gave a wave. He looked forward to seeing himself and his father once the painting was finished.

* * *

Jobe pushed down on the spinning top and watched in wonder as the colourful elephants that decorated its surface blurred into an unbroken line of red. He caught the plunger in his right fist and pumped it again, the mechanism converting his reciprocating motion into a rotational one. An image entered his mind, not so much an idea as an inspiration, and he pumped the handle harder, convinced that if he could just get it to spin a little faster it would rise from the ground and hover like the balloon he had seen with his father down by the river. Excited, he grabbed the top and put his full weight on it, attempting to induce as much power and speed as possible. The wooden handle snapped under the pressure and Jobe watched the device skew off on its side across the small foyer and into the dining room where it stopped, one of the red-cloaked elephants looking back at him accusingly.

His mother entered the drawing room with the broken top in her hand. Although she had been baking and was wearing an old pinafore, Jobe thought she was beautiful. She was forced to continuously blow a loose strand of dark hair from her deep blue eyes as she spoke to him, her elfin face contorting as she did so.

"D'you know how many children in the street I grew up in would kill for just a single spin of this top?"

Jobe sensed his mother's genuine emotion and wondered at it. "You've no idea of how lucky you are. Toys like this are precious," she continued.

"I was just trying to make it to fly, Mother," said Jobe, his explanation only serving to turn his mother's sadness to anger.

"So you threw it up into the air, is that it? You need to learn to appreciate what you've got and how lucky you are to have it." Kitty said as she proceeded to collect the toys Jobe had scattered over the thick rug that covered the floor, returning them angrily, but carefully to their box, which she then put on top of Albert's bureau.

"You shan't be having these back until you learn to respect your belongings," she chided him.

Jobe was about to speak when he heard the front door close, and a second later his father entered the room.

Albert immediately sensed the strained atmosphere. "What's all this? Have my two angels had a falling-out?" he asked, bemused.

"Oh, Albert, I'm worried he's becoming spoiled. He's broken his new spinning top. He's no regard for his belongings. I want him to know the value of the things he has."

Albert tucked the rogue piece of hair over his wife's ear and kissed her on the forehead before turning his attention to his son. "Well, that's certainly not like you, Jobe. Let's have a look at it. Maybe it was faulty." Albert looked around the drawing room floor. "Where is it?"

"It's up on your bureau with the rest of his toys. It's not faulty. He's thrown it into the air to make it fly. I've taken them all away until he learns their worth," explained Kitty.

Albert located the box and reached up for it. "Come now, Kitty. Haven't we agreed we don't want him to be deprived or to know want?" Albert nodded towards Jobe quietly sitting on the floor. "Just look at him. Not once has he interrupted or attempted to plead his innocence, and look at the rest of these toys, they're immaculate. How did he react to you taking his things? There was no tantrum or beseeching, I'll wager?" Albert was on his knees now, sorting through the box of toys. He took out the top and its broken drive shaft, fingering the splintered wood where the break had occurred. He looked at Jobe. "Can you tell me how it broke, Jobe?"

"Mother is right, Father. I was trying to make it fly," he confessed. "I didn't throw it in the air, though," he quickly added. He knelt forward and took the two parts from his father, explaining his aim as he provided a reconstruction.

"The top spins so fast that I fancied if I could make it spin just a little faster, it would take off, lift from the ground. So I pushed down on it as hard as I could, but it snapped instead of spinning." Jobe released the broken top to the floor and knelt back sadly. He looked at his mother. "I wasn't trying to make you sad, Mother. I'm sorry. I try to treasure each and every one of my toys."

Albert brought his hand to his forehead. "The boy is a genius," he said, more to himself than his wife or son as he scooped Jobe up and spun him in the air. "Eight years old! An absolute genius!"

This time, he did address his wife. "Don't you see, Kitty? He was trying to create enough downward pressure to enable the top to hover." He noted his wife's total bafflement and smiled. "Never mind." He kissed his son on the forehead as he placed him back on the rug before standing and taking his wife in his arms. "We've created an absolute genius," he said again as he bent and kissed her.

Jobe looked happily at his mother and father, glad that everything was harmonious again. His mother looked down at him, smiling now.

"Well, Master Genius, just be more careful in future, that's all."

* * *

Albert took out his pocket watch, aware that there had barely been time for the hands to move since he last checked, but unable to stop himself. He was also well aware of the hungry glances his watch was attracting, but for once decided to discard his caution.

He had more serious concerns. He scanned the bar again. Being at least a head taller than the rest of the clientele in the poorly renovated parlour, he was in no doubt that Potter wasn't in the room. Potter was never late. And the onset of worry began to gnaw deep within him, an odd sensation that he didn't enjoy. Deciding it was time to leave he drained his glass, flinching at the hot, unfamiliar liquid burning his throat. Why did people drink?

That question became more pertinent when, on opening the ramshackle door leading into the street, he was greeted by a man lying prone in the doorway. Albert shook his head but still bent, about to heave the drunk into a more comfortable position when he noticed the lice that crawled through his exposed chest hair. He retracted his helping hands and stepped over the obstruction. Without a word being spoken between them, three men who stood around a hogshead barrel drained their glasses and followed Albert.

The sun shone brightly above the street but neither its warmth nor light permeated into the dank and narrow canyon that remained in constant shadow. The black tenements on either side so high that the air itself was inert, creating a noxious atmosphere that Albert could almost feel pulling against the exposed flesh of his hands and face. His mind spun as he navigated his way through the refuse, sewage and uneven cobbles with a dexterity that belied his ignorance of the street. He wondered if he had misread Potter's note, but immediately disregarded the thought, Kitty had also read it and indeed directed him on how to reach the venue scrawled on it.

Potter, as tall as himself but even broader, enjoyed their clandestine meetings and wrung all he could from them by insisting they use a different public house for each of their monthly rendezvous. It seemed to Albert that the pubs had grown seedier and rougher over the course of the years, each one located deeper in the entries and alleyways than the one before. Albert often wondered how Potter carried out his reconnaissance and could only venture that he remained in the localities long after Albert had left. He couldn't blame the big man for attempting to wring maximum excitement from what must otherwise be a mundane existence serving Albert's parents on the Wirral peninsula.

His usually reliable and self-preserving powers of observation and awareness were heavily diluted by the tumult of anxious and apprehensive thoughts that cascaded through his mind and he failed to notice as mothers ushered their protesting, emaciated children out of the gutter and into the tenements and cellars on either side of him.

A heavy thud to the back of his head caused an instant explosion of stars before his eyes. His knees buckled, and he was on the verge of sinking to them. He shuffled forward, some unconscious strength keeping him upright, a desperation to avoid falling into the filth that covered the street as much as any sense of self-preservation. He spun around and, again more through instinct than sense, threw a wild and heavy haymaker just as the lead pipe was about to make contact with his head for the second time.

The wielder of the pipe was bewildered that the toff, big as he was, had somehow remained on his feet. He prided himself on his strength and ability to bring down an opponent with a single blow of his two-pound lead pipe. It always fell to him to land the blow that got the job done. The kicks and punches that followed, thrown by all three of them, as their prey lay prone and penniless, were purely for pleasure, fuelled by spite and hatred. For one of his victims not to collapse instantly into the gutter was nothing short of miraculous, especially when he had the element of surprise on his side. The thoughts raced through Bernie's mind as he trotted forward the couple of paces needed to deliver the second, and surely, killer blow. They also served to slow and weaken the strike that was aimed at the same spot on the back of the head but never reached its destination. Bernie was helpless to avoid the crashing blow from the huge right hand that brought his flow of thoughts to an abrupt end.

Albert leant forward and retched the fiery liquid he had just consumed on to the cobbles, adding to the plethora of human and animal waste that already festered there. With both hands on his knees, he looked up at the two remaining assailants. "I'd give it a bit more thought if I were you," he managed to croak.

The two men looked at their fallen comrade face down in the filth and then back at the colossus in front of them, who was busy straightening himself up to his full height, taking the time to wipe his mouth with a handkerchief as he did so. They glanced at each other for an instant before, decision made, they ran full pelt back to the safety of their abandoned hogshead.

Albert, unsure of his legs, waited for a second before approaching his assailant to pull him out of the filth he was quietly drowning in. The villain was a dead weight and it took all of Albert's diminished strength to drag him from the scum-covered-puddle and prop him against the soot-covered-wall.

"Yer wanna leave him in the gutter where he belongs. Nothing but shite anyway."

Albert slowly turned his head in the direction the voice came from; the movement still too immediate for the liking of his aching skull. It felt as though his attacker had found his way inside it and was busy hammering away with his lead pipe. Albert retched again, but his stomach was empty and his ribs ached with the exertion. The old woman who the words belonged to stood in the shadow of a doorway, her shape and face hidden by a swathe of black rags that seemed to float around her. Something about the woman affected

Albert more than an army of assailants and his heart sank. Children who had been dragged indoors by their mothers now flooded into the street and approached the unconscious ruffian cautiously. On seeing that he was no threat, they descended on him and in a silent frenzy tore at him, removing anything of value including the lead cosh.

His earlier dexterity and demeanour forgotten, Albert half-ran, half-staggered through the dank entry, buffeting from walls and splashing through pools of filth. He burst out of the alleyway and into the relative security and sunshine of Great Howard Street with such force that he shocked a match-seller who stood on the corner into dropping her basket of wares.

* * *

Kitty had just finished basting the roasting piece of meat and was flushed from the hot stove when she heard Albert come in. She entered the parlour where her husband was sitting before the unlit fireplace.

A wave of relief flooded over her whole being and her nerves ceased their continuous jangling. She understood the necessity of his monthly meetings with the mysterious Mr. Potter but couldn't for the life of her imagine why they took place in such surroundings.

"Kitty, do you know where this public house is, dear?" Albert would ask, unfolding a luxurious piece of paper in front of her. Kitty would take the paper and although the scrawled street name would cause her stomach to lurch, and more often than not provoke a flurry of memories, she couldn't help but marvel at the exquisitely fine paper.

As often as not, she knew of the pub, or if she didn't was always at least aware of the court, street or entry it was in. The meetings were always in the worst parts of her old parish or even less desirable neighbouring ones, and she would blanch as she gave him his answer and then directed him on how to arrive there by the safest and least unsavoury route. She had stopped trying to talk him out of having his rendezvous in such areas for fear he would stop asking her advice.

"Well, Kitty, if you're going to worry so, I shall have to stop asking your advice and not share my whereabouts with you," he had told her.

She instead mollified her anxiety by forcing Albert to repeat her directions at least three times, which would, please Lord, negate the need for him to spend longer in an unknown area, going deeper into the depths until he was lost in the honeycomb labyrinth of tenements, alleyways and courts. Still, she couldn't help trying to curtail Potter's risk-taking. "It's just common sense, Albert. Why not meet in the town? Why can't your father's man just come here?"

"It's Potter's prerogative, dearest, and if anyone were to see us… If Mother found out she'd stop our stipend and Potter would be in as much trouble as Father. More. She can't sack Father!"

Kitty put down her tea towel and, looking at Albert, noticed that his face, usually so rugged and robust, was pale and clammy, his breathing shallow. She sat on the arm of the chair he sank further into and stroked his brow. "Albert, are you hurt my love, whatever's the…Oh my…" Kitty tailed off as her hand traced the huge lump on the back of his head. "What happened…"

This time it was Albert's interjection, a raised hand, which caused her to trail off. She fell to her knees in front of him, hands in his lap, waiting for him to speak.

"I'm fine, dear, I promise. Physically, at least. I'll let you fuss over me all you want in a moment or two, but first please hand me Potter's last envelope from the bureau in the drawing room."

Kitty, although shocked and with a hundred questions that needed answering, got up and carried out his request. She returned with the envelope her husband had brought home a month ago stuffed with the precious pound notes. Now all that it contained was the beautiful paper with a pub's name and street scrawled on it in a terrible hand. It reminded her of Jobe's, although even at eight his writing was better. Thank God he was at school now and couldn't see his father in this state.

"What does the note say, dear?" asked Albert.

Kitty knew from memory, having given Albert directions at the beginning of the month and again that morning, but looked down at the note anyway. "It says Nonpareil, Luton Street," she said. She brought it over to Albert and again sat on the arm of his chair. "You see, Nonpareil, Luton Street," she repeated as she held the note in front of him while he held his hand up to his eyes.

"Yes, I knew already, and it's the one off Boundary Street, just under the railway arches?" he asked, his hand still massaging his eyes.

Kitty's nerves began to jangle again but she forced herself to stand, tall and bright. "Yes, that's the one, Albert. Now, c'mon, I want a proper look at this head of yours, and to know where and how you got such a coggie, although I can well imagine. Didn't I warn you they call the place Sebastopol on account of how rough it is!"

* * *

Kitty flinched on numerous mental levels. The sheer size of the man was cause enough; he was bigger than Albert even—hugely tall, long-limbed and broad in the chest—though none of his intimidating size was portrayed in a face that shone with geniality. He was obviously from, or sent by, Albert's family over the water. And that was where the greatest shock lay; he was addressing her as Madam.

"May I speak with your husband, Mr. Albert Warburton, please, Madam?" the big man repeated.

Kitty, to an extent, recovered herself. "Yes, that is, I'm sorry. Please come in." She stepped back and opened the door fully. Although the doorway was large enough to accommodate him, the man stooped in order to enter. From habit, Kitty thought, then mentally rebuked herself. C'mon now, Kitty, get a grip of yourself girl, this is important. She had entered into the habit of chastising herself soon after being estranged from her family. Although she had never been wantonly scolded by any of them, her habits always left room for minor chiding, and as nobody was around to do it for her, she did it herself, out loud when she was alone or with Jobe but inwardly at all other times. She saw the man in the hall looking at her, awaiting direction. God! Now, c'mon, Kitty, will yer!

Potter sat facing Albert. His sympathies were obviously genuine, and Kitty found herself liking the man. Albert held on to the china cup in his hand so tightly that Kitty feared for it. Even though she shared the full pain of her husband's bereavement, she couldn't bear to see something so delicate and precious damaged. Her prudent nature took over. "Here, my love, let me take that for you." She gently removed the full but cold cup from Albert's grasp.

He looked at her as if waking from sleep. "And the funeral was last month." He stated rather than asked, looking at Potter but speaking to no one.

"I'm so sorry, Albert. He passed a few days after I had delivered his latest stipend to you. Your mother has ensured that I remained busy, which wasn't difficult given the circumstances. She knows I was your father's man and has always had her suspicions that we met on his behalf. He always spoke about wanting to accompany me..." Potter tailed off. He could only speculate at what was going through Albert's mind. He wondered if the anguish of the news had given way to pragmatism. If not, the grief of losing his father must soon be accompanied, if not outweighed, by the worry of losing his regular stipend.

"I can't believe she never let me say goodbye." Albert's words interrupted Potter's musings, and he saw that Albert was addressing his wife.

Potter took the opportunity to study Kitty unobserved. Her beauty was startling. He had been taken aback by it when she had pulled open the heavy front door. Only his ingrained politeness and years of service had allowed his face and voice to remain unaffected.

He had been well aware of what enticed Albert back to the Merchants Coffee House on Water Street, and he knew it wasn't the quality of their beans or the panoramic views across the Mersey. Potter had heard of the serving maid's beauty but hadn't witnessed it first hand; he fully expected that either the sating of Albert's lust or the continual rejection of his advancements would bring the visits to an end. He was as shocked as anybody when Albert announced his marriage plans to his distraught parents.

He now appreciated Albert's decision to defy his mother's authority in order to make the serving girl, Kitty, his bride. Albert's mother, as always, had been unwilling to have her totalitarian habits queried and responded brutally to her only son's deviation from the path she had prepared for him. Her decree that Albert be ostracised by the family, and deprived of the benefits of belonging to it, had met opposition, but when it was learned that his intended was a Catholic cellar-dweller from Liverpool, even the boldest opposition, that of Albert's father, melted away. It was a heavy price to pay even when the banker's draft Mr. Warburton set aside for his son to start a new life in America was taken into account.

Potter blanched at the theatrical clearing his throat that intimated he had something further to add. Albert and Kitty both looked at him and for a second he blankly returned their gaze. Unwilling to add to their burden but having no other option, he looked Albert in the eye.

"I'm afraid the last will and testament has been read, Albert. Your mother was the sole beneficiary."

* * *

Fergus's permanently stooped back became even more pronounced as he tackled the steep brow. His knees screamed in protest with each step of his threadbare but heavy hobnail boots. The impact of the gradient of the hill on his physical condition was equivalent to that of the vicinity on his mental state. His sensibilities grated as he travelled further into orange territory. He'd never crossed the invisible divide between Scotland Road and Great Homer Street into the Protestant enclave before Kitty, his only daughter, had been banished.

He crossed Byrom Street and followed the ever-ascending Richmond Row across its junction with St. Anne Street and so on to Everton Brow itself, his whole body tensing as he crossed into what he considered staunch orange country. Ready to defend himself against the angry horde of Orangemen who could gather at any minute to dislodge him, the Irish Catholic, from their territory. As usual, the outraged mob never materialized, the people he encountered too busy with the daily grind of their existence. The huge majority of their problems mirrored the struggles those of his own parish faced.

Fergus turned his attention to the real battle ahead: Everton Brow was an unmerciful climb, and given his physical condition, it was one he was never sure he would conquer. He took his mind off the task by attempting to observe the O's in their natural habitat, without ever being caught looking. The better quality of air and life offered on the hills didn't permeate to these lower reaches of the climb and Fergus only ever encountered the types of people he would on his own doorstep. Still, they were queer fish. Sure, there were the odd few Catholic families scattered in the enclave of Protestantism, but to Fergus's mind, their continual exposure to the O's had somehow tarnished them. 'Tinged with tangerine' as his Nelly would put it.

Nevertheless, it had been wrong to ostracise his youngest daughter and so force her into orange clutches. He had tried to intercede on her behalf, attempted to make his wife see sense, and so in her eyes 'went against her', something she would never forget or forgive. It was how she viewed Kitty's marriage to a Protestant: a betrayal so heinous it could never be rescinded. Kitty didn't stand a chance. Nelly had not stopped rocking in her chair for an instant, as was her wont when she was perplexed.

"But, Mam, if you'd just give him a chance," implored Kitty.

"A chance! A chance! Did they give us a chance when they were setting fire to the roof over our head? Did they?" responded her mother.

"But, Mam, what's that to do with Albert? He's never even been to Ireland. He's loving, kind and gentle."

"Ah, well, isn't that always the way with the devil until he's tricked you out of what he wants?"

"Well, he's had it, Mam. I'm with child, we're to be married next month," blurted Kitty.

Nell's rocking stopped, and she pointed at her daughter as though she were cursing her. "Then you'll leave this house, Kathleen Flynn, and you'll never darken its door again! I'll have no bastard orange in this house!"

Fergus almost collapsed against the set of railings that surrounded the pleasure gardens on Shaw Street. The melancholy that settled over him, instigated by his haphazard swirl of thoughts, had accompanied him up the hill like an extra weight.

A group of young women with bonnets and babies in perambulators sat inside the fenced summer seat, casting the odd furtive glance in his direction. Fergus gulped in a lungful of the fresh spring air. It couldn't hold a candle to the good clean Irish air he'd been raised on, but compared to the fug the rest of the town was forced to inhale, it was an elixir.

With any kind of choice in the matter he'd have preferred his daughter remained in America but on receiving word that she was home was relieved to find she was still a married woman. Kitty was better off up here, away from the degradation and despair of the slums, even if she was surrounded by O's. He dragged his callused palm across his sweating forehead before wiping it against his trousers.

He'd had to get involved when he realised the enormity of the tragedy facing his family. "Well, hang on there, Nelly. If the girl is pregnant and to be married then this is a situation that needs discussion, not hotheadedness."

His wife had twisted on him like a viper, her rocking regaining its momentum. "Hotheadedness, is it? Is that the hotheadedness that got us out of our burning house as they barricaded us in? Is that the one? Sure, Fergus, you'd have had a hot head all right, never mind just a singed one, cowering inside as you did! Wasn't it my hot head that broke us out and lambasted the landlord's agents?"

Fergus had spent years trying to impress on his wife that he hadn't been cowering at all but in fact protect his youngest from the burning thatch that had begun to fall upon them. "I'm just saying—"

"Well, you'll say no more, Fergus Flynn, or you'll be out on your ear with her." Nelly scooped up the quart of ale from the table, filled her pot and fixed her eyes stubbornly upon it. Her rocking gained an extra impetus but she didn't spill a drop.

Kitty had looked at her da and, seeing there would be no further intervention on his part, ducked under the lightly laden washing line and ran from the dimly lit room.

Nelly kept her eyes averted as Fergus took up the quart of ale and emptied its remains, every last drop, into a jam jar on the table then stood over her and swallowed the contents in one go. He slammed the jar back on the rickety table, making it tremble; confident his point had been made, which was verified by Nelly's lack of protest in the face of such blatant antagonism, he left the room. Nelly picked up the quart jug and threw it against the opposite wall, where the heavy pottery smashed into pieces.

There was no way Fergus would ever sever ties with any of his children, let alone his youngest daughter, of that he was sure. He hadn't fought all these years to keep them alive just to forsake them when they made a decision that went against the grain.

It was true he had had to fight far harder to protect his eldest children from the grasps of death. From the very outset, it had been against all the odds that any would live, and he had to concede that without the strength of his Nelly, there wouldn't be one of them left.

Vincent had been born to great joy just before the first blight. Fergus, who never drank, went into the village and celebrated in style in O'Shea's that night, ensuring that everybody in the tavern, fisherman and farmer alike, shared in his joy, standing them all at least one jar of poteen each. It would prove to be the last true celebration the village experienced. Fergus could still put a name to the face of every man that congratulated him with a slap on the back, shake of the hand or a toast to his firstborn son's health that night.

The first blighted crop had been a disaster. Rotten black stalks replaced healthy green ones overnight. There was no warning, no opportunity to rescue any portion of the yield. Fergus had experienced bad crops before, as had everybody else, but this one was different. News of spoiled fields was coming from every corner of the country. It seemed the whole potato crop of Ireland had been reduced to a pile, no, a mountain, of dry, black shoots whose foul smell pervaded the entire island.

Taverns—there had still been enough potatoes or corn to make poteen then—were full of talk about a bad fog that had blown in and settled over the fields at the worst possible time. The optimistic nature of the locals decreed that a toast be raised to the easterly wind that would ensure the fog didn't settle the following harvest.

"Have no fear, boys, and raise a glass to the easterly that'll blow that accursed fog straight across the sea to the Godless English's fields."

Fergus wasn't so sure. This was something he had never experienced. It was as though there were an invisible and island-wide pestilence. He worried it didn't bode well for the next year's crop or the one after.

His young wife had not only detected his fears but also acted on them. She spent every spare moment collecting and preserving every scrap of food nature's larder had to offer. She would be seen up in the hills, on the coast and in the woods with Vincent strapped to her back, a sack in her arms. Every vessel she could put her hands on was utilised, sanitised and made airtight. Everything she collected she would somehow preserve by salting, pickling, drying or smoking and then bury in the cool, dark mud, sowing the earth with a bounty that had no chance of growing but would provide sustenance when so many others were starving. Blackberries, turnips, mushrooms, herring, shellfish, even roots, nettles and seaweed all found their way onto the Flynn table while others were laid with nothing but broths made from roadside weeds and grass.

"Good God, Nelly! Is there no end to these jars?" Fergus would say in mock exasperation each mealtime.

"You'll know about it when they're gone, Fergus Flynn," would be her stock reply.

The situation became worse as each succeeding crop failed. The village and surrounding farms, although spared from the viciousness of the food riots and influx of English soldiers that the bigger towns and cities were experiencing, was still subjected to the hated landlords and the barbed pangs of hunger that heralded slow starvation.

Fergus and Nell, together with their neighbours, watched the ships loaded with Irish oats and grain sailing up the coast to feed the English armies around the world while they watched and starved. Then they observed as the village itself depopulated daily. In the majority of cases, there were only two destinations on offer: one was to follow the oats and grain into the world, namely Liverpool; the other didn't bear thinking about.

And so it was either on the coast or in the cemetery, on a steamer or in a coffin that Fergus had bade his family, friends and neighbours farewell. Both were heartbreaking. In days gone by, he had known people who travelled for new starts in the relatively close city of

Liverpool and, those that could afford it, further afield to exotic places like America and Canada. But such was the news coming back about the degradation and disease that festered in Liverpool that he was of the opinion it would be better to stay and be buried in his local and ancestral cemetery than a strange English one and the cost of travelling to America was so prohibitive he had more chance of taking Nelly and the nippers to the moon.

In the end, it was the landlord, or rather his hired mob, that forced the issue. The opportunity to transform the hovel and potato-pit-strewn land into lucrative fields full of cattle and sheep was not one to miss for the landlord. Tenant farmers up and down the country had found themselves evicted from their land to make way for livestock.

Nelly ensured that the landlord's agent never left the Flynn door without his monthly dues. Just as she produced meals from the barren coastlines and thin air of misty hills, so she conjured up pennies she'd saved behind a loose brick in the blackened fireplace in order to ensure the roof over their head was one that would remain. The landlord, frustrated by the lack of arrears, which he could manipulate to his advantage, had tried to pay the family's passage to Liverpool. When that didn't work, his agent employed one of the many gangs who had been sent over to Ireland from England to evict and terrorise tenants. Bigger towns had begun to form gangs to defend their own against this threat, but in the small village and its surrounding farms, there wasn't the strength in numbers or bodies to fight, such was the shortage of food.

It was his Nelly alone, just as she liked to remind him, who had confronted their particular persecutors. As he cradled the three-year-old Vincent and his baby brother Bog into the protection of his body, she smashed her way out of the barricaded front door with their only knife in one hand and a poker in the other, scattering the group of English who, although not wanting to come within striking distance of the flame-haired banshee, had retained their masculinity by laughing and calling obscenities. The following day, they were on board a steamer looking at their Ireland grow further and further away as England loomed ever nearer.

Fergus looked down on the city and traced the line of the Mersey back to its mouth. He stared into Liverpool Bay and wondered where it was that the Irish Sea began. Unaware of his vacant expression, the passage of time or the people of Everton deviating from their routes in order to avoid the bedraggled stranger, he simply stared as the events of a different life tumbled through his mind. He unconsciously licked his lips in anticipation of the pints that would numb, if not flush away, his melancholic mood, to be bought with the money he would allow his youngest daughter to force upon him.

"Da!"

Fergus straightened as his daughter ran the length of the fence and threw her arms around him, forced to strain against her weight or risk falling back against the railing, such was the power behind her embrace. He felt her body begin to rattle as sobs shook her slight frame. Bewildered, he stroked her hair and patted her back. "Hey now, what's all this? My brave Kathleen all of a fluster?"

Kitty remained nestled in the rough fabric of his overcoat. The smell redolent of her early years, and the sobs became audible.

"C'mon now, let's have a look at you, get your head out of this stinking coat."

Kitty allowed her father to gently grasp her cheeks with his rough hands and look into her eyes. "Oh, Da, I'm so scared, I don't know what we're to do." She gained a modicum of control and disengaged herself from her da, instead taking him by the hand. "Are you OK to walk a bit, Da?"

She led Fergus out into the rolling pastures where the population dwindled and they could talk alone and undisturbed. "Albert's father has died, Da."

Fergus was surprised that Kitty was showing so much grief for an in-law who, to his knowledge, she had never met. He removed his greasy cap, and Kitty ruffled the flat hair that was pasted to his scalp. Now that it had been disturbed, the gentle breeze played among his jet-black locks, which were incongruous sitting atop his worn, narrow face. "Well, God rest the man, I'm sorry for your husband's loss." He sat down in the field, his knees cracking loudly, and looked up into the unbroken sky for a second, marvelling at its blueness. "But I'm a little surprised that you're so upset, Kathleen?"

Kitty sat next to him and, knees tucked under her chin, replied, "I am grieving for Albert's loss, Da, but it's not him losing his father that has me in such a state."

"I don't understand, Kathleen. What is it yer trying to tell me?"

Kitty rested her forehead on her knees, obscuring her face. "He was our only source of income, Da. Albert received a monthly stipend from him. It's what's kept us for all these years."

"But I thought he was a writer?" said Fergus as he replaced his cap on his head.

"You should leave that cap off for a bit, Da, let some fresh air at your head. He is a writer, but for all the money it brings in it might as well be in a voluntary capacity. You'd make more for a day down the docks. We've no income, Da. All we've got is what I've put away."

Fergus was still struggling to grasp the situation fully. He looked across the Mersey and over to the rolling hills of the Wirral, the home of his daughter's wealthy in-laws. "Am I remembering right, he's the only son?" he asked.

Kitty nodded her confirmation.

"Ach, Kathleen, then you're worrying over nothing. He was a rich man; there'll be a will. You'll be better off than you are now." Fergus furrowed his brow in consternation as his words only served to reduce his daughter to tears again.

"No, Da, the will has been read. His mother was the only beneficiary. Albert suspects trickery, but we're powerless to contest it. We could never afford a solicitor." Kitty sniffed and wiped at her eyes with her cuffs.

Fergus blinked as his daughter regressed into the little girl from Holy Cross; he half expected her to drag her sleeve across her nose.

Kitty felt the need to explain further. "His mother is like mam, Da. Stubborn to the core. Only she's worse—she's rich and powerful. He didn't even get to pay his respects. She's never forgiven him for marrying a Catholic, and a slummy to boot. He's in the same situation I am, Da, ostracised by his family, and now his father has gone, the last tie has been severed."

Fergus had difficulty deciphering the torrent of information but was able to grasp the situation. He glanced furtively around, ensuring there was nobody in earshot. Even though the fields were empty, he spoke in a whisper. "They're a queer lot, Kathleen, you've always known that."

Kitty stood up in exasperation and paced around him. "Oh, Da, you sound like Mam. Albert couldn't care less about any of that nonsense, it's what he writes about. Satire, he calls it. Isn't it him who's forfeited a life of luxury to be with a cellar-dweller like me? But it's not us I'm worried about, Da, it's Jobe. This is the only life he knows."

Fergus held out his hand so his daughter could help him to his feet. "He's a lucky man to have you, Kathleen, and don't you go letting him think otherwise." He brushed the grass from the frayed backside of his trousers. "And if all he does with his writing is poke fun at the sectarianism in this town then it's small wonder he makes nothing from it! He must be the only person I've heard tell of that reckons it a joke." Fergus took his daughter in his arms and kissed her head. "Now c'mon, will yer walk an old fella a little way down the hill, give him safe passage past all these bloodletting O's?"

Kitty smiled for the first time that day and, as she always did, wordlessly opened her da's hand in order to slide a few coppers into it.

Fergus kept his fist tightly shut and closed his other hand over hers. "You'll be all right, girl. You've more of your mam in you than you'll ever know."

* * *

Albert stared at the pile of notes and coins that Kitty deposited on the table before dragging his hand through it in wonder.

Kitty slapped at his arm."Be careful now, Albert, you'll scratch the surface," she scolded.

Albert straightened up, removing his hand from the money and looked at her.

Kitty immediately licked her thumb and wiped at a small scuffmark on the polished wood.

"But how?" he asked. "I don't understand!" He brought his hand to his face and played it along the length of his moustache.

Kitty detected his discomfort. It reminded her of the night he had informed her they had to leave their home in Boston but she made no mention of America and instead attempted to downplay her achievement. "Ah, c'mon, Albert. You've been giving me a small fortune for an age now. What d'you think I do with it all? The house is furnished. You know I refuse to waste money on hiring help. Apart from food and fuel, the only real outlay is the rent and Jobe, his school fees, clothing and such, oh, and the toys you insist on spoiling him with, of course. When you've had nothing all of your life, it's only common sense to put a bit away for a rainy day."

Albert looked at her. "You truly are a wonder to behold, Kathleen Warburton." He looked at the money again, remaining utterly confounded until Kitty broke his reverie.

"C'mon, let's count it together and then we'll decide how it's best spent." She fell to her knees before the low table.

Albert took her hand and pulled her up and into him. He nuzzled her head as he spoke. "I promise you now, Kitty, I will begin writing in earnest. No more of these pieces for pamphlets or newspapers, or my own vanity, come to that. I will earn the money to keep us in the life we're accustomed to."

Kitty looked up at her husband and kissed him on the lips. "There's not a bone in all of my body that doubts you will, my love."

Chapter II

1888

Jobe wished more than ever that there had been a toy or two alongside the solitary tangerine and handful of walnuts in his stocking this year. It would have been no hardship to sacrifice those toys, he told himself. The task he faced now was an impossible one. How could he possibly choose? He started the process again, knowing it was futile but feeling he had to be doing something to gratify his parents, especially his father. He picked up a steam locomotive and scrutinised it for any flaws before placing it back on the floor and rolling it forwards and backwards. Content that its wheels ran smoothly, he stroked it reverentially before placing it in his toy box and repeating the process with another of his treasures.

Kitty looked from her son to her husband, who was drumming his fingers on his knee, a habit he had developed whenever he was growing agitated. She was about to kneel down and help Jobe point out some of his particular favourites but froze when his small fingers closed around a spinning top. An inertia-inducing memory of Albert triumphantly lifting Jobe in the air like a trophy flashed into her mind and she was forced to stifle a sob.

Albert eyes darted to his wife and he sensed her reluctance to interfere with the endless charade. "Come now, Jobe, enough of this procrastination," he urged less diplomatically than he had intended.

The severity in his father's tone caused Jobe to abort his mock inspection of the spinning top and he sat as if frozen.

Albert silently berated himself. The situation was no fault of the boy's, but lately he found it increasingly difficult to keep his patience in check. He knew the boy went to great pains to behave in a way his once tolerant father would appreciate, but the constant cautiousness and tiptoeing around only served to infuriate Albert further, which in turn fed his guilt, serving to make him even more abrasive.

Jobe placed the top on the floor. He would usually make every effort to satisfy his father, quell his newfound temper and subsequent raised voice, but on this occasion found he could summon no pretence. It rarely worked anyway. "I can't choose, Father, I'm sorry."

Albert stood up from his rickety chair so he towered over his son. "Look over there, Jobe. That's right—on the far wall. Can you tell me what is missing?" he asked, his voice steel.

Jobe looked at the bare space and, happy that he was able to oblige, answered at once. "The piano, father," he smiled nervously.

"And here, where I'm standing, what's missing?"

Jobe was again eager to please and his nerves fell away. "Your armchair, Father."

Albert pirouetted around the room, almost dancing; as he conducted Jobe's gaze, his movements serving to stimulate his son further. "On the mantelpiece there?"

"Mother's candlesticks and vases!" chirped Jobe.

"And here under our feet?"

"The rug, father, the rug!" Jobe was practically singing out the answers now, unaware of the path his father was leading him down.

Kitty watched as Albert became almost manic, until she could tolerate no more. "Stop, Albert! In Heaven's name, stop!" She sank to her knees on the bare but varnished floorboards.

It didn't take long before the implication of his father's questioning dawned on Jobe and he looked around the empty room, seeing its bareness for the first time. Without speaking, he knelt and carefully placed each one of his toys into their large storage box. When it was full he looked up. "I think I'm a little old for toys now, Father."

* * *

Albert, his back straight, jaw set stood in the high arched doorway of the Mercury, unable to stop himself from looking up at the newspaper's crest carved into the sandstone wall of its offices; A liver bird perched on a scrolled shield that bore Mercury's wand and horn entwined by serpents. But it was the banner below that caught his eye, the legend Libertas etched into it. The Latin word for Freedom. To Albert the word signified freedom of action, freedom from restraint, independence and rights, personal and social liberty. His lip curled into a sardonic smile, the editors at the paper obviously didn't interpret the Latin in the same way.

He looked down at the sheaf of papers he grasped in his hand. He had been in such a hurry to leave the offices that he had failed to file them back into his briefcase. The thousands of words represented weeks of work. He held them behind his back, crossed the road to the small brazier of a potato seller and pushed the papers onto the coals. Ignoring the remonstrations of the vendor as he made his way down Wood Street.

He decided to prolong his journey by taking the not-so-scenic-route out of town. In no rush to see the expectant look on his wife's face that nevertheless plagued his every step. His inability to procure a means of living from his writing meant that he could no longer meet the eyes that had once captivated him. He soon found himself on Scotland Road whose fame, or was it infamy, reached all the way to the harbour and docks of Boston.

Albert could see why. It was a city in itself. An unending stream of cabs, buses, carts, wagons, barrows, drays, traps, carriages and gigs maneuvered for position as they delivered, dropped off or deposited their goods. Nimble, businesslike boys scuttled about on all fours, dodging between wheels and hooves with battered scoops and brushes, trying to keep the carriageways clear of the steaming mounds of manure that the horses unceremoniously dumped on the cobbles.

The organised chaos of the road was mirrored on the teeming pavements, where business and pleasure jostled for supremacy. Vendors, navvies, clerks, dockers, hawkers, drunks, beggars, shoppers, merchants and meanderers milled around the plethora of chandlers, grocers, pubs, boarding houses, butchers, chemists, workshops and warehouses that lined the road in an unending concertina of discord.

Albert negotiated the disorder. The sights and smells clearing thoughts of Kitty from his mind until the magnificence of the Rotunda Theatre loomed up from the mélange of madness. He looked up at the music hall that rose above him. The much-lauded comedian Albert Loyd was appearing and Albert momentarily considered calling in to the box office and purchasing two tickets. A night out would do him and Kitty good. Go a way to relieving some of the frustrations that had built up between them. He was about to go inside when he realised he couldn't afford it. That his marriage was suffering because of the realities of a life constrained by financial hardship. He quickly walked from the shadow of the building not slackening his pace until he reached the bottom of Everton Valley and, for the sake of saving shoe leather as much as anything else, turned towards home.

A bedraggled but sizeable crowd headed along Netherfield Road and given their direction he had no choice but to walk alongside, careful to maintain his independence of it. Albert appraised the crowd as he walked. The men in it were mischievous rather than violent, behaving like children given an unexpected day off school. Most of them wore working clothes, betraying the fact that they had left their yards, counters or benches in their pursuit of excitement and Albert speculated as to the cause of their assembling.

His musings ceased on reaching the railings of the pleasure gardens on Shaw Street and he stopped to look beyond the manicured shrubs and hedges, to his house on Westbourne Street. It looked the height of respectability; the huge front door with its gleaming brass work, the heavy drapes that hung at every window. He was glad he had ignored Kitty's pleas to pawn the drapes rather than Jobe's toys. 'The drapes are a façade, our defence. If we allow it to be breached, to let the outside world in…don't you see? If that defence is lost, so too are we.' His wife had followed his words but not his reasoning.

He tried to turn his mind back to the crowd but couldn't help imagining the scene playing out behind the drapes. Kitty and Jobe in the kitchen, chattering incessantly between themselves as his wife concocted whatever travesty she would call dinner. All the time unaffected by the disconsolately bare floors and walls that surrounded them.

The crowd had moved on, reaching the junction with Soho Street. Boos and hisses rang out and Albert sensed an opportunity to postpone his return to the desperation, despondency and depression that would engulf him as soon as he put his key in the front door. He joined the crowd to see another mob entering Shaw Street from Soho, realising that the Chapel of St. Francis Xavier was the object of their jeering and he watched as more than one missile was launched at the church.

They passed into the shadow of the Collegiate Institution. Albert felt a pang of guilt as he looked up at the imposing building. He had long harboured dreams of Jobe attending and honing his obvious intellect at the Institute, but his building excitement refused to allow him to dwell on such matters and he returned his attention to the crowd. Although he had no idea of their intent or destination he was fully commited to their cause. He turned to the man next to him. "I say, what's the carry-on?" The man, his leather foundry apron soot-streaked looked Albert up and down before looking away with a snort. The response shocked Albert and he paused for a moment unsure whether the slight was through ignorance or arrogance. He was about to reach for the singed shoulder strap of the apron when a ruddy faced man wearing a butchers apron decorated with still-glistening flecks of offal and blood took it upon himself to enlighten him. "It's that new pastor. He's holding an open-air rally in the square. I've got out of work early 'specially to see him tell it like it truly is. He's got a special way with words, he doesn't half stick it to them Catholics and Irish lovers."

Albert had heard of Pastor George Wise and his incendiary sermons. He was no advocate of the man or his beliefs but the crowd had burgeoned and Albert was being carried along by sheer weight of numbers with no opportunity to turn back even if he had wished to.

The crush became intense at the entrance to Islington Square as other mobs converged from Brunswick Road and Erskine Street to the east, Moss Street to the south, and west from Carver Street and Islington itself. There was electricity in the air, and Albert was glad he had made the decision to join the mob. He used his sheer brute strength to shoulder his way into the square where the multitude fanned out and there was at least room to catch a breath and look about freely. The crowd continued to surge like a confused tide, and Albert, having no agenda, allowed himself to be pushed, first one way and then the other.

A spontaneous cheer erupted as an unassuming man in his early thirties took to the steps of a building on the corner of the Square and Shaw Street, not far from Albert's vantage point. The horde descended into a fervour of jostling before a relative calm established itself. The man, Pastor Wise Albert assumed, stepped up onto a small platform that had been erected between two white Grecian pillars that guarded the entrance of the building. A thick moustache covered his face, meeting and combining with his heavy sideburns so it hid his jowls but left his chin exposed and bare. The round metal eyeglasses he wore seemed too small for his face, and he looked over them as he addressed the eager crowd. "Brethren, welcome. I thank and applaud you for your attendance here this evening."

The crowd cheered and clapped and the pastor allowed the applause to continue, until with his finely tuned ear the pastor detected the first hint of the raucous approval abating and held up his arms in a signal for quiet. Although a few of the panting, sweating faces in the crowd continued to call out he began his eloquent oratory. "Once more we are forced to gather together... to illustrate how fervently opposed we are to the Fenianist ideals we are force-fed each and every day by those who think they have a right to dictate to us...but were no more than human ballast when they reached this great port!" On the resulting cheers dying down the pastor continued. "We cannot, nay must not, wait for the Established Church or the mealy-mouthed politicians to protect us or impress our rights...for they will not...and if we do not act, if you do not act, then our very Church, our very society, our very moral code will be a thing of memory...The ritualistic Romanism that is encroaching on our worship grows every week! Many of you are experiencing the idolatry to such an extent that I'd be amazed if you don't wonder yourselves papists every time you attend church!" More cheers greeted this, and the speaker continued in his alluring singsong baritone. "Is it not enough that we already have to swallow..."

Albert was jerked from the powerful delivery of the speech by a hand on his shoulder and he turned around to see a grinning face that he recognised well.

"Albert, how are you?" asked Potter as he peeled off a leather glove and held out his shovel of a hand.

"I'm fine, thank you, Potter, it's good to see you. How are you?" replied Albert, only too aware of the cold, raw hand he proffered. "What the devil are you doing here?"

A man in front of the pair turned round, his intention to tell the chattering toffs behind to shut up but, on seeing their size, returned all of his attention to the speaker.

"I'm with him," replied Potter, pointing over to Pastor Wise. "Listen, I can't talk now, but make your way over to the steps when the crowd clears. We'll have a drink and I'll explain." Potter clapped Albert on the shoulder as he made his way to the front of the crowd and discreetly took a place a few feet to the side of the speaker, surveying the crowd in front of him as he did so.

* * *

Albert failed to register the two men who busied themselves removing the temporary platform or the traffic that traversed the now empty square. He leaned against one of the Grecian pillars, ruminating on the points the speaker, Pastor George Wise, had raised. The problems the town faced had consumed Albert's intellect for a long time. The majority of his writing was aimed at ridiculing those who insisted religion or immigration, particularly the Irish influx, was the root cause of every problem the city and the country at large endured. He satirised the ignorance of the fundamentalists who believed the great unwashed were in any way perplexed by the manner in which a church service was conducted or a mass delivered. Chided their disregard for the myriad of socioeconomic problems that kept congregations in poverty, which was, as far as he was concerned, the origin of society's ills.

Although it caused Albert a distinct discomfort to acknowledge it, there was a great deal of logic behind some of Pastor Wise's words. Words that, try as he might, he could not contradict. There was no denying the man was a fundamentalist, and a fanatical one at that, but Albert had to concede that not only was he incapable of opposing Wise's arguments, he agreed with the majority of them. He tended to view himself as a progressive; an enlightened soul regarding such issues, and the conflict raging within him soon led him to question the legitimacy of his writing. Had his marriage and personal circumstances created a bias that must pervade his work as conspicuously as a lightning bolt? The realisation evoked an unprecedented sensation of shame that emanated from deep within his gut and quickly traversed his body. Conscious that it had reached his face, which must be burning a deep crimson. His feeling of discomfort was only enhanced when the door of the building opened and Potter emerged.

"Ah, Albert, you're here. Good man," said Potter surveying the Square rather than looking at Albert. Seeing there was nobody in the immediate vicinity he beckoned out the speaker, who emerged, flanked by two heavyset men who, compared to Potter and Wise, looked incongruous in their rough and frayed clothing. The trio descended the steps, where Potter commenced with the introductions. "Pastor, Albert Warburton. Albert, Pastor George Wise."

The two men shook hands, and Albert got the impression that the pastor was conducting a surreptitious scrutiny of him. Already ill at ease, he broke the handshake a little too hastily. "An eloquent sermon, Pastor," he complimented, attempting to cover his faux pas.

"Thank you, Mr. Warburton. A pleasure to make your acquaintance," replied the pastor. Albert was again alert to the fact that he was somehow being measured, and his tongue evaded him.

Potter interceded. "Until next week, Pastor, good evening." He shook hands with the pastor and then addressed the men who had remained behind the pastor. "See Pastor Wise safely home and then get yourselves off. I'll be in touch." With that, he turned to Albert, "Shall we?"

* * *

Potter led Albert down Islington as far as Commutation Row where they passed the Wellington Monument and joined the thoroughfare of Lime Street which was, as usual, well lit and alive. Every demographic the town had to offer was represented on the busy artery. Well-heeled gentlemen, their top hats brushed and bristling, linked arms with their immaculate ladies as they headed to an evening of dancing in St. George's Hall or a show at the Royal Court or Empire Theatre. Barefoot children, faces and hands as black as their feet, flitted between them in the hope of a few pennies, the lucky ones depositing their gains with mothers who waited around the Stebble Fountain in anticipation of the paltry windfall. A commotion broke out around the fountain as a belligerent husband arrived, demanding the pennies his wife and child had begged. As hawkers, one eye on potential customers and the other looking out for coppers, stood with baskets full of goods or pushed barrows brimming with wares, animal, vegetable and mineral from every corner of the globe that had never been intended for sale in Liverpool but were smuggled from the docks for that very purpose.

Men, those who had finished their day's work, traversed the street on their way home or to the next pub. Those who had failed to find work or the loafers who had no compulsion in doing so, idled on corners and emitted a casual air of threat. Clerks and other office types poured in and out of Lime Street station oblivious to the danger of the horse-drawn trams and carts that they cut between. Those jettisoning the station for the first time stood, slack-jawed, as they surveyed the scene before them.

Albert and Potter bypassed the raucousness until they reached and entered the relative tranquillity of The Vines public house. Albert looked around and was impressed by the surroundings as well as the clientele. The long, gilded bar was matched in length by huge ornamental mirrors that reflected the busy barmen and their prosperous patrons. "Well, it's better than the pigpens you used to frequent," he said.

Potter laughed and slapped him on the back. He pointed to a table. "Take a seat, I'll get the drinks."

Albert sat at the round, marble-topped table and watched Potter cut his way through the cigar smoke and revellers to the bar. The walk to the Vines had been a relatively quiet one, littered with patchy small talk. Potter had sensed Albert's humour and was happy enough allowing him to mull, while Albert felt comfortable enough in Potter's company not to feel obliged to blather instead choosing to reflect on his earlier contradictions.

Potter returned with their drinks and dragged over a stool. He sat down heavily, as if tired and, after taking a drink, addressed Albert. "I could see your mind was weighing heavy on the way here, Albert, but you must have some questions for me."

Albert took a hesitant sip of his drink, his face contorting.

Potter laughed. "I see you've not lost your fondness for a drink."

Albert smiled. He was eager to put to one side his conflicting emotions, and he did indeed have questions that needed answers. "Where to begin? How are things on the sunny Wirral, and, forgive me, how is Mrs. Potter?"

"Mrs. Potter has the constitution of an ox, and as long as she is in the service of your mother, is happy, thank you, Albert."

"And my mother, Potter, is she well?" he asked.

"She is well, Albert. She mourned your father for a long time, and even now she remains in black, but she prospers. In fact she is quite the philanthropist, very respected. She sits on a number of boards and committees." Potter reached for his drink as Albert digested the information.

"She's never instructed you to reach out to me?"

"I'm afraid not, Albert. Forgive me, but you're well aware of her obstinacy."

This time it was Albert who reached for his drink, taking a large gulp without sign of any adverse reaction. "She knows you're in Liverpool?" he asked as the burning liquid settled in his chest.

"I'm here at her request. She's quite taken with Pastor Wise and has become a staunch supporter. He delivered a sermon in Birkenhead last month. She met him afterwards, and on hearing about some of the skirmishes his addresses have caused on both sides of the water, grew concerned for his safety. She put me at his disposal. I spend a lot of my time in the town now, organising his security."

Albert raised his eyebrows at the news, although on reflection it didn't surprise him that his mother was an admirer of the pastor and his incendiary views. The pastor's surveying of him entered his mind. "Wise was aware of who I was," he said, more statement than question.

"I informed him of your parentage, yes. I apologise if you take offence." Potter spun his glass on the table in half revolutions.

"Not at all," shrugged Albert. There was something different about Potter. He was more at ease, happier.

"What did you make of the pastor, Albert?"

Albert's response was delayed by a young girl who approached the pair selling cockles and mussels from a basket she carried around her neck.

Potter gestured towards the girl. "Albert?"

Albert used the interlude to take a drink. "No, thank you, Potter."

The girl looked dismayed at the loss of a potential sale.

"Ah, come on, Albert," Potter cajoled. "You were always fond of your seafood, and you're looking a little gaunt." He leaned to one side, enabling him to fit a hand into his pocket while remaining seated. "Two trays of mussels if you will, Miss, both with a generous helping of vinegar."

Potter took out a handful of coins and, finding the one he wanted, gave it to the girl as she laid two trays in front of the pair. The girl took the coin and began counting out change. Potter dismissed her, a mussel already halfway to his mouth. "No, no, for you. Away you go now." The girl gave a little curtsey and continued on her round.

"So, Albert, Pastor George Wise?"

* * *

Malachi marvelled at the spire of St Francis's towering over the multitudes gathered below it. "Watch out for him, lads, the big bastard there," said Driscoll cutting into his vision.

Malachi tore his eyes from the spire. "God almighty, but he's big."

Driscoll looked and saw that Malachi wasn't looking in the direction that he was discreetly pointing. "No, not him, although look out for him as well. He's auld, but all the same… No, look, the other big brute there. He's the real enforcer, a dirty, mean bastard he is."

Malachi followed the discreet nod and gave an audible gasp. "That's the fella who turned Bernie Hopwood into a vegetable down Sebastopol. One punch is all it took him. He took Hopwood's lead pipe to the skull and didn't blink! I was there. I saw it with me own eyes."

Driscoll and the rest of the gang looked at Malachi, and he nodded confirmation as he wrung his hands, still looking across the crowd at the big man, who suddenly looked in their direction as if aware he was the object of their attention.

Malachi quickly averted his eyes. "Oh, Jesus," he whimpered as he looked at the ground.

Driscoll tutted at him. "Have a look at yourself, Mal', will yer! Once the div'l begins with his sermon, all hell will be let loose. Just make sure you stay out of the big bastard's way. Sure, isn't he big enough not to miss?"

Malachi wasn't convinced. He could have kicked himself for allowing Driscoll to twist his arm to join the gang who were going up to Everton to stop the O's and their new champion from desecrating the Church of St. Francis Xavier. He couldn't give a toss for St. Francis's or any other church for that matter; he knew for a fact that the majority of the lads had pissed up against the wall of St. Mary's more times than they had been to mass in it. He suspected it would be the same for the fellas from all the other parishes who would be making the crusade up to Everton. He had told Driscoll as much. "Ach, I can't be arsed traipsing up that hill for no good reason, Driscoll. Let the O's do what they want. Sure, it's their parish. Worse goes on in ours."

"Ah, c'mon, Mal. It'll be a hoot, and you'll never get a better chance to crack a few O's. We're all going up, and when we get back we'll have a few jars to celebrate." Driscoll looked at him slyly. "I'll stand you a few if you haven't got the coppers." That had been the clincher for Malachi, although Driscoll continued, "We'll be a regular army by the time we arrive. Why, they'll be walking down Scotland Road in droves as we speak. What'll it look like if the parish of St. Mary's, The Mother Church, the oldest Catholic Church in the city, isn't represented? The meeting point'll be Scotland Place. We'll collect the Holy Cross boys as we pass through, not that they're ever much use! It's a parade, a regular carnival, and you should see the O's tremor as we go marching through their territory unopposed."

Malachi licked his lips. "I'll work up a raging thirst banging those orange heads in. Are you sure you can stand me a few jars to slake it?"

Driscoll smiled as he replied, "We'll return conquering heroes. I'll be surprised if we don't drink the house dry!"

Malachi looked over at the big man again, his memory reverting back to the day when he had left the Nonpareil to steal the toff's watch. He'd left his drink unattended on a hogshead barrel. It would be light work. He winced as he remembered Bernie Hopwood's cosh thumping the back of the big man's head but he reacted as if nothing more than a fly had landed on him, turning and with a single punch leaving Bernie a vegetable. The crack of Bernie's jaw snapping reverberated around Malachi's head, robbing him of his last ounce of bravery and he looked around, desperate for an escape route. He wondered who was friend and who was foe but there was no way of telling. Apart from the few well-dressed heavies creating a cordon in front of the chapel, everybody looked as ill clad, ill shod and ill fed as the boys from St. Mary's. The last thing he wanted was to wander into one of the many gangs of O's in the crowd. He continued to wring his hands as he turned full circle when a booming voice caused him to jump.

"Do priests drink Holy Water?" George Wise took to the soapbox placed outside the Chapel of St. Francis Xavier and ignored the cheers of the crowd as, fist clenched above his head, he repeated in his baritone. "Do priests drink Holy Water?"

"No they drink whisky!" The well-rehearsed reply, or lack of one, easily distinguished Catholic from Protestant with one short sentence and the simmering suspicion that pervaded the street was transformed into knowledge. Battle lines were drawn as pockets of the rival sects re-established their positions, ensuring they were not left on the wrong side of the divide. Minor scuffles broke out and kicks and punches were thrown, but the unannounced truce held and all eyes returned to the pastor, who, after his deliberate and illuminating pause, continued.

"Brethren, I see we again have guests among us. One wonders how the Right Honourable MP for Scotland Ward continues to afford to reward them all with a pot of ale on their return to the slums."

This was greeted by exaggerated laughter from his supporters and a seething silence from his opponents.

"Well, maybe for once, they can act in a civilised, decent manner and we'll reward them with a bit of schooling?" He looked to the Catholic section of the crowd. "What do you say, boyos?" On a lack of response Pastor Wise turned his gaze back to his own supporters. "They look worried! Well, they don't need to fret so, there won't be a test!"

Again, his supporters replied with derisive, delirious laughter. A stone thumped against the wall, far enough away from George Wise to suspect one of his own followers had thrown it.

"Ah, they have reverted to stoning their own places of worship now, I see. Is nothing sacred to them? I think we know the answer to that! Well maybe if I don the idolatry of their priests, I can get away with any amount of sinning, just as they do?" With these words, Pastor Wise took a set of rosary beads from his coat and put them around his neck. From his other pocket he pulled out a crucifix and held it aloft. "Here now, do these idolatries allow me to say my piece? Don't they allow those who wear them to say theirs without censor? To fornicate with members of their congregation! To gamble in the courts! To drink and drink and drink!"

A single stone hit one of those in the protective cordon in front of Pastor Wise. Thrown from a group just to the left of the St. Mary's gang, who Malachi thought he recognised from down St. Augustine's, it was the catalyst for mayhem..

There was an audible intake of collective breath followed by a roar full of indecipherable insults and hatred as those at the front of their respective lines charged, wielding sticks and knives, hacking at anything immediately in front of them. George Wise took his cue and, flanked by half a dozen thickset men, made his escape up Soho Street to the safety that the Presbyterian Chapel on Shaw Street offered.

The air filled with flying debris as both sides threw whatever missiles they had collected en route. Pieces of slate, stone and rock rained down on unprotected heads and bodies. Bottles smashed, shards of glass splintering into legs and torsos. The injured staggered or were dragged to the rear of their respective territory.

The St. Mary's contingent had escaped the airborne peril unscathed. Malachi had taken no part throughout, either offensively or defensively. Instead, he had watched as Albert, his nemesis, had escorted the pastor up the hill toward Shaw Street and out of sight. He was still on his tiptoes looking when the crowd around him reacted to a surprising and unplanned enemy charge.

Aside from the lunatic fringe, those at the very front of their respective lines, an all-out attack was a rarity in the exchanges, with those on both sides preferring to throw insults and missiles from afar and therefore enjoy a relatively safe, inexpensive evening of entertainment. Only occasionally, if the odds were favourable, did the opportunity arise to give a rival group a good kicking. This particular charge was a consequence of the pastor's supporters who, having gathered toward the top of the hill, were enjoying the advantage of the steep incline. They placed their hands on the comrades directly in front of them to maintain balance as they bent to gather the slates, rocks and stones that had been launched at them, their weight forcing their companions forward, causing a ripple effect that gave those in the vanguard no option but to stagger forward in a disharmonious straggle.

Their opposition, sensing the impending attack, reacted by rushing headlong at their aggressors. Malachi almost lost his balance and was at risk of being trampled in the ensuing stampede when Driscoll grabbed hold of him. "C'mon, Mal, snap out of it! Get stuck in, yer bastard, or there'll be no ale for you."

The two groups came together in a flurry of kicks and punches, those who carried weapons wielding them indiscriminately, as likely to bring their planks, sticks and pokers crashing down on the head of a friend as that of a foe. Screams, curses and howls filled the air, replacing the earlier missiles. The attending police officers watched in mild astonishment as the situation suddenly intensified. Heavily outnumbered, they remained neutral on the edge of the ad hoc battlefield, cudgels drawn, ready for anybody who strayed into their vicinity.

Malachi's reluctance and Driscoll's badgering cost the pair, and they found themselves cut off from their group. The impetus of the initial charge had not abated, and they could only flail at their opponents who flashed by, aiming their own strikes and blows which the pair were forced to dodge or parry. It was only when congestion ceased the charge that the fighting began in earnest with both mobs finding themselves face-to-face with their antagonists. Malachi and Driscoll had been forced far through their enemies' frontlines. It was difficult to exact any telling blow such was the press and a melee ensued.

It suited Malachi and he whooped with delight as he found himself among those who habitually avoided any meaningful violence and injury by remaining at the rear of the crowd. It was those who clung to the coat tails of the mob that had inadvertently caused the impromptu charge and were now reaping the consequences in the midst of the retaliatory attack. Elbows, knees and short upper cuts cleared them from Malachi's path, while Driscoll remained in the safety of his friend's wake, gouging at eyes and fish-hooking those his comrade had winded, wounded or debilitated in any way that left them defenceless to his malice.

The remaining lines turned and fled in any direction that offered sanctuary and Malachi didn't end his pursuit of them until he reached the crest of the incline. He drew breath and looked down into the fray from his elevated position. It was on the verge of petering out. The majority of those taking part had either fled or lay prone. Only a hard core remained, and the fighting among them was intense.

"Jesus, but we gave them a pasting, Mal," said Driscoll as he put a hand on his friend's heaving shoulder. "We need to be getting back among our own, though. It does us no good to be this far up the hill. C'mon, let's give them lot a wide berth and get home. The coppers'll be here in force soon enough."

Malachi wasn't listening. His face, which had been flushed from his exertions, drained of all colour. He had seen the giant in the middle of the fight, swatting men aside as he prodigiously rained blows with his right hand and swung a gold-topped walking cane with the other. Without a word Malachi spun around and tore up what remained of the hill towards Shaw Street.

Driscoll blanched, torn between being left alone or running further into orange territory. "Mal, come back! What about yer pints?" he screamed.

* * *

Albert drained his glass in one and slammed it on to the bar. "Another toast! Landlord, another round here," he shouted.

"Albert, we've toasted everything from failing potato crops to your walking cane. What can possibly be left?" asked Potter, exhaling a lungful of cigar smoke.

Albert picked up one of the glasses the landlord had just deposited on the bar and held it in the air. "To Potter!" he exclaimed before draining it in one go. The cheers of the entourage were, on this occasion, full of genuine gusto. The majority of them owed their turn in fortune to Potter. Clad as they were in the attire of gentlemen, their tattered clothing and matted hair hidden by overcoats and bowler hats obtained from pawnshops with money given to them by their benefactor, they toasted him with exuberance.

Albert draped an arm over Potter's broad shoulder. "There, hear how your army adores you?" he slurred.

Potter ignored the compliment and unwrapped Albert's arm from around his neck. "It's you that's their hero! Although you're going to end up getting yourself on a murder charge, the way you've been tearing into the papists these past months," Potter semi-scolded.

Albert laughed. "Come now, Potter, do I detect a hint of jealousy? God knows you've no need to worry. There are enough of them to go round. Isn't that the real point of Pastor Wise's wrath?"

Potter shook his head. "It's no laughing matter, Albert. Granted, the odd one needs a good seeing to, but a short, sharp smack is sufficient for the majority of them. They're either malnourished, drunk or both. The way you go laying into them with that cane of yours…why, it's only a matter of time before one of them ends up dead."

"Well, that'll please the pastor, at least. One less Fenian to corrupt and threaten the good and pious of the town," laughed Albert as he raised his hand to attract the attention of the landlord.

"It'll be no joke when you're on the gallows, Albert," sighed Potter, knowing his advice was falling on deaf ears as Albert forced another drink on him.

"Come now, Potter, less of the old woman act. Another toast!" he roared.

* * *

"Who is Pastor Wise?" Jobe had heard the name tossed between his mother and father during their frequent arguments.

His mother stood over the scullery sink scrubbing at one of his father's collars. She turned and looked at Jobe for a moment before answering. "Ooh he's St. George to your father, Jobe, but really he's a demon. A horrible, nasty devil of a creature intent on bringing misery to this town. Would you like to hear what the good and God-fearing people chant to him as he's walking the street?"

Jobe wasn't sure he wanted to know. There was a hint of madness in his mother's eyes, a hatred in her voice that he had never heard before. She had never addressed him in such a manner, and it unnerved him.

Abandoning his father's collar so it fell to the floor, she stooped and approached Jobe as she spat out a verse. "Pastor, pastor with yer quack, quack, quack. O go to the div'l and don't come back."

Jobe turned and fled from his mother's unrecognisable features but could still hear her repeating the verse, the words of which became branded on his brain.

A few days later, it not being too cold, his mother had allowed him to sit outside and draw with a rogue piece of chalk he had found jammed between the skirting and floorboard in his bedroom. Jobe's tongue protruded the corner of his mouth in concentration. The drawing was of his mother and father hand in hand while he sat above them on his father's shoulders. He replayed the scene he was catching in chalk. The last excursion he had enjoyed on his father's shoulders, revelling in the rocking motion his giant but seamless strides created and the incessant commentary he provided regarding everything they witnessed or experienced on their travels.

"You see there, Jobe, the mighty Albert Dock. It shares its birthday with me. It's forty-two years old today, but on the day I was born, it was only ten and the greatest dock in the world. Prince Albert himself came to open it."

"That's who you're named after," cheered Jobe.

"You're right! Well, I like to think I'm named after both."

That day, his father's birthday, was the last time Jobe could recall seeing him happy. The sun that had shone on the hills and on his life had been replaced by grey skies and cold winds. For a long time he had fretted that he was responsible for the change in his father, but he observed that his mother had also fallen from favour. He took solace from the fact that he wasn't responsible for the decline in his father's temperament, but that relief was diluted by the sympathy he felt for his distressed mother who endured his father's mutating humour with her usual stoicism. The angry exchanges that now took place between them unsettled Jobe, and although he wasn't frightened by the cross words and raised voices, they weighed heavily upon him.

He gave his head a gentle shake as if to rid it of the negative thoughts, re-concentrating his efforts on the drawing. He began to tunelessly sing the words of the rhyme he had learned from his mother under his breath giving extra emphasis to the 'quack, quack, quack.'

Jobe felt a shadow fall across him and looked up to see that his father had stopped in the gateway to observe him. Jobe, under the impression his father had paused to admire his work, continued with his sketch, carefully adding three huge smiles to each of the off-scale faces. He was forced to move his hand quickly as his father's boot came crashing down and landed squarely on his mother's face, scuffing the chalk and ruining her smile. He was knocked off balance as his father brushed past him and into the house.

"Kathleen! Kathleen!"

Jobe knew there was to be contention on hearing his mother's full name bawled around the house. He cringed in the doorway as his mother entered the hallway from the kitchen, wiping her hands on the stained pinafore she wore.

"What is it, Albert?" she asked as sanguinely as possible.

"What is the meaning of teaching my son those filthy Fenian lyrics?"

Jobe wondered at the word Fenian but knew it couldn't be proper from the way the blood drained from his mother's face.

"Are you forgetting, Albert, that your son is one of those filthy Fenians?" she spat.

"I allowed you to christen my son a Catholic to assuage your irrationality, but we agreed that this was never to be a religious house." His father towered over his mother as he stood twisting his moustache.

"It is only you who has raised the issue of religion in this house, Albert. Do I not attend mass without making any fuss about it? Have I ever once attempted to force my beliefs on you? Well, have I?"

"Yet I come home to find my son singing insults about Pastor Wise."

"Oh Pastor Wise again is it? That great ambassador for religious tolerance! Wasn't it him who stirred up the trouble last week that ended up with Father Riley being hurt?"

"Hurt? A mere trifle! Why, Pastor Wise was almost lynched by a rabble at the weekend."

"Well, I'm sorry to hear it was only almost. He could do with been strung up! Isn't it him reigniting all the old tensions?"

"Old! Old! Are you so naïve? There is a fight for survival taking place this very moment, right now. It's impossible for a good man to find a job, walk the streets in safety or even go to church in peace, thanks to the feckless imbeciles that continue to pile into this town by the day..."

Jobe returned to the front step, closing the front door behind him. He began to drag his foot across his drawing, distorting the chalk lines until they were unrecognisable. All the while doing his best to ignore the raised voices coming from inside.

It had taken Jobe a long time to get to sleep that night and the reverberation of the front door slamming dragged him from his dreams and back to the discomfort of his pallet. He turned on his back and looked at the ceiling. There was enough moonlight filtering through the uncovered windows to watch his breath as it evaporated into the cold, still air. He tried in vain to find a position that didn't expose a jutting bone to the surface of the unforgiving pallet. His mother had covered it with old blankets and newspaper in an attempt to provide a modicum of comfort, but Jobe imagined that even a half dozen of his old horse-hair mattresses wouldn't make any difference to the hard and unyielding pallet he now called bed. He lay awake, trying to make sense of the troubling events that had taken place around him. His main cause for concern wasn't the removal of his iron bedstead and mattress, which his father had manhandled down the stairs a few weeks after he had taken the box of toys, but the change in his parents' behaviour, especially that of his father, who had become a stranger to him. After a while he heard the muffled voice of his mother.

Kitty heard the front door closing and blew out the solitary candle so she sat alone in the enveloping darkness. The remnant of wax that remained would be saved to wake Jobe and see him off to school in the morning. Albert entered the parlour and Kitty wrinkled her nose as the potent alcohol fumes pervaded the room, superseding the remnants of candle smoke. The glare from the glow of the candle flame had long since diminished from behind her eyes, but the darkness was so complete she could only sense Albert floundering about in it. "The candle's here. I'm sorry but there's only enough left to see Jobe off in the morning." Kitty took the box of matches from her lap and silently placed them under the wooden chair she sat on.

Albert had assumed his wife would be upstairs asleep and that he was therefore alone. Regardless of the total darkness he suddenly felt exposed. He was about to feel his way over to Kitty but dismissed the notion. "Well, I hope it'll be enough to see us all off. I'm afraid we're due to be evicted next week, and I, for one, will not be around to experience that particular pleasure."

Kitty stood but felt as if her insides remained where she had been sitting. "But, Albert, we've sold all we had in order to live. The money that I had saved…we agreed it would be used to pay the rent. There was more than enough. Surely we have a few months yet?"

The couple looked towards each other but remained veiled from sight by the consuming darkness.

"Yes, well that specific…venture never came through, dearest," slurred Albert, rocking on his heels in order to keep his balance.

Kitty scrabbled under the chair and grabbed at the box of matches. She stood and struck one, at the same time holding it out so she could see her husband's face. The phosphorous flash illuminated the short space between them and Kitty closed her eyes against the flare.

Albert gazed at the vision before him, the glow of the match lending his wife's beauty an ethereal quality that caused his breath to catch in his throat and almost choke him. His resolve wavered, and he wanted nothing more than to reach out and caress her cheek, to reassure her that he would always be at her side and there was no existing entity that could separate them.

The match spluttered out and Albert heard Kitty scraping another along the side of the box. Her eyes opened and his breathing was checked for a second time, so sharply that it caused him to take an involuntary step backwards. Her eyes emanated a hatred that he didn't believe she could possess. Framed within the beauty of her face, it seemed to him she resembled a harpy from the childhood tales with which Mrs. Potter had regaled and terrified him. A surge of irrational fear tingled up his spine, causing him to shiver.

"What's that, Albert? Someone trampled over your grave? Well, I'll make you a vow right now. If my Jobe…our Jobe! If he suffers from the ills of this world because of you, I will put you in your grave and God forgive me, I will dance. I will dance upon it, Albert Warburton!"

Chapter III

1889

The boy left the steps of The Adelphi and ran the short stretch to The Vines pub where he took a battered orange crate from under his arm and set it down. "'Ere, you don't wanna be putting your foot on his block, sir! I'll warrant he told you he'd shine your shoes for a copper?" he chirped at a ship's captain as he efficiently pulled out an arrangement of threadbare brushes and cloths secreted around various parts of his person.

The bespectacled ship's captain, his foot already resting on an upturned crate, looked at the newcomer in surprise. Confused by the sudden complication he raised bushy eyebrows at the shoeshine in front of him, as if inviting some conflicting statement.

"Oh, he'll black 'em and crack 'em, but he'll never get a shine on them. All he's got there is soot and vitriol, vitriol and soot, his father's a chimney sweep, you see," continued the interloper as he meticulously spread out the tools of his trade in front of his orange crate. He took a lavish step back to survey them correcting the angle of one or two, until finally satisfied, he looked towards his competitor for the first time. "Deny it if you can, Jonny, protest to the good captain here."

Jonny seethed but remained mute as the captain removed his boot. On his silence continuing the captain shrugged at him and moved over to the effervescent boy, placing his left foot on the upturned crate.

The boy's chatter didn't abate as he rubbed, scrubbed and spat at the high button black leather boot, his eyes never leaving it. After a minute or two he leaned back on his haunches to admire his work. "Here you go, sir, somewhere to see your face without the need of a looking glass…and all for the aforementioned copper," he said with a final flourish of his rag.

The captain looked down. The boy's boasts held some legitimacy, he could indeed see his blurred features in the toe of his boot and he gave a slight nod of acknowledgement as he lifted his other foot to the crate.

"That's right, sir, let's have the other one and I'll do it for sixpence," said the boy solemnly.

The captain pulled his half-cocked right leg back from the crate, almost losing his balance. "Sixpence? Why, you said you'd shine them for a copper. The boy there," the captain looked to the space his initial choice of shoeshine had left empty in pursuit of another customer. "Was charging me a penny," he trailed off.

"Well, he'd have blacked them for a copper, I can believe, but if it's a matching shine you want, it'll cost you sixpence. Which I'll take in advance if it's not too much trouble?"

The captain bristled as he begrudgingly handed over the coin and placed his foot on the crate.

The boy, noting the captain's frown, grinned at him. "Don't take it too hard, sir. You wouldn't expect to catch a weasel asleep, would you now?"

Kitty watched the whole scene play out. Her concern for the two boys, younger than Jobe, out at such a late hour shining shoes for pennies unable to keep the ghost of a smile from her lips at the quick wits of the boy.

She wasn't the only one who had been surreptitiously observing the episode. A stick-thin gentleman dressed in black velvet had paced the road opposite throughout, his vexation apparent as he paced first up then down muttering to himself while stroking his chin.

Kitty wondered at the miserly behaviour of some of those with money. Surely a simple shoeshine did not warrant such rumination. Without warning, the man strode out into the road, oblivious to the existence of an oncoming tram. His countenance was unnerving and Kitty was suddenly worried for the little shoe-shines. She prayed that he would pass into the public house behind them but mustering her courage, prepared to check the man if his conduct was too outrageous. Hadn't she already endured leering looks and coarse, lewd remarks for the majority of the evening? Her heart sank to her stomach as the gentleman came to a stop directly in front of her and she lowered her eyes so they became fixed on his shining, laced-up boots.

"May I enquire as to the services you are willing to participate in?"

Kitty gasped and looked up to find herself looking into features that seemed ancient and conveyed doom and malevolence. Strands of wispy white hair escaped from under the old-fashioned stovepipe top hat that crowned a very long, very old and very thin face. She tried to take a step back but found she had already pressed herself flat against the public house wall and she was powerless to stop herself from making the sign of the cross.

A smirk started at the corner of the old man's mouth and his tongue flicked out, playing along thin, bloodless lips as he stroked his wrinkled cheek with a gloved hand. "Hmm, very pretty, very interesting. Now, what say we end this charade and you accompany me across the road to the hotel there?" He broke off his conversation as the door to The Vines swung open and a small group of men decanted onto the street. One of them drew his company's attention to the incongruous spectacle before them and they continued down the street laughing loudly.

The old gentlemen cast a disdainful glance in their direction before continuing. "Before you reply, let me inform you that I will make it very much worth your while if you are willing to acquiesce to my small requests."

Kitty froze and watched as the hand stroking his cheek moved towards her own.

"Kitty?"

Albert stood resplendent, the silk top hat he wore lending him even more stature so he towered over the scene. Kitty remained against the wall, terrified that any movement would bring her into contact with the gloved hand that had become static but remained hovering in front of her face. "Oh, Albert," she said, her tone beseeching.

The old gentleman, his thin bloodless lips pursed, glared at Albert before he silently withdrew his hand and made the short walk to the Adelphi Hotel, disappearing inside without a glance back.

Kitty remained fast against the wall unable to move.

"Kitty?" repeated Albert.

She looked at Albert, magnificent in his top hat and tightly tailored overcoat and peeled herself from the wall with as much composure as she could muster. She subconsciously patted down her dress. Feeling the weight of the disparity between them even though she had put her hair up and was wearing her best. She became aware of the two men accompanying Albert. They too wore hats and overcoats but Kitty noticed patching to the bottom of one of the men's trousers and the worn docker's boots of the other. She found herself wishing that Potter were in attendance. "I'm sorry, Albert, I had to find you," she explained.

Albert took out a gold pocket watch that Kitty had never seen; he looked at it before returning it to his breast pocket.

"We've received a telegram, Albert. Jobe has passed the scholarship test for the College. He's been accepted." She became breathless as she delivered the good news.

"Liverpool College, a scholarship? Well, well!" he replied as he passed his gold-topped cane from one hand to the other.

"That's right, Albert! Isn't it wonderful? His future will be assured. Who knows, he may end up at Oxford or—" Kitty was cut short as Albert suddenly interrupted.

"And why, may I ask, the haste to track me down?" he asked, not looking at Kitty but monitoring the smooth momentum of his cane.

"Well, we've to send a telegram of acceptance before the week is out, Albert. Time is of the essence."

Albert suddenly took a grip of his cane and brought it down hard against the ground, startling Kitty. He looked her in the eye. "Forgive my obtuseness, but what, may I enquire, do you mean when you say…we?" His question asked, Albert proceeded to afford his full attention to the cane as he continued to pass it from hand to hand.

Kitty blanched, her worst fears being realised. "But, Albert…it was always your dream for him…we…"

Albert again snapped his head up. "There it is again, that word— we!" This time, he took an intimidating step forward and stared into his wife's upturned face. "Do I understand its implication correctly?

That you are implying there exists a you and an I? A partnership? An association? An…Us!" Albert spat each term with such unadulterated revulsion and vehemence that Kitty, for the second time that evening, found herself shrinking back against the wall of the Vines. Her tongue grew leaden in her mouth until she felt it would choke her and she was unable to check the apologies that tumbled from her lips.

"I'm sorry, Albert, forgive me. But this isn't about us, it's about Jobe. I could never afford his uniform, books—I haven't the money, Albert," she stammered.

Albert's face lit up in mock enlightenment. "Ah, so there we have it. Money," he said, resting his cane against his leg so he could bring both hands together in a slow clap.

Kitty felt her timidity fall away as her blood rose, flushing her cheeks. Responding to his intimidating step forward and the threatening tone of his voice, she forced herself from the refuge of the wall until she was almost under the brim of his hat.

"It has been months since you forced your wife and son into the slums, with not a thought for their welfare. Have I come to you for a penny in that time? How dare you accuse me of begging?" Kitty stood her ground as she awaited his response.

"And how dare you accost me regarding the education and advancement of a papist," he responded.

"He is your son. It's his only chance! It is your duty, Albert."

"My duty? To fund the intellect of another Fenian mouthpiece?"

"Ah, it's the religion. That's your excuse again, is it, Albert? I wonder, is it the Wise Pastor who pays for your finery, or are you back suckling your mammy now that you have rid yourself of your Catholic family and the associated shame?" Kitty roughly fingered his overcoat, looking him up and down as she spoke.

Albert was taken aback at Kitty's touch and the mention of his mother but quickly regained his composure. "I say, if the desperation to educate your son is of such import, perhaps you should have paid more attention to the codger's proposition. If it was his age that caused your squeamishness, I'm sure one of my men would cross your palm with a few shillings." He turned to his associates, and with a blitheness one would attach to remarking on the weather, offered them his wife. "Lads? I have the means to provide a sub if needed," he offered, nodding towards her. "I can attest that it's nothing special. You know how Catholics are. But it would pass the time, and I'm sure the landlord would allow you use of the barrel-keep for a copper."

Kitty turned toward the two men as their vacuous faces lit up in understanding. She pushed herself past Albert and bolted along Lime Street without looking back.

* * *

As she turned off Marybone into Marlborough Street, Kitty saw that the short walk to her court was in darkness. She hoped the gaslight had broken again and that the High-Rips hadn't put it out so they could lurk in the shadows and use the cover to creep up on their victim.

She chided herself, only too aware that the newspapermen had helped to create the High-Rip myth by sensationalising the deeds of a few ragtag delinquents. Every crime or act of violence was attributed to them and splashed across the front pages. As a consequence, even the skinniest miscreant could strike fear into the most burly of men by hollering the battle cry Hiiiigggghhhhh Rrrriiiiiipppppp!

The sky was clear, and the glow of the half-moon lit up the cobbles enough for Kitty to find her way to the entrance to Number

4 Court. The moonlight was cut off as she entered the narrow passage and didn't return when she entered the court. A single gas lamp feebly illuminated the gloom and she kept to the wall until she reached the steps of the cellar she now called home, her ears intent on picking out the slightest noise. The fear of a High-Rip attack had subsided now, replaced by the worry that someone would swing open the privy door located at the top of her steps, forcing her down them. She had already lost count of the times the men of the court, those who had the decency to use it, fresh from the pub, had misplaced a step on leaving the privy and arrived at her front door in a tangled heap.

Instinctively holding her breath, she reached the top of the steps unimpeded. The constant stench that permeated the area near the privy made it impossible to breathe freely without gagging. Kitty had done her best to rectify the issue, but her efforts bore little fruit. She had tracked down the night-soil men and through charm alone persuaded them to attend to Court 4's privy and then, unable to afford the coal to boil the water, she had used buckets straight from the standpipe to sluice out the pit and scrub the bench, her hands blue and numb from the cold water. The matriarchs of the court had poured scorn on her attempts to sanitise the privy: 'Suppose them from up the hills have shite that smells of roses, don't they?'

The children of the court, those who were allowed to approach the *snob from Everton*, revelled in refilling Kitty's bucket from the tap in the middle of the court. Each time they struggled back with their load, Kitty would delight them with the mythical stories from her childhood or the verse of a song that kept them occupied throughout. Those children not allowed to help or even approach Kitty sat sullenly watching events from afar until, once their mothers' backs were turned, they would join the other children in the fight for the privilege of fetching Kitty's water.

The sanitation was now a weekly occurrence, and although none of those who patronised the privy ever offered to help, their dexterity had greatly improved when depositing their night-soil, and some of the children now brought buckets of hot water that their mothers had heated over the fire.

Kitty, her lungs bursting for air tried to open the front door quietly, not wanting to wake Jobe but she fell into the room, gulping in a great lungful of the staleness within.

Jobe had heard his mother coming down the steps, and from behind the curtain that partitioned the one small room into two tiny ones, repeated the question he had asked the previous three nights. "Did you find him, Mother?"

Kitty silently scowled at herself, under the impression she had woken her son. She popped her head around the thin sheet of material, although the inky blackness obscured everything. "Not tonight, but I'm sure I will tomorrow." She was glad of the darkness that cloaked her lie and her tear-stained face. She knew instinctively that there would be another question on Jobe's lips but stopped it on them. "Not now, sweetheart, it's late. Sleep now and we'll speak in the morning. Goodnight and God bless." She readjusted the sheet and, after feeling for it with her foot, sat down heavily on a crate that was her only seat. There was a candle next to the remains of the loaf her da had brought her, lying on the upturned bucket that served as a table, but she remained in the dark.

Jobe still struggled to eat the dry, stale bread, gagging as he attempted to swallow, but if she could get a small fire going in the stove, she would be able to toast some of the staleness out of it, and it would suffice for breakfast. Kitty sat in the impenetrable dark, unable to see her hand in front of her face or her tears that fell silently to the cold, flagged floor.

* * *

Jobe looked around the court, only his forehead and eyes visible above the top step, which in the strictest terms was breaking another of his mother's 'not to do's' but scarcely enough to be conscionable.

"Don't set foot upstairs into the court, Jobe," she had said. Again he had protested.

"But, Mother, I'll be a prisoner in this cell." His mother had tutted, and he had appealed to her anxious tendencies, declaring dramatically, "I'd wonder if I didn't die from the lack of fresh air!"

"Ach, Jobe, it's just for a while, and there's not much fresh air up there anyway! Remember, it's like one of your adventure books, and look…" She went and pulled the sheet of dirty fabric so that it gathered along one end of the string it hung from. "Didn't Mr. Duncan tell us it was two rooms?"

The narrow slice of sky he could see above the court was just gaining some colour. It was difficult to measure time in the cellar, such was the lack of natural light, but it must have been hours now since he had heard the court noisily come to life as those with employment left on their long walks to reach it.

His mother had left their room early, creeping around so as not to wake him. Taking advantage of her absence, he opened the door and crept out onto the narrow, damp steps that led up into the court.

The court was a tiny walled in square, not more than fifteen feet across. The narrow passageway through which he had entered on his first day the only access for both people and air, and he imagined neither of those that passed through could be very salubrious. He noted with a hint of satisfaction that the court was almost an exact parallel; four dilapidated doors faced each other, one on each side of the court. These doors were seemingly the only entrance to the four floors above them, which he noted, with neck craned back, by counting the cracked, grime-caked windows. Many of them were broken and had been stuffed with yellowing paper or dirty rags in an attempt to keep the chill out.

A thin layer of soot covered everything, including the steps upon which he sat. Even though the dampness of the court encouraged the dust to settle, Jobe fancied he could feel the black matter entering his throat and nose as he drew breath. The privy was just to the right of his head, and though his mother had enticed the muck-men to empty it with regularity and scrubbed it out herself each weekend, the smell coming from it was still enough to make his eyes sting. On each of the dozen or so occasions she had cleaned it, he had begged to be allowed to join her up in the court, but to no avail.

"Remember I warned you about the stray dogs, Jobe? Well, these children can be just as vicious and then some. Let me get a feel for them, see who's who, and perhaps next week I'll introduce you."

Jobe hadn't been satisfied and it was torture to listen to the sloshing of water and the children shouting and shrieking as his mother regaled them with tales of Cliodhna, Queen of the Banshees or taught them verses of the old songs.

He continued his reconnaissance of the decaying foundations that made up the court, following a scum-covered trickle of water back to a dripping, rusted standpipe that protruded at an angle from stained and cracked cobbles in the middle of the court. Then he saw the dog.

It must have been still for a very long time because he couldn't have failed to notice its movement in the tiny space; he wondered if it was asleep. Most of the dogs he had known of were small, and although they sometimes yapped loudly, their owners would easily control them with a reprimand if it were a man, or a comforting word if it were a lady. He tried to remember a time when he had seen a dog without its owner but couldn't. Dogs were one of the things his mother had warned him of the day they had arrived in their new home.

"Look, Jobe," she had said as they were led down stairs that were covered on one side by raw sewage leaking from the privy at the top of them. "It's just like one of the caves from your pirate stories. I wonder if there's any buried treasure in here?"

Jobe thought it very unlikely and held his nose and stepped over the witches brew of faeces, urine and rainwater that had found its way under the door.

Mr. Duncan was a small balding man. His face so badly burnt that the thick scarring covering it dragged his mouth down until it almost met with his chin. He failed to conceal his pretended ignorance of the filth by stating in his lisping guttural voice, "Hmm, I'll have a word with schuperintendent of the night schoil-men. You will get usched to the schmell, and I can asschure you that even during the heaviescht downpour, the privy upschtairsh will not overflow. But you musht impressch on your neighboursch the need to be more shalubriousch with their schecretionsh."

Duncan had shown his mother a small wood-burning stove and then pointed to a dirty sheet that was held up by a string that spanned and, when drawn, separated the room. "You schee, it has a partition here, I really schould be charging you for two roomsh. I could eashily rent thish half to another family." He pulled the sheet across to illustrate his claim. He spoke as though his nose was blocked and dabbed at a trail of spittle that leaked continuously from the side of his mouth. Jobe wondered if the man could smell anything through his melted, fused nostrils.

Duncan left them alone in their new room, and his mother beckoned her to him. She held him closely for a while, and although she was silent, he could feel her body shuddering and knew she was crying. When she released him, her eyes and cheeks were glistening but she was smiling. "Now look here, you, although this is going to be a grand adventure, a holiday, there still have to be rules. You know most of them because they're the same as we've always had, but there are some more here because this is like one of your fantasy stories." She took pause and became very serious, holding Jobe by the shoulders. "You know, Jobe, how sometimes there can be danger in your favourite stories, and if the heroes aren't clever and careful they could be killed or taken prisoner or have their princess kidnapped?"

Jobe nodded his understanding.

"This is just like that," his mother continued. "You need to be clever and careful all of the time. Promise me you will, Jobe."

On his promising and ensuring he had understood her message, his mother had proceeded to give him a list of do's and don'ts, mostly don'ts.

"Don't ever go out alone. Don't ever go off with anyone—"

Jobe had interrupted her. "I'm sorry, Mother, these are all the rules from our old house."

His mother had agreed. "OK, remember all of them and add the new ones, don't ever go into the privy upstairs…"

Eventually, she had arrived at dogs. "Beware of them, Jobe. They're not like the wee yapping fellows from the pleasure gardens. These are sneaky, intelligent creatures, like the hungry wolves from your old picture books, especially when they're in a pack. You make sure you give them a wide berth."

Jobe didn't know how he was supposed to run into a pack of wolf-like dogs if he wasn't allowed out, but he didn't interrupt his mother as she carried on with her list of not to do's.

This dog was big. It lay taking up a ridiculously large space in the corner of the court. It still hadn't moved. He was about to ascend to the top step and contravene a plethora of his mother's don'ts when two smartly dressed men entered from the passageway.

Jobe wasn't quick enough to dodge out of sight and one of them noticed his head poking out from the cellar steps as they cast furtive glances around. "You there, rouse your neighbours, tell them to congregate around the standpipe here," he called.

Jobe looked at them and remained mute. Not only because he felt a rush of irrational guilt at being caught on the steps but also to obey another of his mother's don'ts.

"Don't you ever talk to strangers, Jobe!" she had ordered.

"But Mother, Father always told me to respond when spoken to. It is rude and ignorant to do otherwise," he had protested.

"Not here, it's not, you're not to speak to strangers, Jobe, understand?" she had insisted and Jobe had nodded his acquiescence.

"You, boy! Rouse your neighbours I say!" On receiving no response the man shook his head, taking Jobe for a simpleton. Unbeknown to the man every household that the court comprised was now aware of the two official men who had entered their domain. After a minute or two, the men realised they were being observed but purposely ignored. "Ho there, we're from the corporation. We've come about your court being photographed," he called out to the court as a whole.

No sooner had the words been spoken than doors opened and faces appeared at the filth-caked windows overlooking the tiny square. Jobe ducked out of sight and crouched on the steps, his mouth perilously close to the black sludge. He wrestled with himself internally before reaching a decision, cautiously projected his head back into the court. His view of the standpipe was now blocked and he marvelled at the number of people who had spilled out of their front doors into the small quad, packing it tight. He was even more surprised when, looking up, he saw those who couldn't push their way into the court or were too infirm to try, appear at each of the cracked windows, competing with one another to obtain a view. The corporation men made no effort to make themselves heard and Jobe struggled to pick out a single word. Those who had been forced to the back of the crowd and found themselves next to the privy glanced curiously at him before diverting their attention back to those delivering the information. The only clear words that Jobe was able to discern came from the men as they were leaving the court.

"And for goodness' sake, can somebody get rid of that dead dog!"

* * *

Marge O'Grady cackled her mispronunciation of the name Rathbone. "Ratbones, funny name for a family of toffs," she screeched. Immediately becoming stony faced and eyeing Kitty malevolently as she cleared the passageway and entered the court.

Kitty ignored the looks and continued to the cellar clutching a net of oranges her da had given her. Only stopping to give a piece of fruit each to the half dozen children who sat just inside a decrepit doorway next to her cellar steps. She was exposed to an odour akin to that of the privy as she bent to deliver her gifts. On receiving their

79

bounty the children retreated into the bleak interior, already ripping at the peel with their teeth.

So it's the Rathbones behind it all she thought as she descended the stone steps. Kitty had attended their charity events with Albert, met some of the altruistic family and even knew some of them enough to say hello to. Although happy that a glimmer of excitement had entered the lugubrious lives of her neighbours, that they had something to look forward to and be proud of, Kitty herself couldn't care less about the news the men from the corporation had proclaimed to the court; that it was to be photographed for a study being carried out by some philanthropists intent on finding solutions to the overcrowding, poverty and lack of sanitisation in the slums. To allow the subjects of their study a modicum of dignity, and no doubt to avoid muddying their boots, the Rathbones themselves were not going to come prodding and prying into the slums and courts but would use photographic evidence to help compile their data. Although Kitty was aware of plenty of well-to-do people who weren't daunted by a visit to the slums. Not just the religious zealots who doled out their bread as reward for attending a prayer meeting but those who fed their morbid fascination with poverty and degradation by observing it firsthand. Using those unfortunates who dwelt in the slums for cheap entertainment and even, in some cases, to slake their immoral tendencies. She had seen the groups of slum-watchers congregating at the railings of the pleasure gardens awaiting their guide for the evening. Although they made efforts to dress down and become inconspicuous, they still resembled royalty in comparison to those they were hoping to infiltrate.

Court Number 4 Marlborough Street had been selected as one of the courts to be photographed. The news had spread like wildfire, not only among the other courts that lined the street but also through the parishes of St. Mary's and Holy Cross, which the little thoroughfare was sandwiched between. The court had already been the subject of scandal when the gossip that a woman and her son from Everton had moved into it had spread. It was only confirmation that it was the daughter of Nelly and Fergus Flynn from Standish Street that had prevented the formation of an outraged mob.

The communal solidarity that existed within the slums and the courts of the area was born from mutual experience. The daily struggle for survival that resulted in the neglect of every other pursuit beyond the mere means of existence. Any difference was magnified. Any deviation from the economic condition or good fortune, regardless of its guise, was met with open hostility. Now that it was perceived Court Number 4 was being shown favour by philanthropic toffs the customary solidarity had been suspended and both parishes and the remaining courts on the street had renewed their sniping with vigour. Accompanied by a healthy dose of jealousy. Those in Court Number 4 would not only be recorded and framed for posterity but would benefit from their court being made over, cleaned and whitewashed. It set them apart from their neighbours so made them fair game. The slights would become topics of conversation wherever a resident of Court Number 4 ventured; in shops, pubs or when passing a janglers wall, the favourite haunts of the gossiping matriarchs. "I wouldn't thank you for it, being gawped at by those do-gooder Bible bashers." "Aren't they all O's anyway? Probably friends of them tangerines from Everton."

The residents of Court Number 4 had all too often been the proponents of petty, seething spite and resentment themselves, and to find that they were, for once, the objects of it presented them with an opportunity to walk with their heads a little higher and their backs a little straighter.

The only positive for Kitty had come when she learned that the walls were to be cleaned and prepared for the coat of whitewash they would be receiving. "I've never understood it, Jobe. If they truly want to capture the filth and dirt people live in then why do they whitewash the walls?"

Jobe had explained that the walls of the court were so soiled and soot-covered, and the deficiency of natural light so stark that the flash of the camera had no chance of working in the usual dank gloom of the court so the walls had to painted. Kitty had nodded at her son, still in total ignorance, but was happy that the court would be spruced up a little.

* * *

The three urchins stood in a circle on one of Great Crosshall Street's ollers, a patch of waste ground adopted by children as their playgrounds. The last drops of urine they could muster splashed on the mud and over their bare feet. Michael began to pull up his crusted cutoffs, wrapping the string around his waist for a second time before tying it tightly.

"Is that your contribution, Michael? Jesus, my baby sister pisses more," piped Jimmy Malone in disgust diverting his steady, but reducing stream, toward his friend's feet.

Michael wasn't fussed. He had purposely not pushed too hard. The last time they had played jelly and custard he had strained so much that his head had spun and he had almost fainted. The other lads finished and pulled up their pants.

Michael already had his piece of stick inhand and had begun to stir the urine into the mud. "'Ere, wait for us, Mick. Most of it's our piss after all," stated Jimmy.

The trio began to mix with their sticks. "Jelly and custard, Jelly and custard," they repeated rhythmically, not noticing the man who came up behind them.

"What's all this now? Have you boys no more imagination than to be stirring up piss and mud for your entertainment?"

Michael looked up to see his grandfather.

"Hello, Mr. Flynn," chimed his two companions.

Fergus shook his head sombrely at the three boys. "I'm sorry for you," he said gesticulating over to Holy Cross Church. "Don't you know it's a mortal sin to urinate in the shadow of God's house?"

Jimmy Malone looked worried. "What's urinate?" he asked.

Paddy Goss elbowed him. "It means to piss, idiot," he hissed.

All three looked up at Fergus but it was Jimmy Malone who spoke, looking at the other two accusingly. "I told youse we should have went rabbiting down Leeds Street." He turned his attention to Fergus, fear etched on his face. "Ah, no, Mr. Flynn. Is there anything we can do? There must be something. What if we go to the priests' house and ask can we scrub the step?"

Fergus rubbed his chin. "Well, I wouldn't go telling the priests what it is youse have been up to," he replied, making a point of leaning forward and examining the mush they had created. "Well, that's something at least, it's not dried up yet. I'll tell youse what, if you can get home before this is dry, making the sign of the cross all the way, mind you, and then do your mother a great help, really help her I mean, with whatever chore she sets yer too, the harder the better, youse might, just might, be OK."

Jimmy Malone and Paddy Goss were off down Great Crosshall Street, their right arms a blur as they hurriedly made as many signs of the cross as possible.

Fergus held on to Michael's collar before he could race off. "Haven't I told you about hanging around with those Fontenoy boys. Look at them go, thick as bricks they are," he said as he let go of his grandson's collar.

Michael looked at him. "But the mud, Granda! It's drying!" he protested.

Fergus shook his head. "You see how stupidity is catching? C'mon with yer now, let's see if there's some jam and bread for yer in the house."

As they walked up toward Standish Street Fergus looked down at his grandson. "Why is it that you never play with your cousin Jobe in the courts?"

"Me da says I'm not allowed to on account of him and his mammy being filthy O's."

"Is that so? Well I'll be boxing the big lummox's ears for him, he should know better than to instill disrespect for your aunt into you. Besides, when they were younger, your da and Jobe's mammy were inseparable!"

"I don't think it is because they're O's at all. I think he's scared that it'll upset Grammy," confided Michael bashfully. His face turned white on mention of his grandmother. "Aw no, she'll kill me. I've forgot her jug!" Michael desperately rifled through the pockets of his cutoffs, pulling out a sixpenny piece with obvious relief. He looked at his grandfather. "She sent me ages ago, what'll I do?" he stammered, his mortal sin against the church forgotten in the face of raising the ire of his grandmother.

"Did she give you a jug to return?" asked Fergus.

His grandson thought a second before shaking his head. "No. I dropped and smashed the last empty she sent me with. I'm to tell Fitzy she'll have me da return his empties."

Fergus smiled conspiratorially and ruffled his grandson's coarse, dark locks. "Here's what's to be done. Give me the tanner."

Michael obediently gave his grandfather the coin.

"Now you get yourself back to your grammy and tell her that I took the tanner off you as you were about to go into the Borough. Tell her I was drunk and made you accompany me all the way down to the Goat's Head on the Dock Road because I wanted your help carrying a package I was picking up from a Russian sailor." Fergus paused. "Have you got that so far?" Fergus watched as Michael relayed the information in his head, his lips moving silently before nodding. Fergus continued. "Now tell her the Russian fella never turned up and I sent you away and went into the Goat. Got it?"

Michael went through the process of getting his story straight, his lips moving as he practised the conversation in his head. "Got it!' he said, smiling. The story was a good one, and as far as he could tell, it would be his granda in all the trouble and not him. He might even get a bit of bread and some milk if he laid it on thick about the forced march to the Dock Road and back.

* * *

Nelly's nose twitched as her husband entered the room. She ground her teeth for the bread and milk she had given young Michael and made a mental note to give him a good whack for his lying when she saw him next.

Fergus ducked under the empty washing line, pretending to falter.

"You can stop your charade, Fergus Flynn. You've brought no more alcohol fumes into this room than was already here." Nelly's rocking was frenetic, such was her choler, but given the lack of missiles, Fergus felt it safe enough to drag an orange box nearer the table and sit down on it.

"I'll tell you once and never again, Fergus Flynn, there'll be no more of my money squandered on that treacherous O' daughter of yours."

"Squander? Nell', have you heard yourself? You're sending out for a jug while our daughter is around the corner starving to death, her and your grandson." Fergus spoke the words softly as his wife continued her rocking.

"Your daughter, Fergus Flynn. Your grandson! What's the do now? Has my prophecy come home to roost? Has her great, grand O' finally consigned her back to the slum she had no right in leaving in the first place?"

"No right? Is that it? Is that your problem all these years, Nelly? Are yer jealous? Would you resent your wee babby daughter doing her best to escape this shite that we've had to endure the last thirty-odd years?"

Nelly stopped rocking and looked hard at her husband.

Fergus dropped his head to his chest. "I've allowed you to become this, Nell'," he said, spreading both of his hands to encompass his wife. "To forsake everything. To sit in that chair and drink yourself into an early grave. I've done it because it was easier, Nelly. Easier than watching you try to survive with dignity in this cesspit. Although you could have. If anyone could, it'd be you." He exhaled sadly and shook his head. "But I couldn't bear to watch that. I'd rather you sat and escaped this drudge by drinking yourself into oblivion. Don't you see it is me who failed us? It's me who dragged us to this godforsaken city. Jesus, I didn't even listen to the advice I received on the boat. Didn't that widow tell me to beware of the Scotland and

Vauxhall Road areas? Do you remember her?" Fergus mimicked the hag, pointing his finger at Nelly in a conspiratorial manner. "'Avoid them both like the plague! Avoid them like the plague, or more than likely it's a plague that'll be your fate.' But I knew best, didn't I? We'll be better off with our own, I said. The city won't get its claws into us I said. Well it did, Nell! It got its claws, teeth and everything into us, ravaged us until we became the husks we are today, both of us staring at those empty jugs and knowing we'd give our back teeth to have just one of them half full." Fergus looked at the empty jugs on the table and unconsciously licked his lips. "And it's not only the two of us but our children as well, the lot of them. Except her, Nelly, don't you see it?" Fergus's tone traversed from remorse to anger to beseeching. He took heart from his wife's lack of rocking and the faraway look in her eyes. "We can't sit by and watch her struggle, Nell'. She's been out of the slums too long to come back and survive. If we don't give her whatever scant support we can, it'll do for her." Fergus fancied that he saw his wife's features soften and continued. "And the boy, Nelly. He's just like her. He's a beautiful boy, too fair to be on the scrap heap at his age. Bright as a button he is. He could do something with his life if we'd just give him what help we can." Fergus leant forward and took his wife's hands in his. Physical contact of any kind was a rarity now. Even on bitter nights during the winter they would lie apart, forsaking the other's body heat. Now, her hands clasped in his, he looked her in the eye. "What d'yer say, Nelly? Shall we do it? Something of consequence, redeem ourselves through them?"

His wife looked down at her husband's gnarled, scarred hands enveloping hers. Remembered the years he toiled on their rocky barren land, cultivating it inch by painful inch in order to provide for her. The sensation of his skin seemed alien to her but she returned his gaze and smiled at him. "You do as your mind tells you, Fergus Flynn, but you ever take so much as a ha'penny from this house in order to furnish those tangerines again and I'll flay the skin from your back and take yer kidneys for the dogs."

* * *

"The Giant O' was here! The Giant O' was here!"

Kitty's mind convulsed at the words little Sally McManus was screaming around the court and her memory regressed back to a conversation she had had with her da a fortnight or so ago, as he walked her to one of her charring jobs. She stood stock still as the conversation played through her mind.

"It'll be more difficult for me to help you now, girl. Your mother isn't a bad woman. She's had it hard and it's turned her hard. I wish you could have known her in Ireland." Fergus's head hung, disconsolate.

Kitty took his hand. "I'll manage, Da. I have my little bits, the slop-work, the charring. This one on Rodney Street is a good earner. They'll suffice, neither of us eat much, and the hovel is almost free as long as I can afford Jobe's schooling..." she tailed off, smiling at her da.

Fergus could see through his daughter's smile but was concerned at her mention of slop-work. He knew many of the unsavoury characters involved in the slop-trade; they employed women to transform rags into clothing with the skill of their needlework. Sailors fresh to shore after months at sea made excellent customers. Regardless of their creed, colour or culture, the seamen would arrive in Banastre Street desperately seeking to rid themselves of their salt-stiffened rags, swap them for functional clothing that they could wear while embarking on emptying their full purses in the pubs, taverns and gin palaces. Those visiting for the first time were amazed that the world-famous Paddy's Market could be contained in the grimy-looking brick shed.

The slop-traders, who jealously guarded their pitches on the earthen floor of Paddy's Market, were perfectly placed to considerably lighten the sailors' purses, not only by providing them with the cheap, but fresh, clothing they craved but by offering another, less salubrious service that the seamen were equally desperate to partake in. The wages the slop-traders paid their army of needlewomen were negligible and they were known to prey on the poverty of the seamstresses to cajole them into less skilled, less time-consuming, but more profitable work.

"Who is it you're slopping for, Kitty?" he asked, unable to keep a tone of trepidation out of his voice.

Kitty was only too aware of his concerns. "Don't worry, Da. It's none of those pigs from Marybone. I know only to well what they're about. I'm working for a respectable Jew from up Pembroke Place way."

Fergus nodded his head in relief. "A respectable Jew, eh? Well there's a first," he couldn't help adding before commencing with the conversation he had been putting off for an age. "Kitty, would you not look at selling your ring, consider pawning it maybe?"

Kitty stopped and Fergus looked the other way, feigning that he was watching for traffic. She recommenced walking. "I can't, Da. What'll I say when he comes back?"

"Tell him you sold it in order to feed yourself and yer child, Kathleen." Fergus's frustration had shown in his tone, and he looked sheepishly at the floor. "D'you really believe he'll come back, Kitty? I mean, it's been months now," he said more softly.

"I do, Da, and I want him to know that I trusted him, to be able to show him I never lost faith in him, never doubted him. He's going to need that. The guilt will eat him otherwise."

"Won't your waiting, your struggling show him that? Sure, you could have your pick of every eligible man in every parish. There's a lot to be said for an economic marriage, Kitty. Your worries would be over."

Kitty swung her da's arm as she had when she was younger. "Ach, don't be silly, Da. He's had it hard. It was bad enough his business in Boston failing and us having to come home, but he dealt with it. His father dying has sent him to the drink and muddled his senses, and the emergence of the Wise Pastor has turned his head, that's all."

Fergus stopped walking and turned Kitty in his direction. Taking her other hand in his, he spoke into her face. "It's done more than turn his head, Kitty. It's turned him to breaking them! Catholic ones! And dozens of them. He's a regular bogeyman! The children talk of him, call him a Giant. The Giant O', they say. He has glowing green eyes, a silk top hat and a gold-topped walking cane that he'll put through your skull."

Kitty shook her head at her da's melodramatics. "Oh, Da, it's not like you to listen to children's prattle. He loves us. He left everything behind for me once, and he will again. I just know it. Until that day, I'll continue to raise Jobe and ensure he gets his education, and the ring will stay hidden away."

Sally's words broke into Kitty's thoughts. "The Giant O' was here! The Giant O' was here," she screeched. Sally was one of the children who always brought a bucket of hot water on what was now known as 'Sanitation Saturday'. No matter how tired Kitty felt after her hard week's work, she always ensured that her half-day off was spent cleaning the privy with the children of the court.

She beckoned Sally over. "Now then, what's all this chatter about a giant, eh?" Kitty was in a turmoil. Her heart seemed to be beating in her throat, but she managed to remain composed.

Sally answered, her breath catching in her throat such was her excitement. "Oh, Kitty, you should see the size of him! He truly is a giant! He has great green eyes and a shining silk top hat and, and he had his walking cane with him, the one he uses to bash heads in."

Kitty could hardly breathe. "What was he doing, Sally? Why was he here? Was he looking for someone? Did he mention my name? Did he mention Kitty Warburton?"

Sally had gone quiet, and Kitty realised she was holding the child by the shoulders and shaking her. She immediately let go of her, instead hugging her to her breast. "Oh, forgive me, Sally. I'm sorry, my love. I'm sorry. Everything's going to be fine now, it'll be all right, d'you hear?" Kitty was blubbering. The defences she had constructed and maintained for so long disintegrated with the news that Albert had finally come to reclaim her and his son, and she fell to her knees, still holding the confused girl. "It's over, Jobe, we're safe now. Everything is going to be all right."

Sally broke free and looked at Kitty, wondering at her sobbing words and the tears streaming down her face.

"He wasn't looking for anyone, Kitty. He came to visit my Aunt Aggie."

Chapter IV

1890

Kitty, still sobbing, followed Sally into Mrs. Keogh's rooms, plotting a course among the multitude of children who sat in the hallway tying bunches of kindling together that they would soon bring into town to sell as firewood.

The walls of Aggie's kitchen were freshly whitewashed, painted from tins that the photographer's engineer had *lost* a few days previous, and covered with paintings of religious scenes. A huge depiction of Our Lady of Majula took pride of place above a roaring fire that gave the room a snug feel.

Seeing the state that the usually composed and confident Kitty was in, Aggie Keogh, her silver hair falling thick down her back, had shooed another group of children who sat around the huge, scrubbed farmhouse table into the already packed hallway with a stream of expletives. Before she settled Kitty into a worn and frayed, but comfortable, button backed highchair and forced a cup of hot tea into her shaking hand, flatly refusing to answer any questions or even discuss her exotic visitors unless Kitty took it and sipped it down.

Once Kitty had swallowed some of the tea and remastered her breathing Aggie Keogh nodded with satisfaction and took a battered silver snuffbox from the deep pocket of her much-darned cardigan. On finding it empty she called out a girl's name who, seconds later, duly appeared from the hallway. "Heidi, here take my box to down to Jenks' and ask him for three penneth of Fine Irish. The money's in the tin there," she said pointing to an ornament crammed dresser. Before the girl reached the dresser Aggie had reconsidered. "In fact take sixpence and fetch me a tanner's worth."

Content the girl had grasped the essence of her errand, Aggie sat in a chair directly opposite Kitty and began to explain the origin of her bounteous visitors. Her John had again been imprisoned, on this occasion falsely, mind you; he was a drunk, and of that there was no denying, but he was never violent, not like they had claimed. While awaiting trial, he had been held in the Main Bridewell at Cheapside, where he was, she admitted crossing herself repeatedly, such a regular that he was usually allowed his own cell. Finding another soul already in there, he had taken exception, but after the interloper had allowed him use of his newspaper and managed to acquire him some cigarettes from the guards, John and his new lodger had enjoyed some conversation.

Her John had a wide breadth of knowledge; he was an avid reader and was a good conversationalist when sober. The two had formed an incongruous friendship, and when John, following his appearance in court, had returned to the cell and informed the man of his six-month sentence, the stranger had told John not to fret about his family, that he would take it upon himself to see to it that his wife and children would not suffer in his absence. John's newfound friend was none other than the notorious Pastor Wise. But he had been true to his word and remained so. Aggie had received several visits from well-to-do gentlemen, all bearing the cell-lodger's well wishes and, more importantly, a quantity of cash. Protestants, every one of them, but courteous and well-mannered Protestants.

"This Albert, the Giant O', your husband. He's only been here the once, and that was today. I've heard the stories that do the rounds about him and Pastor Wise, but I can't help feeling they must be greatly exaggerated. You know what the soft shites around here are like?"

Kitty had waited patiently throughout the monologue, but now that Aggie Keogh had invited her into the conversation she asked the question that was singeing her tongue. "Would you have noticed whether he wears a wedding ring, Mrs. Keogh?"

They had never spoken before, but Aggie smiled at her slyly, treating Kitty as though they were old collaborators. "He removed his gloves to hand me the envelope and he does, Kitty, he does."

Kitty almost slumped off the chair in relief and Aggie mistook her show of relief for faintness and ordered Sally, who had remained in the doorway observing the pair, to cut a slice from a still-hot loaf that rested on the shining stove and slather it with butter. As with the tea, Kitty had no choice but to accept. Mrs. Keogh promised Kitty that if the Giant O' appeared at her door again, she would send the children to find her. Kitty supplied her with a current list of her workplaces; it was a long list, and Aggie Keogh had chided her that she would work herself into an early grave but also promised that one of her large extended family would track her down. Aggie had given Kitty a hug and then forced the remainder of the still-warm loaf and a dish of butter on her before allowing her to leave and share the news with her son.

Kitty, although loath to do so, could see no alternative but to impart her findings about Albert to her son. The conversation with Aggie

Keogh had provided her with fresh optimism, although she remained shaken and red-eyed following the tumultuous and emotional torture she had endured. On returning to the cell she beckoned Jobe to sit down and gave him a thick slice of warm, buttered bread, which he tore into as he sat, cross-legged, looking up at her.

"Your father was here in the court, Jobe," she said, not pausing or drawing breath, and so sparing him the cruelty that she had suffered, she added quickly. "He wasn't here for us, son. I doubt he even knows we're here. He was here to see Mrs. Keogh. He was on the Wise Pastor's business." She allowed the news to sink in and watched as Jobe took pause from greedily consuming his slice of bread. "But he still wears his wedding ring, Jobe."

Jobe continued to look at her, the crust of bread halfway to his mouth still stationary.

"It's grand news, Jobe! If he still wears his wedding ring, his vows must remain dear to him. Although his mind is fuddled, he still considers himself married. Me his wife and you his son."

Jobe looked at his mother wide-eyed, swallowing the last of the bread and stretching out his tongue, searching for the spots of grease that glistened on his cheeks, chin and fingers.

"There's more, Jobe. You know how you like a good story and how you enjoy it all the more if there's a real terrible baddy in it—one that has the ability to scare you before you go to sleep? Well the children around here have no less vivid imaginations. They've got their own bogeyman. The Giant O', they call him. They say he has glowing green eyes, wears a silk top hat and carries a gold-topped walking cane which he uses to bash in the heads of Catholics…"

"I've heard of him," Jobe interrupted excitedly. "I've heard of him!" He had become fascinated by tales of the Giant O', even beginning to concoct his own stories, regaling the children of the court with tales about the green-eyed demon's latest misdeeds. Sometimes they were entirely his own creation, but on other occasions he replaced the Giant O' with the antagonists of the books he'd read or stories he'd memorised. "I make my own tales up about him. I made Nancy Bennett and Mary Miller run home crying with one of them last week," he finished proudly before his eyes widened with realisation. The fingers he had been sucking fell from his mouth and he stared at his mother, unblinking.

Kitty knelt and took Jobe's face in her hands. "I want you not to believe a word, Jobe. Your father is the gentlest man alive. Sure his mind is fuddled and he's helping to protect the Wise Pastor, but the only reason he would ever strike anybody is if he was in mortal danger himself." Kitty gently shook Jobe's head and then lightly slapped his unflinching face to rouse him from the comatose state he had entered.

Jobe's eyes rolled in their sockets and Aggie Keogh's bread and butter came back up to cover the front of his blazer.

* * *

The group of boys unenthusiastically kicked around a tightly bound ball of rags, the narrow passageway to Court Number 4 their goal. Not one of them sported shoes, and occasionally, there would be a cry of pain as a toe stubbed against a jutting cobble or an opponent's shin. Sporadically, one of them would turn and look up the short distance to the junction with Marybone. "He's late. I reckon he's sneaked past us."

"Don't talk shite, how could he? We've been kicking our heels here for an age."

"Maybe he's played the wag today, stayed indoors."

"More shite. He'd have to be at death's door before his ma'd let him off a day. D'you know how much money she wastes sending him to that shiteing school?"

"Why don't we give him a pass today, go down the docks, see if there's any untended carts about?"

"Ah, you would say that. You're only scared of upsetting his shiteing ma."

"Am not! She's nice, that's all, didn't she bandage my leg the other day."

"Well there'll be no pass for him. We'd be a laughing stock if we allowed a little shite from Everton amongst us, one who attends that shiteing college to boot, without any molestation."

"But what about Michael Flynn? He's his cousin, isn't he one of us?"

"That shiteing traitor Flynny? Isn't he always off down Fontenoy ways playing with our enemies? Sure, didn't he sneak some of our bonfire wood last Guy Fawkes night!"

"What if we've waited all this time and his granda is with him? There's no work down the docks, they're all on strike."

"He's right. Me mam almost put me da's hook through his head last week when he told her he wouldn't be crossing no picket line."

"Pah, what are we? A shiteing janglers wall? Let's get over to Great Crosshall Street. We'll cut him off there."

* * *

Jobe was unsure how to proceed. Running wasn't an option. The cap that had been wrenched from his head had been earned by his mother, who charred and scrubbed so hard during the day that some evenings she was forced to abandon her needlework for fear the material she worked with would be damaged by her raw and bleeding fingers. Her hand in a bowl of cold water, she would fret over the deductions to her pay the missed deadlines would elicit.

Even if he was willing to abandon the cap, he doubted he would get very far; the majority of his tormentors were both bigger and stronger than him. The adults that meandered about seemed to have no inclination to help him, and judging by their look would have proved incapable anyway. His mother's words came flooding back to him.

"A group of wild and hungry wolves, Jobe." He had understood her characterisation from his first venture into the court. The children within had ceased their play, viewing him with ravenous eyes while they sniffed for any perceivable weakness.

She had utilised one of her now famous and anticipated Saturday sanitation afternoons to introduce him, remaining at the bottom of the steps wringing her already raw hands on the rusting handle of her bucket, ears pricked, before finally emerging. "Everyone, say hello to my son Jobe. He's been suffering from a terrible chill this last few months and has had to remain indoors," she stated before inducing a mini-melee among those who didn't possess a bucket of hot water by placing her empty one on the ground. His novelty status and his peers' affection for his mother had carried him through his initial few outings. His manner, sense of humour and, most importantly, his ability to tell stories had cemented his place among the court's children.

The group now blithely tossing his cap from one to another was more reminiscent of a cauldron of raptors, and he sensed their intent was real.

"Are yer lost, little toff?" asked a big, rough-looking girl. Her wiry red hair fell untidily over a face plastered with freckles to such an extent that Jobe wondered if they were one large unfortunate birthmark.

He knew any attempt to retrieve his cap would be futile, only serving to provide the gang with further sport, and—to their irritation—he made no such attempt. "No, I'm not lost. I'm on my way to Number 4 Court Marlborough Street," he said matter-of-factly.

"Oh, so you've come to enjoy a bit of slum-seeing, have yer? What was it, did you hear your rich mammy and daddy talking about us while you ate your meat and potatoes last night? Well, you might get away with trespassing on Marybone, but us from Cockspur Street won't have any of it."

The wind rushed from Jobe as, without warning, the girl swung her fist into his stomach and he doubled over in agony. A hand pulled him roughly up by his hair, causing tears to pool in his eyes. He attempted to blink them away before they could spill out onto his cheeks.

"I don't know about meat? He looks like he hasn't eaten for a week," the owner of the hand commented, betraying a hint of concern. He released his hold on hearing an angry voice behind him, allowing Jobe to return to his prone position.

"'Ere, what's all this shite?"

Clutching his stomach, Jobe fought to regain his breath and rid his eyes of tears. He recognised the deep, monotonous voice and groaned inwardly. Could things get any worse? He looked up to see that half a dozen boys he recognised had turned on to Great Crosshall Street and joined his initial tormentors. The voice belonged to Tommy Molloy, self-appointed leader of the Marybone Boys who were all older than

Jobe but not much bigger, stunted as they were by hunger and ill-health. All except for Molloy. He was a huge, hairy beast of a boy and had led the gang's persecution of Jobe since he had emerged from the relative safety of the court in order to make the long walk to school, with his grandfather when possible, but alone if necessary.

Forming a circle around Jobe, they would push him from one to the other as they chanted, "Ha-ha-ha, ho-ho-ho, lookie here, it's the shiteing O'!" or other lyrics of a similarly inane nature. The group would rifle through his bag, taking any remnants of food they found and waving any books he was allowed to borrow in the air, but on his liberty and bag being returned to him, he would always find that his books had been put back inside with a well-measured deftness. The pushing was as physical as things got, and Jobe had stopped attempting to outwit the gang, finding it more tiresome than the actuality of being apprehended.

"I said what's all this shite?" Tommy Molloy commanded instant respect and the majority of the initial group cast their eyes downwards.

The freckled girl wasn't one of them. "What's it to you, Molly? We've caught ourselves a slum-seer and we're going to teach him a lesson," she sneered.

Tommy Molloy looked at his companions and laughed before turning his attention back to the intruders. "It's Molloy, and you're on our side of the road, that's what it is to me," he snarled.

"You know the law, *Molly*. All boundaries are null and void when it comes to O's and slum-seers. He's ours and we're taking him back across to decide what's to be done with him."

"Is that so, Freckles? Well, the whole shiteing country knows what you get up to on that side of Vauxhall Road, don't they? What'll you do? Murder him for shiteing sixpence like you did poor Richard Morgan? They should have hung the whole cowardly shiteing lot of you. Two was never enough!"

The whole Cockspurs Gang bristled at mention of the murder of Richard Morgan that took place twenty-odd years ago, had outraged the whole of the country and remained a stain on their parish.

Freckles struggled to compose herself. "Everybody knows that the ghost of Thomas Cosgrove was to blame for that!" she spat through gritted teeth, her face turning crimson.

Molloy seized on her chagrin and sought to press home his advantage. He turned to his gang and pointed up the road. "Ah, Cosgrove! Another shiteing murderer from that side of Vauxhall! Too cowardly to face the music for killing his wife, he done for himself with a draught of shiteing poison."

"That's right," confirmed Freckles. "And Morgan died exactly where Cosgrove was buried." Those behind her nodded solemnly at her words, but Molloy wasn't satisfied.

"What you're not making mention of is that Cosgrove was buried at shiteing midnight with a stake through his shiteing chest so he could never rise and make mischief again. So you can't use him as a shiteing excuse for your backward, murdering ways."

Jobe looked up at the girl whose fingers were digging into him, noting that her skin, those patches not already covered by freckles, was steadily turning a deeper shade of crimson at each insult.

"So I hate to break it to yer, " continued Molloy. "But you shiteing Cockspurs'll be taking him nowhere. We'll be taking him back to his home."

Freckles shook herself. "As if you would know where he lives, yer big pudding," she retorted.

"Oh, I know all right. Yer see, this little toff here is no shiteing slum-seer. He lives in Court 4 on Marlborough Street—same one as Ged here." He turned to a boy whose cut leg Jobe's mother had cleaned out and dressed the week before. The boy still had the rag tied around his knee, but now it was grey and greasy looking.He nodded his confirmation. "Yeah, that's right, Tommy. He lives in our court, in the cellar," he pointed to his knee. "His mam…" he continued but trailed off on noticing Molloy's frown.

"So you've got two choices, Freckles. You can go back to your shiteing side of Vauxhall Road empty-handed, or you can go back empty-handed and bloody-nosed!"

Freckles wasn't appeased and retained her hold on Jobe's blazer.

Although Molloy had no qualms when it came to hitting girls, especially ones as big and ugly as Freckles, he, for once, engaged his brain rather than his fists. "His da is the Giant O'!" he said blithely.

Freckles let go of Jobe as if she had just heard he was riddled with leprosy. She looked at him with awe and then turned to Molloy. "The Giant O's son?"

The legend that the Giant O's son lived among them had spread like wildfire around the surrounding parishes. It was the reason behind Freckles's and her gang's expedition from Cockspur Street across Vauxhall Road and into enemy territory. The excitement of a chance encounter with such easy prey as Jobe had caused all thoughts of the Giant O' and his son to evaporate.

Tommy Molloy took the opportunity to pull Jobe back and deposit him behind his gang. "So what's it to be, Ginger? Are yer leaving of your own shiteing choice or is it to be fisties?"

Freckles bristled and Jobe noticed both gangs' postures subtly change as they prepared for violence. He pushed his way through the protective line in front of him and calmly approached a boy with a slate-shaped head who flinched and blinked in surprise when he realised he was the object of the Giant O's son's interest. He clutched the cap he held more tightly, before, looking down, understood Jobe's intent and threw the cap to him.

Jobe caught the cap and slowly lifted his hand in the direction of Vauxhall Road. "Go," he ordered his voice was almost a whisper. Each of his tormentors reacted to the command as if it had been roared directly in their face. As one, they turned and fled back toward Vauxhall Road, a shock of ginger hair bobbing at their front.

Tommy Molloy looked at Jobe as if he were a Maxim machine gun. He grabbed Jobe and swung him onto his shoulders with ease. He had found a new weapon in his fight to protect the Marybone Boys' boundaries from the ever-encroaching shites of Vauxhall and Fontenoy. "Three shiteing cheers for the Little O'! Hip shiteing Pip…"

An avalanche of memories cascaded into Jobe's mind as he was hoisted onto Molloy's shoulders and he was powerless to quell the tears he had refused to release not a minute before.

* * *

"Why don't you piss off, Bacon Face! We're not paying a ha'penny more!"

Mr. Duncan swivelled to his left, his colourful handkerchief swishing through the air, lending his turn an extravagance. It was impossible to detect from which of the cracked windows the shout had emanated. He dabbed at the side of his perpetually dribbling mouth with the handkerchief before turning back to the despondent residents at the standpipe. They listened to his lisping voice in dejection.

"The schmall increasche in rent ish the direct reschult of the vascht improvementsch that thish court hash benefitted from." Mr. Duncan illustrated the improvements by pointing as he spoke. "It hash been whitewasched, the night-schoil men are collecting regularly, and I'm reliably informed that the gash lamp there ish bright enough to illuminate the whole parish."

It was true the court, although still decrepit and barely fit for human habitation, had enjoyed a slight renaissance.

"And why it is that you should profit from any of these improvements?" came a voice. "What is it that you have contributed to any of them?"

Duncan again swivelled on his heel but couldn't see an adult among the emaciated children who squatted on a step behind him. He looked closely; although the voice had been childlike, he was sure it must have come from an adult. The extent of the burns to his face made it incapable of expression and belied none of the hatred he felt for his tenants. He returned the baleful stares of those children brave enough to look at him before turning again to face his grudging audience. "I think you'll all agree that the very modescht increasche of—"

"I asked why it is that you should profit from any of these improvements."

Duncan spun around, intent on identifying his heckler. A boy had emerged from the group of children and now stood independent of them. Duncan still couldn't believe a child had posed the question and he scrutinised the boy through eyes bereft of lashes or brows.

He spoke again. "What is it that you have done to improve the quality of life for the tenants of this court?"

A shout of encouragement came from one of the windows. "You tell that greedy ham-faced bastard, Jobe!"

Duncan didn't deign to discover the destination of the insult and instead looked at the boy, perplexed. "And where in the court do you live?" he asked as he again dabbed at his mouth. He hoped the impertinent boy had a large family and relished the moment he would inform each and every one of them that they were evicted with immediate effect.

"I live below the latrine, in the cellar there," replied Jobe, pointing over the landlord's shoulder.

Mr. Duncan nodded, his melted face revealing no clue to his burning frustration. There would be no eviction. He had found the cellar unrentable since its last occupants, a family of eleven, had died of fever. It wasn't the revenue the single mother generated but his depravity that was the significant factor behind his decision. The beauty had never missed a payment, but since the day she had moved in he had enjoyed fantasies of the kind of payment he would elicit when the eventuality arose. Existing in the slum had corroded her figure, but in the almost twelve months she had occupied the cellar, there had never been so much as a late payment. A fact that left him ungratified and only served to enhance his base passion.

"Well, then, you've benefitted more than moscht from the improvementsh, wouldn't you agree?" he chuckled with a lisping wheeze so the dribble that escaped his mouth frothed up on to his cheek.

"Yes, as has the whole court, but only as a result of my mother's back-breaking and disease-risking efforts, because you proved incapable of ensuring the night-soil men carried out their duty with regularity." Jobe's words were met with sporadic exclamations of agreement from a few in the court.

"Hear, hear!"

"Well said!"

Duncan brought his handkerchief to his mouth and looked around the court.

Jobe didn't afford the landlord the opportunity to formulate a reply before he spoke again. "The walls you mention have been left to decay to such an extent that they crumble with rot as a result of the soot and damp that has permeated into them and which now leaks into our rooms and into our lungs. The paltry coat of whitewash that the Rathbones financed in order to take their photographs has only served to hide the problem, not solve it."

Jobe's words were met with universal appreciation and Duncan's eyes flicked around the court, giving him a reptilian air as the shouts of support became more malicious. Jobe continued. "And what possible relation does the lamplighter carrying out his duties with a better degree of dedication have to you?"

Duncan was confused by the laughter that rebounded from the tightly packed walls of the court, ignorant of the fact that the quality of lighting was a direct product of Jobe's ingenuity.

Kitty had nervously watched as he climbed onto Molloy's shoulders, wet rag in hand. She had directed him to do nothing more than wipe some of the grime from the glass panels of the gas lamp. But once on his friend's broad shoulders, he had made use of his vantage point, taking the opportunity to examine the inner workings of the supply valve and the three mantles. A crowd had gathered around, not all of them happy with Jobe's meddling.

"What are they up to now? High Rip vandals, is nothing safe?"

"He's going to break it altogether. We'll be falling over ourselves in the dark."

"Leave it alone, why don't you!"

Molloy, unable to see the protesters, his face pressed against the wall as he easily shouldered Jobe's weight, took offence. "Can't you see he's only cleaning the shiteing glass," he had roared in frustration.

Jobe examined the three mantles and the valve that fed the gas to them, discovering that if he unclogged and manipulated the mechanism of the supply valve, he could considerably increase the volume of gas that fed the mantles. The onlookers and doubters had gasped and then applauded as Jobe, finished with his alterations, had touched a smouldering piece of wood to the valve. The mantles came on in quick succession. Flash. Flash. Flash. So that a parchment-like glow illuminated Jobe's smiling face and lit up corners of the court that had remained in perpetual shadow since its construction. The lifespan of the mantles themselves was greatly reduced, but Molloy and his boys entered into their communal service with aplomb. Spiriting Jobe across the boundaries of Marybone and into enemy territory, they hoisted him up lampposts so he could reach and unclip the mantles, returning them to the courts like spoils of war. Their forays had had to grow in regularity; Jobe manipulated the gas lamps of all the courts on Marlborough Street and now the boys were responsible for supplying fresh mantles to them all. The threat of interference from the lamplighter was easily eliminated. Already the subject of abuse and threats in streets that had been in darkness for days, he was only too happy to deviate from the dreaded battle cry of the High Rip that he would hear roared the length of Marlborough Street whenever his bicycle weaved into the vicinity.

The laughter of the court unsettled Mr. Duncan. It was the first time he had ever seen his tenants so animated, alive and actually expressing emotion. They had always presented as the walking dead, shuffling aimlessly in their grey rags, grey faces bowed, in perpetual search of the grave they would discover only too soon. To witness them jeering, catcalling and now laughing, coupled with the absurdity of the articulate slum-dweller who had the audacity to challenge him was unsettling, and he struggled to maintain his grip on reality. He forced his misgivings to one side, refusing to be cowed in such company. "How dare you queschtion my management! Hell will be a cold plasche indeed the day I have to juschtify myschelf to the likesh of you!" He turned on the rest of the court, spitting and spluttering in his indignation, his handkerchief forgotten. "Or any of you! I will evict thish entire court, every man, woman and child within if thish schow of dischreschpect continuesh!"

The tenants who seconds before had openly cheered Jobe attempted to shrink back into the shadows of the court in order to escape the landlord's ire.

Jobe alone remained undaunted. "It would be of interest to know what the Rathbones would make of your threats?"

Mr. Duncan wavered. How could this boy be aware of the efforts he was making to gain access to the higher echelons of the town's society? He had already donated a considerable sum of money to the Rathbone Foundation that he was assured had not gone unnoticed. "And how would a cellar-dweller like yourschelf impart that information? What likelihood is there of you ever scheeing a Rathbone?" Duncan bit his tongue until he felt blood seep into his mouth. How ridiculous to enter into a sparring session with this louse-ridden slummy.

Jobe did not miss the landlord's subtle glitch and allowed himself a smile. "I'm sure a letter to the Mercury would suffice. I hear they're avid readers."

* * *

Kitty grew pale at the thought of being evicted. She put down her sewing, the fear of missing her deadline forgotten, and sucked at the numb tips of her fingers as she listened to Jobe's tale. She hoped there was an element of exaggeration to the exchange but dismissed it, knowing that it was not in her son's nature to embroider the facts. "I know he's detested throughout the court, Jobe, but Mr. Duncan has only ever been courteous and considerate to me. You can't go speaking to the landlord in that way. What'll we do if he decides to evict us for your impertinence?" She rubbed her hands together before picking up the pair of trousers that she was halfway through, again conscious of her deadlines.

"But he has no right to tyrannise the unfortunate of the court, Mother," replied Jobe.

"We're very lucky to have such a landlord, Jobe! Mr. Duncan has always impressed on me his understanding and acceptance of unforeseen situations that could result in a late payment, but that doesn't mean you can go pushing his amiability to the limit by objecting to his rent increases in front of the whole court." She tutted as she was forced to unpick some wayward stitching that even a customer at Paddy's Market would find questionable and sensing that Jobe was ready to argue his case further curtailed him before he could start. "That's enough now, Jobe. The next time you see Mr. Duncan, you'll apologise for your temerity. Now, wash your hands and prepare for bed."

Jobe knew from her tone that she would accept no dissent. He would wait until she wasn't so exhausted to inform her that he had no intention of apologising to the bullying landlord. He understood his mother's concern. Cellars were always the cheapest possible source of accommodation in the slum, especially one that was situated more or less under the privy, and he knew that his mother was approaching total exhaustion and illness earning the money that they needed to survive, let alone the expense associated with his education.

Kitty watched Jobe dipping his hands into the cold pail of water and admonished herself as she continued with her sewing. It was her own fault. She had agonised over allowing Jobe his newfound freedom, calculated each of the myriad of dangers and issues it presented. Now that she had allowed the genie out, she was as powerless to return it to the bottle as she was to return Jobe to the confines of their cell, or the court for that matter. Not only would Jobe himself rebel against it, but so would all of the children, and most of the adults too.

Fear and pride wrestled for the ascendancy whenever she thought of how Jobe had reacted to and overcome their change in circumstances. He was the only living creature she had ever known to blossom in the slums, but she constantly worried about the multitude of risks and threats to which he was exposed. She couldn't imagine what Albert would make of the changes in Jobe on his return. Her Albert, the one of old, she was sure, would feel a sense of pride, revel in the durability, innovation and leadership that his son had shown. And what of Albert? John Keogh's six months were almost served, and if the Wise Pastor was planning on sending his wife and children another allowance before he returned, it must be any day now. Kitty chided herself again. She tried to refrain from thinking of Albert's return, instead using him, and it, as an inspiration to continue striving for their son. It was a source of comfort to her now and then, when she was overtired, or in the extremities of hunger, to take the ring from its hiding place behind the stove and imagine Albert placing it back on her finger. It would not even fit on her thumb now, and the only request that she would make of him was that he buy her a thin necklace on which she could wear the ring until she regained her health and it would fit her again. She fretted about how he would view her. The lack of food, her work and her constant worry, in essence life in the slums, had aged her twenty years. She could feel individual ribs and the bones that poked through her flesh where she hadn't known they existed. But once Albert returned she would soon regain her health and in the meantime her jutting bones would serve as a testimony to the hardships she had borne through her love for him.

* * *

"Can you wrap them for me please, Cook?" asked Kitty.

The cook in Duke Street, a large portly woman who had herself originated from the slums, wiped beads of sweat from her head with her forearm. "Why not eat now?" she asked suspiciously, although she already knew the answer. She looked Kitty up and down. "There's hardly a pick on you, girl. You're wasting away!"

"I'm very grateful for the free dinner, and I know it's against house rules to take food from the premises, but I'll be late for my job on Catherine Street if I don't leave now. I can eat on the way."

The cook wrinkled her eyes and looked into Kitty's before smiling. "House rules, pah. Isn't it me who makes them! Here, I'll wrap these pieces as long as you eat this as I do." She reached over and grabbed a still-warm slice of beef from the silver salver, handing it to Kitty. "Don't ask. I squarely refuse. You eat it there in front of me as I wrap this for you," she admonished, refusing to take her eyes from Kitty.

Kitty smiled, tore off a small piece of meat and placed it in her mouth. The sensation was almost overwhelming. The hot meat caused her to salivate uncontrollably, and she brought the remainder to her mouth and ripped at it with her teeth. She wondered at the energy she could feel seeping into her body.

The cook looked at her. "You ought to take better care of yourself. Those depending on you'll be all the worse if you take ill. How many jobs have you worked today?"

Three, signed Kitty with her left hand, while using the thumb of her right to catch the grease dribbling down her chin.

"Three? It's only just past midday!" screeched the cook in alarm. "No wonder you're stick thin, running yourself ragged all over this town." She shook her head and passed Kitty the wrapped beef.

Kitty smiled her thanks. Praise the Lord I never gave her the real number, she thought to herself.

* * *

Jobe watched his mother carefully unwrap the slices of meat she had brought home and put them on a plate alongside a freshly cut slice of bread.

"Where's yours, Mother?" Jobe enquired as she laid the plate before him on an upturned tea chest.

"Oh, I've eaten, Jobe. I eat mine with the other girls. It's the only chance we get to have a good old gab," she replied, her back to Jobe as she busied herself gathering together the breadcrumbs with her hand. She could feel his eyes boring into her. He hadn't yet started eating.

"What did you eat, Mother?"

Kitty had been waiting for the question and grimaced. She paused from her task and spun around. "Oh, Jobe, how could I forget to tell you? You'll never believe the story that Janey Hopkins told me, have

I told you about her? She's nanny to the Forsyths that I char for. Well, she told me that there were sightings of Springheeled Jack the last two days, up near Everton." She pulled a crate toward him and sat down as she spoke animatedly.

Jobe's eyes were wide. "Springheeled Jack!" he exclaimed. Kitty picked up the scrubbed tin plate and placed it in his lap.

"Here, eat your bread and meat while I tell you all about it."

* * *

The half dozen or so men couldn't fail to catch the attention of everyone they passed. Those unfortunates who did fail and found themselves obstructing the progress of the squad were unceremoniously barged out of the way to create a thoroughfare for the biggest and best dressed among them. Grocers arranging their wares in crates outside their wooden-fronted shops were shouldered aside, their goods spilling onto the road. Children playing on the pavement were skittled in all directions, and the cornermen standing outside pubs in an attempt to intimidate the price of a pint from passers-by found themselves knocked into the gutter on their behinds.

The men all sported bowler or top hats that had seen better days and the onlookers they passed recognised pawnshop attire when they saw it. One hat stood out, its silk sheen radiant. The rest of the men struggled to remain ahead of its wearer, astonished at his knowledge of the streets and alleys he dissected with ease. On passing through Adlington Street those who had made the trip before recognised Standish Street and Marybone.

Kitty barely had the strength to lift her head as she turned from Vauxhall Road onto Pickop Street. The only part of her body she was conscious of was her burning chest. Her clothes were still damp from the rain that morning, and they hung from her, their weight almost equalling that of her body. She was eager to get home in order to dry off and get a bit of life back into her limbs before Jobe returned from school and saw her in such a state. She clutched the wrappings of scraps she had procured for his tea to her chest as she turned into Marlborough Place, a narrow entry linking Pickop Street to Marlborough. Chin on her breast, eyes vacantly fixed on the cobbles as she dragged her feet, she didn't notice the incongruous group blocking the narrow entrance to Number 4 Court.

Only on reaching the passageway did Kitty look up. She paused, staring at the men blocking her path through red-rimmed eyes before comprehension cut through her exhaustion. The blood began pulsing through her veins and her heart beat out of her chest as she staggered toward the men, bumping into one and causing him to falter. She ran to the cellar, the precious scraps falling from her grasp. Once inside the hovel she fell to the ground in front of the stove her raw hands scrabbling at the black hearth. Then she was up rubbing the soot from the ring as she took the stairs two at a time and raced to Aggie Keogh's tenement. Albert appeared at the doorway just as she reached it. The shock of seeing her husband shut off the energy that coursed through her body and her knees buckled. She fell forward into Albert, holding onto his legs, her face against them. "Albert, oh, Albert." She blubbered incoherently, her grating gasps distorting her voice.

Albert looked down in bewilderment and shrugged to the Keogh woman for explanation. Realising his frame filled the doorway he turned his body to one side and allowed her to manoeuvre past him.

"Kitty dear, Kitty, my love. Come on now, up yer get," said Aggie as she attempted to lift Kitty to her feet.

"Kitty!" Albert recoiled as he realised who, or what, was wrapped around his legs.

Aggie Keogh looked up at him from bended knee. "C'mon, yer great lummox, get the girl up!" she demanded.

Albert acquiesced and hoisted Kitty up, unwrapping her from his midriff and holding her at arm's length. He looked into her face. The blood draining from his own as he did so. The beauty that he remembered had gone. Her skin was grey and hung loose as if decomposing and he could almost see her skeleton as it pushed through her features. She was mumbling something that he had to strive to understand. 'Albert, oh, Albert, you've come. I wouldn't sell it. Look, I have it here! It's here, give me your hand!' As if entranced he began to reach out his gloved hand but retracted it in shock as he realised what Kitty held in hers. He brought the tips of his fingers to his mouth, the taste of leather bitter on his tongue, and biting down slid his hand from the glove so his wedding ring was exposed.

* * *

Kitty awoke to find herself looking into Albert's face. His green eyes gazed into her own and she thought she must be dreaming. She closed her eyes again, terrified of waking herself, and attempted to snuggle further into Albert, but couldn't. Something was amiss. She was standing? And why was she so cold? She heard Aggie Keogh's voice but could not understand her words. She was still in the court? The ring! Her eyes flashed open, and she pushed against Albert's embrace, attempting to escape it. He slowly released her, ensuring she didn't topple backwards.

"That ring, Albert?" Her eyes were wide and glistening with tears.

116

Albert returned her stare, transfixed by the beauty he now recognised in the gaunt and ravaged face. The obnoxiousness he had demonstrated all those months before outside the Vines pub was nowhere to be seen, and he looked at Kitty in despair. "I've remarried, Kitty. We're divorced!"

The words reverberated around Kitty's head as she turned and stumbled back towards the cellar.

Aggie Keogh looked at Kitty disappearing down the cellar steps and then turned her gaze to Albert. "She'll not last much longer here," she said.

Albert opened his mouth but found he couldn't speak. He took out his wallet and took out two white five-pound notes. Still unable to find his tongue he held them out to Aggie.

Aggie Keogh took the money. "On the Holy Gospels, she'll receive this, but there's only skin and grief left of her. It'll take more than money," she stated sagely.

Albert didn't reply but tipped his hat to the old woman before striding from the court. The pace he set made it difficult for his men to keep up with him, and they resembled overgrown children, forced to half trot in his wake. He paid no heed to the urchins and young men who had congregated and now followed, hurling insults and missiles.

"Shall we disperse them, Albert?" One of his men enquired from behind him.

Albert was oblivious to the agitators and replied with a curt shake of his head. Memories of Kitty filtered through his mind, and he quickened his pace as he brought his handkerchief to his eyes.

* * *

The strap of the satchel cut painfully into Jobe's fleshless shoulder and he readjusted it for what seemed the hundredth time as he passed the hawkers who inhabited the pavement. Fishwives, their baskets piled with winkles, cockles and mussels. Mary Ellens, baskets of apples and oranges spread in front of their dirty legs and bare feet. The shoeshines, chip-girls and newspaper boys, every one with young figures but sporting old and wrinkled countenances created a cacophony, all trying to bring attention to their myriad of wares and services.

Jobe ignored them all. Using the time it took to make the descent down the hill from Liverpool College back to the slum to revise what he had learned in his lessons before his enforced compartmentalisation of the classroom. Although he relished the discussions and debates he enjoyed with tutors and students, utilising them to stare down men like Mr. Duncan, he had no choice but to relegate them to the recesses of his brain that he didn't allow to accompany him into the slum. They had no place in his reality, and if he attempted to carry them into it, he wouldn't last long. The majority of students and a fair number of his tutors were of the opinion that he had no place in their reality either and barely acknowledged him. Those who were not offended by his threadbare and malnourished bearing, or made the effort to look beyond it, were rewarded with a keen-minded and altruistic individual.

He regarded his academic experiences as a daily excursion into escapism, part of his distant past that he frequented but to which he no longer belonged, a place it was imperative to have fully departed by the time he arrived back in Number 4 Court.

He no longer shared his mother's optimism that his father would return to pluck them from their existence in the court. If, as legend stated, he walked the streets in pristine silk top hats, perfectly tailored overcoats and carried a walking cane topped with a solid gold handle, then why was he allowing his wife and only son to subsist in the slums? Jobe deliberated the issue while witnessing his mother's deterioration. Although it weighed heavy on him, he had decided that he would relinquish his scholarship and leave Liverpool College in order to lighten his mother's burden of acquiring his books, uniform and shoes. He had discussed the situation with his grandfather, who was of a like mind.

"I've tried to make her see reason, son, but I think the thought of your father returning is the only thing keeping her upright," his grandfather had told him. "Your attending the College is as much for him as it is for you."

"I'm thinking of leaving, Granda. Getting a job, removing some of the strain from her," he had said.

His grandfather had laughed. "Well, it'll be over her dead body, but maybe we can broach it with her together. I can certainly get you something down the docks. Your cousin Michael will be starting there if the knobsticks haven't taken all our jobs by the end the strike."

The distant cry of a boisterous crowd seduced Jobe's eyes away from the cobbles and his thoughts. He had reached the bottom of the hill, and looking up, he could just make out a commotion on Great Crosshall Street. The stimulation the slum provided doused his despondency, and in his eagerness to join the excitement, he ran across Byrom Street, eliciting angry shouts from carters and tram drivers. With his bag thudding against his legs, he continued to the junction with Fontenoy Street before coming to a dead stop. Stalking towards him, shielded from a mob of ever encroaching pursuers by a band of burly men, was his father, dressed in all of his Giant O' finery and clutching his gold-topped walking cane.

Jobe remained in his father's path. He had played out this scene in his mind on countless occasions and was formulating his opening salvo when a man with a bowler hat came from behind his father and swatted him out of the way. The door of The Australian had just been opened by a toothless hag sent by those inside to see what all the noise was about, she sidestepped Jobe as he fell unceremoniously into the pub. Regaining his feet and pushing past the hag, he found the crowd had passed him by and his opportunity to accost his father had gone. He clutched his bag to his chest and tore up the remainder of the street in the direction of the court and his mother.

* * *

Fergus mulled over the outcome of the union meeting in Bank Hall. If what could be called an outcome had been reached. The strike differed from those he had supported throughout the seventies and eighties. The newly formed National Union of Dock Labourers provided a sense of cohesion to the struggle, to such an extent that all members working on the north-end docks had downed tools and were all out. The show of solidarity, supported as it was by the coal heavers and carters with talk that the firemen and seamen's union were in discussions about coming out in support, could actually force the ship owners to listen to the timeless demands against exploitation, slave wages and the hated stand where they were forced to gather each morning in the hope of a day's work.

Scabs and knobsticks, the out-of-towners shipped in from other ports, and sometimes the bosses themselves were still unloading ships, but it was slow work carried out by unfamiliar hands, and the unchanging forest of masts and funnels along the waterfront told their own story.

There was, as usual, a contingent ready to return to work, using the caveat that they would only do so for those employers willing to acquiesce to union demands. As far as Fergus could figure, any return to work would only serve to fragment the solidarity of the men and weaken their collective bargaining power. Edward McHugh, leader of the NUDL, had posed the question during the meeting; 'Are we willing to work for such gentlemen who have never been an enemy of the union?' The differences of opinion within the ranks were highlighted when a carter had responded, "Aye, if we get terms then let's go back to work lads!" He was immediately set upon by a huge unionist who ruined his nose with a haymaker of a right before bundling him to the edges of the crowd.

Fergus could feel that something had to give, and soon. On leaving the meeting he had witnessd an unfortunately placed carter attempting to transport a wagonload of grain. A group of boys, ship scalers by the look of them, had stopped the horses and mounted the wagon, spilling the grain to the ground. One of the new meat wagons crammed with coppers had been on the scene in no time, quickly supported by half a dozen mounted police. But on surveying the size and mood of the crowd the decision had been made to leave the carter and sacks of grain to fend for themselves. The coppers withdrew back along Stanley Road, the crowd's cheers and insults ringing in their ears. Fergus knew from old that the retreat was one that would not be repeated.

He had been on his feet for a long time and although his breath was growing more ragged, he held it as he shuffled past the Northern Dispensary on Vauxhall Road. A Mary Ellen sat contentedly outside, her wares almost sold. Fergus wondered why anybody would want to buy fruit or vegetables from such an insalubrious location. He had convinced himself a long time ago that the air surrounding the hospital was contaminated and was always careful to avoid it. Only his aching knees and feet had led him down that particular route: the quickest home. He reached the junction with Marlborough Street, still attempting to regulate his breath and began to wonder at the lack of children or idlers outside the courts. Continuing on, he turned down Pickop Street and on reaching Marybone realised he still hadn't seen a soul. He popped his head into Stewart's Butchers. "Ho, Sid, what's the do? The streets are deserted out here."

Sid, the personification of a big beefy butcher, put down his cleaver and walked around his counter wiping huge hands on an already bloodstained apron. He pointed across to Holy Cross Church. "You've just missed the tail end of them. The Giant O' was here with a group of heavies. The children, and some of the men, are tailing them. Right noise they made as they passed here." As he finished speaking, Fergus, without another word, walked off in the opposite direction towards Marlborough Street. Shrugging his shoulders, Sid returned to his shop and picked up his cleaver.

Fergus limped through the court and was about to start down the cellar steps but came to an abrupt halt on noticing that the front door was wide open. Kitty was pugnacious in her efforts to prevent the noxious air from seeping into the tiny cell, only ever opening the door a crack, barely allowing enough room for admittance.

"Jesus Christ," he would protest. "Can yer not open the door, girl? I know I'm stick thin but..." he would moan melodramatically.

She would respond by pulling him through the narrow opening by his arm. "Will you stop yer whingeing and just get in so as I can close the door, Da."

Seeing it open was both alien and alarming. Fergus set off down the stairs. With each step descended, he heard more keenly a low animalistic mewing noise that was wrought with agony. He shuffled through the open door. The curtain that offered a modicum of privacy between Kitty and Jobe's pallet was pulled closed. The noise came from behind it. Fergus pulled back the curtain, his heart thumping so hard he could feel it in his temple.

Jobe lay face down, his back heaving with silent sobs. Every few seconds, he would emit the unearthly sound Fergus had heard on the steps and he breathed a sigh of relief. The lad must have crossed his father's path on his way home from the college. Had the fears that they both shared confirmed to him by the big bastard. Fergus suddenly wished he were twenty years younger.

He would wait with his grandson, comfort him, until Kitty returned. It might be no bad thing that the truth was out; although it would be raw, they could now hold a proper conversation on what the future held. He approached his grandson, grimacing at the pain in his knees. "There, there, son, come now…" His eyes adjusted to the gloom as he bent down and the words on his tongue turned to ash as he caught sight of Kitty's dark hair trailing out from under Jobe's heaving body.

Chapter V

1890

Fergus cradled his daughter's lifeless head alongside that of his grandson. The cell was in complete darkness now, and he had no idea of the time that had passed since he had found them. His legs had given way, and he had silently slumped to the cold floor, his back against the damp wall. He pulled them both into his lap. Although one of them was breathing, both were dead weights. Jobe had become quiet; only the sound of his breath and rise of his chest separated his countenance from that of his mother. Fergus caressed both of their heads. His tears had long since stopped, and he stared unseeing into the dark. A flicker of candlelight caused him to blink, and his dry eyes stung as their lids flicked across them. He became conscious of a voice that he didn't recognise.

"Oh, Mary Mother of God, no! Oh, Jesus, Mary and Joseph, please no!" The candle came closer as the owner of the voice knelt down.

"Fergus, it's me. John Keogh's wife, Aggie. Fergus, can you hear me? Fergus can you hear me? It's Aggie Keogh. Ah, please God, no," cried Aggie as she knelt before them.

"She's dead, Aggie. My beautiful baby girl is dead."

* * *

Fergus put up no resistance as Jobe was gently eased from the crook of his arm, but when he felt hands pulling at Kitty, he came to life. He had lain for so long with the weight of his daughter and grandson in his arms that both were numb, and although he managed to lift the cramp-ridden limbs, his fingers could make no purchase as Kitty's lifeless body was taken from his grasp. He didn't know how long had passed before he felt himself being pulled up from the cold, hard floor and gently manhandled across the dark court to Aggie Keogh's rooms.

He was brought through to a room where Kitty was laid out on a double bed, a thin sheet covering her. A wooden crucifix lay on her chest, its silver figure of Christ reflecting the candlelight that flickered solemnly around the room.

"She had this clutched to her breast," said Aggie as she put Kitty's wedding ring on a polished occasional table.

Fergus took the ring and turned it in his hand. Revitalised by the warmth of Aggie's fire, he walked over to the bed and pulled the sheet back from his daughter, staring into her face before lifting her arm. He attempted to place the ring on her woefully thin finger and cried out as he realised the ring wouldn't even stay on her thumb.

Aggie came and took the ring from him. "I'll keep it safe, Fergus. I have something else in my possession. We'll discuss it tomorrow." She brought him back to his seat at the table. "You're welcome to stay the night with her, you and Jobe both."

Jobe slept next to his mother, just as he had whenever he had suffered night terrors. He stirred from unremembered dreams, waking to face the nightmare of reality. His mother lay lifeless next to him, and his granda sat wide-awake, still at the table where he had left him.

Aggie had tried to get them to take some breakfast, but neither accepted. "Well, it's for the women now, Fergus. We need to prepare and dress her. It's time."

Fergus knew there was no interfering with women and their duties and took Jobe by the hand. "Come now, lad, let them see to your mother."

Jobe broke free from his grasp but only in order to place a kiss on his mother's forehead.

"I'll send one of the girls for you when we're ready, Fergus," said Aggie as she saw them out. "Don't forget I have something here to give you."

* * *

Although lost in grief, Jobe still felt a foreboding about entering his grandmother's rooms. He was under no illusion how she felt about him or his mother.

Fergus read his thoughts. "Don't you be worrying any, Jobe. You've enough to be contending with. This is your home now."

Jobe looked around as they entered the garret. Each room he passed through was much larger than the cell he had shared with his mother, and a glut of furniture filled every one.

"Go on, son, have a seat. I'll get a fire going and put the tea on." As his granda finished speaking, Jobe heard a woman's voice.

"Is that you, Fergus Flynn? Where in God's name have you been all night? I hope you've been down to them bleeding docks and found out if all that nonsense is over."

The owner of the voice entered the room. She looked at Jobe as she stomped over to a rocking chair near the fireplace. It became organic as her heavy frame filled it, creaking in protest until her excess flesh poured out and settled between the carved spindles so the two became one entity. Her wrinkled face set, she began to rock backward and forward, sucking at the bottom lip that curled into the empty space where strong, sparkling teeth had once inhabited, her remaining wisp of her hair flouncing with the swell of the chair. "What's all this, Fergus Flynn?" she asked after she had built up a continuous rocking motion.

Satisfied that the fire would take hold, Fergus stood on creaking knees, pulled a crate to the table and wearily sat down. "I've some terrible news, Nelly. It's Kathleen. She's gone. She passed last night," he said, without looking at his wife.

Nelly remained silent only her chair and the growing fire made any sound as she rocked back and forth.

"Have yer nothing to say, Nell'?"

Nelly looked at her husband, keeping her eyes fixed on his face as she rocked. She inclined her head towards where Jobe sat. "And I suppose we'll be stuck with her tangerine now, will we!"

Jobe recognised the venom in the words but didn't have time to properly think on them. He watched in horror as his grandfather, moving with a speed and agility he didn't associate with the old man, grabbed a heavy clay jug from the table and brought it crashing against his grandmother's head. Her accelerated rocking seemed to magnify the impact and she was thrown from her chair with such force that they flew in opposite directions, their organic connection severed.

Nelly was just about to spit another barb at her husband when she realised with surprise that she couldn't speak. She had somehow fallen out of her chair and was lying in a heap against the wall. She had refused to heed the groans of the chair for a long time and had now paid the price. Her instinct was to right herself, get herself into an armchair but she found she couldn't move or breathe. Something had fallen on top of her. Crushing the life from her.

No sooner had his wife landed in a crumpled heap than Fergus was on her, his hands clasped tightly around her throat.

The commotion roused a woman Jobe didn't recognize. She entered the room rubbing at sleep filled eyes. Pockmarks ravished the skin that her torn nightgown exposed and she watched the scene playing out in front of her for a few seconds before, realising what was happening, she let out a high-pitched scream. Her shrieks summoned a big lump of a man that Jobe recognised from around the parish. It was his mother's brother, Bog. The newcomer took in the situation instantly and without hesitating stomped over to the far wall. "Da! Da! What are you doing?" he shouted as he tore his father from his mother's prone body.

The pock-scarred woman had tentatively followed Bog across the room and now the condition of Nelly was obvious to her she fled, her hands covering her mouth. "He's done for her! He's done for her! In the name of God, someone fetch a copper!"

"Less of your damn jaw, yer blasted heifer!" shouted Bog to no avail. The woman's shouts for a constable could be heard reverberating around the tenement as Bog turned his attention to Fergus. He shook his father and shouted in his face. "What're you thinking of, Da? What've you done?"

Fergus was powerless to do anything but hang limply in his son's powerful grasp but he turned his head toward Jobe, his breath coming in short sharp rasps.

Jobe, understanding that the old man was in mortal danger rose from the chair he had occupied for what seemed like years but in reality was only minutes. He reached for the bent and soot-blackened poker that rested against the grate, weighing it in his hands as he slowly approached his maternal uncle and grandfather.

Bog continued the relentless shaking of his father, his shouted questions becoming incomprehensible. The fumes of cheap spirit grew stronger as Jobe half closed his eyes and raised the poker, intent on, for the sake of Fergus, contributing to the violence and making it a real three generation, family affair. But before he could bring the poker down on his uncle Bog's head a huge shape entered the room and swatted him to one side.

A burly constable, responding to the screams for help had pushed his way into the garret and, assessing the scene in seconds, grabbed Fergus from his now weeping son and without speaking to anyone, manhandled him from the room.

Fergus was powerless in the grip of the burly copper but tried to reach out to his grandson. His breath had deserted him and he could only mouth his name silently.

Jobe recognised his name on his grandfather's lips and latched on to him in a futile, one-sided tug-of-war that was over in a second.

* * *

Pins broke from the gloom of the tenement and into the early morning sun. He couldn't envisage the short walk to the Main Bridewell posing any significant problems. The woman whose shrieks had brought him inside now concerned herself with ministering to the woman, his prisoner's wife he assumed, and her not insignificant injuries. Only the scrawny boy who had attempted to hold on to the old man had followed him out of the tenement and still lagged behind. He decided there would be no need for a wagon. He would deposit the prisoner at the Main Bridewell before returning to the scene and carrying out his investigations. It would probably be a good idea to bring along an inspector, as, from what he'd been able to take in, it seemed likely the investigation would turn into that of a murder.

Those meandering the streets barely registered the unremarkable sight of a drunk being escorted to the cells to sleep it off. Pins was aware that the culprit serenely accompanying him to Cheapside didn't smell of alcohol and, although his mind remained distant, was walking steadily enough. They were making good progress, and he wondered if he could get any sense out of his prisoner that he could impart to the desk sergeant. He loosened the heavy arm-lock he had initially applied. "What's it all about then, eh?" he asked with as much good nature as he could muster.

The prisoner remained detached, and Pins decided to try another avenue. He manipulated and manhandled him so that he looked back on the road they had taken and the boy who remained on their trail. "Who's the lad?" he asked. He was unprepared for the sudden paroxysm that shook the perpetrator's body as he made a bid to break free of the loose hold. Pins reapplied his initial arm-lock with even more pressure. "Whoa, whoa, calm yourself or I'll hurt yer! What is it? You looking at bashing his head in as well?" His prisoner slumped at the words, and he was forced again to loosen his restraint to prevent snapping the prisoner's arm as he collapsed to the ground. Pins could have kicked himself for initialising the investigation rather than just getting his compliant prisoner, who was now shouting in a hoarse voice, to the clink.

"Jobe, Jobe, come here, son."

Pins sensed the old man he held up was unravelling. His legs had completely given out, and his eyes and facial expression implied that his mental state was becoming detached from reality. Pins knew it was only the boy he could entreat. He looked up at him.

"You! Away now!" he scolded. The tone he used was usually enough to disperse the most aggressive group of cornermen but had no effect on the boy. "Away with you, I say! Go on, beat it!" he shouted, drawing his truncheon in mock threat. "Is it a lick of this you're wanting, because it's what's in store for you." Pins ground his teeth. The spectacle was attracting a crowd, and he despaired at his decision to commence his cack-handed inquiries. He turned his frustration on the spectators that had gathered on the crossroads that linked Vauxhall Road, Hatton Garden, Tithebarn and Great Crosshall Street. "Beat it, the lot of you, now," he snarled.

Those not used to dealing with officers of the law meekly continued on their way, but those who had a regular brush with Pins and his colleagues remained unfazed and with no other pressing business to attend to held their ground. The reputation of the bear of a copper ensured that nobody intervened physically or even verbally, but he couldn't be sure how long that would remain the case, and, at the very least, they were becoming an obstruction.

He had dealt with a similar sized crowd a few months back in Sawney Pope Street. Breaking up a game of pitch and toss, he had suddenly found himself surrounded by a pack of belligerent youths intent on recouping the handful of coins he had scooped up off the ground. He was relatively new to the Holy Cross beat and knew it was imperative to show these kids, who were only ragamuffins after all, that he couldn't be cowed. A few insults, quickly followed by missiles, had been launched in his direction. He responded to neither, but on seeing a number of newcomers removing heavy buckled belts, knew the time for self-preservation had arrived. He toppled the nearest agitator and, picking him up by the ankles, spun him like a dervish. Those that were not skittled onto their backsides fled from the possessed copper, their pennies a distant memory.

He chided himself. He didn't have a prisoner, possibly a murderer, in custody at the time, one he was still supporting from slumping to the ground. The man's head had dropped to his chest and Pins wondered if he was drunk after all, his mind telling him one thing, his nose another. Many were the times he had physically dragged a prisoner to the Bridewell by a foot, but it didn't seem proper with this one. He looked the suspect over, checking for lice before, decision made he hoisted him over his shoulder and continued on his way to Cheapside.

The spectacle over, the crowd dispersed of its own accord; only Jobe was left to follow. The weight of the prisoner was negligible, and Pins' long strides had him approaching the nick in no time. He inwardly chastised himself, paying no heed to the boy trailing in his wake.

Jobe tore down the remainder of Cheapside and along the intimidating wall of the Bridewell, reaching the only entrance just in time for the heavy, almost mediaeval, wooden door to slam in his face. He sank to his knees, forlornly banging his fists against the door.

* * *

The women of the court had shown their disdain for the new cellar-dwellers by withholding from them the habitual warm welcome reserved for newcomers. No well-wishers had appeared at the door before his mother had a chance to unpack or sweep the miserable room, as was customary; nor was there anybody seeking to borrow a pan or a penny or sign her up to the many subscriptions that ran continuously in the courts. The collectors of the funds to bury a child who had just died in one of the top rooms, the raffle to win a pig which was at that very moment being fattened in one of the tenements and the collectors of the penny funeral fund were all conspicuous by their absence. Even those in perpetual search for a new pot-pal, someone who would be able to chip in and make up the price of a jug of ale to share, remained aloof.

His mother had taken the ostracism well, expected it, and explained to Jobe that the slums had their own systems and hierarchies every bit as complicated and convoluted as those of the Houses of Parliament. "They hated me for having the affront to escape the drudgery of the slums, Jobe," she said. "The fact that your father is a wealthy Protestant only fuelled their resentment, but they'll soon come around."

The priest had mirrored his flock's lack of Christian charity; there would be no example of turning the other cheek or celebrating the return of the prodigal daughter from his pulpit. "The shame of the returning, would-be upwardly mobile pervert is a lesson to us all," he had preached on hearing of her return to the parish. His mother had found it difficult to swallow. "Father Connor baptised me, gave me my first communion and confirmed me. Have I ever forgotten my orders? Did I ever miss a single mass in St. Francis'! An upwardly mobile pervert? For Heaven's sake!"

The lack of opportunity to contribute to the penny fund had also incensed her. "We'll never have need of that penny fund, Jobe, praise the Good Lord. The biggest fear of those around here is not for that of themselves or one of their own dying, but that they'll find nowhere to spend eternity but in a pauper's grave." She made the sign of the cross before continuing. "If they won't take my money now then I'll ensure they can't ignore my contribution when your father comes for us. I'll ensure it's big enough to pay for the next dozen funerals."

Jobe placed the bread back on the table without taking a bite from it. His mother now lay in the shell of a temporary coffin that Aggie Keogh had presumably sent for. The women had dressed his mother and said that now, in peace, she had something of her former beauty. Jobe couldn't see it. It was his mother's vitality and spirit that had made her beautiful; what he saw now was nothing more than the coffin she lay in, a shell.

"Your mother wasn't in the penny club, Jobe, but I can arrange for Father Connor to contact the parish."

Jobe looked at the two white fivers that Aggie had lain on the table as she gave him the piece of bread. "Will that be enough?" he asked.

"Jobe, that is all you have in the world. That and her ring. You're going to need it. I could try and see what a collection would fetch if you don't want a pauper's…a parish funeral. Your mother was very well thought of…"

Jobe looked Aggie Keogh in the eye.

"…in the end," she tailed off under his scrutiny.

"I want the money used to provide the best funeral it can, and I want you to see to it that the ring is buried with her," he said.

Aggie Keogh looked at the boy who had taken on the countenance of a man, and although she knew the ring must be worth five times the amount of money on the table, she didn't argue. News of Fergus's arrest and Nelly's demise had spread like wildfire. "What will you do now, son?" she asked.

He looked at Aggie and softened; she owed him nothing, and yet here he was sitting in her room. "Can you see what price pawning my school things'll fetch, Mrs. Keogh?"

* * *

The March winds had blown into April and any protection the dock wall offered from the biting, incoming gusts from Liverpool Bay was diluted by the gale it channeled the length of the dock road. The stand for the Waterloo Dock was positioned alongside the wall, next to the majestic granite turrets that held the gates in place. It had no covering, and the dockers who converged on it, like those at every other stand, were exposed to whatever the elements threw at them.

Old hands burrowed themselves into the throng of humanity, shielding themselves from the worst of the gale. The two distinct classes of dock labourer stood together under the leaden sky. Lumpers and stevedores, responsible for unloading incoming ships or loading outgoing ones respectively, mingled with the porters whose responsibilities included weighing, marking and stowing the incoming goods. Indiscriminate from each other, they stood stamping feet and rubbing hands, swapping gossip, tobacco and snippets of information regarding incoming vessels, what loads they carried and where they would be berthing.

Although the still dark sky showed no hint of colour, the stand was already crammed with between one hundred and fifty and two hundred men. The relative calm and goodwill of those gathered degenerated into a haphazard melee when the first of the foremen appeared at the gates. Conversations ended mid-sentence as the stevedores, lumpers and porters separated into their specific groups. Mufflers were pulled down and cap peaks raised as men stretched up on their tiptoes, grabbing their neighbours' shoulders for added leverage in an attempt to make themselves visible.

The foreman's beady stare raked over the mob as he feigned ignorance to the shouts of the men. He settled his gaze and locked eyes with individual dockers, inspiring a split-second of euphoria, before moving on without acknowledgement, revelling in his part in the pantomime that played out before him. The calls for his attention became more frantic, and friend elbowed friend in a desperate attempt to gain an advantage. Growing bored, the foreman gave those he had recognised and selected from the outset a curt nod. Transgressions would be forgotten as those selected readjusted their scarves and made their way to the gate. Those who were unknown would only be acknowledged if there was a ship with a quick turnaround, or one full of perishables arrived to the dock late, generating a pressing need for men.

As newcomers, Jobe and his cousin Michael were squeezed out to the fringes, adrift from the collective warmth and invaluable intelligence of the crowd. The arrest of their grandfather had resulted in the easy employment he had promised the two boys failing to materialize and they trudged the length of the North Docks, necks concertinaed in a futile attempt to burrow further into the mufflers that protected them from the freezing conditions as they tried to find work. Only on occasions when considerable numbers of men were summoned inside the gates would the cousins, along with the still drunk, simple, old and infirm who haunted the fringes of the stand with them, get the opportunity to advance close enough to the gates to see a foreman up close. Even then, among the dregs, Jobe, given his age and diminutive stature, would remain unseen. Michael, unlike his cousin, took after his father Bog for size, and, looking like the best choice of a bad lot, would sometimes be taken on. He would wink at Jobe and strut through the gate, entering into the clandestine world of the docks in the wake of the old hands.

The Waterloo Dock foremen hired men notoriously early. Wags quipped this was to ensure the foremen could afford the time for the spectacle of a fistfight or two to break out before taking on. The positive aspect of the early draft was that the men who found themselves on the wrong side of the creaking dock gates as they were pulled closed still had a glimmer of hope that they could make one of the neighbouring stands before their foremen had recruited for the day. Those with an abundance of optimism would race off, dodging through the traffic, oblivious to the fact that their last-minute appearance would severely hamper their chances. Those who didn't share their optimism or have the energy or compunction to go haring along the Dock Road watched them them with a grimace, while contemplating what their own next move would be.

There was always the afternoon stand. This offered a second chance at selection, but for those not local, this entailed traversing the Dock Road for the entirety of the morning in freezing conditions in what usually turned out to be a forlorn attempt at earning a half-day's pay. Those with a few coppers burning a hole in their pocket found the lure of a pint or two in front of a burning coal fire was too much to ignore and sloped off into one of the multitude of taverns that littered the Dock Road. Once the escapism of a few pints was tempered by the reality of empty pockets, they would stagger back into the cold armed with a drunken optimism that the second stand would replenish their misspent coppers.

Those physically exhausted from middle-of-the-night rousings and multiple-mile walks, mentally worn out by the constant rejections would stride off without looking back, beginning the long journey home, each step heightening the dread of their children's hungry, disappointed eyes and the resentful, baleful looks from their wives that would be enough to ensure they repeated the cycle the following morning.

Jobe, with nowhere else to go, would bury his face further into his muffler and, head down, shoulders hunched, roam the Dock Road in the hope of gleaning some positive news regarding the second stands.

The five-week withdrawal of their labour had done nothing to ease the dockers contentions. The contemptible but commonplace conditions, insecurity, casual and perilous nature of their work all still abounded. All the strike achieved was to identify those willing to try and break the strangling grip of the employers. On their return to the stands the so called unionists and militants struggled to find an honest day's work and suffered from the spite of the resentful, spiteful ship owners and their foremen. The knobsticks, outsiders shipped in from other ports, and the scabs that broke the strike had learned their roles well during the five weeks of industrial action. On occasions, those who had blacklegged during the strike found themselves working next to those men who had threatened and abused them as they crossed the picket lines. The number of accidents and injuries suffered by the scabs rocketed. As the wounded were led off with a bleeding head or stretchered away with a crushed leg, there would invariably be a docker with outstretched arms pleading his innocence. 'The rope just snapped.' 'My hook slipped.' 'That rigging must be faulty.'

The scabs and knobsticks held an impromptu meeting, the result of which was categorical. They must protect themselves. Wasn't it them who ensured the docks continued to operate during the union strikes? The ship owners would surely realise the predicament and peril they faced and show empathy. They would strike, after all hadn't the unionised men been re-employed en masse. Hearing that the scabs had the temerity to go out on strike and seeing their scantily manned picket lines had caused the first glimmer of a smile to cross Jobe's face since his mother's death and grandfather's subsequent incarceration.

"Jesus, Jobe, that's the first time I've ever seen you smile," his cousin Michael had exclaimed while they waited outside the gates of the Trafalgar Dock under a sky that was just beginning to show a hint of colour. That had been almost a month ago and Jobe had still not managed a single shift.

The winter assizes were held in St. George's Hall. Jobe had never been inside the grand building before. He sat alone in the gallery, the demise of his grandmother doing little to end the ostracism she had imposed upon him. His extended family, taking up the majority of the public benches, behaved as if he didn't exist. Even Michael, in the presence of his parents, had ignored him. The rest of the benches were filled with familiar faces from the parish, a number of them rustling bags of toffee they had purchased from McGhee's Confectioner's on Great Crosshall Street on their way to the court.

The prosecutor for the Crown had urged the jury to reach a verdict of murder, as, in the eyes of the law, a mother and grandmother had been killed by an unlawful act of violence. "It remains murder," he concluded, "regardless of the human emotion surrounding events. For this reason, the prisoner's life must be forfeit."

Jobe had watched his grandfather throughout. He seemed tiny in the large semicircle dock where up to twenty or more defendants could be tried at once. Nothing that was said, either in accusation against him or in defence of him, seemed to register.

Dr. Commins, acting for his grandfather, had summed up by imploring the jury to be mindful of the fact that Fergus was an upstanding, hardworking member of the community. "This was not a wife who was repeatedly stretchered to the infirmary, forced to call on the local constable for protection or reduced to a drudge by a brutal and tyrannical husband. This was a wife who felt the love of a good man, good husband and good father. As the prosecutor himself has stated, there was no premeditation involved here, no drink-fuelled spite, no murderous intention, just a freak blow, doled out spontaneously, while in the very deepest pit of despair. A despair brought about by the loss of a cherished and only daughter."

Judge Justice Day sitting straight as a board throughout, ensconced in polished oak and every bit as intimidating as the Aberdeen Granite pillars that dominated the court, looked down at the shadow of the man in the dock and informed him that although there was no excuse or justification for murder, the immense emotional components of the case that had made the accused indifferent to all consequences bound him to accept the lesser charge of manslaughter the jury had arrived at.

He left Fergus and those observing under no illusion that, if it were not for the deluge of tragedy and raw human emotion that engulfed events pertaining to the case, he would have had no qualms or doubts about donning his black cap before passing sentence.

Jobe got the impression that the judge was disappointed there would be no opportunity to theatrically condemn his grandfather. Neither could he shake the feeling that the gallows would have been a quicker and more humane punishment than the three years' hard labour his grandfather had been sentenced to.

He looked back at the ragged picket line, unconsciously shaking his head. The crowd began to swell as men shifted their positions and Jobe didn't need to stand on his tiptoes to know that a group of foremen had appeared at the gate, clipboards in hand.

* * *

Molloy looked down the road. He was beginning to think that maybe Jobe had finally been taken on when he saw his friend's slight frame turn into the street. He shook his head and readjusted his new Blucher boots before setting off to meet him. "I don't know why you bother, Jobe. If your shiteing face doesn't fit, there's nothing down for yer. Especially if you look as if you weigh no more than a shiteing docker's hook."

Jobe shook his head; half of it remained buried in his muffler. He was frozen through. He had watched as Michael had, once again, sauntered through the Waterloo Dock gates, this time without looking back at him. Jobe, as usual, had walked the length of the docks and then tried again at the afternoon stand. All to no avail.

"Look at yer, shivering. You'll freeze to death before you get a shiteing start, and I suppose that shiteing cousin of yours got took on," Molloy cursed.

Jobe began to reply and realised his muffler was distorting his words. He pulled it down, his face raw where it had been rubbing. "It's a good thing Michael's getting work. He says he'll let the foreman know we're both Fergus Flynn's grandsons," he explained.

Molloy spat into the gutter. "Pah! You can't be trusting that shiteing little shite, Jobe. He'd sell you out for a ha'penny."

Jobe couldn't help smiling at Molloy's ire.

He continued. "When're yer going to see shiteing sense and follow me into the gang?" He took a step back so that Jobe could appraise him fully. "Look at me. New hat, new boots, new strides… Why, me belt alone is worth a day down the shiteing docks. You'd be a dead cert, Jobe. Yer brains are worth more than all of our brawn put together."

Jobe shook his head. "It's not for me, Molloy. Taking from folk who've less than us doesn't appeal to me."

"Are you shiteing blind, Jobe? There's nobody with less than you." Molloy pulled a bundle of tickets from his pocket. "Where would you be without these?" He peeled a ticket from the stack and held it out.

Jobe took the ticket and read it. It was a carbon copy of those Molloy had already given him, but it gave Jobe an escape from his friend's accusing eyes.

'LEE JONES' FOOD AND BETTERMENT SOCIETY'

One Night's Admittance to the Marybone Homeless Shelter Only

"I've enough of these to keep a roof over your head for the next twelve months," continued Molloy as he flicked the tickets with his thumb. "But is that what you want for yourself, Jobe, to be sleeping among the shiteing penny hangovers?"

Jobe folded the ticket into his pocket. Before Molloy had, by whatever means, acquired the bundle of priceless admittance chits that ensured he would have a roof over his head each night, Jobe had, on more than one occasion, spent the night strung up against one of the penny hangover benches. Those unfortunates who were not deemed deserving or desperate enough by the army of volunteers who scoured the slums handing out chits entitling the bearer to a bowl of soup, a pallet and a coarse blanket on the packed floors of the Marybone shelter were not entirely ignored by Lee Jones's charity. The opportunity to purchase a penny hangover was always on offer.

On the first of these occasions, following a bowl of hot soup, Jobe was intrigued to be led down a dank set of narrow stairs into the bowels of the shelter to the entrance of a damp, low-ceilinged room that was perfectly square and had what appeared to be high-backed church pews against each of the walls. On arriving at the entrance to the cellar, the men and surprisingly more than a few women were informed that it was imperative to retain an orderly line. Despite this, the queue disintegrated before long as men and women jockeyed for position. It reminded Jobe of the melee on the stand, and he was bemused by the obvious determination and desperation to be first into the room. A minor scuffle broke out, more verbal than physical, and a voice that startled Jobe boomed out.

"Anybody judged to be cajoling or causing consternation will be escorted from the premises. Pennies will not be refunded!"

Following this directive, the dishevelled line regained a semblance of order. On being allowed into the room and finding a seat on one of the unforgiving benches, Jobe instantly understood the clamour to be among the first to reach the pews. Those lucky few were already rolling up rags they had secreted somewhere on their person to use as pillows on the overhanging ends of the benches, whereas Jobe and his peers who found themselves with a neighbour on each side had no option but to remain stiffly facing forwards.

When everybody was in place, crammed shoulder to shoulder, a dwarf entered the room. His large head seemed too heavy for his body and swayed precariously from side to side with each step. Four pieces of rope trailed behind him, each one as thick as his forearm. One after the other, the ropes were stretched across the benches at a height so arms could be draped over them and the ropes secured from one end to the other. After completing his task with well-worn practice, the bulbous-headed dwarf surveyed those seated with a scowl, as if daring someone to raise a complaint. Content that his captives were secure, he stomped out of the room. The sound of his heavy footsteps ascending the staircase dissipated, and men and women began to writhe and wriggle, to the chagrin of their neighbours, in a futile attempt to gain an inch more space, which might afford them even a modicum of comfort.

Jobe could never have envisaged such a reality. He was amazed to find that as well as the usual suspects, the drunkards, vagabonds and beggars who he was expecting, there were working men, their clothes betraying their profession. Painters' overalls, porters' coats and even a postman in full uniform draped themselves over the ropes. The women scattered about the benches offered no outrage to the fact that they were sandwiched between two men and focused only on finding the comfort that would prepare them for sleep. Jobe knew with certainty that his penny would only serve to keep him warm and dry; there was no chance he would be visited by the luxury and escape of sleep in such circumstances. The man immediately next to him had already slumped forward and only his rhythmic breathing indicated that he was still alive.

Yet Jobe had awoken with a start the next morning among a writhing and wriggling mass of humanity who, like him, had pitched forward onto the cold floor when the rope supporting them had been untied without warning.

"It is five o'clock in the morning," the dwarf called in his booming voice as he stomped from the room the lengths of tar stained rope trailing behind him.

Jobe stirred from the chit and the memories it induced and looked up at Molloy. "It's only until I get myself fixed down the docks, Mol'."

Molloy softened his tone. "I look up this street at the same time day after day, hoping I won't see you coming down it. That you'll have been took on for the day and my waiting'll be in vain and I'll only be ordering one plate of bacon and eggs from Ma Boyle. I'm sure that if you did get a day, you'd be running the whole of the dock system by the end of it, but it's never happened, Jobe, not once. And it's never going to," he said with finality.

Jobe considered his only friend in the world for a second; Molloy never ceased to surprise him. After a second he shook his head and grinned. "You're still standing the shiteing bacon and eggs then?"

* * *

Jobe looked round and estimated his odds against the bedraggled crowd who stood around the Stanley Dock gate. The stand was heavily populated as usual, but the main body of fit and able men was missing. In all likelihood, they were at another stand where it was known the need for hands was high. Jobe actually fancied his chances of getting a day's work and although hopeful of being selected in their absence, cursed that he wasn't privy to the information that rippled between those in the know. Union buttons and badges were slowly superseding the secret handshakes and passwords that had been prevalent throughout the century, but the priceless information was no more forthcoming because of it.

The opportunity to push through a mass of elderly, infirm and still drunk men was one that had never presented itself before. Jobe slunk his way through what would usually be an invisible barrier jealously guarded by elbows, cursed warnings and on occasion fists, until only a couple of rows of men stood between him and the dock gate, which was creaking open. The foreman weighed up the rabble with undisguised disappointment visualising his cutoff line markedly.

Jobe reckoned, with rising excitement that he was easily within the foreman's eye line and he became mesmerised by the pencil that began to blur like the baton of an orchestra conductor. Within seconds a dozen men had been selected from the ranks Jobe himself stood in. The foreman's hand came to a pause as he surveyed those remaining in front of him. He hesitantly started to dip an index finger at Jobe, but before he confirmed the command, a group of twenty-odd men burst from Lightbody Street and sprinted towards the stand. The foreman, his index finger still lingering over Jobe, raised his left hand to counter the decree.

Jobe ignored the obvious excitement of those who pushed past him and on through the dock gate at the behest of the visibly relieved foreman. Their hysterical babble making no mark on him.

"Did you see the little bastard I clobbered? He'll not remember his name for a week."

"The little shites won't be lurking in the shadows for a while, that's for sure."

Jobe wheeled away from the gate before it could come to a shuddering halt in his face. It was time to submit to his friend's constant badgering.

* * *

Molloy led Jobe into a narrow entry situated between a row of tenements and an old, dilapidated warehouse whose roof had caved in. Its rotten remains, wooden beams and moss covered slate, created a barrier that had to be carefully negotiated to access the passageway. Jobe maneuvered the length of it when it abruptly ended at a soot-covered wall that stretched into the sky.

Molloy moved aside a tar-stained board and ushered Jobe through a hole in the wall and into an abandoned, ramshackle room. The smell of frying sausages wafted from somewhere, competing against the sickly scent of damp and mould. There was a paneled door in the wall directly opposite the hole and Molloy approached it. "They're a shiteing hard bunch, mind, Jobe, so don't get nervous or worried. You're with me and that's enough," he said as he raised his hand and gave the door a heavy rap with his knuckles. The door opened and Jobe was amazed to step into a parlour that was warm, well lit and well furnished. A huge pan of sausages sat precariously on a bent and rusting stove in one corner, sizzling and spitting away. Lounging around the room was a group of boys, a good number of who were nursing injuries of varying degrees. Jobe looked to Molloy for introductions but his big friend only stood gaping, for once lost for words. Jobe wasted no more time waiting and assessed the situation, putting aside his surprise at the comfort within he made a visual scan of the bloodied noses, blackening eyes and possible broken bones. Following his brief appraisal he approached a boy who had a lump that was almost an exact replica of his bulbous nose protruding from the dead centre of his forehead. He appeared to be drifting off to sleep. "Ho! Ho!" shouted Jobe into the boy's dirty face. "C'mon now, wake up, that's it, look at me! How many fingers am I holding up?" he continued as he knelt down in front of him.

Jobe's shouting shook Molloy from his trance. "What in the name of Mary and shiteing Joseph has happened here?" he asked, his voice barely above a whisper.

"I'll tell you what happened," said a young man sitting in a high-backed chesterfield chair. He held a blood-soaked rag to a cut on the side of his cheek but still managed to look composed and authoritative. "Check the sausages, Rodger," he motioned to a boy before continuing, "We were ambushed by the Logwood Gang, that's what happened. Sneaky bunch of motherless bastards that they are. We gave a good account of ourselves though, isn't that right, boys!"

The proclamation was met with muted groans of pain and sniffling and the youngster rose from his chair. "The fight'll go down in history," he roared as he shadow-boxed in a neat circle, his dirty rag flapping about. "The Battle of Silvester Street, they'll call it. Like something from the Crimea, it was." He looked around, noticing the lack of enthusiasm for his words and feints and sat down again, clutching the rag to his open cheek and gesturing to the boy poking at the sausages to dole them out.

Jobe, having ensured that a relatively unharmed boy sitting next to his patient understood the order not to let him drift off to sleep, stood and looked at the boy in the chair, who was just taking first pick of the sausages. He was among the smallest in the room, and although his face was pinched and wizened, it projected a jocular, mischievous quality while his penetrating brown eyes brimmed with intelligence. "The Logwood Gang? Isn't that just a name for a group of working men, dockers in the main, who refuse to allow the High Rip to take their hard-won wages without a fight?" he asked blithely.

Molloy shook his head and put it in his hands, looking through his fingers at his cousin in the Chesterfield who managed to chew on his sausage while assessing his accuser with a philosophical air. He mulled over the newcomers words as he took another bite of his sausage and, having chewed and swallowed it slowly, smacking his lips loudly and dabbing at them with an imaginary handkerchief. "And who, may I ask, are you?"

"My name is Jobe. Pleased to make your acquaintance," replied Jobe, smiling and holding out his hand.

After a second, the young man stood and, with a smile of his own, took the proffered hand. "I'm Silky. Honoured I'm sure."

Removing his head slowly from where he had placed it in his hands on hearing Jobe's tone, Molloy blinked unbelievingly. "At last I can get rid of these shiteing Lee Jones chits. Teddy Kilbane has been pestering me for them for an age. He can have the shiteing lot for tuppence a go!" he pronounced gleefully to nobody in particular.

Silky looked at his foul-mouthed cousin quizzically before, with a shrug of his narrow shoulders, he sat down and returned his attention to Jobe. "The High Rip, as you call them, don't exist. There's no such gang. They're a figment of a newsman's imagination, something to strike ghoulish fear into their readership. Of course, I won't deny using the call from time to time. It's been a useful fabrication to me and my boys."

The hidden away house served as home to the majority of the Blackstock Street Boys that Silky alluded to. Even those who had somewhere to reside would, more often than not, spend their nights in The Den and during the weeks that followed, Jobe became accustomed to their habits of sitting late into the night and sleeping late into the day, although he didn't partake in their heavy consumption of alcohol or their equally extensive tobacco smoking. Their late nights were often dictated by the kind of crimes, what Silky referred to as *jobs*, they were carrying out at any given time, although a good proportion of the jobs were carried out in broad daylight.

Jobe spent his time appraising every facet of the gang's operations and when the time was right approached its leader. Silky listened to his proposals, even evolving some of them, with good grace, but remained sceptical of the new direction Jobe advocated for the gang.

Silky had decided that Jobe's ideas needed further discussion. Understanding that The Den was refuge to the majority of his boys, he never ordered anybody out so that he could think or speak, instead preferring to go on walks or, as on this occasion, retreat to one of the snugs in Ma Shanks'. His trusted lieutenants Molloy and Face were invited along to discuss Jobe's ideas.

"What's the boys' biggest fear?" Jobe asked the three lads who sat around the unsteady table.

"Coppers," they all replied at once.

"Not the ones who're content to give you a lick of their truncheon and send you on your way," Face elaborated. "No, it's the jobsworths who'll drag you to the Bridewell and see you before the madge."

Jobe still couldn't help staring at Face whenever the opportunity arose. Molloy had informed him that nobody, not even Face himself, could remember his real name. So unfortunate were his squashed and upturned features that he constantly resembled a hungry boy pressed up against a baker's window as if attempting to smell and taste the wares on offer through the glass itself. The tip of his nose pointed towards his right ear, stretching the left side of his face so that it appeared flat, the nostril on that side an enormous black hole in the middle of his face, almost as large as one of his eyes. Some buck had christened him 'Face at the Window' in the distant past and he now went by the simple abbreviation of Face.

Jobe forced his attention away from the peculiar visage and directed his attention to the trio before him. "And who is it that supplies the police, the madges and the courts with the information and evidence that condemns us?" he asked, continuing without waiting for a reply. "The people, that's who! Despite your best efforts to cow and intimidate them, there's always one morally upstanding citizen who is willing to speak out, and there always will be!"

The three boys around the table looked at each other nodding. There was no disputing Jobe's logic.

"So you agree but don't see the answer?" he asked.

His three companions looked at him, blankly, inviting one.

"Rather than take what little those around us have, we give! Rather than bully and harass, we support and we help! We look after the people, which in turn gives them a reason to look after us."

Face was mortified, unable to stop his mouthful of beer from spraying out of his lopsided mouth, which contorted to such an angle that the spray shot vertically, straight into his own eye, almost blinding him. He wiped and blinked away the beer as he roared his umbrage at Jobe's plan. "So you're saying that not only should we stop taking what we want, from who we want, when we want, but what we do take we give away?" he asked incredulously.

Silky took a deft swig of his pint, smacking his lips loudly as he swallowed. He held up a hand to his friend. "Just a mo' now, Face. I sense your ire, but indulge me if you will."

Face brought his hands to his eyes. He knew Silky had heard something of influence.

"Say it was to transpire that you found yourself in front of the Beak with a charge sheet as long as this arm," Silky held out his silk-clad arm and began tapping his finger at certain points, as if to illustrate Face's name on the imaginary charge sheet. "Your name dotted all over it. Oh, the Beak is listening to all your transgressions, just itching to sentence you to twelve of the best and a good spell in the Kirkdale, but shock horror!" Silky camply brought his index knuckle to his mouth and bit on it. "There's nobody on the witness stand to describe or testify to your villainous acts! Oh my, the madge is in a right pickle now, isn't he? So there you are, on the stand smiling and waving to your friends and family, readying yourself to be reacquainted with their joyfully accepting bosoms. The madge is beginning to feel a prickly heat, he's almost passing out with rage, but hang on a mo', he's gone and forgot all about his loyal boys in blue, his good old friends from the constabulary, who now, together and in unison, concoct a way of snapping you away from the warm bosom of your friends and family, dragging you back, kicking and screaming from the sunny jaws of freedom and locking you away in Kirkdale with a back that's been striped by a dozen!"

Silky had brought both Face and Molloy to the edge of their seats with his words and delivery before sending them slumping back into their seats as if they themselves were waiting for a meat wagon to transport them along Stanley Road to the gaol. He let the pain of the imagined defeat sink in before continuing. "Now let's imagine the scene again. Our friend the madge has got a witness on the stand, but rather than each nod of their head condemning you to another lash, they're telling His Honour how you couldn't have been involved in the frightful acts the constable has described. It just must have been someone else, because right at the time that crime was taking place, you'd been unblocking their stove pipe or manfully struggling along with a peck of potatoes on your back, reducing the suffering of the chronic rheumatism that haunts their nights and blights their days. 'Why he deserves a medal, not a whipping, Your Honour!'" Silky finished his dramatics and addressed Face directly. "Can't you see it, Face? If there's anything in what Little Jobe here says, we can turn the snitching slobs into alibis! They'll become an insulating layer between the coppers and us. It won't just be The Den that'll be our lair, it'll be every street in the Parish!"

Face could see the logic behind the argument but was afraid of ceding ground to the little snot-rag who had only just come among them. "Pah, it's nothing but a load of me arse. There'd be no end to what the mugs around here would want from us. All they'd do is take and take and take! Well, they'll be getting none of my share, that's for sure," he vented.

Molloy, who had been an observer throughout, became suddenly animated making Silky jump back in mock fright. "It'll shiteing work. It has shiteing worked—he's done it before!" he stammered before launching into an account of how Jobe, and by association the Marybone Boys, had become heroes of the courts by doing nothing more than making a few gas lamps glow a little brighter.

* * *

For Jobe's hopes to become reality it was imperative a peace was brokered with the Logwood Gang. The gang had been formed by groups of dockers and other workers for their own protection from the gangs of youths who found lone sailors and dockers, foreign and domestic, easy pickings and plagued them. The shriek of 'Highhhhh Riiiippppp' became synonymous with having up to a dozen miniature raptors emerging from the shadows swinging pipes, knives and belts. Even the most hardened of dockers was vulnerable to having their hard-earned wages and anything else of value stolen while the violence involved usually left them in such a state that there would be no chance of earning for a long time to come. It was just another injustice to be borne by the honest and hardworking. Primarily organised for defence the gang was not averse to carrying out reprisals against any youngsters they thought may be affiliated to, or part of, the High Rip, and although they made efforts to retain an element of anonymity, Jobe was aware of more than a few who participated in the loose vigilantism and knew where he could find them en masse.

The industrial discontent that had threatened to blossom again eventually bloomed, taking root in its spiritual home on the docks. Jobe was well versed in the injustices faced by those who earned their living on the waterfront. His grandfather's stories and opinions had been the beginning of his education but his own time spent on the stand had left him only too aware of the unrest and chagrin of the long-abused workers. The issue of pay and conditions temporarily diluted the sectarian troubles that plagued the city and hundreds attended the meetings organised by union firebrands such as James Sexton. The slums and pubs were full of talk of the strikes that were taking place in Southampton, Bristol and London. The general consensus was that another strike would soon be called in Liverpool.

The National Union of Dockers League was predominantly made up of unskilled Catholics. Members of the Logwood Gang would inevitably be among the numbers and Jobe planned to utilise the solidarity of the meetings to approach various individuals and broker a truce.

The parley finally took place on the outskirts of a dockers meeting. Jobe informed the sceptical dockers that, although his gang were not the only ones behind the muggings and he could only speak for the parishes they roamed that they were exploring differing ventures and eager to atone for mistakes of their past, namely, the mistreatment of their hardworking neighbours and comrades. There had been a pause in the discussion in order to listen to an address from James Sexton. On applauding Sexton as he stepped off the gantry, Jobe added the caveat that the truce didn't hold for child or wife beaters.

The dockers were incensed. "Who d'you think you are to instruct a man on how to treat his wife? It's nothing more than a ploy that'd leave most men open to your filching, filthy little fists," came the retorts.

Jobe was adamant. The majority of boys who sought the safety and security of The Den had fled from beatings doled out by violent fathers, lovers or customers of their mothers. Violence bore violence and the boys revelled in the opportunity of returning the savage beatings to the men who wore the same filthy moleskin trousers and dirty jackets as their own assailants. The sour smell of stale ale so redolent that they could close their eyes and imagine they were returning the spite in full.

"Then they'll mend their ways! Any wives or mothers who're carted off to the Northern in the middle of the night will wake the next morning to find their husband is in the next bed to them, with injuries thrice as grievous." Jobe's demeanour, added to the fact that he had sought the men out alone, lent gravity to his words and after conferring among themselves the men agreed to the truce.

The gang was unhappy with the development, not only at seeing one of their most lucrative and relatively risk-free lines of operation closed off but also because there would be no more of the punishment beatings that offered them, unaware of it as they were, a cathartic venting for the violence visited on them in the past.

Silky sat in his high-backed chesterfield attempting to fix a gold-rimmed monocle into his right eye as he addressed the gang. "The Logwood Gang is becoming more of a threat to us every day. They're showing people round here that we're not flawless. A simple scream of High Rip won't cut it anymore. Look what happened on Silvester Street a few months back! Why, it's only a matter of time before they come charging in here with their four-be-twos! There'll be new jobs that won't just yield enough for the odd pint and pan of sausages, times are changing, and it's us that are changing them," he said as he finally mastered the monocle and, theatrically screwing his left eye shut, surveyed his compatriots through it as if inviting their defiance.

The new peace with the Logwood Gang paid dividends from the off. The dockers inside knowledge of what was transpiring on each dock provided the gang with unprecedented returns while at the same time reducing the risks involved. The initial discomfort that the gang felt about the truce with their enemies was soon appeased.

Docks could be targeted with a precision that negated the randomness, risk and waste of effort associated with pilfering from a random cart or wagon. The certainty of the yields gave fresh impetus to the effort put into the planning of jobs. It had always been a loose railing, crumbling wall or laxly guarded dock that dictated their targets, but furnished with information and knowledge, Jobe and Silky were able to formulate plans on how to access specific wharfs.

Never one to overlook ability it was Silky who had hit on the idea of hiring boats and utilising the sailing skills a number of the gang had accrued while serving time aboard the Catholic Floating Reformatory Ship Clarence. Under cover of darkness and using stealth, a tiny fleet of rowboats could cruise straight into the mouth of a dock before leaving in the same way laden with ill-gotten and lucrative spoils. The ease of their piracy resulted in an over-exuberance that became their only adversary. Soaking feet signalling that a boat's weight capacity had been overloaded and precious cargo had to be thrown overboard before the boat was scuppered and sunk by their own greed.

Jobe was always careful not to overload a boat he was in charge of but the fear of capsizing was always real. Especially when sharing a boat with two or three other landlubbers under the orders of a captain straight off the Clarence, were the education of 'the sailors' was not always watertight. A fact the particular 'captain' Jobe found himself with now seemed eager to prove with a level of panache. Even before the small lamp on the bow of the boat was extinguished, veiling the boat in complete darkness, he had seemed intent on sinking them. The flickering orb of light had provided a modicum of comfort and on its dousing the anxiety on the small boat became palpable. The river and the seawall that served as a guide toward the entrance to the Sandon Basin merged into one and the small white tops that slapped against the hull of the boat suddenly seemed heavier and louder. It came as no great surprise when the small boat suddenly shuddered, sending all hands pitching forward. It took a second for the initial furore and hissed insults on-board to subside; once it did it became apparent that they hadn't crashed into the dock wharf but had in fact collided with another vessel, bringing both boats to a grinding halt.

Jobe's suspicions were immediately aroused. His mind raced; who else could be inching their way along the granite harbour wall in complete darkness? Was another gang imitating their unique ruse? He would find out which of the Logwood Gang had betrayed their trust and there would be a heavy price to pay. He lifted the oil lamp from the bow and put a match to it, illuminating the faces on the other boat. His mind stumbled into incomprehension when he saw his cousin Michael staring back at him from the other boat. It was only when he discerned the panic and the accents of those telling him to dim his light that he realised they had collided with a boat full of scabs bypassing a dock-gate picket and dropped the lamp overboard with shock.

Jobe cancelled the planned raid, and judging by the direction the scab boat took, he imagined their day's work had also been brought to naught. The scabs on board had probably mistaken them for union men intent on capsizing their vessel. Jobe mulled over the chance encounter but on deciding there was nothing he could do about it forced it from his mind. He gave no further thought to his cousin's disposition.

Jobe was totally estranged from his family, and his move further along Vauxhall Road, away from Marybone to The Den on Blackstock Street, meant that he didn't even see Michael in passing. To think that he had become a scab illustrated the complete breakdown that must have occurred within the family following the departure of their grandparents.

* * *

Pins didn't resent having a larger than usual beat. As far as he was concerned it was a direct consequence of his ability to do his job, and anyway it wasn't as if he were forced to plod the whole lot of it. His patch overlapped that of other bobbies, his remit being to ensure that his presence was felt in the largest possible locale. He was good at his job and everybody knew it, colleagues and crooks alike. He wasn't a notebook copper, not by any stretch. He understood that his job didn't just involve nabbing criminals to hand over to the Justices and magistrates who sat in their chambers, oblivious to the trials and tribulations of real life. They couldn't remove the shadow of crime or fear of violence that hung over people's everyday lives like a heavy shawl, just as they couldn't alleviate the poverty from which it was born.

Sure, Pins served up his fair share of scum to be sent down; the murderers, pimps and con artists who were better behind bars than lurking on the streets. But he also knew when his own rough justice was more conducive. The opportunistic thief. The drunk. The cornerman. The young hooligan. They just weren't worth the paper, besides didn't it do more harm to remove the breadwinner from a family? A few cuffs around the head sufficed as a punishment and had a less detrimental effect on any dependents. He'd seen too many wives and children who, innocent of any crime save being related, were sentenced to a prolonged period of starvation before the workhouse or death became their only choices.

He liked to think he made a small change to people's days, if not their lives, whether they knew it or not, appreciated his efforts or hated him for them. He limited at least some of the negatives of people's lives, as only he could. But that was only part of his role. He put as much effort into getting to know which of the snot-nosed, scabby-kneed kids rolling in the gutters were particularly destitute as he put into catching criminals. Nobody in the force appropriated more chits from the Policemen's Benevolent Fund than he did. Every one of them would be distributed justly. He knew coppers who used the chits to curry favour in the community, not particularly bothered if they were going to those most in need or not. His were in no way intended as sweeteners to the desperate, but at times, relationships made through them invariably did lead to information that he could use while doing his proper job.

One area that had transformed itself into a relative area of peace and tranquillity was the usually notorious area within the triangle of Vauxhall Road, Marybone and Blackstock Street. There had been times he couldn't get out of the area such was the deluge of incidents. But as if by a miracle, reports of muggings, burglaries and violent crime had all but diminished overnight until they had become virtually non-existent. It had been an age since he had heard the slip-slap of bare feet on cobbles only to turn and be greeted by a wide-eyed child who, too breathless to speak, dragged at his sleeve in their desperation to get him to the room where their father was bashing in their mother's brains.

Dilapidated doors, behind which he knew anything but the cheapest bread was a luxury, were replaced with new ones, and his nose twitched at the rich aroma of roasting joints of meat that wafted through them. The Benevolent Fund chits he collected in advance remained in his pocket for longer periods of time. Children who usually sat on sooty steps, too exhausted to play and so emaciated that he genuinely worried whether they'd still be alive on his next beat, frolicked in the gutter, the slight hint of colour in their cheeks lending them an almost healthy glow.

The St. Patrick's Day festivities had been something to behold. The main roads remained untouched, but it seemed that every street and court was decked out in green and white, each one having at least one trestle table that was laden with bread and butter, biscuits and cakes. There was an air of true celebration and cheer rather than the usual simmering antagonism and encouraged hostility.

He was aware he had the natural and accepted arrogance of one who was head and shoulders above his peers professionally, but he wasn't so pig-headed as to think he was behind the comparatively seismic shifts, and he had no desire to begin enquiring or investigating what was behind the changes in fortune, happy that at least a small portion of his beat was prospering. Even the local hooligans were keeping themselves quiet and out of his way.

His shroud of self-imposed ignorance was ripped away by a snivelling wretch from Holy Cross. The voice came from the shadows of an already dimly lit entry. "I've got information that is watertight. It'll give you two gang leaders—Jobe Warburton and Tommy Molloy."

Pins reached into the shadow and pulled out a well built but ill-dressed young. Although he was big enough to put up a struggle he allowed Pins to take his chin in his hand and angle it toward the weak lamp light without any resistance. "I recognise you. Didn't I arrest your grandfather for the murder of your grandmother?" he asked.

"It was manslaughter," came the haughty reply. "Do you want my information or not?"

Pins ended his shift early that day and made his way straight to the Steam Engine in Edge Hill, not far from where he lived. He drank so much that night he had to be carried home by the landlord and his son. His excesses were all to no avail. He woke the next morning having retained every piece of intelligence he had been fed. Regardless of the seemingly boundless benefits it was sowing for the downtrodden and desperate of his beat, his professional conscience couldn't ignore direct evidence, especially regarding organised crime.

He was amazed that kids, hooligans, could pull off anything so sophisticated.

Chapter VI

1891

The cutter pulled its way clear of the heavy river traffic, its single mast bereft of sails. Six boys, no older than Jobe, battled manfully against the current. Unperturbed by the boat's motion they lifted the broad, glistening oars and rowed with ease. Their jauntily positioned glazed hats lent credence to their unruffled demeanour, remaining perfectly in place even though Jobe's head lolled about like a drunk sitting on the Sailors' Home steps. Thick, woolen Guernsey's made them impervious to the freezing cold that numbed his exposed face and neck and the hems of their immaculate blue trousers somehow escaped the lagoon that sloshed about their ankles and splashed up his calves.

Screeching gulls, intuiting that the small boat's wake would provide them with little opportunity of feeding, had long since circled away to follow the steamers that churned up the waters, exposing a variety of marine life that was defenceless against their insatiable beaks.

The strong tidal pull existing within the murky depths of the river wasn't represented on its placid surface and the boat cut serenely through the gentle surge. Jobe experienced the individuality of each tiny ripple, his stomach rising and falling with each swell that slapped lightly against the hull. He imagined his internal organs tumbling about like apples and oranges in a Mary Ellen's basket and he was forced to grit his teeth against the urge to throw up.

He looked over to Molloy, who he knew would be sat bent forward, head buried between his knees in an attempt to avoid the gut-wrenching effects the boat's movements were having on him. Before their nautical escapades with the gang, Molloy had never so much as set foot on board a ferry to New Brighton for a bank holiday picnic and was always the subject of merciless ribbing by the other raiders aboard the rowboat who revelled in the lack of retribution his passive state afforded them. 'Ha, is that Tommy Molloy with his head between his legs and his eyes clasped tight? Well, it's a bit late to be praying for your sins to be forgiven now, isn't it Molloy?'

Jobe leant forward, his intention to mimic Tommy in an effort to alleviate some of his own symptoms. He placed his head between his knees but his inner balance was so badly impaired that the small readjustment caused him to momentarily lose all kinetic cohesion and he pitched forward, sprawling uncontrollably into the midriff of one of the officers who traversed the boat from bow to stern as if on a Sunday stroll. The officer caught Jobe by the shoulders and gave him a swinging cuff. Jobe's face was so numb from the cold that the blow didn't register but still sent his head reeling so he fell back to his bench. A slight tingling sensation buzzed along his jaw as it began to swell and Jobe used it as a source of distraction from the churning in his guts. He felt the blood throbbing in his temples, and although his new position didn't assuage his tumultuous stomach, it at least reduced the chances of meeting one of the officers' eyes and receiving another thump for impertinence.

There were four officers moving about the cutter. Each dressed in similar attire to the boys, the only difference the blue blazers they wore over their Guernsey's, each of the gilt buttons polished to such a shine that they managed to dazzle even in the murky gloom of the Mersey.

"Aye-aye, what's all this shite? Are you taking us for shiteing O's now, is that it?"

Jobe lifted his head on hearing Molloy's raised voice and took in a breath. The cutter had come alongside a ship. It was an enormous square-rigger, its hull ascending into the sky. He'd seen hundreds if not thousands of ships, both at the docks and out on the Mersey, but being so close to the hulking entirety of a full rigged ship took his breath away. His awe was broken by Molloy's voice; a hint of anxiety had entered into it, causing it to break, transforming the shout to a shriek.

"Ho! You louse-ridden shiteing maggots! We're not dirty O's, I tell you! Why're we aside the Akbar? What's all this about, eh?"

A heavy rope ladder, thrown from the deck of the Akbar, crashed into the midships with a wet thump. Without a word one of the officers immediately reached for Jobe, grabbing him by the armpits and hoisting him into the air in one fluid movement. Jobe had a sickening sensation as he hung in midair. Time seemed to freeze as he looked down at the oarsmen back-rowing to maintain their position as the Mersey foamed between the two hulls. He flailed for the slick rope ladder, which he caught hold of, immediately freezing into the foetal position.

Molloy's inertia snapped on seeing Jobe thrown onto the ladder, and he lurched up from the bench his lack of sea legs instantly apparent as he pitched forward. Panicking to compensate he toppled backwards and tottered, arms flailing, before landing in a heap. The three remaining officers had weighed Molloy up, he was as big as any of them and they were loath to initiate a wrestling bout on board the small cutter. But now they were quick to take advantage of his vulnerability, and three of them sprang forward, landing on him in a flurry of knees and elbows. The fourth, after ensuring Molloy was sufficiently restrained, began to buffet Jobe around his haunches and backside, forcing him to forgo the safety of his entwinement and climb the stinking, slippery rope. The battering to his legs continued until he reached a height that allowed the officer to begin his ascent behind him. The cessation of the beating to his legs and the added weight of the officer pulling the glistening rope ladder taut made it easier for Jobe to climb the thick but fraying rungs and he allowed a modicum of his concentration to wander and worry about the fate of his friend. He knew the cutter was moving away from the Akbar from Molloy's shouts, which were growing fainter with distance although still distinguishable over the creaking of the hull and his own and the officer's grunts of effort. "No, you've made a mistake! It's me who's the shiteing O'! I'm the O', I tell you! Turn this boat around, you shiteing nancies or I'll choke the lot of yer!"

Jobe, almost at the summit of the ladder climb, reached for the taffrail of the Akbar eager to complete his climb and look for Molloy. He was dragged over the side and dropped to the deck like a fish released from the nets. Quickly heaving himself up he looked overboard to see the cutter had moved a good distance away. He couldn't see Molloy but was aware of the space his friend must occupy within the boat. He watched in dismay as the three remaining officers continued to rain blows down upon it.

* * *

The sherry was warm but Rebecca still shivered inwardly as she drained the remnants of the glass. It was imperceptible to the man standing in front of her save for a slight trembling of her hand as she leant to place the glass gently on the occasional table at her side.

Simmons took it as his cue to speak. "The boy is safely ensconced aboard The Akbar, ma'am," he stated stiffly. He wasn't immediately graced with an answer and remained standing to attention, a line of sweat beginning to form on his top lip.

His mistress surveyed the shelves of books that lined the wall directly opposite her, as if searching for a specific title. "Everything is in order?" she asked, her gaze still fixed on the far wall.

"Yes, ma'am. He is to remain isolated until he accepts the change."

"And if he opposes?"

"There are provisions in place to deal with that eventuality."

"And our man can be trusted?"

"Irrefutably, ma'am," answered Simmons. His top lip was beginning to itch, but he kept his hands clasped tightly behind his back.

His mistress mulled over the information she had been furnished with as she again scanned the rows of books. She created a steeple with her hands and, lightly resting her chin on it, dismissed her servant. "Thank you, Simmons. That will be all," she drawled.

The man didn't relax a single muscle as he turned and made the long walk to the imposing French doors through which he could exit the library.

She leant over and refilled her sherry glass from the crystal decanter; as the dark liquid neared the brim she spoke. "Unless he refuses to accept his new surname, I never want to hear mention of him again."

Before the first syllable had formed on his mistresses' lips Simmons had already come to an abrupt stop. He turned his head to look back at her. "No, ma'am," he replied before turning and striding out of the doors.

The inception of the Liverpool Juvenile Reformatory Association had caught the imagination of Rebecca Warburton, always an indefatigable volunteer for charitable organisations. The Association had been formed in 1854, following the Government's Youthful Offenders Act, which, for the first time, recognised lawbreakers under the age of sixteen as a different group from their grown-up counterparts, providing the opportunity to separate them from criminally minded adults. The chance to reclaim at least a proportion of the juvenile delinquents who infested the streets and swarmed around the docks had been championed by the town's philanthropists for years, and Liverpool was, amongst other things, a city that put its theories into practice with gusto.

Rebecca, with a verve and zeal for fundraising, had been welcomed into the group of progressives with open arms. Her efforts had been instrumental in bringing the first reform ship to the Mersey. The teak-built Indiaman purchased from the Admiralty had an illustrious past, serving on the Indian, Pacific and Atlantic oceans. Her hard life was illuminated by the costs incurred to repair her rotting hull and fit her out in order for the first fifty boys to be brought on board with the remit of being morally reformed, educated and furnished with an industrial training that would provide them with the opportunity of becoming useful members of society.

Such was the ineptitude of those charged with purchasing and making the ship fit for purpose that the Akbar had lasted a mere six years before her rotting, worm-infested timbers were judged to be a hazard to life and limb and she was towed to the breaker's yard. Rebecca Warburton was adamant that such effort and expenditure would never be so frivolously squandered ever again. With the whole project in the balance, she had canvassed hard to be appointed to the committee responsible for acquiring a new ship, utilising her influence, money and contacts in order to gain a seat.

Having illustrated her prowess for efficiency from the inception of the venture, it was with her blessing that Captain Sualez took fifty boys overland to Plymouth and sailed the new Akbar around the coast to its berth on the Mersey, a third of a mile off the Rock Ferry shore. The risk-laden journey had proved fruitful. The ship had enjoyed a less illustrious past than its predecessor, spending forty-one of the forty-five years of her Royal Navy career safely docked in reserve. Rebecca had procured the society a ship that, although nearing her half-century, appeared as new as if she had just been launched.

The costs incurred to billet the boys were astronomical and a constant threat to the project. Like a thrifty housewife, Rebecca discovered that it was in the minutiae that the most effective cuts in expenditure could be made. Not content in shaving pennies from the cost of bushels of potatoes or replacing expensive shin beef with bullocks' head, she never tired of finding other cost-cutting methods. Boys re-soled their own boots and sewed their own clothes; the ship's barber was given notice, his duties passed to the cook; drives were organised to urge the well-to-do from both sides of the river to transform a portion of their botanic-like gardens to the production of seasonal vegetables to sustain the insatiable appetites on board.

By the time the Catholic dignitaries of the town, having witnessed the success of the floating reformatory, began to instigate the commissioning of their own vessel, Rebecca had gained such a reputation for proficiency in the art of penny-pinching that the famous Father Nugent civilly sought her advice.

A fierce proponent of the old adage, 'keep your friends close and your enemies closer', Rebecca facilitated all requests, answered all queries and offered innumerable and immeasurably valuable suggestions. All the time gaining influence for herself through contacts, associates and agents within every level of administration and personnel, both on deck and on shore. It was in this way that she became aware of a boy that shared her own, and unusually Protestant, surname of Warburton who had been sentenced to three years' service aboard the Catholic Reformatory Ship Clarence.

* * *

Jobe sat on a narrow crossbeam, which although hard and unforgiving at least kept him out of the lake of brine that sloshed about the floor of the hold he had been locked in. Fits of fear coursed through his already shivering body as he listened to the creaking of the timbers, trying to ascertain if it was growing louder or nearer. Heightening his horror, and sometimes hope, that the hull was about to be gouged open by the frothing Mersey which would crash in and drag him to his death and at the same time release him from his misery.

The officer who had harassed him up the rope ladder, once having gained his footing on deck, had dragged him down into the bowels of the ship and thrown him into the dark hold without uttering a word. There was no way of telling how long he had sat in the damp darkness, but during that time, he had been given, and eaten, three meals of dry ship's biscuits served with a watery gruel.

As well as convincing himself that the hold would be reduced to kindling at any second, he passed his time worrying about Molloy, hoping his big friend was faring better than he. What was behind their separation? Whatever it was didn't bode well for him, that was for sure. Molloy had told Jobe all about the prison ships that anchored over the other side of the river. They were cold, bleak, dismal places. Those on board suffered such hunger that they fought over the old coconut husks that they used to scrub the decks.

Molloy had described to him the keen air of sectarianism that festered on the Protestant Akbar and Catholic Clarence, which often spilled into violence whenever hands from either boat came together on dry land. The bi-annual sports day was a favourite. The athletics and football trophies that created so much pride for the governors of the respective ships paled into insignificance next to the unauthorised, undetected events of gouging, fish-hooking and kidney blows that the boys contested among themselves and which were the real victories of the day. But it was what Molloy had said about boys who had been placed on the wrong ship that caused Jobe the most consternation. "The very worst thing that can happen to a lad, Jobe, is him being placed on the wrong shiteing ship and his fellows finding out that he's of the opposite colour. He's liable to find himself floating face down on the river before long."

Jobe comforted himself that his very Anglo-Saxon surname would offer him a veil with which to hide his Catholicism and he tried to recall every snippet of information Molloy had taught him about the ships. He reflected that his time spent locked in the hold was the longest he had spent apart from Molloy since he had been lauded as a hero for seeing off the Cockspur Street Gang singlehandedly on Gt. Crosshall street years before.

Lost in his thoughts as he was his ears didn't discern the noise of the key scraping in the lock, and he sat up in surprise as the door swung open and lamplight illuminated the damp hold.

"Jobe Flynn?"

Jobe couldn't see who addressed him from the doorway, hidden as he was behind the flickering glare of the oil lantern. It was the first time since coming aboard that anybody had addressed him directly, and he hesitated before answering, his throat feeling, and his voice sounding, alien.

"My name is Warburton, sir. Flynn was my mother's maiden name."

The heavy door slammed shut without another word being said. Unnerved, Jobe remained in the darkness wondering at what had just passed, a feeling of dread emanating from the pit of his stomach.

The exchange was repeated, over and over. The same sharp spoken question, delivered in a West Country twang, followed by the door slamming shut on Jobe's response until he changed his answer, the fear being he would never see the light of day again.

"Yes, sir, Jobe Flynn, that's me."

"You? But you're Jobe Warburton. If you've told me once you've told me a dozen times."

"No, sir. There's no Jobe Warburton in here. I'm Jobe Flynn. I'm sorry if I've led you to believe anything aside from that."

"Is it stupid you're taking me for, boy?"

"No, sir. Excuse me, sir, it's just that my name is Jobe Flynn."

"There's no Jobe Warburton in here then?"

"No, sir."

"And there never was?"

"No, sir. Never, sir."

"You ever heard tell of a boy by the name of Jobe Warburton?"

"No, sir. Never, sir."

"Well, then, Flynn, my lad. What is it you're doing all alone in the dark and the damp? Let's get you fed, warmed and dried, shall we?"

Jobe straightened up and moved towards the door, his knees and back cracking in protest. As he approached the lamp, near enough to be bathed in its light and feel a flicker of its warmth, a hand clamped around the back of his neck. He couldn't see the face but could smell the rum-soured breath and feel the flecks of spittle that showered his ear and neck.

"Now if a boy should all of a sudden become confused about his name again, he may find himself overboard and alone in the freezing water. 'What a pointless attempt at escape,' they'll say. 'Why choose such a cold night, one with no moon?' they'll say."

"I can't see any chance of confusion, sir, I've only ever been known as Flynn."

Jobe was taken down a set of steps to what he was informed was the lower deck.

"Pick up 776. In there is your uniform and that next to it is your hammock."

Jobe looked to where his gaze was being directed. Stored neatly in the middle of the floor was a pile of hammocks. Next to them were bags stamped with numbers. He found 776 and hefted it up. The bag, although seemingly empty, was heavy and cumbersome and looked as if it had been sewn together from scraps of old sail.

* * *

The wind whistled across the deck. Jobe stood naked, his duffel bag at his feet, shivering in front of those who had been assembled on deck. He imagined it must be the ship's full complement. Officers stood on the quarterdeck while boys watched from various vantage points, some even swinging from the rigging like bald monkeys. He had initially tried to stop his teeth from chattering but was afraid that his jaw would shatter with the effort and so stood under everyone's gaze while his teeth rattled away. A hogshead barrel had been filled with river water and placed on the deck; a plank leant against it served as a bridge from the deck to its lip.

"Officers! Gentlemen! This here is Flynn, our new shipmate on the glorious Akbar!" The West Country twang reverberated around the ship, and Jobe saw boys look at each other, eyebrows raised.

"Like all new mates, Flynn here has been blessed with the gift of a clean, warm uniform, but just like you afore him, before he can don it and come among us, he first needs to clean the filth of his landlubber past that clings to his every pore!"

The announcement was greeted with lusty hurrahs.

"C'mon then, young Flynn. Let's get you used to the water, shall we!"

Jobe saw no point in prolonging the spectacle and so stepped onto the plank, which was upset by his weight, and his arms flailed as he attempted to maintain his balance. The screams of pleasure and derision were instant. Jobe triumphed in his battle for balance and continued carefully up the plank. On reaching the barrel he refused to hesitate or wait for an order before plunging straight in. The water was almost at freezing point and his spine constricted as he submerged his whole body so it filled his ears and suppressed the caterwauling from the deck. He remained under the water for as long as possible before exploding out, replenishing his lungs with fresh air before immersing himself again. The shrieks and howls had ceased a long time before it was suggested that the landlubber filth of his past had been sluiced from him and he was allowed to climb from the hogshead and stand on the deck to dry. "It's a good thing there's a strong northwesterly. With any luck, you'll be dried and dressed before one of these here seagulls swoops down and attempts to peck away your maggot."

The well-used jest was greeted with mirth. Jobe, intent on playing no part in the show stood unabashed his hands at his sides, happy in the knowledge that he had at least curtailed a part of their entertainment.

The diversion was the last in a long list of chores that the boys had endured before it was time for their hammocks. Jobe found it easy enough to sling the hammock, but his attempts to climb into and remain within it were another matter. The exaggerated whoops and cries of glee echoed around the lower decks, and after enduring the ice-cold immersions with a stoicism that had diminished their enjoyment on deck, Jobe now found himself providing the end-of-evening cabaret.

His eagerness to end the spectacle turned to fervour that only served to prolong his torment. Jumping from a standing start, taking a run, diving head first from an angle all ended with the same result. He would grab the hammock before his weight spun him over and he crashed to the floor. On the rare occasion he accomplished his task and actually made it inside the canvas hammock, his negligible weight would again betray him and he would be flipped over, landing flat on the floor again. The boys screeched until the exhaustion of another long day overwhelmed them and they were lost to sleep, leaving him to his fruitless attempts. When the majority were breathing rhythmically, a short, fat boy approached him. Jobe had never seen anybody with such a perfectly round face.

"Here," he said, smiling and manoeuvring Jobe to one side. The smile creased his small eyes until they seemed closed, and his face took on such benevolence that Jobe had visions of the saints his mother used to tell him about. Despite his obvious weight, and being only a head taller than the hammock the boy simply flopped into it, laying for a second before rolling out and standing aside. Jobe mimicked his actions until, on the third attempt, he was lying snugly in the hammock, marvelling at the comfort it afforded. Carefully he turned, intending to thank the boy who had saved him from another night on an unforgiving wooden floor but he was gone and sleep took Jobe before he could wonder where his hammock was strung.

It seemed like he had only closed his eyes for a second when loud shouting snapped his eyes open. "Lash and stow, you lazy lubbers, lash and stow!" The pre-dawn wake-up call that tore Jobe from his first sound sleep in days was enough to engage his brain but his body struggled to interpret the messages sent from it and his fingers fumbled at the ropes and knots that secured his hammock. He was powerless to rid his eyes of their heaviness or shake off the lethargy that made his movements slow and ponderous regardless of the officer who stood next to him and barked orders straight down his ear. By the time he unslung the heavy canvas the other boys had already lashed and stowed theirs.

His exhaustion and humiliation stirred memories of his daily eviction from the Marybone shelter and his mind wandered back to those mornings before he joined the gang, when he was ousted onto the cold street to begin fruitless journeys to the dock stands. As the other boys were savouring their hot porridge and pint of black coffee, Jobe was forced to sling, unsling and stow his hammock over and over, the voluble officer's face, and breath, so close to his ear that he felt the stubble covering the cheek brush against his lobe more the once.

On the bell ringing for the end of morning mess, Jobe was allowed to join the other boys as they filed into an airless cabin for education. The droning schoolmaster seemed intent on sending Jobe back to sleep and his eyelids fluttered closed on several occasions. Only repeated pokes in his side snapped his head back up from his chest and stopped him dropping off completely. The fingers that dug into his ribs belonged to the fat boy who had helped him master the hammock the previous evening. Each time Jobe tried to whisper his thanks, the boy remained impassive and paid even closer attention to the monotonous tutor at the front of the class.

Following the torturous three hours of schooling, the boys were set to work. Jobe and a number of others were provided with old coconut husks and designated an area of deck to scrub. Jobe scrubbed at the deck with the husk, bemused by the hairy fruit he held in his hand as he wondered why they weren't using sandstone for the task. Seeing the bulk of the boy who had helped him with his hammock the previous night and to stay awake during *education,* he sidled over to him. He received some kicks on his way but the boys who delivered them were never looking at him and he couldn't be sure if they were accidental or dealt on purpose. "I'm sorry I didn't thank you last night. I was so exhausted I must have fallen straight asleep. But thank you."

The fat boy continued scrubbing the deck, paying Jobe no heed. Although it was a cold day the exertion of scrubbing had caused a sweat to break out and glisten on his round face. His expression was so vacant that Jobe wondered if he could be the same boy whose features had transmitted such warmth and personality the previous evening. "I'm sorry—"

"Sh! No talking! If you're caught talking, they'll find something worse for you to do and I'll be for it too. We'll speak at mess," he wheezed between laboured breaths.

Jobe's sluggishness had cost him his morning meal and his stomach grumbled as he looked around at the hundred or so boys who were led into the mess hall to line up around its sides as the mess captains, boys who were deemed to be adhering well to the rules and principles of the ship or who granted certain favours to those officers with a penchant for them, oversaw the lowering of tables that were lashed to the ceiling.

`Once lowered the boys were allowed to sit around the dozen trestle tables. Jobe sat next to the boy who had schooled him in the art of the hammock and waited for the mess captain who followed the galley cooks, ensuring each boy received his portion of salted bullocks' head meat, thin soup and ship's biscuits which were accompanied by a pint of black, unsugared tea.

The scraping of metal on metal filled the hall as each boy bent to the task of clearing their tin plates and filling their growling stomachs.

Jobe's neighbour cleared his plate of sliced bullocks head and was busy crumbling dry biscuits into his thin gruel. There was no trace of the vacant expression he had sported earlier as he focused all of his attention on ensuring every crumb entered his bowl. He spoke to Jobe while he ground. "I'm Horatio. Eat your meat. It's easier to chew when there's a little warmth to it." He smiled as he lifted the bowl to his mouth and began to suck down the mush he had created.

"Horatio, eh? That's a name apt for the environment."

"My real name is Horace. The others have nicknamed me Horatio on account of me being such a bad sailor," he explained, his smile temporarily disappearing as he looked down hungrily at his empty bowl. Seeing it was completely empty, he shrugged his shoulders and looked at Jobe as one of the captains, the only boys allowed to walk around freely at mess time, leaned between the two, forcing Horatio to shift to one side. Jobe could see the definition of the captain's well-built upper arm muscles and smell the rank sweat that leeched through his thin undershirt. Jobe looked up at him as he spoke to the other boy.

"Well, well, Horatio, finally found a friend, have we?" he said as he took hold of the boy's fleshy jowls, twisting the skin before letting go and watching his white finger marks being erased by the blood rushing back to the rosy cheeks. He turned to Jobe. "We don't get many Flynns around here. Catholic name, isn't it?"

The question was asked with the utmost geniality but Jobe recognised the malice in the captain's clear blue eyes. The boys on Jobe's table, having satisfied their immediate hunger, were now looking up from their plates as they swigged their tea. Jobe saw no advantage in attempting to deny what could only be taken as an accusation. "I'm Jobe Flynn, and yes, I suppose I am a Catholic, although I've always been too busy surviving to take lessons from men in cassocks on the rights and wrongs of the world," he looked away from the captain and pulled his plate of bullock cheek towards him, picking at the meat.

The captain, unable to compute the response was stunned into indecision and he could only watch as Jobe wrestled with the tough meat. He recovered from his stupor but, finding he was still at a loss for words, hocked a gob of spit into his mouth that he allowed to slowly leak between his lips and dangle over Jobe's plate. The weight of the globule finally became too much and the string of sputum snapped, sinking into the already unpalatable bullock's cheek. "We don't like papists eating *our* meat on this vessel. I'll be seeing you later!"

Jobe looked up as the captain sauntered away with a wink to his audience and saw that the officer with the West Country accent had witnessed the episode.

"If you were to just slice that piece..." Horatio's words were accompanied by an index finger that hovered over Jobe's plate to illustrate his meaning. "That piece just there, see? The rest of the meat is untouched," he advised.

Jobe looked at the plate for a second before sliding it across to Horatio, who, nodding his thanks, immediately set to work with his spoon. Jobe's train of thought had been interrupted but he refocused his attention on the mess captain as he approached the serving hatch to claim his own meal. The officer with the West Country twang followed him and was now whispering into his ear as he received his victuals.

Horatio looked up from his plate following Jobe's gaze. "Don't concern yourself too much with Cameron," he said, his mandibles working overtime to chew the tough meat that had gone cold. "He's nothing but a bully. I used to get it from him something terrible, but now that he's been made a captain, he's got a full mess to persecute," he said, his face creasing into yet another smile.

* * *

The muscles of Jobe's arms trembled uncontrollably as he lay in his hammock. Days of ceaselessly scrubbing the decks resulted in him being barely able to lift his victuals to his mouth by the time evening mess arrived and he had taken to lapping at his pints of stewed tea like a dog until he could risk lifting the mug without the contents slopping over the sides in his shaking grasp. It reduced the chance of the steaming black liquid spilling down his front and giving Cameron yet another opportunity to vilify him, not that he needed an excuse. Cameron had remained a constant pain since the day he had spat on his dinner, a malevolent spirit that haunted his every move. The attention the mess captain paid him eclipsed the petty menacing that those with position coupled with inclination revelled in meting out to the unfortunates in their thrall. It was specific enough to leave Jobe in no doubt that he was receiving orders from Mr. Wilkes, the officer with the West Country twang, who no doubt, Jobe reasoned, had somebody on shore whispering in his ear while at the same time lining his pockets.

In his discomfort, sleep evaded him, and although exhausted it at least presented the opportunity to exercise his brain and again contemplate his position on the Akbar. The conclusions he reached never offered any comfort. Did his father really view him as some sort of risk to his new life? So much so that he felt it necessary to strip him of his name and condemn him to a reform ship? He had kept a close ear out for tales of the Giant O' during his time in the gang. The streets were always awash with news of his deeds. His father, along with his pawnshop henchmen, had taken to frequenting Union meetings, his sole purpose to interrupt and intimidate those who supported calls to strike.

Following his diplomatic sorties to members of the Logwood Gang, Jobe had endeavoured to keep abreast of all news and developments, and continued to attend meetings, listening to speeches while constantly hoping, and fearing, to catch sight of his father. The nature of his father's appearances led him to thoughts of his extended paternal family. Before her death his mother had informed him that the Warburton's came from old money but wasn't sure where their interests lay. Did they extend to shipping and storage, or did his father pimp himself out to the ship owners as he did to the Wise Pastor? Jobe wondered if his father's cameos were nothing more than an opportunity to assuage his basest tendencies, namely cracking the skulls of Catholics.

He contemplated his own Catholic skull, which had been in danger since Mr. Wilkes, content that Jobe had neither the stomach for, nor the audience with which to share his true identity, had ended his sentinel-like observations, happy to allow the dark lugubriousness of life aboard the Akbar and the spite of Cameron and the rest of his shipmates to grind Jobe down.

His initial anticipation of mastering the sails, masts and wheel had dissipated. It had quickly become apparent to him that Wilkes would not allow him to learn so much as the most basic of knots. He was classified as one of those boys who showed no compulsion or understanding of sailing and were kept well away from the rigging, masts and the ship's wheel; instead, they were enlisted to the purgatory of picking apart old ropes for use in caulking the ship or, as in Jobe's case, scrubbing and swabbing the decks.

The only light that Wilkes, he himself or Cameron and the rest of his peers couldn't extinguish was that which was emitted from his friendship with Horatio, who had become his constant companion, although Jobe had attempted to avert the first hints of friendship after witnessing the toll Horatio was paying. His excess weight and lack of dexterity regarding anything maritime had led to his ostracism long before Jobe arrived aboard, but his acceptance and befriending of the Catholic was beyond the pale, and Cameron punished him unmercifully on every occasion that allowed for it. His lack of nautical ability was surpassed only by his inability to defend himself, and where those attacking Jobe knew they were in a fight, Horatio proved to be nothing more than a punch bag, which did little to dampen the efforts of his tormentors.

"I think it'd go easier for you if you looked on your own tasks and left me to mine from now on, H," Jobe said as he dabbed at a cut over Horatio's right eye. It was unusual that Cameron and his cronies would aim blows to the head or face, preferring to leave no visual evidence of their assault.

Horatio pulled his head away, a hurt expression on his face that bore no relation to his injuries. "Why would you suggest such a course?"

"The beatings you receive are because of me, H. It would be better if you publicly fell out with me, began to shun me, accost me at mess, something like that," Jobe explained.

"Nonsense, Jobe. These bashings are nothing compared to the whippings I used to take from my father. Why, they'd have to throw me overboard to keep me from the side of the only true friend I've ever had."

"That could well be on the agenda, H. I know they'd do for me if it wasn't for Wilkes."

Jobe had tested his theory that the officer was in the pay of somebody on shore by feigning to throw himself overboard. Mr. Wilkes was still keeping him under close scrutiny at the time. Jobe had worked his way over to the rail, husk in hand. Ensuring Wilkes was in attendance, he stood and climbed onto the rail, blithely looking down into the river. Within seconds, he found himself in the arms of Wilkes, who maintained his crushing bear hug until he had Jobe below decks.

"What is it that goes through a boy's mind to have him acting in such a foolhardy manner?"

Jobe didn't reply, waiting for the officer to do the talking.

"Notions of escape, is that it? Well, only an escape from life itself lies down that path. There'll be no more of it. Why, I'll ensure that your back is ribboned if there is any repeat of such behaviour!"

Jobe sensed the concern emanating from the officer, and he knew it had nothing to do with his welfare.

* * *

Jobe threw the last of the husks into the pail.

The initial conundrum of why the usual sandstone used for scrubbing decks had been replaced by the alien shells of the exotic fruit were now well apparent. His raw hands were testament to the amount of scrubbing the deck received; his efforts alone were enough to reduce the hulking square-rigger to nothing more than a raft if sandstone were employed, and he detested the sensation of the hairy husks against his cracked palms. The creaking of a deck-board interrupted his thoughts and he tensed before spinning around with the heavy pail fully extended so it smashed into the midriff of a boy who was only a few paces behind him. Quickly taking a step back, he saw that boys from his mess surrounded him in a semicircle, numbering not quite half a dozen.

Jobe having nothing but the pail with which to defend himself took another careful step backwards, thus cancelling out the risk of any of his tormentors coming at him from behind. The boys waited, unsure how to advance and Jobe took advantage of their hesitancy and swung the heavy pail in a wide-reaching arc as if to illustrate its range. The pail was heavy, and the boy who had been hit hung back on the fringes, nursing an arm that could well be broken. The boys were used to Jobe utilising whatever was at hand as a weapon, and although the pail looked incongruous in his hands, it was heavy and nobody seemed willing to be the first to step into the wild arcs that were Jobe's defence.

"Cameron told us to make sure we do for him good," one of them said without taking his eyes from the pail. The boys looked at each other, particularly their wounded comrade, and with a shrug of their shoulders began to step backwards. "Nothing urgent, Irish, we'll be seeing you later," said the last of them to file through the doorway.

Jobe slumped in relief. His rubbed his tanned arms. His biceps, as with the rest of him, had shown small bursts of growth, but he knew he couldn't have swung the pail for much longer. The twelve-hour working day that dominated the boys waking hours was enough to exhaust even the most zealous of attackers, and Jobe was safe in the knowledge that the next time he spied his would-be assailants, they would barely have the strength to sling their hammocks. He just hoped that H' would fare as well.

Horatio had remained true to his word, refusing to forsake his friend regardless of the beatings that neither concerned nor cowed him. Jobe took heart from the example set by his effervescent friend. Nothing about the hardships of life aboard the Akbar affected Horatio, even the hunger that gnawed at him constantly was mitigated by his daydreaming.

"Oh, it was a sight to behold, Jobe. My father was like Rumplestiltskin. His bakery was always full of whatever you fancied! Pies! Pastries! Sweet or savoury! You could eat and eat to your heart's content and it would never empty." H' would sigh as he scrubbed at the deck, his eyes wistful and faraway. Sometimes his features would temporarily darken, like a cloud blocking out the sun. "But if he caught you filching…" The darkness never lasted long, and he would lick his lips, his smile returning. "It was always worth it, no matter what form of torture he could dream up."

Jobe would permit H' his mental excursions, never interrupting, allowing him his escape from the despair and drudgery of his existence aboard the Akbar. He resolved to repay the steadfast friendship H' had shown him, but he was powerless to offer protection from the spite and malice of Cameron and other boys, and so he set his mind to solving H's biggest torment: his own stomach. He was determined to find a way of assuaging his friend's constant hunger, although he did have grave doubts about whether H's appetite could ever be sated.

"What if I could offer you something as big as your father's bakery?" he asked one evening as Horatio finished verbalising his favourite daydream. Darkness had stolen over the ship. A tall, unctuous boy named Scully, who had recently been promoted from a mess captain to a petty officer, was busy lighting the oil lamps that hung from the three masts and were dotted at intervals along the rail. Jobe and Horatio were pulling up their final pail of water with which to swab the foredeck, their hands raw and numb.

Horatio looked at him uncomprehendingly.

"There's no pies or pastries," Jobe said. "Well, not to my knowledge anyway, but there's plenty of other victuals."

Horatio let go of the rope as he contemplated Jobe's meaning and Jobe was pulled against the rail by the unexpected extra weight.

Scully spun from his oil lamp and eyed the pair suspiciously.

H' took up the rope again and began pulling in earnest. "I haven't the foggiest what you're getting at. Is it a ribbing you're giving me?" he asked.

"I've got a key to the stores," whispered Jobe.

The bucket again clattered down the side of the ship as Horatio released his hold for a second time. "The stores!" he said, his voice breaking with excitement so that he only emitted a barely audible squeal, which was just as well, as they now had the full attention of the petty officer.

"Ho, what's all the commotion over there?" shouted Scully. "Stop with your japes and get that deck swabbed or it'll be a report for the both of you!"

Horatio concealed his excitement and pulled up the bucket with uncommon gusto.

* * *

The problem of how to access extra rations for H' consumed Jobe, offering him a mental diversion from the crushing banality of his daily chores, and with his mind reactivated, he found that he began to flourish mentally as well as physically.

Ideas presented themselves constantly but, after careful consideration, he was forced to discard them all. He watched, coconut husk in hand, as the fresh goods were delivered from the Liverpool docks by barge; but the milk, butter and specific fancies of the officers were closely monitored, checked once as they were taken on board and again as they were stored in the hold. Even if he could concoct a way of extracting a portion of the goods, he would then have to repeat the same feat the following week, and any discrepancies would result in a search, placing H' in the line of fire.

Jobe concentrated every ounce of his intellect; there was certainly no other strain on it, trying to solve the problem. One solution presented itself repeatedly and refused to be dismissed, regardless of being fraught with jeopardy. Access to the stores themselves would provide a route to the dried goods, fruits and vegetables that were plentiful and so accounted for in a more haphazard fashion. Any discrepancy, if noticed at all, would be minimal and probably put down to spillage or rats. But there was only one way in. Jobe had never attempted to pickpocket anybody before, although he'd received schooling from a master.

Silky had refused to abandon his favourite and most lucrative earner on the gang modifying their activities. He had evolved his practice into an art, which he loved to use in and around the business district of Dale, Water, and Castle Streets disguised as a sweep, porter or butcher's boy.

"The most important part of the whole play is not to allow the mark to see you as a threat, and by virtue of their pompousness, you'll remain invisible to them, even when you're right under their nose," Silky had informed Jobe as he tiptoed around The Den, squinting through his gold-rimmed monocle which he held between his thumb and forefinger as if it were evidence of his hypothesis.

But even taking the arrogance and lackadaisical nature of the officers into account, Jobe was aware that his dipping skills were not even as good as second-rate, and he was sure any attempt would be folly. He would need to prosper from some sort of diversion before he could even risk trying. A melee or a crush would have to occur where he would have the time not only to steal the heavy bunch of keys from an officer, but also remove the stores key before replacing them. He would have discounted the idea if he had not already exhausted every other possibility. He couldn't risk confiding in anyone else in order to manufacture a distraction, and his refusal to place Horatio in any danger meant that he would just have to be patient and wait until an opportunity presented itself meaning he would be forced to act without notice or planning. Or so he thought.

"It's bloody freezing. It's too late in the year," protested the squeaky voice.

"What d'you mean, freezing? Summer's only just ending. Besides, I'll be in there as well, won't I?"

"What'll you be doing in there?"

"Well, ready to save you of course!"

"You needn't bother. I'll be dead from the chill."

"Listen, it's the last chance for a slap-up meal at one of the governor's houses, isn't it? Did you see the way Swigger and Higson were treated the last time they pulled it? Why, that compass they were given will be worth a pretty penny when they're back on shore, engraved or not!"

"Yes, but they pulled it when the sun still had some warmth in it, didn't they? We'd be offering up a lot more than they did."

"Yis but old Braddock said we'd be on the foremast tomorrow, all we have to do is ensure we're on the fore course and it'll just be a small drop into the river. We'll be pulled out in no time at all," he cajoled, noting the look of doubt on his co-conspirator's face he continued. "Look here, we've a long miserable winter stretching ahead of us. Don't you want a day on shore being treated like a lord? I'll easily find someone else if you don't."

"I still don't know..."

"You said yourself, the time is now. It'll be getting colder by the day, and you're right about that, of course you are! We'll go tomorrow."

"I didn't say that, did I?"

"Think of all the lauding. We'll be heroes. Well-fed and well-rewarded heroes!"

"OK, tomorrow it is!"

Jobe listened from inside a cargo hold that was used for the storing of swabbing mops, pails and bolts of lichen-covered canvas that looked Jurassic. He had heard tell of the old ruse of falling overboard. Shouts of 'man overboard' would reverberate around the deck and echo from any ships that happened to be passing. Before the warning bell could be rung, one of his shipmates, always a strong, capable swimmer, would be overboard without any thought for his own life or limb and bravely keep afloat his spluttering, thrashing colleague until a buoy could be thrown out to them and they would be dragged up to the deck as heroes.

The boys would be the toast of the ship. Proof that the floating reformatory was indeed influencing the morality of boys who, before their berthing on board, would think nothing of rifling through the pockets of a drowning man before watching him go under. The Committee was only too ready to spread the word and lavish rewards and gifts on the said heroes. Jobe knew the fraudulent pair's plan would present his best opportunity and hoped that neither they, nor he, would get cold feet.

Following noon mess, Jobe ensured he remained as close to the rail as was possible without raising any suspicion. He felt sure that the planned 'rescue' would go ahead. Both boys had landed themselves jobs on the lowest spar of the foremost mast, thus providing them an easy drop into the river below. Jobe felt his stomach tighten; he had high hopes that his partners in crime, albeit that they were ignorant of the fact, were committed to their part but wondered if he would be able fulfill his own. The omens were positive; old Braddock was the officer on watch, a dithering old sailor who had served as long as the inaugural Akbar and one of the officers on-board who extracted certain *favours* from certain boys.

As he was weighing up the possible outcomes, an image blurred within his peripheral vision followed by a splash and a cry of 'man overboard'. The ship's bell hadn't reached its third peal before another boy had splashed into the water. The warning bell being rung was an open invitation for all hands to rush to the starboard rail. Jobe timed his movement, waiting for Braddock to limp to the rail. There was already a throng leaning over it, shouting encouragement to the two boys so that Braddock was forced to use both hands to part the cheering crowd that had gathered to watch the two boys splashing in the river, trusting the denseness of the crowd to bear his weight and keep him upright until he reached the rail and could see what was going on in the river.

Jobe saw his chance and, pressing his body against that of the old sailor, snaked his hand into his pocket. He retrieved the bunch of keys with ease. Keeping his hands low, his fingers tracing the shape of the keys like a blind man. He had only seen the stores key once but had committed its shape to memory. A lifebuoy had been thrown overboard, and by the changing dynamic of the crowd Jobe knew that the heroes were being hauled back aboard. Time was waning. He recognised the key, older and more rusted than its companions, and manipulated it from the chain, sliding it into his waistband.

The initial excitement of the rescue was subsiding by the second. Other officers had arrived and were busy marshalling the boys away from the rail and back to their places of work. Jobe had kept himself pressed against Braddock, whose attention was focused on what was happening in front of him. He lurched forward, as if being pushed from behind, feeling the officer take a step forward against the added weight he forced his hand and the keys back into the baggy pocket.

Braddock spun around and looked directly down at Jobe just as he removed his hand from the damp pocket. There was a look of admonishment on the old sailor's face and Jobe smiled in response, raising his eyebrows suggestively before taking a step backwards and out of the startled officer's personal space. Braddock's features remained creased with censure before they softened and he rewarded Jobe with a smile and a lecherous wink.

Jobe moved away from the rail and returned to his dried coconut husk as a blanket was thrown over the two boys, who remained huddled together in the buoy, teeth chattering. He didn't look up from his scrubbing as the ship's captain made a rare appearance on deck, clearing his throat as he buttoned his long, thick overcoat. "I was of the impression that these charades had concluded with the summer, but I see they have not! Very well. The next boy who falls into the river will receive a dozen lashes on being brought back on deck. The boy who rescues him will receive double! Do I make myself clear?"

The boys chattering and shivering could not hide their dismay at the words; there would be no celebration or lauding of their shifting moral compass.

The key dug into Jobe's stomach as he grinned down at the section of deck he scrubbed.

* * *

The constant cold. The continued enmity of his crew-mates. The continual berating of the officers. And the mundane nature of Akbar life; Horatio was immune to them all. Even on the nights that he and Jobe found no opportunity of sneaking into the stores and he fell asleep hungry, it contented him to know that all of the foodstuffs on board were at his disposal. In his view, Jobe was a little too cautious about visiting the stores, but he had to admit his friend did have an eerie knowledge of the movements and habits of everybody on the ship, which made it easy to trust his judgement. Besides, he had no choice, Jobe wouldn't even consider letting him have possession of the stores-key.

"I'd put my life in your hands without blinking, H', but I wouldn't trust that stomach of yours with so much as a crumb. The temptation would eat you up until you had no choice. Besides, if it's me who is found with the key, you're away, scot-free."

H' understood the logic behind Jobe's words; he wouldn't trust himself with the key either. He knew it was his ability to consume huge quantities of food that had booked his berth on the Akbar. His father had deliberately left the unsealed letter addressed to the Committee of the Floating Reformatory Akbar next to a tray of freshly baked hot-cross buns. The scent of cinnamon had drawn him in from the entry where he had been skulking, awaiting the opportunity to pilfer something hot. Savoury or sweet, it made no difference.

The letter beseeched the Committee to take his Godless, villainous and feckless son aboard in a bid to transform him into a worthwhile addition to society; it offered to pay the costs of his son's board plus a monthly contribution towards the upkeep of the ship. Although the letter terrified Horatio, it didn't sate his appetite and he polished off the full tray of hot-cross buns two at a time right there in the kitchen, grunting and beating the table as he struggled for breath through the mush of warm pastry that blocked his airways. The obligatory beating for consuming the pastries failed to materialise, illustrating his father's contentment with the fear and anxiety he had created with the letter. His father was at constant pains to introduce new methods of punishing him, and H' hoped the letter was just that, a ploy to torment him psychologically in another bid to curtail his appetite.

Horace Brent had moved his expectant wife from the coarseness of Kirkdale across the boundary to Bootle for a better life. Although the burgeoning town was becoming ever more intertwined with the metropolis to its south, the former village still retained a modicum of its rural origins, a direct contrast to the smoke-filled filth of the city Horace had left behind. The town officials were eager not to replicate the mistakes of their encroaching neighbour, and the aspirations of the town were reflected in the naming of the rapidly expanding streets. Those not named after the grand colleges of Oxford were given the names of Shakespearean characters in an attempt to imbue pride and ambition in its residents.

It was on the corner of Balliol and Stanley Road that Horace proudly created his new bakery. He watched over the sign writer like a hawk as he added the legend '& Son' to the priceless sign he had brought with him from his old premises.

"What if it's not a son I'm carrying?" his wife chided, receiving nothing but a knowing smile as a response. The birth proved his intuition to be sound, and he named the boy Horace, in his own honour. Following the birth of his son, Horace could do nothing but watch in despair as his wife began to waste away. She tried valiantly to appease the babe who continuously worried at her teat, but it was never satisfied and seemed to be suckling at her life energy. After her death, Horace ceased to notice the child, and when he finally ventured from the comforting cloak of grief that had shielded him from the world, the boy had abandoned liquid and noisily sucked on sweetmeats. He didn't seem to be troubled by the void his mother's death had created, only becoming agitated if there was nothing at hand to stuff into his mouth. Horace wondered what crime he had committed to be tainted by such a curse.

H' was sure he couldn't have been born greedy. His mother had died when he was still a baby, and he often wondered whether the lack of mother's milk had created the insatiable appetite within him, but thought it more likely that the constant ire of his father was responsible for his love of food. He grew up surrounded by the perpetual waft of temptation, a by-product of the pies, pastries and cakes that his father produced for his shop. It became a constant itch that he couldn't help but scratch. The incessant harassing, chastising and bullying of his father completed the vicious circle, and food became his only solace, his only comfort, the only warmth and comfort he could find in a cold, cruel world.

H's stomach rumbled loud enough to disturb his immediate neighbours and he added to their consternation by calling to his friend. "Jobe," he whispered. There was no reply but he was unsure whether Jobe was testing him. His knowledge regarding the movements and habits of every soul on board, although benefitting H', frequently also unsettled him. It just wasn't natural. "Jobe," he whispered again, stuck in the limbo of wanting to be sure his friend was asleep but at the same time scared of waking him. His stomach rumbled again. It had been days since they had made a midnight sortie to the stores.

"So tell me again, Jobe. Does Braddock know you have the key?"

"Well, he wouldn't mention that the key was missing outright, H'. That'd be admitting he's culpable for losing it," sighed Jobe in reply. He hadn't relished telling his friend that there would be no visit to the stores for a while. "He'll have given the keys to the next officer on watch. They never bother with the formalities involved with the handover. They're supposed to check and sign for the keys, sign that all boys are accounted for, sign that everything is ship-shape on board, but they never do. Who knows if Braddock is even aware it was him who lost the key?"

Braddock had impeded Jobe as he was about to swap his bald, cracked coconut husk. "What's the problem, Flynn?" he croaked.

"Nothing, sir, This husk has had it, that's all. I'm just replacing it," Jobe held up the smooth, split husk.

Braddock took the husk from him, turning it over in his hand as he inspected it. "Yes, you're right. This one's had it. Before you get another, I've got a job for you below decks."

Braddock led Jobe to the brine-soaked hold he had been locked in on first being brought aboard. As the ageing officer advanced towards him, Jobe hurriedly informed him that he was Wilkes's boy. "Someone informed him of my advances towards you on deck the day of the man overboard, sir. Maybe one of your own boys, insecure and jealous of the development."

Braddock halted his advance.

"In turn, Mr. Wilkes has warned me to stay away from any other officers and demanded that I inform him of anyone making advances towards me."

Braddock squinted at Jobe as if trying to penetrate his mind. He recalled Wilkes had covered the boy like a rash when he had been brought aboard and chuckled squalidly to himself as he licked the tip of his filthy index finger. "I knew that so-and-so was no paragon," he said, as if thinking aloud. He looked at Jobe as if only just realising he was still there. "Oh, well, shame, real shame," he muttered as he looked Jobe up and down before turning and shuffling away.

Jobe continued to explain his reasoning to the forever-hungry boy who was twisting his earlobe in concentration. "Cook is responsible for accessing stores to fulfil the needs of all messes. It was only when the fresh goods were delivered today that it was discovered the key was missing. I was scrubbing the deck when Cook realised he'd left his key locked in the galley. Mister Stones attempted to open the stores for him, he looked a little perplexed, but then he simply went and replaced the missing key from the bunch of spares that are locked away in the captain's quarters. A hundred handovers have taken place since I took the key, so no-one will be sure who lost it or how, but the officers must have caught it from the captain. They've completed the handover impeccably all day."

"So nobody knows you've got it for sure," repeated H' hopefully.

"The likelihood is that they're not even aware that anybody has the key, H', but we can't be too careful. Just a few days, that's all. A few days."

During those long days, it had seemed to Horatio that the portions on his tin plate had shrunk, leaving more and more of the chipped plate exposed. "Jobe," he whispered for the third time. He got a response but not from his sleeping pal.

"Shut your fat pie hole, Horatio, or I'll come over there and shut it for you!"

H' waited for a defensive challenge from Jobe, and when it was not forthcoming decided that he really was asleep. He allowed the time to crawl by before eventually rolling quietly from his bunk.

He unlocked the heavy door as if in a trance, pausing before pushing it open. He didn't like to betray Jobe and understood the danger involved in the course he was set on. He briefly debated locking the door, returning the key to its hiding place and tiptoeing back to his hammock but after a second dismissed the thought and in the blink of an eye was inside the stores, locking the door behind him.

Jobe woke with a feeling of dread in the pit of his stomach. Something wasn't right, and he knew without looking that Horatio wasn't in his bunk. The absence of H's light snoring had troubled his sleep, and a glance to his right confirmed his fears. His hammock lay empty. Jobe immediately rolled out of his hammock but no sooner had his feet touched the floor than the light of an oil lamp appeared and the familiar cry of "Lash and stow, you lazy lubbers! Lash and stow!" rang out. Jobe was unsure what to do. There was no chance of sneaking off to the stores without being seen, and he only hoped that H' was aware of the time and right now making his way back to the lower deck.

The hammocks were lashed almost as one, and H's, hanging all alone, became incongruously blatant. It soon became apparent to the petty officer that H's bunk was empty.

"Well, well, Horatio already up and at his duties, is he? Forever the diligent sailor, that one," he quipped, smiling. "Where is the barrel of lard?" he asked Jobe, his smile becoming a grimace.

Jobe was quietly queuing to stow his hammock, doing his utmost to remain inconspicuous. He was powerless to assist H' in any way except for keeping his mouth shut. Cook would be discovering the sleeping, possibly still gorging H' at any second and the game would be up. He remained mute, his hammock playing across his hands.

The officer stalked over to Jobe and pulling the hammock from his grasp, threw it to the floor before grabbing Jobe by the ear lobe just as the deck bell began ringing indiscriminately. Jobe shouldered the officer aside and raced for the lower-deck steps.

* * *

The dead weight that was transferred between the two officers continuously forced them to stop, pause, heft and readjusted their grip with each laboured step across the deck. Their quest to find better purchase resulted in the tightly wrapped canvas coming loose, and the hands that had been gathered on deck gasped as a naked arm fell free, its flesh pallid.

Cameron elbowed Jobe and nodded towards the dangling arm. "Is it my imagination or has your chum lost a bit of weight?" He grinned at the lads in his immediate vicinity, glaring until they acknowledged his quip with embarrassed laughs and nods. All hands watched as H's body was unceremoniously bundled into a cargo net and hoisted onto a waiting cutter below. Jobe responded to the petty officers' whistles and trudged over to where he had left his swabbing mop, wondering all the time how the baker from Bootle would react to receiving the shrouded body of his greedy son.

Chapter VII

1892

The candelabra that hung low from the ceiling trembled with each heavy step, causing shadows to stretch and shrink as they danced around the small room.

"The damned impertinence of the man. He has no doubt organised this whole shenanigan to his own end. A martyr, they're calling him! Martyr indeed! Am I not a martyr? Have I not martyred myself? Ministering in this city for over a decade, protecting good God-fearing Christians from the ritualism of Rome!"

Potter watched the pastor's fleshy jowls quiver with rage and fought hard to suppress the smile that seemed determined to break out on his face. The only way he could contain his amusement was to refrain from looking up at his charge as he paced the floor of his rooms. The pastor had been bristling for over a month, since John Kensit Jr. had appeared in the town, but on hearing the news of his jailing, Pastor Wise had become apoplectic.

Kensit Jr. had arrived in the height of summer and along with his Wycliffe Preachers had been espousing the dangers of ritualism in Church of England services at open-air rallies up and down the country, a territory the pastor felt was his own. Potter fancied the two were pages from the same book, attracted to Liverpool for the same reason. More concerned by the number of Irish Roman Catholics, the highest in any city of England, than the number of High Anglican churches employing idolatry and altar boys.

The younger Kensit had been welcomed into the city. The Protestant Truth Society that his father John Kensit Sr. had established was viewed as a credible organisation formed to preach biblical truth and awaken people to the spiritual dangers of the day. He was even scheduled to speak in St. George's Hall, another reason for Pastor George Wise to feel aggrieved, before the authorities became aware of the consternation his meetings were causing. The meetings had presented Potter an understanding of how Kensit Jr. could afford to graciously decline the offer, by his mistress, of protection from Potter and his men. The Wycliffe Preachers, bibles forever in hand, were such biblical zealots that they acted like warrior monks of old rather than the unassuming church curators they resembled. The disturbances they caused were so raucous that young Kensit had been summoned before the magistrates. He was offered the choice of being bound over for twelve months or jailed for three. Quoting the virtues of free speech, Kensit Jr. had elected to serve three months. Pastor Wise had been offered the same choice the previous summer and chose to retain his liberty.

"Yes, he has created this farce to make me look the Iscariot, well aware the public outcry will negate the need for him to serve his time! Kensit the Elder himself has already made plans to descend on us, Mrs. Warburton was only too happy to inform me, almost swooning with the news! Is her wanton behaviour seemly, I ask myself!"

Although Potter was the only other person in the room, the pastor was not addressing him. He aimed his outrage at inanimate objects:

the mantelpiece, fireplace and bookcase became his audience. Potter interjected regardless. "Excuse me, Pastor, but is this not an opportunity to show that you are the bigger man?"

The pastor stopped his pacing and looked at Potter.

"It is no secret that you have not seen eye to eye with young Kensit and his preachers," Potter continued. Why not organise a protest meeting against his jailing, a rallying cry against the gagging of free speech? Ingratiate yourself with his sympathisers? By the time old Kensit arrives, you'll be integral to any campaign calling for his son's release." Potter watched with relief as the pastor rubbed his chin, the only part of his lower face not covered with bristling hair, a visible sign that he was deep in thought.

He aimed his response at the thickly draped bay window. "The Widow Warburton has organised an event to welcome Kensit Senior for the twenty-fifth. Over the water in Birkenhead, strictly invitation only. I'll orchestrate a nationwide outcry demanding his son's freedom before then. I'll concentrate the nation's ire on a meeting in St. Domingo Pit."

* * *

The Indian summer continued and the sun retained enough warmth for those gathered on the front lawn of the Claughton Music Hall to continue enjoying the drink that had become the fashion of that summer. Potter stood discreetly aside from the group, smiling as he watched Albert sip at his Pimm's, the elegant glass tiny in his huge hand. He wished the men he had brought over on the ferry, and who had been consigned to wait in the stables at the back, could catch a glimpse of their hero now. He knew Albert was extremely uncomfortable attending any events that the men would be called upon to secure. He didn't like them to be reminded how far removed from them he was, failing to understand that the men idolised him even more because of the gulf in class.

Potter's mistress had forbidden his men, the very men she financed through him, to attend, only acquiescing to their presence on hearing of the furore at a meeting four days earlier, which, according to reports, had been stormed by in excess of three thousand Catholics who had caused serious harm to those present. Potter had given strict instructions that there was to be no animosity shown to the Wycliffe Preachers regardless of any provocation but had nevertheless felt the urge to make frequent visits to the stables where both groups had been billeted to ensure his orders were being followed.

Albert found himself linked on both sides; his mother on his right, the new wife she had foisted upon him on his left. It was the left link he frequently broke to sip his drink. Rebecca Warburton once again held the control over her son that she had been helpless to relinquish but had never given up hope of repossessing, and her preening showed no sign of abating. The wife she had inflicted upon him, pretty enough by the day's fashion, provided him with the means to re-establish his standing and reputation within society but offered neither the love nor light with which to lead him from the darkness that enveloped him like a dense river mist.

Potter read the discomfort etched into Albert's features and knew that he would give anything to be ensconced in the stables with the rest of the rabble. It was just as well he wasn't; the tensions between the two groups would have erupted into violence within minutes, and Potter would have been powerless to stop it.

Since learning of the death of his first wife, Kitty, whom since her demise Potter himself had come to view as something of a paragon,

Albert's craving for carnage knew no bounds. Not content with partaking in the pitched sectarian battles that had rattled through Everton all summer, he had taken to quenching his insatiable appetite for violence by infiltrating the burgeoning union meetings that were endemic in the dockland. Albert's interference left a sour taste in Potter's mouth. He hadn't forgotten his humble beginnings in a village on the outskirts of Ormskirk, and he more than empathised with those who fought for the right not to be violated or abused at the whim of their employers.

The plight and problems that faced the working classes had been obscured for too long by the sectarian strife and struggle that burnt through the city, the flames of which were assiduously fanned by those they served most. Potter's whole family, along with the majority of his village, had earned their wages down the pit, the pittance barely enough to keep them from the workhouse gates regardless of the backbreaking, life-reducing work involved. He had itched to be one of the boys who lugged the coal up in tubs, only their eyes visible through faces covered in black dust, never noticing that they grimaced instead of smiling, coughed instead of laughing.

His mother had first led him by the hand into the pitch-black, half-flooded tunnel. She had tears in her eyes as she warned him to stay by her side. "Don't do anything unless I tell you! Keep your eyes closed and your mouth shut, and don't go breathing too much." As they descended to the coalface, they passed boys, too small to be hurriers, sitting with their backs against doors that served as ventilation shafts. He would never forget the growing tap-tap of handpicks clinking against the seam or the coughs of the men who wielded them. His father and the rest of the men had gone down at first light, the women and children waiting for as long as they could before penetrating the depths to collect the black fruit of their men's labour.

She had shown him how to fill the tubs with the jagged rocks as quickly as humanly possible without cutting his hands to ribbons, before scuttling back to the surface, crouching the whole time, dragging the heavy tub behind. "Ignore your knees. They'll last longer than your back will," his mother had scolded as she helped him the last few yards to the surface, dragging her tub behind her with her other hand. As he broke from the entrance to the pit, she slapped him repeatedly on the back. "Don't breathe it in. Cough, lad, cough."

Potter had leant forward, hands on aching knees, and retched, black sputum flying from his mouth, black dust from his nose.

"Every time you come up from the pit, blow that out, cough it up and spit, and look, do this," she said as she twisted her back from side to side and rolled her hips. "Every time!" she repeated, before beckoning him back toward the tunnel mouth. Only the seam being exhausted had saved him from the physical deformities and mental degeneration that had blighted both her and his father.

But the gurgling screams of his peers, boys no older than six, and the shouts of those trying to save them still woke him in the dead of night. The sounds continuing to echo in his ears while images of the desperate men attempting to squeeze through impossibly narrow passages played behind his eyes long after he had shaken off sleep and was sitting bolt upright in bed. The only grace the lack of light in the dark tunnel that masked the contorted expressions of those attempting to rescue the boy whose leg a cart or ventilation door had crushed before he became too exhausted to maintain his own weight and sank below water level.

"What's this, Potter? Not too cold for you is it?" asked Pastor Wise, shaking Potter from his reverie. He unconsciously rubbed his rough, lined hands that hadn't engaged in manual labour for decades but served as a constant reminder of his past.

The pastor looked at him quizzically as the big man emerged from his trance. "Mr. Kensit is enquiring as to some of the landmarks that are visible across the water. I was wondering if you could come and assist?"

Seconds later Potter was inviting Mr. Kensit to follow his index finger, which, with a few swishes, was broadly encompassing the eight miles of docks across the water. He pointed out the Customs House and Sailors' Home before bringing his audiences attention to the civic gems of St. George's Hall and, next to it, the Walker Art Gallery. Before he could continue, the presence of Kensit's wife, a mole of a woman, interrupted the man with a tug at his elbow.

"Ah, Mr. Potter. If you don't mind, could we postpone the tour for a second? My wife has been so eager to be introduced to the good pastor."

Potter responded with a nod of his head and stepped back.

Mrs. Kensit shook the pastor by the hand. "Such an honour, Pastor Wise. We are eternally grateful for your ongoing efforts. We heard twenty thousand turned up at your meeting in support of our son, John's liberty. Such a number."

Pastor Wise accepted the praise. "To quote your heroic son on accepting his sentence, 'As long as I have breath, I shall continue to oppose error.'" He raised his glass. "To John Alfred, a true Crusader!"

A chorus of "John Alfred!" rumbled across the lawn.

Old Kensit caught Potter's eye. "Thank you for the tour, Mr. Potter. I'd be grateful if we could conclude it following the meeting."

Potter found himself looking forward to it, having decided that John Kensit Sr. was as genial a man as one could wish to meet, every ounce the bookseller he was by trade.

* * *

Kensit Sr. had not raised his voice once during the meeting, which went off without a hitch. Uttering every word as if he were in the reading room of a library but forcing nobody to strain to hear the words he spoke. He was certainly a man of books and letters, a true wordsmith and Potter's only concern throughout was how things were proceeding in the stables.

"Are you sure you won't stay with us the night, Mr. Kensit?" asked Rebecca as they walked down the steps of the music hall.

"You have done more than enough, Mrs. Warburton, and I thank you from the bottom of my heart, but we must decline your kind offer. I hope to lead a procession to the prison at first light to demand the release of John Alfred and to build on the sterling efforts of Pastor Wise here," replied Kensit Sr. offering the pastor a half bow.

"In that case, we'll see you to the ferry, won't we, Albert? It's a beautiful evening, after all," said Rebecca. She turned to Simmons who hovered in the wings. "Please have the motorcar rendezvous with us at the pier, Simmons."

Albert responded to his mother, giving her all his attention, his wife a mere spectator. "I was planning on staying in the city, Mother. I have business to attend to this evening and was hoping to be part of Mr. Kensit's procession in the morning."

His mother bristled at the information; only those who knew her noticed the almost imperceptible signs, knowledge of which would have had her aghast. "Of course, my dear. Attend to your business and accompany Mr. Kensit on his procession." She turned to Albert's wife. "Felicity can travel home with me. I'll expect a detailed report of the procession at dinner tomorrow," she finished, by way of exerting her influence.

The walk down to the pier was a pleasant one. Potter's men filed discreetly on one side of the group, the Wycliffe Preachers on the other, both near enough to offer their protection but far enough away not to be in earshot of the conversation, which centered around the effort to have John Alfred released.

Approaching the waterfront, they became aware of a group of youths. They were vociferous but presented only a minimal risk, which was reduced to less than negligible by the separate groups of bodyguards who converged upon them. As a distraction from any possible unpleasantness, Rebecca brought the attention of the small band to the incoming ferry.

"Did you know there has been a ferry service from Birkenhead since 1150. It was known as the Monksferry," she stated proudly. "And oh, look, you can see the floating reformatory perfectly. You must come for a visit, Mr. Kensit."

Kensit Sr. never got the chance to decline or accept. A metal file came spinning from within the group of youngsters, striking the older Kensit above the left eye. Potter pushed past the screaming women, his mistress wasn't one of them, and knelt at the side of Mr. Kensit. He passed Albert the metal file, which must have weighed all of two pounds, a concerned look on his face. It was his mistress who took control.

"Quickly, Potter onto the ferry with him. The infirmary in the town will be better suited to treat his injury."

* * *

It had been a long summer and the tragedy involving Kensit Sr. produced a natural lull in Potter's duties to Pastor Wise. Mr. Kensit had seemed to be recovering from his injuries, but the onset of pneumonia coupled with blood poisoning finally proved fatal and he died on October 6th. The respite from his duties presented Potter with the opportunity of keeping the company that he had been craving for what seemed like an age, namely his own. His mistress was content to accept the pretence of his presence being needed in the town. She had a trusted company of retainers carrying out her every whim and was quite happy to permit her husband's man to meander in the town while retaining the companionship of his wife, who was now a servant in name only.

Potter did have duties to perform in her name, mainly maintaining the core group of trusted bodyguards he had spent time financing and establishing. But he was happy to leave them to their own devices for a short time.

He drained his shot glass, quickly followed by his jar, and waited to catch the landlord's attention. The pub was packed to the rafters with seamen, dockers and, judging by the number of untended wagons obstructing the entrance, carters; the very men Albert was helping to keep under the heel of their paymasters. Potter looked around, used to being head and shoulders above the crowd but surprised to find that a good number of the men equalled him in size, especially those of a dark complexion. He scanned the room, lost in his bleak thoughts and in no particular hurry to have his glass replenished when he spied a scene that had him questioning his own eyes. There, in a secluded corner, was Simmons, deep in conversation with a pugnacious-looking sailor, whose tidy uniform was made even more resplendent by its direct contrast to his visage, so much so that

Potter was sure the original owner of the bright-buttoned blazer must be lying in a gutter somewhere with either a cracked skull, a blade between the ribs or both.

Potter was no fan of Simmons, who, in his humble opinion, was nothing more than their mistress's panting lapdog, but he held enough grudging respect for the man not to want him to end up in some back-alley jigger like the previous occupier of the officer's uniform. Potter traced a way through the throng to the table. "Simmons? It is you! I thought my eyes deceived me," he said brashly, interrupting the duo's consuming conversation.

Simmons's shock caused him to look up before he had fixed his customary mask in place and Potter didn't miss the concern etched across the man's face before he managed to gain control of himself. "Potter, my good fellow. I had an idea our paths might cross among the spit and sawdust. You haven't a drink, I see. Let me just part company with my cousin here and I'll accompany you to the bar," he said smiling, his eyes attempting to read anything Potter's features projected before turning to his confidant. "Farewell then, Sam, regards to Aunt Beryl. Tell her I hope her gout becomes more manageable," he said loudly, standing and proffering his hand to the uniformed man.

Potter almost laughed at the pretence as the rogue in the uniform sat slack-jawed, gaping at the open palm in obvious confusion.

"Take care, Sam," said Simmons as he withdrew his hand and guided Potter away from the table. "Dropped on his head as a child, a terrible burden to my Aunt Beryl," he said from the side of his mouth.

* * *

Potter woke a little later than was his custom. The only impairment he suffered from the previous evening was a cracked tongue and a parched throat, his usual reaction to a night of excess. He reached for the jug of water on the bedside table and surveyed the room Simmons had procured for him as he filled his glass. It really was top notch, in fitting with the evening as a whole. On draining a second glass of water, he settled back onto his pillow, reflecting on the previous evening. Simmons had been on excellent form, remaining with Potter until the landlord of the Cross Keys had called last orders and then insisting they visit a club that he claimed was so exclusive he'd warrant Potter had never heard of it.

To Potter's amazement, Simmons was right. The club was a stark reminder of just how powerful and influential their mistress, Rebecca Warburton, was when even Simmons, no more than an employee of hers, could access such grandeur in her name. He had walked past the merchant's offices that took up the floors of Sir Thomas Buildings a thousand times, never suspecting its basement was a gilded hideaway where the rich and well-to-do of the town enjoyed fantastically late suppers and some truly bizarre cabaret, which had climaxed with a purring bout; the most anticipated and main attraction.

Potter remembered tales from his childhood about the rough men of the mills and mines who took part in purring, the art of kicking at each other's unguarded legs and shins while wearing traditional wooden clogs. The sport had been made illegal decades before and although he'd heard whispers that it continued in the deepest parts of Lancashire his jaw dropped, and the clientele erupted, as two naked women walked onto the stage. The contrast between the two was stark, and Potter watched a bookmaker dissecting the tables, his arms a blur as he accepted bets.

Simmons laughed at Potter's incredulous gape. "Care to make a wager?"

Potter looked back to the bookmaker.

"We'll leave him out of it, you wouldn't believe what his minimum stakes are. Choose your horse," Simmons added with a nod to the stage.

Potter appraised the women. One was an enormous specimen. Her giant breasts spread across her massive stomach and under her arms, forcing them up into the posture of a pugilist, which was in keeping with her features. The other was much more pleasing to the eye, a fraction of the other's size with everything in proportion. Potter feared for her. "Bit of a mismatch, wouldn't you say? But if you insist, I'll have the navvy there. Shall we say a pound?" he said, proffering his hand.

Simmons laughed again. "I didn't realise our mistress rewarded you so well! A pound it is."

The bookmaker held up a hand to a man standing between the two women and the main candelabras hanging from the ceiling were dimmed while those on the main stage brightened, intensifying the fog of cigar smoke that idled around the two women. The man between them stepped backwards and a heavy clacking of wooden clogs echoed around the now-silent basement as the big woman, 'St Helens Sally', and the smaller girl, 'Warrington Wendy', began to dance around each other.

Sally seemed content to allow the smaller competitor to dart in and catch her with lightning strikes to her shins and calves. Even with the slight frame powering them, the blows caused considerable damage, and it wasn't long before blood began to flow freely from Sally's shins. Wendy's clogs soon developed a sheen that matched the glaze of perspiration on her naked, sweating body. With each kick, flecks of blood flicked off her shining clogs, speckling those on the tables nearest the stage, who, to Potter's amazement, pawed at the blood with the tips of their fingers and sucked it off with obvious delight.

Wendy landed blow after blow on her static opponent and Potter was resigned to losing the wager. He watched as Sally finally made a move to defend herself, holding up her right leg in an attempt to evade the constant kicks. Wendy sensed victory and stepped in, aiming three quick kicks at the standing left leg. The third didn't land. Sally of St Helens brought her right leg crashing down onto Wendy's shin and the crowd gasped deliciously at the sound of breaking bones. Sally's first assault left her opponent writhing on the floor, the screams of pain drowned out by the cheers of the jubilant crowd, Potter amongst them. Sally bent down, grabbed a handful of her prone opponent's hair and wiped her bleeding shins with it before approaching the front of the stage, both arms held aloft, her still-bleeding legs spread wide.

Potter had allowed himself to enjoy the evening thoroughly, changing his estimations of Simmons by the hour. He would have no qualms about proposing a repeat, and soon. He accosted himself for allowing his perception of Simmons to be defined by the relationship he shared with their mistress; after all, hadn't he been prepared to walk over hot coals for their master while he lived?

He was disturbed from his thoughts by the knock of a chambermaid. He permitted her to enter but remained stretched out on the bed. "Any sign of life next door? Have you managed to rouse my associate?"

"The room next door is empty, sir. I'll warrant the bed hasn't been slept in."

Potter was about to question the maid's assertion when 'Cousin Sam' sprang into his mind. He brought his hand to his forehead.

The whole night had been a sham, an exercise in concealment. He recalled his initial impression that Simmons had been in danger from the miscreant in the officer's garb but realised his assumption had been well wide of the mark, Simmons' concoction of *simple cousin Sam* as a cover story illustrated as much. The off-beat location of the meeting reminded him of his own clandestine meetings with Albert from a different age, and he could almost feel the silkiness of one of his mistress's intricate webs. He sprung out of bed, intent on finding out what it involved and whom it concerned.

* * *

Simmons stomped along the upstairs landing of the Saddle Inn. One of the haunts he knew the ship's officer frequented when granted leave from the Akbar. "Wilkes! Wilkes!" he yelled, banging on each and every door he passed. The Saddle was the sixth pub Simmons had forced entry into, paying no heed to the remonstrations of any one of the landlords. There was no sign that he had been up all night, drinking for the majority of it. Both his presentation and countenance remained immaculate, and went a long way in numbing the various landlords into inaction.

He had not even entered his suite in the Ship and Mitre, where he had procured he and Potter rooms. On bidding an inebriated Potter a goodnight he had immediately hurried to the pier. Paying a sleepy bargeman a huge sum to ferry him across the river and wait for his return. The Karl Benz motorised car was parked in a well-maintained coach yard, and Simmons had been forced to wait impatiently while the driver cranked it to a start.

The drive to the estate had been frayed. He was on the cusp of failing his mistress for the first time. He wouldn't allow it to happen.

She had appeared without a hair out of place, only seconds after being woken by her handmaid.

"I'm afraid there is every possibility that the location of the boy has been breached," he stated. The muscles needed to deliver the news were the only ones that moved in his whole body.

Rebecca remained unmoved. "Albert?" she asked.

"As good as," replied Simmons.

"Potter then? Damn that infernal man!"

As efficient as ever, Rebecca simply stated her orders. "Put the contingency plan into place. Ensure it happens away from the Akbar, Simmons. Have him put ashore under the guise of an escape. I want it carried out on land with no connection to the reformatory."

"Yes, ma'am."

"Your man on the ship…"

"As soon as possible, ma'am."

"Goodnight, Simmons."

* * *

The Sunday morning Dock Road traffic was only a token of its weekday counterpart, and Potter enjoyed the relative peace along with the stiff breeze that blew off the river. If, as he suspected, 'Cousin Sam' was on some kind of shore leave, there was a chance he would have made a full night of it and sought out a hair of the dog before presenting himself back at his ship. The odds were long but he decided it would do him no harm to have a look while partaking in a hair or two from the same dog.

A junior brass band passed by Potter heading in the opposite direction towards the Pier Head landing stage. Potter half chuckled at the belligerent scowls that greeted his warm smile. The boys were

216

spick and span in their spotless uniforms, but the phrase 'wolves in sheep's clothing' sprang to mind. He had walked another twenty paces before registering the officer who led them. He wore exactly the same uniform as Cousin Sam. Potter changed direction and followed the band to the landing stage.

The officer bent down, fussing over a smear of soot on his toecap, presenting the opportunity for one of the scamps in the group to blow a loud raspberry. The officer, his face beetroot, straightened up and spun around, searching for the culprit. His gaze found Potter and he eyed him suspiciously.

"Excuse me, sir, I was just marvelling at your fine young fellows. Where is it they're performing, might I ask?" ventured Potter as it dawned on him that the boys must come from one of the floating reformatories.

"I'm afraid you're out of luck. They've already performed," answered the officer.

"Ah, is that so? I would have liked to have heard them for myself. I've heard great things about the Clarence brass band," he exclaimed loudly enough for the boys to hear.

"Oi, we're no dirty Paddies," quipped one of the rascals. The officer spun around to hush the culprit.

"Apologies, my boy. The Akbar then. I thought from the uniform…"

"The uniforms are quite distinct," stated the officer, puffing his chest out pompously. "The Clarence's are a different hue of blue entirely."

"Again, my apologies," said Potter as he gestured towards Annie Garvey, a permanent fixture on the landing stage since Potter himself was a boy. The old shack she squatted in had never changed, and Potter must have eaten a ton weight of the apples and oranges she sold during his life. "Allow me to purchase the boys a piece of fruit to enjoy on their crossing. They look so grand after all." After buying enough apples and oranges to go around Potter distributed the fruit to the grateful boys, his mind racing as he did so. He had always hoped to assuage the grief that was eating Albert alive by reintroducing his estranged son back into his life, but his surreptitious attempts at locating Jobe had come to nothing and Potter constantly rebuked himself for not having ensured the boy was safe and supported at an earlier date. Perhaps then Albert would not have transformed into the empty husk he had become. Recognising the opportunity for redemption, he quickly made the short walk to Covent Garden, saying a silent prayer to anybody who may be listening that Albert had stayed true to form in scorning his frigid wife and was lying with one of his favourite barmaids from the Pig and Whistle.

* * *

Albert tumbled down the narrow staircase that led from the rafters of the Pig and Whistle and burst out onto the street.

Potter was forced to chase his half-naked form down Chapel Street, passing him items of clothing as they semi-trotted to the landing stage. Potter was impressed at Albert's reaction to his hypothesis. On opening the door to one of the small loft rooms he had been greeted by the snoring form of Albert, a girl half his size draped around him. But on finely waking Albert and imparting word of Jobe the sluggish, indifferent loafer was transformed into an animated blur. Hence, Potter scurrying at his side like a schoolboy handing Albert garments of clothing while relaying specifics of the theory that had resulted in his unseemly appearance in the loft of the Pig and Whistle.

The handful of notes and coins Albert held out on reaching the pier meant they had no trouble finding a craft to carry them across to the Sloyne off the coast of Rock Ferry. Albert stood in the small boat and looked wistfully at the three square-riggers in the murky distance. "Which of them is the Akbar?"

* * *

The vicar enjoyed the opportunity to breathe fire and brimstone over his congregation of incarcerated boys. His ninety-minute sermons were infused with carefully planned, sometimes rehearsed, stagecraft and histrionics. It wasn't his usual style of service, but he had spent the whole of his childhood picking oakum in a Belfast workhouse. The memory of his bleak existence, the ruthlessness of the regulations and the eternal merging of day into dismal day were etched on every face and reflected from every eye that he looked into. He hoped his weekly cameo was a welcome escape from their suffering and prayed that in later life the boys present would recall his dramatic interludes with fondness and associate them with the Church and the true word of the Lord. The boys sat content throughout, knowing that the twisted and tar-stiffened pieces of ancient rope, coconut husks and swabbing mops would remain locked away for the remainder of the day, and that, after making repairs to any damaged clothes or boots, they would be left, in a fashion, to their own devices.

Following the mass Jobe retired to a collection of, pointedly disregarded, benches that were set aside for reading. He remained in the relative peace until, on hearing the midday mess bell; he laid down the dog-eared Old Testament that he had borrowed from the

Akbar's minuscule library. He had already read and re-read both the Old and New Testaments, the only books contained in the small chest that was unlocked each Sunday.

The excitement around the tables was palpable as the boys waited for their usually tar-black tea to be transformed by a luxurious splash of milk. "C'mon, Peters, get a move on with the moo-juice would you. My tea's going stone cold here."

A splash of milk wasn't the only luxury that the boys enjoyed on a Sunday, and Jobe felt his stomach sink as an extra slice of bullock-head meat was placed on his tin plate. He couldn't look at either without a surge of despair and guilt flushing over him. The memory of Horatio's enthusiasm regarding his pint of milky tea and extra portion of gristly meat settled on him like a weight, stripping him of his appetite. He had continuously warned his companion over the amount of the dried goods he consumed. "Go easy, H'. The stock-take isn't over-exuberant but neither is it non-existent. Besides, you're going to make yourself sick!" Horatio would look up at him, the half-masticated food he was shovelling into his mouth escaping from the sides. 'Mnnmmn mnnom,' he would reply, gesticulating wildly at the brimming shelves before setting his hands back to the task of cramming food into his mouth. To imagine him eating enough dried oats to swell and burst his stomach made Jobe feel as if his own belly were on the same course. He looked at the tin plate that clattered down in front of him but, unlike his peers, simply stared at the food, showing no attempt to eat. He could almost hear H's hopeful tone as he gestured to whatever remnants of food remained on his plate. "What's that, Jobe? You're not letting that go to waste, are you?"

Without looking up, he slid his plate to the empty place beside him and patted the gaping space on the bench. It was wide enough to accommodate at least two of the boys who sat squashed around the table, their elbows knocking as they ate, but Jobe had decreed that the space was H's. It was a scant memorial, but there would be no other paid to his memory.

Jobe had had to earn the right to proclaim the space as H's memorial. Cameron had whimpered as he lay on the floor looking up at the possessed demon standing over him, bloodied paddle clutched tightly in a pale fist. Watched as the dark red blood, his dark red blood, trickled slowly down the thick handle to the flat wooden blade and, although his head pounded, enthusiastically nodded his acceptance of the terms that were being spat at him.

"You can continue to be the officer's dog. I know the vile acts you participate in to gain your grubby perks, but if I hear tell of you snitching on any one of your comrades, hear of one beating carried out at your hands, I'll kill you! This is my mess now!" Jobe remained standing over Cameron but looked around at the wide-eyed crowd of spectators, purposefully fixing gazes with captains of other messes, not looking away until they had lowered their eyes. "D'you all hear me? This is my mess now!" He paused, inwardly praying that they would remain transfixed by the image of the toughest bully on board lying at his feet like a wounded animal. One voice of dissent would bring everything crashing down and he would more likely than not be lynched there and then. He turned his attention back to Cameron. "Now I remember our first meeting. You spat on my meat, proving yourself a devout and pious Christian, did you not?"

Cameron lay in the foetal position unaware how best to respond. He hesitantly nodded confirmation.

Jobe smiled. "Good, good. Then just like Jesus, you can atone for the sins of your brothers who are gathered here today." He turned back to the crowd, their macabre expressions of fascination signalling their total deference. "You have a saviour! One who will atone for your many sins! But beware—this is a one-time cleansing. Anybody who repeats a sin will receive immediate and frightening retribution!"

The blood that had traversed the length of the wood began to crawl back in the direction it had come as Jobe silently hefted the paddle above his head and brought it back down again and again, heedless of Cameron's screams.

* * *

Wilkes cursed himself as he climbed the rope ladder back aboard the Akbar. He hadn't even slept off the drink before that jumped-up butler Simmons had stormed into his room above Ye Hole in Ye Wall and ordered him back to the ship.

"I've wasted the best part of the morning searching for you, you oaf! Up now, on your feet and back to the ship there's not a moment to lose!" he had roared as he grabbed at the bed sheets.

Wilkes had sat up, unsure where he was and unable to comprehend the intrusion, his mind still blurred from the drink he had only recently stopped consuming. The instructions imparted to him as he dressed had a more than sobering effect. He was to put the boy in a cutter and deposit him on shore with immediate effect. And that would be that! An abrupt end to his high living. "But just last evening, you were of the opinion his staying aboard was of no consequence! You said you had faith in my stock, my ability to ensure the boy remained nothing but Flynn!" Wilkes had become immobile as his frenzied brain attempted to retain his lucrative earner.

"The situation has evolved. Now move, man! Time is of the essence!" Simmons had snarled growing ever more animated.

Wilkes remained stationary. "I can see his neck snapped and have him found floating in the river," he whispered, his hushed tones an attempt to seduce his paymaster.

Simmons froze and looked him in the eye.

Wilkes continued blithely. "We've discussed it before. It can be arranged for a small fee, a final payment."

Simmons contemplated the idea for a heartbeat before dismissing it. His mistress had ordered that the act be carried out on dry land, away from the Akbar and potential recriminations. "There's no time. I've already told you, the situation has evolved."

Wilkes had prospered by ensuring the runt remained incarcerated on the reformatory ship and kept his real identity to himself. It was money for jam, and everybody knew jam could be preserved for as long as was needed. To that end, he hadn't saved a single ha'penny with which to realise his ambition of retiring back to Bristol, away from the northern filth he'd been surrounded by for over half his life. But there had been no rush; here was an opportunity to live fast and free before saving for his later years. The plan had been to keep the boy aboard the Akbar even after his three-year sentence was up. Violation after violation could easily be concocted to ensure the boy remained on the ship, into his dotage if needs be, but now it had all come to nought. He hadn't even managed to get into the drawers of Lucy, barmaid in the Cotton Picker, although he was sure he was on the cusp with his big-spending ways.

He clambered up over the rail and made his way across the deck, passing the hogshead barrel that some shaven-headed scamps were filling with pails of river water ready for a new inductee. A sudden rage overcame him, and he aimed a heavy boot at the barrel, which rocked back and forth before finally tipping, spilling its contents on the deck. The boys watched the water seep over the freshly swabbed deck and shot daggers into the back of the officer's head.

His encounter with the hogshead dragged his mind back to his last real contact with his charge. As was customary, Wilkes had gathered to observe the inauguration of the latest new cadet. His usual indifference to proceedings more marked than usual, thoughts of the inroads he was making to the defences of his favourite barmaid leaving little room for anything else. He looked around the quarterdeck wondering whom he could bribe to take his watch that night, thus allowing him to continue his bombardment. The conservative demeanour of the crew had tugged at his subconscious, but it wasn't until the new detainee was ready to walk the barrel and was standing naked before his peers that their silence hit him. Officer Daniels, charged with overseeing proceedings, was visibly shaken by the lack of response to the well-versed jokes, and his patter tailed off so that the only sound was the wind whipping through the masts and the flapping of untethered canvas.

The Catholic counterpart of the Akbar, the Clarence, had narrowly averted a mass mutiny just weeks earlier, and, sensing the mood of the boys, the captain had already given the order for pistols to be distributed to those who stood beside him on the quarterdeck. Wilkes rebuked himself as a loaded pistol was pushed into his hand; he had been so lost in his own fantasies that he had been completely unaware of the silent menace.

Officer Daniels brought proceedings to a close, ordering the dripping, shivering cadet to put on the uniform at his feet in hushed tones. Once he was dressed, the officer dismissed the crew in as resounding a tone as he could muster, his voice breaking mid-sentence. Nobody moved, and Wilkes was primed to face down a rebellion. The captain stepped up to the quarterdeck rail and in a tone filled with authority demanded that all hands go below decks and lash hammocks. His order fell on deaf ears, and Wilkes heard more than one pistol cock.

Just as the captain was about to be forced into the ignominy of repeating his order, one boy stood and moved towards the hatch. As one, his peers rose or climbed down from the rigging and followed him. In his disbelief and clamour to confirm what his own eyes were telling him, Wilkes had almost bundled the captain over the rail. It was Flynn who led the ragbag crew down the hatch.

Wilkes had contemplated keeping the information to himself but was aware that his paymaster's grapevine was a large one. Simmons, or whoever employed the jumped-up butler, would no doubt find out that the boy had become a strong and uniting influence, and he'd be for the chop. His cushy number on the floating reformatory would be over and he'd be thrust back into the hardships of life on the open seas. He'd rather forfeit his earner than risk that happening.

"Didn't expect to see you back on board until later this afternoon, Mr. Wilkes. Shat in your bunk again, have you?"

The light-hearted jape brought Wilkes back to the present and he looked up at the joking officer who stood at watch on the quarterdeck. The officer, named Brent, was one who was always ready to cover his shifts if the price was right. "Is midday mess over yet?" asked Wilkes before disappearing down the main hatch without waiting for an answer.

The boys expectantly waiting for their splash of milk were shocked to see Wilkes stomping down the steps with murder in his eyes. He scanned the mess for an instant before making a beeline for Jobe Flynn. Jobe remained staring at the plate he had just slid into the empty space beside him while patting the bench reverently. Wilkes came up from behind and, without a word, lifted Jobe bodily from his place on the bench.

Jobe had a strange sense of déjà vu. Wilkes had hoisted him up against his will in the past, throwing him onto the stinking, slime-covered rope ladder that had begun this whole nightmarish episode of his life. Without thinking, he rammed his head backwards with all his might, catching the spirit-soaked officer plumb on the bridge of his nose. Wilkes, shocked by the impact, brought his hands up to his face in reflex, releasing his grip on the boy.

Jobe finding himself free from the clutches of the man who had brutalised him these past months stood and aimed a kick at the privates of the prone officer. Again his aim was precise, and the pain, coupled with the shock, brought Wilkes to his knees. Jobe became aware of the spoon in his grasp and manipulated it so the handle protruded from his hand. He prepared to jam it into his nemesis's undefended eye when a bevy of warning cries came from the tables.

"Beware, Flynn! Behind you!"

Jobe spun, but too late to avoid the blow to the back of his head. Senses swimming, he sank to the floor. Before losing consciousness, he looked up to see Cameron standing over him, a metal platter in his hands and a smile on his face.

* * *

"Come on, man, put your back into it," demanded Albert.

Potter had already had to pull him back from the prow of the boat for fear of Albert falling overboard, such was his eagerness to reach the Akbar. When they were only a few yards away from the hulk, Albert began hailing the ship at the top of his voice.

"Ho there, Akbar, I say, Akbar!" The lack of wind meant that he was answered just as the small rowboat touched the hull of the square-rigger.

"Ahoy down there?" came the response.

Albert and Potter looked up at the face peering down.

"Let down a ladder at once. I demand admittance aboard," shouted Albert.

"Can I ask the nature of your business, sir?"

"My son is being held falsely aboard that ship. I demand access!"

"This is the HMS Indefatigable sir, a training ship. Nobody is held here. Why, it is a privilege to be aboard."

"The Indefatigable? The Indefatigable, you say? Is this not the Akbar?"

"No, sir. This is the HMS Indefatigable, The reformatory ship Akbar is the next ship along."

Albert turned, red-faced, to the oarsman. "You fool! Quickly now, to the Akbar."

The oarsman pushed off without looking up at the belligerent giant who loomed over him. As they approached the Akbar, a small cutter came from around its prow, heading towards the city. Albert tapped Potter, bringing his attention to the cutter.

"You there, ahoy!" called Potter, as a small sail was unfurled from the single mast. "You there, coming from the Akbar! What is your business?" Potter's voice carried easily to the other vessel.

"And what business is it of yours?" came the response of an officer standing in the prow of the boat.

Albert ignored the officer. "Ahoy, any boys in the boat…are there any boys aboard the boat? Jobe, Jobe Warburton, are you aboard that boat? It is your father here!"

On receiving no response, Albert looked at the boatman, who had stopped rowing. "To the Akbar, man."

By the time Potter unceremoniously pulled himself over the rail of the Akbar Albert was already standing on deck. He had made short work of the climb and was surveying the scene on deck. Potter regained his legs and straight away saw 'Cousin Sam' from the Dock Road. He couldn't believe that the scoundrel truly was an officer. He raised his arm and pointed towards him.

Within a dozen strides, Albert was holding the man by the throat. "Where is my son?" he growled as he tightened his grip.

The officer's face, which already bore the marks of a struggle, turned bright red as he fought for breath.

Potter reached Albert's side. "Perhaps if you release your hold, he can answer your question, Albert."

Albert looked at Potter before loosening his hold and returning his caustic gaze to the officer. "My son?" Albert could see the man's mind turning but was in no mood for procrastination. He dragged the officer bodily to the rail and tipped him over, holding him by the ankles like a rag doll. "Where is my son?" he shouted.

Wilkes felt the blood he had swallowed, but refused to settle in his gut, seeping back up his oesophagus. The sensation made him baulk, and he found himself choking, his panic causing him to thrash about so Albert struggled to maintain his hold.

"Are you Flynn's father, then?" piped a small voice beside him. Mention of his wife's maiden name caused Albert to suck in his breath but he managed to nod. "He was taken unconscious aboard that cutter there."

Albert followed the boy's finger to see the cutter he had hailed earlier halfway to the Liverpool landing stage. He heaved Wilkes back up onto the deck where he lay flapping, dragging lungfuls of air through his flaring nostrils as the captain appeared on the quarterdeck.

"I say, what the devil is going on here?"

Albert paid him no heed. "I'll be back for you!" he snarled at the mess of a man he had left on the deck before swinging his leg over the rail and following Potter down the rope ladder. He tore the oars from the boatman and began to row for all he was worth.

* * *

Jobe came to with a start but too late to avoid the second pail of water that was thrown into his face. Spluttering and fighting for breath he lashed out with arms and legs, his brain struggling to recall events. He had just been ready to turn out Wilkes's right eye with the handle of a spoon. He regained his breath and opened his eyes, bracing himself for whatever reprisals were coming his way. His eyes closed again, the blue sky harsh after the gloom below decks. He had been brought up on deck. It would begin with a flogging then, he thought. The blast of a tugboat horn forced his eyes open again, and he registered the clamour of sounds around him. He was lying on the floor of a cutter, a clear blue sky above him.

"C'mon, be off with you. Up you get and be gone!"

Jobe recognised the voice of Officer Corrigan. "I don't understand? What's happening?" he asked, struggling to his feet, one hand searching out the lump on the back of his head.

"Your privileges aboard the Akbar have been annulled. You're to be reconciled with this land-lubbing filth," the officer said as he swept his hand towards the town. He stepped towards Jobe with the notion of physically forcing him onto the landing stage, but hesitated as Jobe's body stiffened and he ceased rubbing the back of his head.

Realising freedom awaited him Jobe didn't need to be invited twice and he was soon standing transfixed, watching from the southern end of the Landing Stage as the cutter pushed off and began to negotiate the river traffic.

He fought to calm his whirring mind as it attempted to comprehend his new situation. He paid no heed to the small skiff, a relative dot, heading towards the pier, in which a giant was rowing for all he was worth.

* * *

Potter feared Albert's heart would burst through his efforts. He also had one eye on the steamers and tugs that Albert paid not the slightest attention to but which had the power to smash their little craft to kindling. They had already felt the full wrath of a ferry captain who, realising the small boat wasn't going to give way, had had to take evasive action. "You're flagging, Albert. Let me take over."

Albert, sensing his strokes were slowing, moved over, pushing Potter into his place. "Quickly, man. Don't lose the momentum," he said as he shielded his eyes and looked to the pier. He blinked, shaking his head disbelievingly on spying a boy, no, a young man, standing on the quayside. His heart quickened as he noticed how the boy held himself, his bearing reminded him so much of himself but he could also see his wife…his ex-wife…his dead ex-wife he remembered, catching a moan in his throat but clearing it quickly. Now was no time for self-recrimination. "He's there look, we haven't lost him. It's not too late. Row, Potter, for pity's sake, row, man!"

The small boat continued inching towards the stage, the swell of larger vessels sending it off course and hampering its progress. Albert kept his full attention on the boy who seemed captivated by the river and suddenly fancied it was he who was holding his attention.

"He's saw us, Potter!" he exclaimed as he began to wave his arms above his head. "Jobe…Jobe…Jobe Warburton!" he roared in a futile attempt to conquer the sounds of the river. "No, Jobe, wait! Wait for me, Jobe, I'm here!"

* * *

Simmons stood in one of the covered waiting rooms that were spread the length of the landing stage. Detached from the cacophony of the crowd, he watched as the boy retreated towards one of the iron bridges that connected the landing stage to the mainland before turning his gaze to the skiff that was being rowed doggedly and was only yards from the pier.

Jobe unconsciously backed away from the uproar of the landing stage, seeking a refuge from the crowded quayside. All of the ideas and intentions he had imagined to while away the hours spent scrubbing decks, the fantasies he had conjured while swinging in his hammock had all centred around his freedom; the people he would see again, the places he would visit, the wrongs he would right. All of them, now within touching distance, seemed further away than ever and he had no sense of the liberty he had been granted as barrow boys, chandlers and the hundreds of emigrants waiting to embark on liners that would take them to America, their luggage, both physical and mental, lugging behind them, cajoled and jostled him up the gangway in a dozen different languages. He uncorked from the bottleneck of the gangway in a daze and stood frozen in shock and awe at the city directly facing him.

* * *

Potter read Albert's mind. There was no way he could make the jump, not from a standing start. "Wait, Albert. A few more seconds, that's all," he advised, his chest heaving from exertion. They had watched forlornly as the boy began to back into the crowd that was obscuring him from their sight with alarming rapidity. Potter physically felt Albert leap as he pushed down with all his weight and then sprang. The boat became instantly lighter and darted towards the stage with fresh impetus. Potter worried whether he retained the strength to pull Albert from the river and knew the opportunity to reunite father with son had gone, wasted by Albert's all too familiar impatience. He was astounded when Albert cleared the churning water and landed on the stage on all fours before springing up and knocking a post-boy from his bike, the letters and parcels in his basket exploding into the air like oversized confetti. "To your right, Albert!" he shouted as the boat glided alongside the pier, guided to perfection by its pilot, so that Potter could hop off with ease before the pier-master could question the illegal drop-off. "He was heading south," he bellowed with the last of his breath. He watched Albert scanning the crowd and, puffing and blowing, reached his side just as he dashed off, scattering those around him like kindling.

* * *

The events of his life cascaded over Jobe like a tidal wave, and he fled to escape them, unknowingly following the path his search for work at the docks took him. With no destination in mind he headed towards Mann Island and the Albert Dock, weaving in and out of the throng in a futile attempt to outrun himself, becoming more frantic with each stride, ignoring those who turned to curse him. He swerved right to dodge a cart full of coconuts but, unable to tear his gaze away, thumped into a man wearing a sandwich board and bounced back onto the seat of his pants, still unable to drag his gaze from the mesmerizing mountain of hairy fruit.

"Well, I've had plenty taking me up on my offer but none so eager as you, sir," said the man with the sandwich board as he redistributed the weight of it across his shoulders. He bent as much as his constraints allowed him and was about to help Jobe to his feet when a man came from nowhere and smashed the boy across the head with a cobble.

"Aye-aye, now…" The man cut his remonstrations short and eyed the white five-pound note being waved in front of him.

"Take this and put the boy aboard your wagon. On its departure, there'll be another one for you."

It took a second for the man to step out of his sandwich board and replace the weight across his shoulders with that of a lifeless Jobe. Simmons looked down at the legend on the chipped whitewashed board.

DOCK WORK in HULL

ALL MANNER of SKILLS REQUIRED & RESPECTED

FREE PASSAGE

* * *

"Smallpox outbreak! Smallpox outbreak! Three quarantine hulks to be towed to the Mersey! Smallpox outbreak! Smallpox outbreak…" The words died on the newspaper seller's tongue as a huge man came bounding towards him. The vendor closed his eyes, knowing that the collision, which would surely reunite him with his parents in Heaven, was unavoidable. When he opened them again, he saw the man had somehow skipped around him and was approaching the man with a sandwich board. He shrugged his shoulders and carried on bringing attention to his papers.

Albert stopped running and began to swivel around so his head jerked as if he had some illness of the mind. At a loss, he called to a man crawling under a stationary sandwich board. "You, man! You there! Have you seen a boy pass by? Thirteen years of age or so... he'll have been running...he's my son, my only son."

The man brought himself from his knees, and fixing the board on his shoulders surreptitiously looked over towards Mann Island, making sure the toff, who had a white fiver belonging to him in his possession, was still there next to the wagon that waited on the cobbles. The wagon driver cracked his whip and clicked his tongue so the two mares shuddered in their traces and pulled the coach off with a jerk. The sandwich board man shrugged his shoulders. "Nobody of that description has passed this way, I'm afraid, guv'nor," he replied.

Albert hoped Potter had fared better but sank to his knees as he watched his friend heading towards him, alone.

Potter looked at the man with the sandwich board before reaching down and helping Albert to his feet. "C'mon, Albert. Let's see about getting you a drink."

Albert allowed himself to be helped up but turned to Potter, his jaw set. "There'll be no more indulging in drink, Potter. My only aim in this life is to be reunited with my son."

Chapter VIII

1893

Jobe groaned. The brilliance of the blue sky above him penetrated his eyes each time they flickered open, lancing deep into the recesses of his skull.

Turning away from the glare, he opened his eyes fully and was greeted by a row of dirty, scuffed boots only inches from his face. He turned his head to face the other direction, only to be confronted by a similar collection of filthy footwear. He had the sensation of being back aboard a boat but registered he was being bumped rather than swayed.

"Hold up, he's coming round. C'mon, move along, give us room to get him up." The request was greeted by muffled groans and expletives. "What's the matter with youse? Don't expect the poor lad to remain on the floor, do you?"

The owner of the voice bent forward and pulled Jobe up towards the row of seated men. Jobe's head swam as he rose, and he baulked as if ready to retch. Those already seated, sidling along a fraction at a time so as to surrender as little space as possible, suddenly squirmed from his path, creating an ever-widening space that was big enough for Jobe to be pulled into.

"Charlie Doyle," said the man who had pulled him from the floor as he busied himself wrapping Jobe in a thin, greasy blanket. "There's a warmth to the sun, but the wind is biting due to us being so exposed," he offered in explanation.

Jobe glanced around the open-air wagon. There were a dozen, a baker's including him, men crammed onto the benches that looked as though they were made to seat eight at the very most. They all looked cold, the blankets and sacking that they wrapped around themselves did little to keep out the gusts of wind that whipped across the open moor. Jobe's wits slowly returned as the man next to him, with one last tuck of a course sack, finally seemed satisfied that only Jobe's face remained exposed to the wind.

He looked past the men facing him, the green expanse that surrounded them shocking his senses after so long aboard the Akbar and, with a start, he stood up. "Where am I? What's going on?" The blanket of sacks fell to the floor, and he would have toppled out of the wagon if his neighbour's reflexes had not been so quick.

"Now, now, don't want another bump to that noggin, do we? C'mon, Fred lad, down we come. There we go."

Jobe was coaxed down into a sitting position. The man who had introduced himself as Charlie began fussing around him with the sacking again, tucking here and there, while Jobe sat numbly, trying, to no avail, to make sense of his situation. He calmly began to help the man who was busy covering him. "Where am I?" he asked, the neutrality in his voice causing Charlie to look up at him with a furrowed brow.

"Well, I don't know where we are exactly, Fred lad," he answered despondently. "But I know where we're headed," he continued brightening up instantly. "We're on our way to Hull!" he exclaimed as if it were the best news he had ever imparted to anyone.

"Hull." Jobe was indifferent to their destination, his face blank.

"Now you've got it," answered Charlie happily, nodding his head to the other men as he gesticulated at his new partner with his thumb. "There's a pretty penny to be made on the docks up there. The Humber's bottlenecked with ships queuing up to dock and not enough hands to unload them."

Jobe looked blankly at the man. A simple "Oh," all that he could muster before another question formed in his still rattled brain. "Why am I going to Hull? How did I end up on the wagon?"

"Well, you were lucky to make it, that's for sure! If those two beauties up front had been a bit quicker with their old nosebags, there's no telling where you'd be," said Charlie animatedly.

Jobe looked at him, waiting for him to continue.

"Well, we kicked up a right stink when Ted hauled you onto the wagon." Charlie looked to his surly travelling companions for an affirmation that wasn't forthcoming. He dismissed them with a wave of his hand. "Pah, miserable buggers!" he spat toward them before turning back to Jobe. "Ted, the fellow with the sandwich board? Well, he doesn't exactly run this operation, but he makes sure there's enough backsides on the benches before the wagon sets off to Hull. Well, as I say, we were only waiting on the nags finishing their dinner when you flop at our feet. Oi, I says to him. Oi, what's all this then? Pressing now, are we?" He rubbed his red nose, almost taking his own eye out as the wagon went over a bump. Jobe's blanket flapped down exposing his throat, and Charlie tucked it back in before carrying on. "Well, Ted—that's his name—says to me, to pacify me like, 'The lad's in peril. Look to the bumps on his head if you doubt my word. His name's Fred and he needs out of the town, he does.'

Well, I has a look, and your old noggin is in a bad way. The claret's not exactly flowing, but there was a trickle, all right."

Jobe freed his hand and brought it to the back of his head. His hair was stiff and matted with dried blood, and he traced his palm across not one but two lumps.

"By the time I'd put a bit of a rag to your head and laid you down there, old Ted was back at his board and we're pulling away, and do you know what?" He paused for effect, pushing his face closer to Jobe's. "There's only a big toff talking away to him, all frantic and animated like. Massive, he was! Well, unsure of Ted's resolve, I shouts to the driver up front, 'Hurry up then, Bert, let's get up to Hull and don't spare the horses!'" He tapped his nose knowingly before continuing. "A couple of these oafs, those that can form an opinion, reckon you to be a runaway from one of the reformatory ships, judging by your attire, like! But I says to them, 'Who absconds from a ship in only a thin undershirt and no Guernsey?' Whatever's been going on, whatever that big fella wanted with you is of no business to anyone but yourself." A dark cloud settled on Charlie's features, aging him ten years. "There's none of us on this wagon with the right to judge another, not one of us without our own sack full of tales and trauma," he said as he looked wistfully across the open fields the wagon travelled between. "But I reckon you had a near miss, Fred, my lad! A lucky escape and no denying," he declared, once again smiling benevolently at his new charge.

Jobe looked up into the big mess of a face unable to make sense of the stream of words that were escaping from it.

* * *

Rebecca heard the heavy, purposeful footsteps of her son approaching the walled garden where she sat looking into a moon-shaped pool that was frozen around its edges. Composing herself, she took a deep breath, inhaling the scent of the Damask roses that surrounded her, making a mental note to have a bunch placed in her rooms. Simmons had informed her of proceedings aboard the Akbar and her son's ensuing pursuit of his urchin. In preparation of the confrontation to come, she had dismissed all of the gardeners and informed all servants to remain indoors. Even so, she had ordered the ornamental fountain to be turned on, ensuring that any raised voices would be muffled and distorted by their melancholic burble.

Albert stooped through the arched entrance to the garden and spoke without greeting. "I must congratulate you, Mother. This time you have really outshone yourself. Surely even you have never before woven such an intricate web of deceit and intrigue," he delivered the words looking straight at his mother, who, rather than meet his eye, watched him through his distorted reflection in the rippling pool.

Rebecca, unaccustomed to being economical with the truth, had already decided that refuting Albert's allegations would only debase her righteousness and looking up, she accosted him with her glare. "You speak as one who is enlightened, yet you remain ignorant of everything barring the slightest strands of what you aptly name my web. You estimate it to be a recent undertaking? You have no idea of the magnitude of the interventions that I have made on your behalf, all of which have been executed in your best interests. What did you suppose, Albert, that I would allow you to renounce your legacy for the love of a Catholic slum-dweller? Each one of your American enterprises withered at my touch. If my authority over you couldn't be diluted by the width of an ocean, did you really believe that the width of the Mersey would be a barrier against my attentions? How could you have been so criminally callow?" The tone of her voice was mirrored by the caustic glint in her eye, and Albert, unprepared for such a frank admission, turned and took a seat on a stone bench.

He looked at the gravel under his feet and shook his head as he attempted to formulate a reply. "It is you who has committed the crime, Mother. Did it cause you such grief to think of me happy?" His head remained bowed, and he didn't not see his mother's lip curl into a snarl at his words.

"Do not have the temerity to question me on the subject of happiness or grief. Is there not an ounce of respect in you for the black you see me wearing day after day?" Rebecca rose and strode over to her son and grabbed him by the jaw. Holding him firm in her cold, wrinkled hand she forced him to look her in the eye. "Ask yourself, Albert. Whose fault is it that I am forced to wear these mourning colours?"

Her meaning dawned on Albert, and he grabbed her wrist, its flesh even paler than the pearl bracelet around it. Forcibly removing her hand from his face he stood, his mother's translucent wrist still in his iron grip. "Do not speak in riddles, Mother. Explain yourself!"

"Did you imagine I was ignorant of the monthly stipends that encouraged you to remain in your squalor?" she spat, shaking herself free of his grasp and smoothing out her ruffled dress before looking Albert in the eye once more. "That I would sit idly by and permit my only son to rot amongst the lowest classes of the toiling multitudes?"

"You killed my father, your husband, in order to restore your control over me?" Albert whispered the question, his tone muted through disbelief rather than any fear of being overheard. On seeing his mother roll her eyes at his bearing, he stiffened his resolve, discarding the speech he had prepared, understanding that nothing he said could puncture his mother's callousness. His only power over her existed with himself. "I came here only to inform you that I want you to arrange my divorce from Felicity," he said.

Rebecca illustrated her disdain by refusing to justify Albert's demand with any response, focusing her attention on the petal of a rose she had plucked and held between her forefinger and thumb.

"This is no request, Mother. You had my last marriage annulled within a week. My wife is a woman, is she not? The law states that I can divorce of my own accord, and I will."

Rebecca crushed the petal between her finger and thumb before allowing it to drop into the pool. "A woman, yes, not that your uncertainty surprises me. But Felicity is no Catholic whore from the slum. She is from a family of good standing. There will be no divorce, no further scandal."

Albert's hand unconsciously went to his moustache, which he twisted. "Speak of my departed wife in that manner again and I will see you hang for the atrocity you have conducted, regardless of whether I have to drape the noose myself," he said his hand retuning to his side, the look of shock across his mother's features appeasing his temper. "But you speak the truth, Mother, and I will, like you, concoct and hatch, plot and plan, just like a common rough. My wife, Felicity, will come to see my son as her own. Her wealth will be the vehicle of your destruction! Scandal, oh yes, there will be plenty, and I assure you, I will continue to shovel it onto your grave long after you are dust and bones, forgotten by all bar me."

* * *

As the sun began to set, the stream of words continued to spew forth from the shapeless face and showed no sign of abating. The throbbing in Jobe's head became more concentrated and he wished that the sporadic complaints of his travelling companions would have some effect on his communicative neighbour.

The last shaft of light disappeared from the sky as the wagon turned off the well-worn road that intersected the bleak moor and bumped along what was little more than a dirt track. The moor came to life, and the calls of its nocturnal inhabitants drove terror into the men in the wagon. Even Charlie ceased his continual babble, better to hear the approach of any wild animal intent on snatching him from his perch.

It had been dark for a long time and a cacophony of snores had joined the chorus of animal calls when the wagon finally came to a stop. Jobe looked around, not noticing the house that was moulded into the gloom until a shaft of dirty light escaped from an upstairs window. Somebody must have heard the wagon and was now holding a candle up to the glass. The window returned to darkness, and after a minute or two, the same flame illuminated the entrance as the front door was pulled open.

Nobody emerged from the dingy opening, but a scolding voice carried to the wagon. "Arrived, have we! Well, I hope you're not expecting hot food. It'll be nothing but bread and butter for supper!"

The men in the wagon remained stationary. Following hours of griping at the wagon driver and straining their eyes in the hope of seeing their overnight billet, not one of them moved.

"What is it you're waiting for? An invite from the Lord himself? Up with the idle lot of you, some of us have work to do!"

The men trailed out of the wagon and, as one, traipsed up a gravel path to the barely illuminated front door.

Charlie looked back to the wagon. Bert had climbed into the back, busy gathering all of the blankets together. "You coming, Bert?"

Bert looked up from the wagon. "Horses!" he called by way of an answer. "Besides, I like to take advantage of the night air," he muttered.

Charlie shook his head and followed the waning glow of the candle that was proceeding through a narrow hallway and into a kitchen. The candle, the only source of light in the room, was placed on a long table and the men took their place on the benches around it. Without any audible conference, they arranged themselves exactly as they had been positioned in the wagon.

"I won't bother remaking the fire as it'll be bed following supper."

Jobe looked towards the grate that didn't have even the slightest glow of dying embers.

"Well, what about the tea?" asked Charlie from beside him. "It's all that's got me through that bog and all the hooting, the thought of a nice cup of tea."

"Yes, yes, there's a pot on the table there. Here, I'll light the lamp, shall I?" The candle temporarily illuminated the landlady's face as the she lit an oil lamp from its flame and banged it back on the table. Sharp cheekbones accentuated sunken eyes and a puckered mouth lent to an overall look of shameless brutality and the smell that permeated the room thickened with her proximity until Jobe could no longer stop himself from gagging. He was sure he saw something scurrying from the light and back into the safety of the shadows but his head was still spinning and he was loath to strain his eyes.

The solitary candle, finally supported in its battle against the gloom, so the man nearest to the pot grabbed at it and filled a jar that was next to him. Not bothering to pass the pot on to his neighbour, he slammed it back down, and after a haphazard journey around the table, it reached Charlie.

"Pah, it's not even lukewarm and thick as treacle but weak as piss," he spat, wiping his mouth with his sleeve.

The response was caustic. "Take it or leave it. You city folk coming up here with your fancy ways!"

Charlie nudged Jobe. "Our fancy ways? Tell you what; happen we're lucky that we're blinded by this gloom, Fred lad. I wouldn't like to see what lays behind it."

Jobe found himself unable to do anything but nod. A platter of bread and butter clattered onto the table. As with the teapot, courtesy was abandoned, and the salver skittered across the table as hands from all directions descended on the mound of sparsely buttered bread.

"I've cut it extra thick and there's more than a slice each."

Charlie's hand shot out and grabbed two slices, one of which was proffered to Jobe. Jobe folded it, conscious of the indents caused by fingers and thumbs that didn't belong to him. He hoped they were Charlie's and bit into it, immediately feeling a sharp pain in his mouth. He manipulated his tongue and worried a piece of grit free of his molars, a sure sign that the bread was of the cheapest kind.

"It's almost snapped my tooth!" shouted Charlie, experiencing the same thing as Jobe. He brought a hand to his offended mouth. "Pah, I'll not bother with this. I think I'll retire, if you don't mind," he said, half rising from the bench.

"No, you don't! I'll not have you all lumbering up the stairs one at a time, disturbing my other guests. They're well-to-do gentlemen, local, loyal customers. I'll not have you waking them."

244

Charlie was forced to sit in simmering silence until the men had eaten their bread and drank the cold tea. Realising there was no form of recreation on offer, they began theatrically to clear their throats.

The landlady approached from wherever she had been lurking in the shadows. "I suppose it'll be bed for you now, will it? Well, some of us have work to do. I'll show you up and then I'll be back down to clear your mess, shan't I. Quiet, mind, I don't want my regulars disturbed."

The whole staircase shuddered as the men tramped their way up it. The landlady led the way carrying the candle and the oil lamp, refusing to relinquish either, those directly behind doing their utmost to angle their heads from her wake. She stopped in front of a closed door and, hanging the lamp on a rusted nail that protruded from a scorched patch of the wall, unlocked it. The smell that emanated from the room making the most hardy of the men to turn their face away quickly, as if in response to a slap from an invisible hand.

"Well, are you planning on staying the night on the landing? In with you," barked the landlady as she reclaimed the oil lamp from its hook, her loyal guests' peace seemingly forgotten.

"All of us in the one room?" contested Charlie.

"Come on, in you go. Some of us still have work to do, can't afford the luxury of sleep, never mind complaining of the machinations of it," ordered the landlady, remaining outside the room, jealously guarding both sources of light.

The men, heads bowed, filed into the pitch-black. A startled shout came from within the darkness. "'Ere, there's folk already in these beds!"

The landlady hung her oil lamp back on its hook and entered the room, beating her free hand down on the beds with venom.

"Shove over, you bleeders. Haven't I warned you about spreading yourselves!" she screeched before turning her ire on the men crowded around the door. "Don't tell me you've never shared a bed before? C'mon in with you! Some of us have work to do."

Charlie grabbed the oil lamp from the hook and shouldered his way into the room. He swung the light across the half dozen double beds squeezed against the walls, paying no heed to the landlady's protestations. Bleached-white faces blinked in the feeble glow of the lamp, the marble orbs of their skeletal knuckles almost popping with the effort of pulling the tattered bedclothes further up to shield their eyes.

"Bless us and save us! What is this place? These men would be better off in their graves!" Charlie could only whisper the words, shock muting his usually booming tones.

The landlady snatched the oil lamp from Charlie's limp hand. "Well I never! In all my time running this establishment...in, the lot of you, now!"

Jobe and Charlie were the only two who did not respond to the order. Charlie hadn't even registered it. He stood in a state of dread. "And the door locked to boot," he mumbled as he shook his cannonball of a head.

"And it'll remain locked! I'll have nobody creeping around under the guise of answering a call of nature. There are two chamber pots."

Charlie came to as if waking from a nightmare. "Yes, and doesn't the smell tell you that both are in desperate need of emptying? Sod this, I'm off to the wagon! It's no wonder Bert opts for the night air! You coming, Fred lad?"

Jobe followed Charlie down the dark unsteady staircase, his hand reluctantly but frequently brushing against the greasy wallpaper for balance and direction.

The landlady, gripped between following the two down the stairs and leaving those milling about the room to their own devices, settled on crouching on the uppermost steps to ensure the two renegades left the house.

On reaching the front door, Charlie spun around and addressed the flickering glow of the candle. "And another thing, missus, you wanna try wiping that arse of yours with a bit of sandpaper!" He crossed the threshold into the clear night air, noisily filling his nostrils with it.

Bert sat up when he heard the commotion at the front door. "What's the matter?" he asked as Charlie gave Jobe a leg up into the back of the wagon.

Charlie's frame, topped by wide, rising shoulders that expanded to his huge head, gave the impression of a man who would be forced to drag his bulk, but his movements were lithe and graceful, and he pulled himself into the wagon in one fluid movement. "We've all grown up sharing beds, if we were lucky, but asking fit and able men to sleep with the infirm and bedridden? I've never seen the likes! That hag must be on to a pretty penny locking them poor blighters up and cashing in their settlement bonds and savings." He paused in reflection. "I'll tell you what, Bert. There's nothing much that's endearing this trip to me thus far, apart from making the acquaintance of young Fred here. If we get to Hull and the promise of work is as far-fetched as everything else, there'll be hell to pay for those who've sent us." He made his declaration as he pulled Bert's covers from him. Ignoring the driver's protests, he counted them before handing him a third of them back. "Don't get up, Bert. You stay on your bench. The lad can take the front seat, he's got littler legs than us. That OK with you, Fred?" he asked as he placed another third of the blankets on the driver's bench.

Silky fingered the heavy iron poker in his hand. His favourite weapon, his belt, with its three sharpened brass buckles that, when whirled about, gathered one by one next to the fastening buckle to create a vicious instrument of violence would be of no use in the confinement of The Den. He closed his eyes, sensing the rest of his boys lurking with intent in the darkness.

Everybody who had a right to know, knew about the jars. Even the lads who came home, their heads muddled by Laudanum, the mix of opium and water, which he had strictly forbidden, remembered the jars. Nobody ever knocked one down accidentally; sending a jar crashing to the floor would alert the whole gang and could well result in being knocked unconscious or worse.

Silky could tell by the huge forms of the two who had entered the room that it wasn't members of the Naylor Street Nasties or the Pumpfields Posse carrying out a midnight raid. Neither of that gang of maggots would dare. Nor could it be the Logwood Gang: they'd disbanded long ago, the need for their vigilantism gone.

The invaders had to be aware that they had set off some kind of alarm or warning system on hearing the shattering jars, but, judging by their confident movements, paid the fact little heed. If they weren't from another gang, they could only be coppers, and Silky was smart enough not to launch an attack against coppers; neither hanging from a jib or spending the rest of his life behind bars appealed to him and he struck a match, holding the flame to an oil lamp. The room was instantly lit. The two men standing before him weren't fazed by the sudden illumination. Silky drew in a breath. He hadn't looked into the peculiar green eyes that stared at him now for what seemed like a lifetime. Memories of penny pies and a hot air balloon rolled into his mind. And that little toff sitting fidgeting on the giant's shoulders was Jobe! Silky shook his head wistfully; I bet that clever little bleeder recognised me from the off. He lowered his poker. "You haven't come looking for your sixpence, have you, cos I'm afraid it's been well and truly spent."

Albert instantly recognised the urchin from George's Dock. How long had it been? Six, perhaps seven years previous? The boy hadn't grown a great deal but had filled out adequately. He was obviously doing well for himself, judging by his attire.

Silky didn't register the recognition in the green eyes. "You don't remember me?" he asked.

"On the contrary. I'm glad to remake your acquaintance, and happy that you have the good grace to recall the liberty I allowed you to retain that day, along with pie and sixpence I furnished you with."

"Perhaps," replied Silky noncommittally. His mind was racing through the gang's recent activities, trying to create a link between those and the man in front of him. It was useless. He could have been a victim of any one of a score of recent jobs they had carried out. Silky looked into the green eyes, searching for a clue as to the man's intentions. There was no trace of the humour that had put Silky at ease on their initial meeting, and he involuntarily swallowed as his mouth flooded with saliva, his Adam's apple betraying his concern.

Albert noted the reflex and moved to put the young man, at ease. "I have no malicious intentions here. I simply come in search of my son, Jobe Warburton."

"Jesus, it's the Giant O' come looking for Jobe!" The outburst from somewhere behind Albert was quickly repeated by the dozen or so gang members around The Den, and whispers of "the Giant O" traversed the room, the boys repeating it in awe rather than to inform their comrades.

Silky threw the box of Lucifer matches to a boy facing him and made his way to his trusty Chesterfield chair, giving no indication of the rising panic he was feeling. The Giant O' in his Den! He sat down, ignoring the urge to take the gold-rimmed monocle from his embroidered waistcoat lest his hands shake and betray his fear. "We've heard no news of Jobe since he was taken aboard the Clarence almost eighteen months past. We're expecting one of our members to be released a fortnight from now. He's sure to have news for us." Silky noted the pained look that flashed across his impromptu visitor's features. "I've no concerns for his well-being, though," he added quickly. "Jobe was sentenced with my lump of a cousin, Tommy Molloy, and he'd fight the devil himself to stop any harm coming to Jobe."

Albert gestured to a three-legged stool. "May I?" he asked.

Silky provided permission with a curt nod of his head. He looked up at the Giant O's companion and, his confidence returning, made a pharaonic gesture with his left arm, inviting him to be seated also. Potter watched a boy who was busy lighting the remaining oil lamps before sitting.

"Jobe was not confined on the Clarence as you suggest, he was placed aboard the Akbar," explained Albert.

Silky recoiled from the news. "Then I'm afraid it's more than likely he's dead. No Catholic could endure aboard the Akbar, populated as it is by treacherous O's." Silky remembered who he was addressing and fought to control his Adam's apple while retaining eye contact.

"You're mistaken," Albert said. "I'm delighted to say. I've been looking for him these last two days, since Sunday afternoon in fact, when he was put ashore from the Akbar. I last observed him racing toward Mann Island but since then have neither sight nor sound of him."

Silky shook his head. "But it makes no sense. He hasn't served even a half of his three-year sentence..."

Albert turned to Potter, who inclined his head slightly. Albert was in agreement with his friend's unspoken endorsement of the boy's reaction. For the second time in two brief meetings stretching years apart, Albert decided Silky was telling the truth; he had no knowledge of Jobe's whereabouts. He pulled a five-pound note from his wallet and gave it to Silky, along with a card.

"My address is on the card. Provide me with news of my son's return, or his whereabouts, and there'll be more of those notes than you and your gang can count together."

Silky stood with Albert and brought himself to his full height, still not coming to Albert's chest. He handed the five-pound note back to the giant but retained the card. "If Jobe wants you to hear of his return, then you'll hear."

* * *

Jobe didn't immediately realise he had woken. Each breath felt cold and pure in his lungs and he lay vacuously watching the stars play out above him. He had never known that they were so numerous or that they could shine so bright. The sense of serenity he experienced was a new sensation. "Jobe Warburton!" he mouthed quietly, before repeating it out loud. His utterance caused him to sit bolt upright as if a jolt of lightning had coursed through his body and he said his name again himself, louder this time. "Jobe Warburton."

"What's that…who…what?" Charlie's arms flailed as he attempted to sit up. "What's the do, Fred lad?" he asked as he finally steadied himself.

"I'm not Fred, I'm Jobe. Jobe Warburton."

Charlie looked across at Bert, who was snoring blissfully, then looked over at Jobe before rubbing his face with both hands as if dry-washing it. "What's this you're saying, Fred? You're name is really Jobe?"

"That's right, Charlie. Jobe Warburton." He shook his head in disbelief. "That's the first time I've said my name out loud for over a year!" he whispered to himself. He cupped his hands around his mouth and stood. "My…name…is…Jobe…Warburton!" he shouted at the top of his lungs.

Charlie sprang forward, finger on his lips. "Shhh, all right, Fre… Jobe lad. That's quite enough of that, don't want to rouse the whole of Yorkshire now, do we?" he whispered. Grabbing his blankets, gestured to the front of the wagon. "What say I come and have a seat up front with you, eh? We'll have a good chinwag while we wait for the sun to come up."

They pooled their thin blankets, producing a thicker layering, which they sat under in silence looking up at the stars.

Charlie fully concentrated on them, broke the silence. "So, Jobe eh? I like it! Better than Fred anyways. I thought you had a bit more about you than a plain old Fred."

The silence continued, as did their vigil of the stars.

"I can remember my mother telling me his story," said Jobe after a while. "He was the most pious man in his village, good and holy. But God, *in his wisdom*, took everything from him—his herds, his land, his family and finally his health. Stripped him of everything in a wager with the Devil. He was persecuted mercilessly, but throughout it all he never lost his faith, always remaining good and pious."

"The Book of Job," said Charlie. "I remember it from church," he declared shaking his head in wonder, as if amazed by the power of his memory.

"I think it was a jibe at my paternal grandmother," said Jobe. "She ostracised my father when he married my mother, kept him from his birthright and me from my legacy."

"You've lost me now, Jobe," said Charlie, after taking in a deep breath.

Jobe started from the beginning; being born in Boston, coming to Liverpool as a babe, the house in Everton, his father, the descent into the slums, the death of his mother and downfall of his grandparents, Tommy, Silky and the gang and finally his term on the Akbar. All the while, he looked up at the stars as they made their arc across the night sky. When he had finished, a silence settled between the two again. Bert's snoring and the odd animal call the only sounds.

"I accused Ted of pressing you," Charlie said after a while. He sensed Jobe take his eyes from the sky and look at him for the first time since they had sat down. He didn't return the look but continued. "You know, like in the old days. The press gang used to hunt down men, mostly drunks. Any who had the misfortune of crossing paths with a press gang would wake up far out to sea with a head resembling yours," he finished speaking and felt Jobe return his gaze to the sky.

"No, I don't think I was pressed. I think someone followed me off the Akbar—Wilkes or, more probably, whomever it was that was pulling his strings on shore. I don't know. It makes no sense. But at first light, I'm heading back to find out."

The determination in Jobe's tone made the hairs on Charlie's neck stand up. He didn't doubt the lad's conviction but was of the opinion that a passage of time might help his situation. "Why not let a layer of time settle on it? For now at least. It sounds to me like your feet haven't touched the floor in a while. Continue to Hull. Think. Plan. Work. Fill your pockets with a bit of brass. It'll make things a lot easier when you do return. Think on it, Jobe lad. C'mon now, what about some shuteye before the cock begins to crow?"

* * *

Jobe's knees cracked as he jumped from the wagon. His headache had almost abated, but it protested with a jagged wave of pain as he turned and looked back at Charlie, who remained seated, pawing at his eyes and cheeks. Jobe brought his hand up to the back of his head and traced it over the still prominent but diminishing bumps as he made his way around the house in search of some privacy in which to answer his ever more urgent call of nature.

He wondered at the piles of rubble that hid in the thigh high grass as he picked his way among them, assuming that they were remnants of an old storehouse. He was shocked when he looked up and realised that they had once belonged to the boarding house itself. The back of the house was just made up of interior walls. The exterior was gone, dilapidated, as if a giant hand had swiped it away and scattered it over the moor to serve as proof that a full house had once existed. Jobe could make out the pattern on the remnants of wallpaper that doggedly clung to the exposed walls. Weather-beaten interior doors now served as part of the outside wall and Jobe wondered if the landlady ever opened them to provide some much-needed ventilation, but judging by the smell of the place, he doubted they had been opened in years. No wonder the sleeping arrangements were so cramped. Had anybody 'creeping around during the night, under the guise of answering a call of nature' ever wandered through one of the doors and found themselves on the lonely moor with two broken legs? Jobe shook his head in disbelief as he wiped his hands on the seat of his pants.

On his return to the wagon, Charlie was replacing the blankets on each of their travelling companions' perches. Jobe doubted they would be needed, the sky was a perfect blue and the sun already had a warmth to it. He turned toward the house on hearing a loud rapping to see Bert hastily scuttling back up what served as a path before the front door could be opened.

"Soon be setting off, Jobe lad. If we make good time, we should be able to get half a day's pay in, more if the light lasts," Charlie said as Jobe climbed back aboard.

The silence was total as they continued their journey across the moor; even Charlie was absorbed in his own thoughts. The uplands suddenly turned into the outskirts of a town without any warning, the two piebald mares took a small ridge in their stride and on cresting it the dirt track became cobbled. A flurry of low grey housing sprawled down towards the River Hull, which meandered through the town before feeding out into the Humber. The attention of the men was pricked by the change in terrain, but they remained tight-lipped and in possession of their own counsel.

They hadn't travelled far through the town when, nearing midday, the wagon came to a halt outside a rundown public house. A trio of burly men lounged on a bench against its poorly whitewashed wall, their sleeves rolled up to expose rough tattoos. They paid no attention to the men in the wagon or the landlord who appeared as if he had been expecting them, hurriedly buttoning a bottle-green overcoat that he wore over a pair of brown buckskin breeches. "Welcome to Hull," he said in a thick Yorkshire accent as he cast his eyes over the men in a way that Jobe had seen charge-hands do at the dock stands and he realised the man must be their ganger.

The landlord turned his attention from the men and ducked in order to pop his head back inside the pub doorway, calling instructions to someone inside. "Thirteen halves if you will, Trudy." He ducked back out, beaming at the men. "We know how to treat our guests in these parts! A quick stretch of your legs, a wetting of your whistles and then we'll see about squeezing in half a day, shall we? You'll be needing the price of a pint when we get back!" he boomed, collapsing into a fit of coughing and wheezing as he shook his head, enjoying his own joke.

A thin girl appeared through the doorway holding a tray with half a dozen pots. Jobe thought back to the commotion caused by cold tea and grey bread in the guesthouse; he didn't fancy the girl's chances, but the sombre tone that had been a constant companion across the moor remained prevalent and the men waited quietly for their glasses.

"Is there any chance of a cup of tea, mister?" asked Charlie hopefully. The landlord looked at him quizzically before noting that the girl still had one full glass on her otherwise empty tray. Bert looked expectantly, but the landlord paid him no heed, instead ushering the girl through the small doorway. He followed, re-emerging with a silver canteen and two cups. "You'll never drink tea again! I'm not usually so free with my Colombian beans, but seeing as you're a guest…"

Charlie took the proffered cup, examining the ink-black contents. He took a sip and with a shrug of his shoulders held up the cup to the landlord in a toast.

Jobe didn't relish the half pint he found himself holding, but such was his desperation for something cold to drink he drained the glass in one, to the delight of the landlord.

"Ha, you might be a youngster but you drink like a true Liverpudlian. Let's hope you can work like one as well, eh! C'mon then, muckers…" He entered into one of his laughing, coughing fits with this utterance and could only wave them towards the wagon, his bottle-green sleeves shimmering in the sun.

The thoroughfare they followed was a busy one. Trestle tables lined both sides of the street, creaking under the weight of the fresh fish that was piled upon them. The sight of a group of working men in a wagon was certainly not a peculiar one, and Jobe wondered at the baleful stares of those who stopped their appraisals of the seafood or turned from their wares to watch them pass. He was relieved when the wagon turned into a narrow, relatively unpopulated side street, coming to a stop next to a set of rusted gates. The men dismounted, the last one down being the landlord, who had sat next to Bert for the trip. Bert turned the wagon around and, without bidding farewell to anyone, started back on the long journey to Liverpool.

The landlord took a heavy key from his pocket and unchained the gates, which creaked open. The dock itself, and the surrounding warehouses were deserted. The array of weeds and vegetation lent the whole wharf an aura of long-term disuse and abandonment. Jobe looked at Charlie, who raised his eyebrows. The scene didn't fit with his original description of ships cramming the Humber waiting to unload.

The landlord noted the disquiet etched on every face. "Why the long faces? Don't worry, the work's here! Hull's a busy port, but it's not Liverpool. Docks are abandoned now and again. Now c'mon, let's be having you," he breezed as he led the group to the wharf 's edge.

Looking down into the undisturbed water, Jobe saw a barge tethered to a rusting ladder that was precariously bolted to the quay. His stomach sank as he realised why ship owners with a town full of dockers to employ had sent to Liverpool to recruit. "This has a bad feeling to it, Charlie," he said before turning to the landlord. "What's all this about?" he called.

"Don't suffer seasickness, do you? The dock we're working is on the other side of the river," he answered innocently.

"Don't you have bridges in Hull? I've never sailed into a pitch."

"My apologies, button. We're not so enlightened in Hull as to have a railway to ferry dockers about like royalty. Dockers from these parts rely on their legs to get to work. Our pitch is t'other side of the Hull—feel free to swim if you prefer."

"He obviously doesn't know the prices they charge on the overhead railway," said Charlie in an attempt at breaking the tension. "But to be fair, it does serve as a decent umbrella for those who can't afford the price of a ticket."

"Times a-ticking, men," continued the landlord, pointing up at the sun. All tones of virtue had left his voice and there was no doubt the sentence was an ultimatum.

Jobe watched as the tightly huddled dockers approach the ladder as one. He wondered whether it was just habit that they grouped together like sheep or something darker and more depressing born out of generations of servility. He shouted at the group, anger straining his voice. "Listen! We've all seen boats like this unloading knobsticks on the docks back home! They're the worst kind of scab, if scabs are worthy enough to warrant a pecking order that is!"

"Hark at him! Bright little union button I've been saddled with here," smiled the landlord through gritted teeth. "There's nothing untoward here. Those that want an honest day's work, with plenty following, look sharp. Those that don't…"

The men began to file towards the ladder, disappearing down it one by one.

"Jobe, lad?"

Jobe forced himself to look into Charlie's mishmash of a face. "Did you know, Charlie?"

"Well, I had an inkling but was hoping it wasn't the case. I'm sorry," he replied, unable to meet the youngsters eye.

Jobe paused before taking hold of one of Charlie's massive hands, clasping it in both of his.

Charlie pulled the boy to his breast. "I won't ask you to come or understand," he said as he hugged him.

"Don't do it, Charlie. Never mind what kind of shoes you find yourself in today, they'll be walking a new path tomorrow. This decision will taint your steps forever. You're a good and honest man—too good to become a scab."

One of those about to broach the descent called to Jobe. "What about the likes of us what've been blackballed by your union? Shut out because we're happy to pick up a day's work when it's available. You can't expect the bosses to pay us for sitting on empty crates using our last coppers to send for ale." It was the first time Jobe had heard the man utter a word.

Charlie broke the embrace with Jobe and turned to the man. "Down the ladder with you," he hissed. "Looking for a boy to redeem you from your nefarious doings." He turned back to Jobe. "Go home, lad. Go now, reclaim what's left of your family. See if you can catch Bert and the wagon. If he tries to stop you getting on board, tell him he'll have me to answer to!"

Jobe turned and ran without looking back.

The landlord had locked the gates, but there was enough slack in the chain for Jobe to push the gates and squeeze through the gap he created. He jogged up the quiet side street, slowing to a walk as he entered the busy thoroughfare. The malevolent looks its occupants had shot at the group of knobsticks in the wagon made sense to him now, and he quickly retraced the route it had taken, being sure to give a cursory glance at the pubs he passed in case Bert had tethered the mares outside one of them.

He still hadn't caught sight of Bert on arriving back at the landlord-cum-ganger's pub. Already out of breath, his heart sank when there was no sign of Bert. The three were still lounging on the bench and Jobe guessed they were heavies employed by the scab-ganger to protect his interests. They supped at the foaming mugs they held, paying him no attention until he made to enter the pub. "Oi, weren't you on that scab wagon?" asked a thickset man without getting up. The peak of his filthy cap covered the top half of his face so all Jobe could see was a dirty unshaven mouth and chin.

"Has the wagon that brought us passed back this way?" Jobe asked hopefully.

"Off with you, scab!" came the unhelpful reply.

He had been hoping for at least a glass of water from the thin serving girl. His race to retrace his steps had left him tired and he hoped he could charm her out of something to eat without the landlord's eagle eye on them. An image popped into his mind of Bert licking his lips in the hope of a half pint that wasn't forthcoming. Of course he wouldn't stop where people were aware of the cargo he carried. He ran from the pub, leaving the final rows of squat slum housing behind him, and struggled up the small rise the wagon had rolled over earlier that day. Reaching the crest, he took in a breath. There was no sign of Bert and his piebald mares on the road, and Jobe's Adam's apple bobbed in reflex to the enormity of the journey that lay before him. Everything that stretched ahead, for what seemed like an eternity, was green. He never appreciated how expansive the space was from the wagon. The sense of exposure added to his discomfort, and he had half a mind to turn back into the shelter of the grey anonymity he had just left. He could scrape along in Hull as well as in Liverpool, after all, but images of Molloy and Silky, Fergus and even the Giant O'—his father—crowded his mind. There would be no replacements for them in Hull. Scattered though they may be, they were all at least somewhere in his hometown.

The memory of the servile men and their meek descent down the ladder steeled him. All they knew was a life of servitude. They would be better as serfs; at least then their lord would prosper from them and have a reason to keep them alive and fed. Those men had given the best of themselves, for little reward, to employers who used and discarded them like rubbish. Memories of their appeasement of the landlady, tolerance of the wagon drive and complete compliance to the scab-landlord filled Jobe with a burning rage. They watched as animals were given better treatment, and yet they still responded to the whim of their employers, usually to the disadvantage of their fellow workers.

Jobe took in a lungful of the fresh Yorkshire air. He wouldn't capitulate. He would crawl back to Liverpool if need be. He would maintain his liberty. The gang would become an avenging force, taking from those who prospered from the burdens faced by his class. If the gang no longer existed, he would simply form a new one. One that would target the ship owners and landlords and strike fear into the black hearts of their ilk.

Jobe hadn't held money for a long time and the selection of shillings and coppers felt heavy and strange in his hand. Charlie must have deposited the coins during their farewell embrace. He tried to recall if they had passed any kind of house or farm on their journey to Hull but couldn't recall anything that had disturbed the barrenness of the moor following the departure from the grisly guesthouse.

He wished he had been able to persuade Charlie from the clutches of the scab-ganger and the stain that he would never be able to cleanse from his conscience. His easy manner and light-hearted banter would have provided a welcome aside from the bleeding soles and yearning stomach that were sure to be his companion the whole way home. In his haste to catch up with Bert, he had not even had the sense to pilfer a few apples or a loaf of bread to see him through the first miles of his long journey. He realised that the only thing he had eaten or drunk in almost three days was the grey piece of bread in the guesthouse and glass of ale outside the pub.

Once his mind became conscious of this, it persecuted him by sending constant messages to his stomach. The pangs of hunger were almost unbearable, but he retained the hope of coming across fellow travellers that he could hitch a lift with or a farmhouse where he could purchase some food, perhaps even rent a room for the night. But for now the moor extended unbroken as far as the eye could see, and to pass the time he absent-mindedly counted the money over and over as he walked. The novelty of having it in his possession soon diminished, and he would gladly have swapped it all for a piece of bread and cheese to placate his rumbling stomach.

As the light began to fade, he thought it better that he should stop rather than stumble through the dark and risk losing the road. He ventured into the calf length scrub until he found a small trough in the ground. He couldn't imagine that it was natural. It seemed that a heavy rock had been left there for a long time, or that it had been dug out. Even in his exhausted state, Jobe couldn't help but wonder. Regardless, the grass was long, soft and served as an excellent mattress. He fell into a deep, dreamless sleep, waking just before sunrise, his legs and back stiff, but his mind refreshed.

The moor grass was heavy with dew and his feet sunk into the shallow peat as he made his way back to the road. The pitted, uneven track had decimated the sole of his right shoe. The hours spent mending and stitching it while aboard the Akbar counted for nothing and the sole flapped open, allowing stones and rocks in that made every step a painful one and constantly threatened his footing.

The road remained empty in either direction. Jobe couldn't understand the dearth of traffic. Hull was a gateway to the continent and the east. The flow of goods in and out was considerable but on the sun approaching its midday zenith he still hadn't encountered a living soul. Keeping his head up became a struggle, and he was powerless to stop it from sagging to his chest. The effort of placing one foot before the other became his own personal purgatory and he developed a limp, his body's attempt to protect his right foot, which only served to place added pressure to his left leg and cause it to ache. The terrain remained monotonous and unchanging so it became impossible to judge his progress.

His stomach gnawed at him, the rumblings seemingly keeping time with his steps. He thought of H' and how he had become a martyr to his stomach. His energy waned, and his once-confident strides were reduced to a scraping shuffle. The two lumps on his head throbbed and he rubbed at them intermittently in an attempt to gauge whether they were growing, imagining his dehydration was causing them to swell. His mouth was as dry as the clumps of Sesleria that covered the moorland, the ale he had drank the day before a curse, its stale redolence making him retch.

He took out the coins Charlie had secreted in his pockets. Not to count them but to hold them in both fists like charms. Now and again he would allow his eyes to close and cup his hands together his hands together so he could shake the coins and enjoy their jingling.

"Ey up, sounds like a few bob thee's got there, petal!"

Jobe's hands and eyes opened in shock and he stood blinking as the coins spilled onto the ground. He looked at them scattered around his feet but made no attempt to pick them up. A dozen or so men had appeared in front of him as if from nowhere. He had developed a keen instinct for danger aboard the Akbar. Encountered enough belligerent boys to detect when the threat of violence was imminent. Senses that had become dull with fatigue now tingled with foreboding, there were no boys among this group; each one of them was a grown man with hair and muscle beneath their buttoned shirts and shabby waistcoats. He looked around, whether for an escape route or to fathom where they had appeared from he didn't know.

"Has thee addled so much that thee can afford to go throwing Godspennies into the dirt to get all clarty like they're nowt but trammel?" said the man who had first addressed him. He was a good head shorter than Jobe but so well built that he resembled a cube. He was the only one not wearing some kind of hat. His mane of blonde hair was combed back so that it flowed and merged with side-whiskers that hung well below his jaw line and resembled large muttonchops. A blade of grass hung from the side of his mouth and vibrated when he spoke.

Jobe could barely decipher his thick slang or brogue and was forced to answer intuitively. "No, it's not that. I just got a fright that's all," he stammered, kneeling to retrieve the coins. Taking his eyes from the men was excruciating, but he forced himself to scan the track for the fallen coins.

"I can well imagine, my ansum. Thee must be capt to encounter owt on this dwine of a road?" said Muttonchops, an air of sympathy in his voice. The sarcastic tone helped Jobe dissect the sentence and it became clear why he hadn't seen a soul. He had been following an uninhabited back road that Bert had used to cloak their arrival into Hull. Why hadn't he considered as much? He felt like crying for his aching feet, stomach and head. How many miles had he wasted following a winding unpopulated dirt track across the moor?

"It's known as the Scab Road these days," confirmed Muttonchops matter-of-factly. He was the only one who had spoken and obviously the leader of the men who bristled behind him, barely able to contain themselves.

Jobe knew there was only one conclusion to the encounter; there was no chance of escape, but if he could just engage his tired mind, there may be a chance of rescue. Muttonchops seemed to be enjoying the game and Jobe's only hope, no matter how slight, was to keep him enjoying it until somebody came along the road; hopefully it would be a wagon full of scabs. He struggled to gather his senses. "We call them knobsticks in Liverpool. The worst kind of scab, those who travel in from other towns to break the pickets," he said, as he furtively deposited the coins into his pockets.

"Knobsticks, is it? Happen we should rename this snicket into town the Knobstick Road then?" The blade of grass dangling from his mouth reverberated as he laughed.

Jobe waited until he had stopped, squeezing every second from the exchange. "I'm no scab. I didn't earn this money. It was given to me," he said, trying to keep his voice even.

Muttonchops turned to the men gathered behind him. "By all his blether, happen our new ansum here is of a mind that we're all gauvies."

Jobe wasn't sure what was said but knew by the resentful looks shot his way that it couldn't be good. His energy was fading fast, and he was too tired to feel relief when Muttonchops turned and continued the conversation, his countenance remaining cordial.

"Think on, petal. You'll gain nowt for thissen by trying to marlock us. A lot of these men are in a right mullock. They, me an' all, have watched a lot of friends clutter up in the Bastille because of thee and tha *knobsticks*!"

The stress of the situation coupled with the exertions of deciphering what was being said to him drained the remnants of Jobe's energy. His head began to thump. Lights danced before his eyes. His confidence waned; he understood there would no chance of redemption from what awaited him. "I'm going back to Liverpool. I was brought here against my will. I've never scabbed and never would," he tried to explain, the words sounding hollow in his own ears.

"Always a bad job when good Yorkshire silver leaves the county in the britches of fugglins. I dassent allow it to, petal. These taistrils wouldn't abide it. They'd have my entrails for their snap if I let so much as an 'aporth aht," explained Muttonchops, his tone almost apologetic. He took the stem from his mouth, shaking his head as he examined it carefully. The act was an unspoken sign, and before Jobe knew it, the men were rushing at him, obscuring Muttonchops, who stood aside engrossed in his blade of grass.

* * *

The sun was high in the sky when Jobe woke. Dry blood clogged his nostrils and he began to choke as he became aware that he couldn't breathe. His lungs almost burst until some sense of self-preservation caused him to simply breathe through his mouth as he had for the time he had been unconscious, bringing a sudden end to his panic induced self-suffocation. He lay gasping as his lungs filled and deflated. A sharp pain in his chest caused him to emit a low groan and he brought a hand to his cracked, or possibly broken ribs. The viciousness of the beating that had taken place and robbed him of consciousness played through his mind. The recollection of each kick and punch opening the floodgates to a wave of pain that engulfed his body and forced him into a constricted ball of agony. He tentatively brought his swollen hands to his puffy eyes before tracing them carefully over his thumping head. His tongue protruded limply from his mouth and he attempted to run it over his teeth but it was so swollen and numb that he couldn't ascertain if any were broken. He rolled onto his back, looking for some relief from his pain but the movement only made him cry out and impeded his breathing so he was forced to roll onto his left side where he remained, slipping in and out of consciousness. Some semblance of lucidity found its way into his mind as the light began to diminish and he forced himself to half crawl, half roll off the road and into a patch of bracken that lined the side of the track. His chest rose quickly and a cold sweat broke out all over his body with the exertion.

The sun was directly above him when he woke. The foliage he lay under shielded him from the worst of its glare but the tongue that he played over his cracked lips was still swollen and dry; he attempted to swallow but his throat wasn't functioning the thick slime that caught making him gag and retch. He knew he had to get up and move on but the simple act of licking his lips was enough to expend all of his energy. He allowed his eyes to close, just for a second to clear his head.

He felt better with his eyes closed. Images of his mother played behind his heavy lids. She called to him in her singsong voice and he could see her standing before him, smiling as she blew the willful strand of hair that refused to be tamed away from her deep blue eyes. The corners of his blood crusted mouth curled into something that resembled a smile, the effort involved registering as a grimace of pain across his bruised and swollen eyes.

* * *

"It's the bloody Trades Council that's bringing all the Liverpool men up here, Jim, I guarantee it."

The words interrupted the panoramic views of Liverpool Jobe was enjoying from his father's shoulders.

"I tell you, when we find proof, we'll flay them with it," the voice continued entering Jobe's mind fully and dragging him back to something approaching awareness. He peered through the bracken, to see a man standing before him, filling his pipe. The man was addressing a pair of legs that were poking from underneath a carriage and on lifting his head a little Jobe could see that there were in fact two men under the coach, repairing something.

"Will you give it a rest, James! Why is it I'm on my back in the mud and you're there enjoying the scenery, no doubt filling your pipe as you do? Wasn't it you who didn't want to take the train?"

Jobe rolled onto his front, a small army of insects abandoning their temporary resting place, and began dragging himself through the bracken, grunting with the pain and effort. Dirt clung to him, and the bracken scratched his already damaged face and hands as he crawled through it. The man with the pipe turned at the rustling and grunting, letting out a scream as he set eyes on the picture of horror that slowly emerged, the contents of his freshly stuffed pipe flying through the air. Before they landed, one of the men working under the carriage had rolled from under it and onto his feet in one fluid movement. The man with the pipe manipulated himself so that he stood behind the bigger man, who was huge and scanned the area with a spanner held aloft. On seeing the figure of Jobe dragging himself towards them he dropped his impromptu weapon to the ground.

"Are you soft in the head, James? It's just a boy! And a badly injured one at that. Water, now!" he admonished his companion as he ran towards Jobe. "Grab the flask also," he called over his shoulder. "Here, you're all right, son? Can you understand me?" he asked as he knelt and supported Jobe's head and shoulders in the crook of his well-defined arm.

* * *

Jim cleared the dried blood from the boy's nostrils and then brushed the leaves and twigs that nestled in his hair before lifting him in his arms. Jobe's body draped listlessly across the man's strong forearms and his head lolled to one side so the man feared the worst as he carried him to the carriage.

"James…the water! Quickly, now!" He held the water to Jobe's lips, and after the first few drops escaped from his mouth, Jobe grabbed weakly for the bottle. "That's the way. Easy now, a drop at a time," he said as he gently lifted the bottle from Jobe's grasp.

Commotion over, James busied himself refilling his pipe and watched as his companion ministered to the boy as best he could. Bringing his pipe to his mouth, James struck a match and began sucking and puffing, blithely throwing the match over his shoulder.

The big man turned his attention from Jobe to reprimand him. "Haven't I told you this whole journey you need to be more careful with your matches, James? This moor can become a tinder-box, your carelessness could cause a heck of a fire."

"Ah, behave, would you, Jim? Did you not see me blowing it out?"

As Jim looked through his friend's billowing smoke for a telltale sign of the match, he spotted a man running toward them. Something in the man's manner immediately put him on guard and he lay the boy down on the ground as gently as possible. "Get behind me and watch over the boy, James. There's something about this fella's gait that I don't like the look of!"

James looked over his shoulder and quickly followed Jim's advice. They both watched the sweating man advancing, his pace, if anything, growing. "Do you think it could be the boy's assailant?" asked James.

Jim didn't answer but absent-mindedly began to roll up his sleeves before realising he had already done so to work under the carriage.

The man stopped a dozen or so paces before the coach. The sweat that streamed from his brow mingled with the dust that covered his entire front, but his breath was steady and even. He looked past the two men in front of him to the broken boy lying on the ground. "Have you run him down?" he asked.

Jim picked up on the menace in the man's voice, sensing that he was on the edge of violence. "We found him like this, or rather he found us. He crawled from the bracken there," answered Jim, pointing to the side of the road. "We were just in the process of cleaning him up and finding out how he came to be in this shape." The words changed something in the man's demeanour and Jim felt no threat as the man approached him.

"You're from Liverpool!" stated the sweating man. "So is the boy there. His name is Jobe." He passed the two men, wafting pipe smoke from his face.

"Who did this to him then?" asked James in between puffs of his pipe. He received no reply as Jim and the newcomer knelt over the boy.

"He's suffering from exhaustion as well as the beating, but I think he'll be OK. Are you from Liverpool as well then?" asked Jim, tipping water onto his handkerchief and wiping at Jobe's face. He wet the handkerchief a second time before passing the container to the man next to him.

The man nodded his thanks and took a huge draught of the water before replying. "Yes, I'm from Liverpool. My name is Charlie. Charlie Doyle," he said, holding out his hand, which Jim and James shook in turn. "Me and the boy were taken to Hull to scab, but he refused to do so, preferring to attempt the walk home, I stayed to work...to scab, but it proved harder than I imagined."

James and Jim looked at each other.

"Who was it that brought you to Hull?" asked James, his pipe forgotten.

"All right, James, enough with the questions. Let Charlie rest. We know enough for now. There'll be plenty of time on the way home for questions," Jim said as he picked up Jobe and placed him in the carriage.

"We're taking them with us?" asked James, a horrified look on his face.

"Well, we're certainly not leaving them here," said Jim. "I'm Jim Larkin. My pleasant colleague there is James Sexton." He held open the carriage door so Charlie could clamber inside.

* * *

The wind battered the side of the coach as it made its way across the dark moor. Jobe's head rested in Charlie's lap, who was at pains to stop it bouncing with the creaking coach. Occasionally, he put a handkerchief to the neck of the water flask, squeezing drops onto Jobe's cracked lips. James and Jim sat opposite, listening as Charlie related every event, leaving nothing out, from Mann Island to Hull.

On the ending of the tale, the three men sat in silent reflection. It was the first time silence had dominated the coach, and the driver could be heard encouraging the horses through the dark night. Charlie focused all of his attention on the window, although it was so dark outside that all he could see was his own reflection flickering in the lamplight.

"Charlie?"

Charlie looked down to see Jobe looking up at him through eyes that were no more than slits in the puffiness and bruising. Charlie smiled, although his eyes betrayed his guilt at allowing Jobe to leave the dock alone. The boy attempted to sit up but couldn't. "Yes, it's Charlie, Jobe lad. Shush now, save your energy."

When Jobe woke, the sun was streaming through the open window of the carriage, and the three men were eating bread and meat from a small hamper. Jobe made no sign that he had woken, instead choosing to observe Charlie and the two men opposite him.

The man they called Jim was speaking animatedly about the burgeoning support of the workers for representation and organised labour, sometimes remonstrating with his colleague, James, or defending his own points from James's remonstrations. The clear blue eyes that shone from dark heavy brows were quick, and Jobe imagined they observed everything, missing nothing. Prominent cheekbones and a powerful, stubborn chin framed the fleshy nose that housed cavernous nostrils.

Jim, feeling he was being watched, looked in Jobe's direction. "Ah, we've woken our young friend with all of our blather," he said reaching across with the contents of the basket. Charlie took the basket and ripped up small pieces of bread and meat, which he gave to Jobe.

Jobe felt the urge to bolt down the food but several of his teeth and his whole jaw ached with the effort involved. He chewed both meat and bread deliberately and felt almost human once he had eaten his fill. The men let him break his fast in peace but on finishing it asked him to relay the events of his time on the moor. Charlie had ground his teeth but held his peace as Jobe recounted his run in with the Hull dockers.

It was Jim who broke the silence on Jobe's story ending. "I hear from Charlie here that you were willing to walk all the way back to Liverpool rather than scab the dock," he said with something like admiration in his voice. "What a lad." he stated wistfully. "Having said that, d'you know I walked to London when I was nine!" He grinned. "Nine, and alone!" He nodded, his grin growing.

James Sexton snorted. "I feel like I walked it with you, the times I've heard the tale! Now, what are we to do with their information?"

he demanded. "I'm of the opinion that we should pose he of the sandwich board a few questions?"

"I think the youngster'll need some medical attention first James, wouldn't you say?" said Jim.

Jobe held up a hand. "I'm truly grateful to you, Jim and yourself Mr. Sexton, it's no exaggeration to say that you've delivered me from deaths door, but once we return to the city I've got business of my own, of great importance, that I must attend to immediately. If you could see yourself to doing me one more favour and instruct your driver to deliver myself and Charlie to Vauxhall Road? Blackstock Street to be precise."

Jim nodded, much to his colleague's visible consternation. "We'd be happy to, Jobe. After the story you've told us it's of no surprise that you have more than a few of your own questions that you'd like answering."

THE BOOK OF JOBE

A TALE OF VICTORIAN LIVERPOOL

II

Chapter I

1893

The puffs of cloud that clung stubbornly to the night sky had long since reflected the last rays of sunlight and were now illuminated by a full moon that bathed the moorland below in an unbroken silver sheet. The mysterious life of the night stealthily scampered along timeworn tracks, scurried over clods of earth or bustled its way through thistle and groundsel as it busily discharged nocturnal routines, until, as if one organism, it froze. Distracted from impulsive errands by a distant but fast approaching rumble, a gentle vibration that swelled swiftly to violence.

The horses hooves that beat against the ground were followed by ironbound wheels that churned up the dust dry earth and created minuscule valleys in the surface of the dirt road. Two lanterns hung from either side of the carriage, their light flashing through the long grass and bracken, momentarily illuminating its inhabitants in the very moment that millennia of innate caution was thrown to the wind. An explosive riot of activity and abandonment filled the undergrowth as the crawling horde attempted to escape the immediate vicinity of the reverberating road. A communal and primordial action that caused the hushed whisper of invisible wings to amplify into a throb as a colony of bats descended from on high to gorge on the unexpected offering. The disregarding drumbeat of hooves and mechanical groan of the carriage's axle moved on inexorably to drown out and disrupt other secret noises of the night.

Jobe woke from a fitful sleep to find the occupants of the carriage asleep, bar one. The flitting and disturbed dreams of his sleep dissolved into the deep recesses of his subconscious as his eyes opened and he was instantly aware of his surroundings. The lamp in the carriage had been extinguished but his head still rested on Charlie's knee. He looked up into the shapeless face bathed in moonlight.

Charlie smiled down at him. "How's the pain, Jobe lad?" he whispered, removing a damp cloth from the boy's forehead.

Reminded of his injuries, Jobe steeled himself against the tide of pain that washed through his body as he began to stretch and test his stiff muscles. "Why were you planning to scab?" he asked through clenched teeth, speaking the words before they or their consequence had formulated properly in his mind.

Charlie kept his eyes fixed on Jobe's and brought his index finger to his lips nodding over at the two sleeping men who had allowed them into their coach, before looking out of the carriage window at a landscape that was painted silver blue by the full moon and he fancied stretched on forever. In stark contrast to the opposite journey, was it really only a day or so before, he had lost himself in the vastness of the silent, deserted moor as it inexorably passed him by. Had allowed himself to be soothed by the cathartic clip-clop of hooves and the rhythmic rocking of the carriage. He wondered if it was the roof over his head that had allayed his primitive terrors or the presence of the young man who lay across him. A boy he had known for scarcely two days but who had influenced him in such a manner that he had torn up all of his well laid plans without a second thought. He looked down at Jobe. How had the boy prevented him from committing the sacrilege of scabbing? And in doing so, led him back to Liverpool, a city where only danger awaited him and his loved ones. "You ok sitting up, Jobe lad?" he asked, responding to Jobe's slight nod by carefully helping him into a comfortable upright position and attempting to rub some feeling back into his own numb thighs.

They both found themselves looking directly at the two men opposite them. The coach was built for the rough terrain of the moor and the sleeping men were rocked like babes in a cradle, a smart bowler resting on the lap of one, a cloth cap on the other.

Charlie looked back out of the window and although he spoke in hushed tones Jobe had no difficulty hearing his words. "Unlike you, it was no accident I found myself heading to Hull, Jobe lad, I was going by design. I needed to earn money and quick," he snorted in derision. "I still do, well, who doesn't, but mine's not to stave off the rent man or settle a tick bill at the grocers or butchers. I need to earn enough to pay my board to New York, along with my wife and littl'un of course." Charlie felt the need to avert his gaze from the sky and train it on his companion. "I'm a marked man, you see. Wanted. Not by the law, you understand. I only wish it was. At least then my wife and littl'un would be safe." He looked again at the two men facing him; ensuring James and Jim were still asleep. After listening to their rhythmic snores for a few seconds he turned back to the night sky. "I've always been an honest man, Jobe lad, but I've never worked with honest men. I suppose that's only natural if you work outside the law." He paused as if the concept was new to him. "I've worked a sight harder than many of those that work inside it mind you!" he continued, bringing his hands up and throwing a few mock jabs and hooks. "I'm a fighter see, or used to be, a good one. Bare-knuckle. Travelled all around the country, up and down I did. Never beaten, not fair and square anyway. Time come when my reputation meant I didn't have to travel no more. My backers were having to turn fighters away, some from as far afield as Dublin and Glasgow, and still I'd sometimes fight twice in one night! Won a lot of men a lot of money, damn sight more than I ever won for myself, but men are never content, they get greedy see, always looking for a sure thing." He paused, as if reflecting on his statement and after a few seconds turned to Jobe. "Have you ever been to an unlicensed fight, Jobe lad? Dangerous places. A lot of unsavoury elements. The ring-keepers have to be as tough as the fighters, armed with staves and belts to maintain order. Jesus, some of the sights I've seen, situations I've found myself in! Drained canals, railway tunnels, church basements, I've fought in them all," he broke off and grabbed Jobe's knee in fright as a barn owl swooped within inches of the carriage window, releasing it with a self-conscious smile. "My last was in the south end, a disused windmill off Park Road. It was billed as my biggest fight, a rematch against this fella from Manchester. I first fought him a few years past in a field just outside Salford. He wasn't a big man, I had more than a few pounds on him, that's the beauty of the unlicensed game see, no weight restrictions, but this fella, he had the art all right, must've caught me with double, treble the punches I managed to land on him. He just didn't have the strength to put me out. We fought to a standing draw, twenty-five punishing rounds. There'd usually be a riot following a draw. Everyone involved, bookies, backers and boxers would have to look out for their hides when an even contest was called. But not on that occasion, we'd put on such an exhibition, you see. We held each other's arm aloft before we were both applauded from the ring." He grew vacant as if lost in the memory, a smile played across his lips before disappearing as he recovered the thread of his tale. "The rematch was always on the cards," he continued. "As I say, it took a couple of years, he, just like me, remained undefeated. It generated so much interest that a dummy bout had to be arranged up on Aintree Racecourse, as a diversion like, fellas were actually paid to go up and attend! He'd bulked up a bit and his punches certainly had more power, but I knew from the first bell I had him, he'd slowed see, his reactions no longer matching his wits. He went from evens to five to one within the space of half a dozen rounds. The ring men had to employ their cudgels and belts to keep back his supporters, they'd bet big on him and were baying for his blood, things could have been so different..." Charlie's voice broke and his head slumped into his hands.

The bench vibrated and Jobe watched from the corner of his eye as the big man's frame shook. He thought back to their conversation on Bert's wagon, had it really only been three nights ago that he'd bared his soul to the stranger? Charlie had remained in silence throughout Jobe's monologue and although Jobe hadn't broke-down there had been moments when the verbal purging had been painful enough to cause the words to catch in his throat. Suddenly uncomfortable looking at the men facing him he fixed his eyes on the roof of the carriage, affording Charlie the time he needed.

"Good Lord, I can't remember the last time I cried, mustn't have been much bigger than a pint pot," snuffled Charlie, as he wiped his eyes and nose in the crook of, first his left and then his right arm. "It was my own corner that done for me. I swung for the cuts man when he began to gouge at an old cut that had opened up on the bridge of my nose, it was only a scratch but he stuck his thumb right in, vicious like." He unconsciously rubbed at the offending area between his eyes as he continued. "I'd have done for him proper if I'd realised the nefariousness he was masking. I can recall the sharp prick in my back as if it were a bayonet spearing my liver now, but at the time, the end of the fourteenth it was, what with my cornerman coming all Little Jack Horner looking for his plum in my noggin and being focused on finishing the job, the needle just didn't register." He shook his head as if still struggling to come to terms with events. He took in a deep breath. "Tea's my only tipple, Jobe lad, and anyone who knows me knows it. I've seen the damage grog does to folk since I was knee-high to a quart jug, it's ravaged my family but, unlike many, I chose to ward it off rather than wallow in it. Well with the laudanum they pumped into my back, it must've been more opium than alcohol; I was soon swinging like a barn door in the wind. Of course the crowd thought it was staged, figured I was planning on taking a fall and it didn't take long for their suspicions to come to fruition. I deserved a medal for managing to stay upright as long as I did!" he exclaimed loudly before bringing his hand to his mouth and looking at the two men opposite. Seeing he hadn't woken them he continued in a hushed tone. "A lot of folk laid a lot of money on me that night, spent their winnings in their heads ten times over before watching me crash to the dusty floor. Well I knew there'd be a price to pay all right. Got my wife and littl'un away that very night. I was still bleeding when we got to the little cottage in the country. I was hoping things'd blow over, that I'd be able to assuage the situation once people's steam had settled. We couldn't stay in the cottage long term, but we should've stayed away, silly of me to think otherwise. I contacted an old pal see; and they still want their pound of flesh. My wife and littl'un, they're in hiding. I had to secrete them away before I left. If those that want me get wind of where they are… they'll take them, Jobe lad. Pimp my Liza out. Have her working in one of their brothels. The clock's against me Jobe lad. I've got them a house well out of the way, but they're alone and it'll only be a matter of time before someone cottons on to where they are and rats them out."

Jim began to stir as Charlie finished his tale, his hand tightening around the cloth cap in his lap, and the first rays of the rising sun began to chase the darkness from the sky.

"I don't know what your planning to do on our return but whatever your plans, Jobe lad, I'll be no good to you in Liverpool."

Jobe looked at Charlie and nodded his understanding as Jim opened his eyes and began stretching. His colleague James had slumped onto the big mans shoulder impeding his movements and he pushed him roughly back to his own side of the bench. "C'mon now James! What is it you take me for, a dock road doxy?"

James almost leapt out of his seat. He looked around accusingly at the men sharing the carriage with him before, gaining his senses he settled back into his seat, although he continued looking at each man with suspicion, only taking his eyes from them to look down at the pipe he had fished from an inside pocket.

Jim looked at his companion and shook his head, before addressing Jobe and Charlie. "Good morning, Charlie, Good morning, Jobe. I trust you both managed to get some rest? How are you feeling this morning, Jobe?"

Jobe brought his hands to his face and head, Charlie's tale causing him to forget about his injuries until reminded of them. He completed his tactile self-examination. "I think the sleep has done me some good, thank you, Jim. My head doesn't bang too badly and it feels as if a lot of the swelling has gone down now," he looked at Charlie for confirmation of his self-assessment.

Charlie gently took Jobe's chin between his thumb and forefinger, carefully swivelling it this way and that both to get a better look and to let the encroaching sunlight improve his view. He turned it in Jim and James's direction. "I'd definitely say the swelling has reduced a bit, wouldn't you agree gentlemen?"

James continued filling his pipe and simply grunted but Jim sat forward in his seat, his clear blue eyes examining Jobe. "I'm no doctor but he certainly doesn't put me as much in mind of poor Joseph Merrick and it can only be a good sign that the headache has receded," he stated as he settled back into his seat.

Jobe didn't follow the remainder of Jim and Charlie's diagnosis. He was transported back through time to the cellar in Court Number 4, Marlborough Street. Standing in a bucket of water, his mother's hand enveloping his, keeping him from toppling over while her other hand scrubbed and gleaned the dirt from his body with an old rag that she periodically dipped into the ever-darkening water as she soothed his protestations with tales of Joseph Merrick.

Her singsong lilt describing the poor man's terrible afflictions and horrific existence while she completed his 'stand-up bath'. "The Elephant Man they called him, Jobe. Gawked at he was, poked and prodded at every funfair and back alley freak show from Lands End to John O'Groats. Ooh if it wasn't for the gentleness and humanity of Dr Treves, the poor wretch would never have known a second's peace, and just look at him now, Jobe, a fixture of London high society. A friend to the Princess Alexandra no less."

Her voice and touch were so clear in Jobe's head that he fancied she was sitting next to him. Exhaustion overcame him and he struggled to focus on the faces in the carriage as his head sunk to his chest. He felt like a leaf torn from the security of its branch. picked up in a gale and tossed through time, with no control over his destination or command of the events he experienced as he passed through them.

Jim noted Jobe's abrupt deterioration and broke off his conversation with Charlie. "We can't be that many hours from home, let's get the coachman to stop so we can break our fast," he said poking James in the ribs, much to his companion's consternation. "This one here can indulge in his foul habit at the same time, he'll become a little bit more human following his tobacco fix, not much mind you, but anything is an improvement on the ignorant swine we have in our midst." James only grunted in response as Jim banged on the carriage wall to alert the coachman's attention.

The sun had risen sufficiently to bask the landscape in a warm glow, drying out the last of the early morning dew and chasing away the final remnants of chill that hung in the air. The horses stamped their forelegs contentedly as they dipped into their nosebags showing no concern for the five humans who stood rolling their hips and stretching their arms taking greatly exaggerated breaths of the fresh, moor air. The hamper was decidedly empty but both Jim and James flatly ignored Charlie and Jobe's protestations that they were not hungry. The driver joined them and added what he had remaining in his handkerchief to the meagre rations before checking on the kettle again.

"It's not much but it'll suffice until we get back to the city," said Jim as he divvied up the breakfast. "What is it you estimate Ed, a couple of hours?"

The driver looked up at the sky and then nodded his affirmation as he took the kettle from the fire.

"That'll see us home before noon, what say straight to Mann Island, see if we can get hold of our 'sandwich board' recruiter?" said James in between puffs of his pipe.

"We've discussed this already, James, the youngster'll need some medical attention first, wouldn't you say?" said Jim after swallowing a mouthful of bread.

"He's a robust lad I'm sure an extra half hour won't kill him, don't you see, Jim, this will provide the proof we need to disaffiliate from those would be aristocratic artisans within the Trades Council once and for all," argued James.

"I'm as eager as you to show the Trade Council's hand in engaging men to break the Hull strike, James, but the boy's health must come first."

Jobe had heard a similar conversation earlier in their journey. Witnessed enough of the two men's debates in the short time he had been with them to know the conversation could go on and on. He interceded by painfully clearing his throat so he could reiterate his earlier words. "I'm truly grateful to you, Jim and yourself Mr. Sexton, it's no exaggeration to say that you've delivered me from deaths door, but, like I said yesterday, once we return to the city I've got business of my own, of great importance, that I must attend to immediately. If you could see yourself to doing me one more favour and instruct your driver to deliver myself and Charlie to Vauxhall Road?"

Charlie looked at Jobe. Jim and James looked at each other, uniquely, each ready to accede ground to the other, but neither with anything to say.

The coach journey resumed in silence and it wasn't long before Jobe, although attempting to devise at least the outline of a plan of action in his mind, had fallen into a deep, dreamless sleep. He opened his eyes and, for a while, drowsily watched as dust-motes danced in a shaft of sunlight before the sounds of the city pulled him fully from his slumber. Realising he was no longer dreaming he grabbed at the door frame and pulled himself to the window just in time to see the enormity of Liverpool College reaching into the sky. He looked along Shaw Street, past the front of the College and into the Pleasure Gardens where he had played so often with his mother. Behind the gardens was his old house on Westbourne Street, where, in happier times, his mother had regaled him with stories of her childhood or anecdotes about her family as she cleaned and cooked, always spurning his father's pleas to hire a maid. He would sometimes come from his study to listen, his huge frame filling the doorway, his booming laughter filling every inch of the high ceilinged rooms.

Jobe's pang of sorrow didn't last, superseded by the sights, sounds and smells that he had been deprived of for so long. Pain forgotten he indulged in the discord of the streets, allowing it to overwhelm his senses. The coach passed through a cloud of smoke billowing into the road from a coal-fired brazier, the smell from the sausages that a fat German was coaxing to a sizzle causing Jobe's stomach to lurch as his eyes swivelled in a forlorn attempt to take everything in. The driver was forced to pull hard on the reins as a line of beefy armed matriarchs, each of them easily balancing a heavy bundle of linen on their heads, passed by. Somehow managing to gossip with her neighbour above the cacophony of the street; carriage wheels against cobbles, the screams of feral children, a tramp plucking a three string cello and the cries of hawkers who stood under the tan awnings of chandlers, tailors, grocers and iron mongers that lined both sides of the road, beseeching anyone who passed not to miss the unprecedented bargains inside their barrows and baskets. Shouting unceremoniously over the respective shop's proprietors while ignoring all efforts to dislodge them.

The coach, navigating the midday throng of carts, trams and ambling pedestrians, was inexorably following the route Jobe himself had journeyed on a daily basis, and he realized with a start that he was silently reciting the college song; just as he had when returning home from the college to his cellar in the slums. Utilising the long walk to commit the Latin verses to memory, his lips and tongue revelling in the exotic phonology as he attempted to master the unfamiliar language.

The coach turned from the thronged Christian Street onto Gerard Street just as a parade of men, women and children dragged a dozen or so worn, wafer thin mattresses into the road. The children began to jump and wrestle each other onto the mattresses as they landed on the ground in a puff of dust, only for the adults to animatedly shoo and manhandle them away. Jobe risked sticking his head fully out of the window as the coach deviated around them. He looked back as one of the men doused the pathetic pile with paraffin before quickly jumping back as a number of lit matches came from the crowd and ignited the impromptu bonfire. Jobe was startled when a voice right next to his ear spoke.

He turned to see that James Sexton had come out of his seat to get a better view, his bushy moustache almost brushing Jobe's ear and his stale tobacco breath almost causing him to retch. "Fear of the cholera," he said, "It's a pity they don't make a bonfire of the landlords who spread bronchitis, tuberculosis and the whooping cough amongst them..."

Jim Larkin pulled him back into his seat before he could finish.

"Will you get your boney backside out of my face, James! Sure, haven't you molested me enough for one day?"

Jobe forced himself away from the window as the coach reached the junction of Byrom and Gt. Crosshall Street. It would do no good for anybody to see him. He had a lot of thinking, planning and healing to do before he made his presence known.

Charlie hadn't forgotten his predicament either. His concern over Jobe's wellbeing coupled with the conversation of the two men he shared the carriage with had provided him with a semblance of escape from the personal problems he faced, but any veneer of normality faded with every yard covered. The worry in his stomach settled into an uncomfortable and constant gnawing, his nerves became stretched as tight as a tourniquet until he felt he might explode, unravel, or both, at any second. He found himself, like Jobe, backing away as far as possible from the window.

Their travelling companions picked up on the obvious discomfort and glanced at each other with raised eyebrows and protruding lower lips. James Sexton shrugged his shoulders and cleared his throat to speak, but before a question emerged, Jim, anticipating the oncoming interrogation, grabbed a lump of thigh between his huge thumb and forefinger and twisted, ignoring James' squeal of pain and indignation.

Content that his colleague had comprehended his none to subtle hint to stay quiet Jim leant forward and drew the curtains on first one window and then the next.

Jobe looked at Jim and sensed the peculiar bond that had grown between them strengthen.

* * *

Silky, as was his custom, flopped into the high backed Chesterfield, the ancient chair wheezing like an old man as air was forced from its litany of rips and tears. Writhing and wriggling he burrowed his backside deep into the cushion until, finally comfortable, he took a small rectangle card from his breast pocket and began to flip it across the flat of his knuckles, from his little finger to his index and then back again. He stopped, gaped at the lettering on the card without reading it, and then stared into a fireplace that contained nothing more than a heap of glowing embers, the roaring logs having long since consumed themselves. For a time the fire had burned bright, matching the raging intensity of Silky's mind but it had become ashes long before the blaze of his thoughts had diminished.

His gaze crossed to the crate that the Giant O' had sat on. The Giant O'! Silky couldn't believe that the real-life, walking, talking bogeyman was actually the giant he'd stood on tiptoes to dip all those years before. It still stung his professional pride that he'd been caught. He'd been careless, disregarding the size of the man. Sure that the swaying of the crowd and the little toff who sat fidgeting on the broad shoulders would camouflage even the most cack-handed attempt at rifling through the pockets of his finely tailored morning coat. Silky unconsciously flexed the hand that had been momentarily crushed in that of the giant.

He'd been sure in that moment on the George's Dock all those years ago that his months long liberation from the misery of the mill was at an end there and then. The shock of the giant flicking a thruppenny bit toward him still hadn't subsided after all these years. And now he'd been hit by another thunderbolt that was even more shocking. The little toff sitting fidgeting on the giant's shoulders was Jobe! Silky shook his head wistfully; I bet that clever little bleeder recognised me from the off.

Images and ideas carouselled around his mind, each one flaring with brilliance before fading to nothing in the blink of an eye, as if imitating the dying embers of the fire. He struggled to contain and control his thoughts in a futile attempt to put an end to his procrastination and formulate a plan. The manifestation of the Giant O', that the Giant O' had actually been in the Den was hard enough to contemplate, but the news that he had imparted; that Jobe was free and somewhere in the city was beyond mind-boggling! Put ashore on Sunday...Put Ashore! So there'd been no escape, no hunting party. The thought of a hunting party slewed his thoughts onto another tangent and he involuntary shivered as the Mill Men added their size twelve's to the legion of boots already marching through the churned up swamp that his mind had become.

For years Silky hadn't passed a waking, or sleeping, hour without at least a fleeting thought of the dreaded Mill Men. Enforcers, employed by the mill owners who, when not pacing the factory floor carrying their 'straight back', two short pieces of rope bound with wax which they brought down with venom on the backs of anyone they found not bent double and at their work, were tasked with hunting and returning those who had the temerity to flee the mill. Following his own escape from the mill deep in the valleys of Lancashire, he had lived in constant fear of a rough hand grabbing his collar and dragging him back to the misery of the mill.

He'd witnessed what happened to those who had escaped and been captured. Compelled to walk to and from the mill, to work in and to sleep in, rusted shackles that rubbed raw to the bone, causing the wearer to leave bloody footprints wherever they went until the passage of time cauterised the skin. A punishment diet of black bread and porridge slops resulted in the returned escapee having to rely on others to share what meagre rations they had or forced them to creep out at night, chains silenced by rags, and steal food from the mill owners' pigs.

The intense fear of being caught, that it was inevitable, was so all consuming that he had been powerless to stop his sister from returning voluntarily to the mill. "I can't live like this Silks. The fear and worry'll put me in the ground before the hunger or cold ever will. It'll only be two years before I can get a paid job or leave altogether and we can be reunited. We'll save and go to America."

Silky hadn't seen his sister since but had still spent every day looking over his shoulder for the Mill Men. He wondered that they hadn't crossed his mind as he'd stood, weighing the cosh in his hand, waiting to repel whoever had the audacity to invade the Den. Even on becoming aware that it was grown men stumbling around in the dark and not a rival gang he hadn't considered the possibility that the Mill Men had come to apprehend him. He had put down his cosh and lit the oil lamp safe in the knowledge that it would be coppers the flickering light would illuminate. Instead it was the Giant O', his green eyes reflecting the wan glow of the lamp.

The image of the Giant O' returned his trail of thought to Jobe. If had been set free, rather than escaped, then what had stopped him from returning to his old stomping ground? Silky couldn't fathom it. If Jobe were free, like the Giant O' claimed, then why hadn't he returned to the Den? To the safety of the gang? Heaven knew they could do with him; they'd sorely missed his influence.

Silky kept the rag-tag bunch together with the promise of a roof over their head and food in their belly, as he had in the past, but the sense of purpose that Jobe imbued within them had withered with his arrest and subsequent sentence. Any sense that they were a force for good within their community had diminished, and with it their sense of self-respect and decency. Silky ensured that their was no return to stealing from their own, especially their old specialty of waylaying unaware dockers, but the gang was always a fluid and transient group and Silky's job in policing them had been made more difficult with the loss of his trusted lieutenants Molloy, who had been sent to the reform ship along with Jobe, and Face, who, always criticical of Jobe's maxim of looking after the community, refused to fully adhere to it and so couldn't rely on an alibi from it when needed. Rather than wait for the magistrate to put him in Kirkdale Gaol with the obligatory striped back, Face had jumped ship to South America.

The Den was also home to those who required refuge but were not officialy part of the gang, local boys who sought sanctuary from the degradations and defencelessness of their youth. Those that found themselves orphaned or cast off, filthy, starving and crawling with vermin that hid rather than join their family as they took the last resort and traipsed up Brownlow Hill to the dreaded workhouse. Then there were those that were escaping the habitual beatings of irate fathers, stepfathers or their mothers' special friends. All were guaranteed somewhere to lay their head. Silky forced nobody to join in what he alluded to as *jobs*. The only rule was that they were from Blackstock Street or the immediate area. The boys were aware, as if from some primeval sense, who should or shouldn't be in the Den and woe betide anybody who attempted to feign membership.

He fumbled the card as one of the gang entered the Den. Recovering it from his lap he looked again at the address and telephone number of Jobe's father, the Giant O', embossed in a flowing, gold Coppergate.

The boy who had startled him made straight for the breadboard and proceeded to saw off a huge chunk from a loaf. He scattered a couple of items on the overflowing table in search of something to spread on it, then shrugging tore at the bread with his teeth. He turned and looked at Silky, his cheeks bulging.

Silky raised an eyebrow quizzically. The boy looked abashed and tried to swallow the chunk of dry bread he was chewing. After finally forcing it down he looked sheepishly at Silky.

"Sorry, Silk' my stomach thinks my throat has been cut! I missed the sausages this morning and I've been right the length and breath of Scotland Road, by God you should have seen the jamboree going on! A docker had brought a monkey up from the docks and he had to barricade himself in the Europa, the women and kids were trying to smash their way in, blaming him and his monkey for spreading the cholera and then..."

Silky raised the card in one hand and pointed to it with the index finger of the other.

"Oh yeah sorry, Silk', no sign of him, not one. I didn't ask anyone, y'know like you told us, I didn't bring any attention to him but nor could I see any sign of him." The boy became uncomfortable as Silky sat frozen in his pose, silently staring at him with his index finger pointing at the still raised card. He looked first at the floor then at the bread in his hand.

Silky remained static.

The boy, unsure of himself, tore another piece from the bread and self-consciously began to chew it. Silky lowered the card and shaking his head, returned to restlessly shuffling it back and forth across his knuckles. "We've no jam left but there should be some butter on the cold shelf," he said absentmindedly.

One by one the human net Silky had cast across the city returned to the Den. Hungry, footsore and with no discernible news of Jobe.

"Each of you get something to eat and then it's back out into the wide yonder until we get some word of Jobe. Remember now keep your ears and eyes open but your mouths shut."

After ushering the last of the boys back out, he took one last look at the card before depositing it in the breast pocket of his waistcoat and after deliberating over which jacket to choose from a hat stand draped in silk, corduroy and leather coats, chose a fur-lined frock-coat, despite the heat, and swinging it around himself like a cape, left the Den.

He knew there was a telephone kiosk on the corner of Hatton Garden and Dale Street but couldn't remember if it was a coin box or whether there would be an attendant to take his tuppence and admit him into the kiosk, he hoped it was the latter as he'd had no previous call to use a telephone.

He strode purposefully towards Vauxhall Road. Decanting those of the lads who were still meandering around Blackstock Street. "Do I need to be dragging you along by the slack of your trousers," he threatened along with a few other choice words. As he approached The Eagle a coach pulled up outside it, its drawn curtains catching his attention. With memories of the Mill Men fresh in his mind he sucked himself into the shadow of the pub doorway watching with baited breath as a heavy man agilely descended the coach steps. Admonishing himself for his skittishness, he was just about to leave the sanctuary of the shadows when something about the way the man checked his immediate vicinity raised his hackles. The man continued to stealthily survey his surroundings and Silky recognised a hunter, or one who was hunted, in his movements. Forcing himself further back into the doorway, he watched as the man leaned into the coach and lifted out a smaller figure that he inadvertently shielded from Silky's view with his sheer bulk.

Another large but smartly dressed man clambered out of the coach, seeming a lot more at ease with himself. The first man moved to shake hands with him offering Silky a glimpse of the smaller of the three. Although most of his face was obscured by a cap Silky couldn't fail to recognise Jobe. He remained in the doorway until the well-dressed man had re-boarded the coach and it had pulled away form the kerb and into the traffic travelling along Vauxhall Road.

Jobe and his companion began to walk in the direction of the Den and toward Silky. The man cast a weary glance at the well-dressed buck in the pub doorway but carried on without a word. The cap Jobe wore and that bulk of the man that partially blocked Silky's view couldn't hide the bruising to his returning friends face and Silky almost choked trying to disguise his sharp intake of breath. He allowed the odd couple to pass into the narrow entry leading to the Den before, anxiously scrutinizing those passing through the street, followed them.

Charlie had placed Jobe into the high backed Chesterfield and they both looked up as Silky entered. Jobe had removed his cap and it hung limply in his hand and Silky could see the grievous wounding to his face, the puffed and yellowing features and the swollen lips that formed a smile.

"Jobe," said Silky as he walked towards him. "You're in my chair!" he exclaimed as if scandalised.

All the disquiet and apprehension that Jobe had experienced passing through his old neighbourhood. The two years of brutality and isolation he had experienced on the Akbar. The near death experience on the road home from Hull. All were exorcised by the familiarity of the face that looked back at him. The dark, intelligent eyes and jet-black hair that clung to the small skull, the wit and mock dramatics in each one of his facial expressions and Jobe broke into a peal of laughter that he was unable to stop. He felt like his lungs were being crushed as the laughter became a maniacal mixture of mirth and misery.

Silky half crouched over the chair and hugged Jobe to his breast.

"I've got so many questions, Silk'. Tommy? Me granda'? The gang..." Jobe sobbed incoherently.

Silky moved his mouth but his attempted interjection was short lived.

Jobe held up his hand, his cap still clutched in it. "Answers, and any questions you may have will have to wait, Silky. There'll be time later but for now we need to do something for Charlie here, his family are in desperate peril. They need our help..."

Silky winced as Jobe struggled to articulate his words. Emotion, exhaustion and swollen lips and tongue made him sound like a man destined for Bedlam. He placed his hands on Jobe's shoulders. "You don't understand, Jobe. I've got news! The Giant O', your father! He was here, right here in the Den not two days ago! He came for you!"

Jobe rolled his shoulders in an attempt to shrug himself free from Silky's grasp. He tried to stand but the effort involved was too much and he slumped back into the Chesterfield and into a state of semi-consciousness.

For once Silky chose not to employ his theatrics and instead, with a nod of his head, brought the iron bedstead set against the far wall of the room to Charlie's attention. Neither man spoke as they carefully lifted Jobe between them and gently laid him on the bed. Once Jobe was comfortable Silky beckoned the older man over to the stove were a battered soot stained kettle sat over a low light.

Silky allowed the silence to stretch as he prepared a pot of tea. The clatter of spoon against enamel the only sound.

Charlie watched Silky surreptitiously, but licked his lips at the promise of tea. He recognised the character from Jobe's asides on the road to Hull and decided there and then that if the lad placed his trust in Silky then he would too. Accepting the mug Silky offered him, and draining half of it in one gulp, he began, after smacking his lips appreciatively, to relay the circumstances of how he first encountered Jobe and the short time he had spent with him. "The wagon was ready to roll see, we were only waiting on the two nags up front to finish their nosebags, when the fixer from Mann Island, heaved this unconscious and bleeding lad onto the floor," he paused, as if inwardly questioning why he'd allowed such a thing to pass. A vertical crease appeared between his eyes as he mulled the issue over, remaining, until content with his conclusion, the indentation smoothed itself and he continued his story. "Well I was the first to remonstrate but on returning to his sandwich board, Ted, that's the fixer's name y'see, well he was accosted by a giant of a man, why it lent credence to Ted's story; that the boy was in trouble. I actually thought we were doing the lad a turn. The big fella buttonholing Ted was so animated, he looked like he was ready to crush the windpipe of the lad laying unconscious at our feet, looked like he could do it with one hand."

Silky's mouth shifted to a circle of shock at the mention of a giant, a man who could only be the Giant O'? Charlie paused, perplexed by the lad's reaction and Silky, inwardly rebuking himself for allowing his surprise to show, motioned for Charlie to continue with a wave of his hand.

"Well we all wondered what on earth the lad had done, him wearing his sailor's Guernsey and slacks an' all. Anyway he remained asleep for the first hour or so of the journey and on waking it was plain to see the lad knew no more of his predicament than we did! The rest of the men took him for simple, but I knew he had more to him see, and I knew for sure he wasn't a Fred, that's what Ted, the fixer, called him, but it wasn't until Jobe's epiphany under the stars that I found out his real name. We'd decided not to spend the night in the boarding house that the rest of them over-nighted in you see," Charlie visibly shivered at the memory of the boarding house, almost slopping the dregs of his tea over the side of the cup. "And it was during the night, while sleeping on the wagon that Jobe came to his senses. We sat under the stars with Bert's snores in the background, Bert's the wagon driver, he must've known about the boarding house from old...well anyway I digress, bad habit of mine, sorry son...that night Jobe told me all about his father's well-to-do family. That them knobs didn't like the fact that his mother, God rest her, was one of us from the courts and they schemed and plotted until his father finally broke, condemning mother and son back to the slums from the luxury of the hills. He told me how his mother worked and strived to keep him fed and attending the college on Shaw Street before the life went out of her. And all about how his grandfather was distraught, and, in his grief, done for his nanna with a jug across the noggin. He told me about you and the family he found amongst all of you here in the Den, how you saved him and then how he found himself aboard the Akbar, separated from the protection of his mate..." Charlie struggled to recapture the name.

"Tommy Molloy," prompted Silky.

"That's the fellow, well Tommy got dragged to the Clarence didn't he, as they both should have, been Catholics and all, but Jobe wasn't fazed, he used that ripe brain of his, planned to use his good English, protestant name as a shield aboard the Akbar only to find it'd been somehow stripped from him. He was locked in a hold, forced to falsely confess that there was no such person as Jobe Warburton, never had been, and he'd always answered to the name Flynn, his mother's maiden name. And so it was that he found himself as Jobe Flynn, a Catholic aboard the Protestant Akbar. He thinks it was done purposefully and that for reasons unknown to him, whoever was responsible for the name change, fancied that the time was right to get him off the ship in order to finish him off good and proper, once and for all. Well that's where it comes full circle y'see, he can remember been put ashore with no ceremony whatsoever, still in his Guernsey and slacks and being so overcome that he ran and ran as if the Devil himself were chasing him, until he come smashing into Ted the fixer and his sandwich board on Mann Island, the next thing he knows he's waking up with a wagon full of navvies on their way to Hull to find work." Charlie stopped talking and made a show of running his dry tongue over his dry lips and teeth, smiling at Silky's offer of a refill. He reflected on his own words as he swilled the tea around his mouth and shook his head as if needing to correct something. "Except we weren't a gang of navvies on our way to find work were we? We were a scuttle of scabs on our way to filch other men's work. We knew it by God, and so did Jobe, the moment we arrived," Charlie paused again, shaking his cannonball of a head. "The lad's got some jewels on him, no denying that, he refused point blank to even travel to the wharf, didn't know if it was picketed or anything, just flat refused to scab, made up his mind to walk back to Liverpool there and then. He put a flea in all of our ears and then he was off." Charlie didn't allude to the fact that he had secreted the only coins he possessed into Jobe's pockets. "I wasn't long in taking his words to heart, don't get me wrong I wasn't happy about scabbing but without Jobe I would have, I'm not proud of it but I know I would have." Charlie put down his cup and rubbed his round face and head with both of his hands, emitting a low rumble from deep in his throat. The head rubbing didn't abate as he approached the end of his tale. "If only I had jewels the size of his I would've left with him, there and then. He wouldn't have met that misfortune on the road. By the time I caught up with him he was almost dead, he'd crossed the path of some striking dockers waiting to bushwhack any scab wagons they could find coming into Hull," Charlie stopped rubbing his head and made a fist of his right hand.

Silky silently marvelled at the scarred boulder that seemed bigger than his own head.

"I only wished they'd have had the good fortune to come across our wagon," Charlie looked past Silky as if he were back on the road into Hull scanning the horizon for militant strikers and Silky wondered who the man regaling him was, as the benign, shapeless face mutated into that of a monster.

Charlie snapped out of his temporary aggression, his face retracting back into that of a benevolent bear. "Well praise be, Jobe had a slice of well overdue luck and he was found by two men, one of them an absolute gentleman by the name of Jim Larkin, apparently he's big in the Union movement," Charlie paused waiting for some recognition from Silky, continuing when it wasn't forthcoming. "Well they fed and watered us, fixed Jobe as good as they could and brought us here," Charlie, finally stuck for words, spread his arms in a final flourish. "And he we are," he said somewhat self-consciously.

Silky had taken in, reflected and digested the information at the same speed the big man had spewed forth the story, and although his rubber face had betrayed all of his surprise, calculation and thought process, he'd remained silent throughout, only moving to refill Charlie's cup. "And what of the peril to you and your family?" he asked.

Charlie scrutinised Silky, reaffirmed his confidence in the strange lad with a nod of agreement to his inner-self. "Jobe's right I'm in a bind alright, although I've not asked him for his, or his friends, help in getting out of it and I certainly never reckoned on finding meself here!" He looked around his surroundings seeming to take them in for the first time. The warm, welcoming and well-furnished room surprised him, more so after remembering that he had entered through what could only be described as a hole in a parlour wall. "Before I left the city I was forced to put my wife and child into hiding," he paused wondering whether to launch into an account of his leaving the city before shaking his head. "It's another long story which Jobe is more than welcome to share with you. Suffice to say I didn't reckon on being back in the city so quick. I had a mind to earn some money before returning and spiriting them away to New York. Events have moved so quickly and in such an opposing direction to those I envisaged that I'm not sure of my next course of action."

Silky took the mug from Charlie's grasp and shook his empty hand vigorously. "I'm grateful for what you've done for Jobe, Charlie. If you're a pal of his then you're a pal of mine. We don't have many outside of our own circle, which is a big enough one, but if Jobe has took it into his mind to help you, then he will. And so will I. For now I suggest you catch up on some sleep and once Jobe wakes we'll sit, the three of us, and plot our next course of action." Silky beckoned Charlie over to the bed Jobe slept in. Take your boots off, make yourself comfortable." He pulled at a shawl draped over the back of a chair and after cracking it like a whip and giving it a few matador like flourishes through the air he lay it on the bed. "And don't worry as soon as Jobe wakes I'll rouse you."

* * *

Silky adjusted his worn brown coveralls. They'd began chafing him before he'd reached the end of Bevington Hill and he regretted his decision not to return to the Den to change them. He'd willingly gone along with Jobe's plan although it had been his own idea to get into character.

"I don't think it'll be necessary Silk'," Jobe had said as he shifted himself up the pillow Silky had insisted on fussing over.

Silky could see that Jobe's face had lost its boyishness and even through the swelling and yellow and purple bruising his features were refined and handsome. "You know me, Jobe, I always work better when I'm in character," he said jumping from his perch on the bed and beginning an exaggerated strut toward Charlie who was standing grasping the bottom of the metal bedstead. On reaching him he proffered his hand. "Charles I believe! Charmed I'm sure," he said, his mocked-up aristocratic drawl extending the vowels of each word. Charlie hesitantly shook Silky's extended hand and looked at Jobe in confusion.

Jobe raised both his hands and shrugged at Charlie for want of an explanation. "But you only need to get up there and put eyes on the house Silk', make sure nothing's amiss and then we can put our plan into place. Get Charlie and his family back together. Set them up somewhere safe until we can get them out of the city."

Silky, absorbed in his own thoughts raised a hand at Jobe and nodded. "Painters coveralls, that'll do it!" he spun around to send someone for his painters coveralls completing a full three hundred and sixty degree turn before remembering he'd kept all of the gang out of the main room since Jobe's return. Mollifying their cries of protest with enough coins so each one could purchase pies and pints. They'd all returned to spend the night on the back room mattresses before being sent out at first light on various errands and jobs, the majority of which entailed resuming their futile search for sight or sound of Jobe. "Painters coveralls, nobody notices a painter. I'll be back in a jif," he said as he skipped around the bed, curtsying to Charlie on his way back past him.

Jobe beckoned him back. "Wait, help me up I need to go into the yard." Silky and Charlie helped Jobe up onto his feet and he stretched to his full height, his vertebrae popping loudly.

Silky stood back from the figure that towered over him, his mouth open in shock. "Bleedin' Hell, Jobe! You're a giant! A regular Giant O' you're going to be," he stopped himself to late. The words had escaped. "Sorry, Jobe," he said bashfully, his coveralls forgotten. "But look, we need to discuss…" Jobe didn't allow him to finish.

"We will, Silk', but this job is our priority for now, as soon as it's over we'll talk."

Now with the coarse material of the coveralls rubbing against the inside of his thigh Silky regretted his choice of painter's coveralls. He was aware the garb of a painter wouldn't afford him the same cloak of invisibility in Kirkdale as it did on Castle Street, but he still enjoyed the chance to enter into a different persona. He'd entered straight into character on donning his costume; offering quotes to a grocer and undertaker to decorate the front of their establishments.

He blatantly ignored the greetings of those who knew him and smiled to themselves or their companions as they mocked. "What is it today Silky? Off to re-touch the Sistine Chapel are we?" Laughing and nudging each other as he strolled by like a stranger frequenting the parish for the first time. Even now when not out picking pockets he had to be alert for any coppers who knew him. The sight of him in workers garb would result in more than just his pockets being turned out. The tug of a copper was a constant danger while out dipping and to remedy it and ensure the copper's searches were never fruitful Silky would situate members of the gang on strategic street corners throughout the business and exchange districts in town, stealthily depositing any ill-gotten gains with them as he passed them by.

He adjusted his coveralls again, winking at a pretty girl in a patterned dress who passed by him as he yanked at his crotch area with both hands. She grimaced in response, spitting on the floor to augment her disgust. Silky shrugged his shoulders. The short walk had caused him no end of grief and he decided there and then that he'd jump on any omnibus that was heading north along Scotland Road toward Stanley or Westminster Road. On seeing a 55 bus he plunged into the traffic and slithered through it, dodging dray wagons and skirting cabs without a turn of his head until with a last confident sidestep he was on the bus.

Ignoring the clicky's remonstrations for him to be seated he scanned the bus and seeing that the only seats available were near the front, too near the horses rear ends for his liking, he climbed the steps to the top deck. The conductor, ticket machine in hand, followed him up the stairs, admonishing him throughout for boarding a moving bus. Silky let the tirade crash over him and passed the conductor a copper as he took a seat at the front where he had a view of every conveyance that navigated the city within a city that was Scotland Road. An unending stream of cabs, buses, carts, wagons, barrows, drays, traps, carriages and gigs maneuvered for position as they delivered, dropped off and deposited. Nimble, businesslike boys scuttled about on all fours, between moving wheels and hooves with their little scoops and brushes, trying to keep the carriageways clear of the steaming mounds of manure that the horses unceremoniously dumped on the road.

The organised chaos of the road was mirrored on the teeming pavements, where business and pleasure jostled one another. Vendors, navvies, clerks, dockers, hawkers, drunks, beggars, shoppers, merchants and meanderers milled around the plethora of chandlers, grocers, pubs, boarding houses, butchers, chemists, workshops and warehouses that lined the road in an unending concertina of discord.

A pale man staggered from the Throstles Nest as the bus slowly trundled past. He didn't pause on the busy pavement but grimly strode purposefully toward St Anthony's Church. On noting the small white coffin the man clutched in his arms Silky removed his emulsion-spattered cap and made a sign of the cross. A group of mourners waited, some of them weeping at the church gates. Silky watched as the women interrupted their sobbing to surreptitiously swig from bottles of stout they had hidden amongst the folds of their black shawls. He replaced his cap as the bus drew past the imposing St Anthony's.

The clicky's cry of 'Rotunda Theatre' pulled him from his melancholic reverie and he looked up at the music hall towering above him. 'The Lily of Killarney' was billed as playing but it was the billboards exclaiming that a new American-Style Bowling Alley had been introduced alongside the billiard tables in the basement that piqued his interest.

The omnibus continued its journey along Stanley road and Silky leapt from it on recognising the road to Kirkdale Gaol. He stuck to the main roads unsure of the short cuts and entries of the area, but knowing his way to the gaol well enough. From there it wouldn't be difficult to locate Rumney Road and follow it onto Ruskin Street. He tried his best to ignore the oppressive presence of the gaol and industrial school as he passed them by and instead focused on the vista across the Mersey and the fresh breeze that blew up from the river. He was enjoying the open pastures until they soon became the usual dense and populated cobbled streets, the newly built two up two downs seeming almost palatial compared to the jumble of humble dwellings he was used to.

For the life of him, Charlie hadn't been able to remember the number of the house. Just that it was next but one to the entrance of the street. Silky didn't have to be a detective to know which house Charlie had concealed his wife and child in. Or that something was amiss. The front door of the house that Charlie had described was hanging off its hinges and Silky watched as anyone who passed by crossed to the other side of the road before doing so. The houses in the immediate vicinity were strangely quiet. Nobody sat on doorsteps while watching their children play and there was no sign of the gossipers such a street usually encouraged. After surveying the empty street for a few minutes and adjusting his coveralls for the last time, Silky quickly crossed from the corner and entered the house. It was impossible to ascertain whether a struggle had taken place, all the rooms were completely bare. Silky reckoned whatever scant furniture there might have been had soon been removed from the unsecured premises. He returned to the battered front door and, leaning on its splintered doorjamb, began to flick a particularly shiny shilling in the air. He hadn't made half a dozen tosses before a woman skulked from a house over the road and sidled up to him. Her long lank hair stuck to her head and as she looked at him her right eye turned savagely in on itself.

"They hadn't been here long, couple of days, queer folk! Didn't answer the door when I came to introduce myself, see if they needed the borrow of anything. And I never seen them go out. Windows covered at all times of the day."

Silky stopped tossing the coin and examined it before repeating the process of nonchalantly flicking and catching.

"Well, I only know what I know, not a clairvoyant am I?" the woman huffed. Silky turned and give the door a gentle nudge with his foot. It proved to be more than it could stand and it clattered to the floor.

The woman jumped backwards, hand on the greasy apron covering her chest. She gave him a look of contempt, her right eye almost burrowing into her head. "Well, what's to say? A group of men came, four or five there was, yesterday dinner. They strode up to the door, didn't bother knocking, wouldn't have got an answer if they had! Just heaved it right from its hinges. In they went and out they came, carrying two women. Well I'd say they was women by their clothing anyway. They had sacking over their head, couldn't see or hear them. The men just troops of with them like they were two pecks of potatoes." The woman finished talking and looked at Silky expectantly.

"Which way did they go?" he asked.

"Well, I couldn't be sure," she stated.

Silky raised his favourite eyebrow in response.

"This is a nice street, new it is! We mind our own here," said the woman turning her gaze to the floor.

Silky was relieved he didn't have to look at her swivelling eye again. "Yesterday dinner?" he asked without looking at her. He sensed her nod of assent and flicked the shilling toward her before setting off toward Kirkdale Station wondering how he was going to break the news to Charlie.

Who, was busy brewing yet another pot of tea.

"How many is that Charlie, it must be approaching a dozen?" asked Jobe looking over the top of one of Silky's newspapers. He'd been reading them all morning in an attempt to grasp at least some of the events that had happened in the city and wider world since he'd been imprisoned on the Akbar.

"Sorry, Jobe lad, you don't think Silky'll mind do you. It's me nerves, I'll certainly replace the tea and milk," he said slowing his stirring and looking guiltily down at the pot.

Jobe couldn't help laughing at his shamefaced, childlike demeanour. "No, it's fine Charlie you can drink until it comes out of your ears, someone'll pinch another box or crate, it's rare we run out of anything."

The explanation worked for Charlie and he placed the lid on the pot, satisfying himself with the dregs in his cup while he waited for the pot to brew. "So what's the S.P. with this place then Jobe, there's enough mattresses in that back room to sleep an army?"

Jobe thought back to his first foray into the Den with Molloy and smiled at the memory of the cluster of miserable and bloodied faces waiting for their sausages. "Silky, started the Den, no-one really knows when or how. He's Molloy's cousin but Tommy told me Silky had been out of the city for years, just disappeared one day. When he turned back up he stayed on his own and didn't let anyone know where." Jobe put his newspaper down and got out of the chair without any trouble, he began taking in his environment as if only just realising he'd come back to the Den following a long time away.

He continued his story as he touched, stroked and picked up various objects. "Turned out he'd found this place, burnt out, dilapidated and hidden from the street by the stables built in front of it. It was a perfect hideout. Silky cleared out a corner and made it his home. He allowed another poor wretch a corner to clear out, then another and another until they were a gang. Silky becoming the leader just occurred naturally."

Charlie listened and watched Jobe move around the room with his boxers eye. He was moving well, just a sight limp on his left caused by a twist or swelling to his right ankle, but Charlie was pleased. The lad was almost recovered. He eyed the empty Chesterfield next to the fire.

"D'you mind if I try that out for size, Jobe lad?" he asked.

Jobe looked from the chair to Charlie and smiled.

"So anyone can just come and go as they please can they?" Charlie asked after he was comfortable, his feet pointed to the fire and one hand balancing the steaming cup on his chest.

"Not anyone, you've got to be from Blackstock or the immediate streets surrounding, or be introduced by somebody who's trusted, like I was."

"But there's no locked doors, we just let ourselves in," stated Charlie.

Jobe turned to look at Charlie as if he'd just invented the telephone. He looked over at the collection of jam jars lining the wall that would be placed on the door handles once it became late, the Den's rudimentary security system. It wouldn't be enough if his fears that somebody was out to get him were right. His mind wondered to the potential culprits. Who could it be? His father? Grandmother? One of their lackeys? There was no point speculating until he could give the problem his full attention. He brought his mind back to the Den and looked over at Charlie sipping his tea and contentedly wiggling his toes in front of the fire. "My God, Charlie, you suit that chair better than Silky does!"

* * *

Charlie sat in the Chesterfield with his obligatory cup of tea but on seeing Silky enter the room, rose and sat on one of the chairs around the table, still clutching the cup in his shovel of a hand.

Silky placed the folded coveralls onto the table but flinching from his still stinging crotch pushed them onto the linoleum-covered floor, nudging them under the table and out of sight with his foot. Making a mental note of where they lay. The inside of his thighs resembled a side of beef and he'd never wear them again, but they'd at least fetch a couple of pawn coppers for one of the women in the street.

"Feel free to sit in my chair, Charlie. I don't think I'll be sitting down for a week, those coveralls have chafed me something chronic," he said pulling at the loose fitting trousers he'd changed into. He turned his attention to Jobe. "I assume from Charlie's serene disposition we've got ourselves a plan?"

"I wish we had time for a plan Silk' but time's of the essence. I've managed to keep Charlie here for just that reason, an hour or so of thought now could mean the difference between success and failure."

Silky was relieved Jobe's reasoning could control the bear of a man, he was certain that nothing else could.

"The good news is that Charlie knows who's taken his wife and nipper," imparted Jobe.

"Well that's something at least, nodded Silky.

"It's the Dead Cormorants," Jobe informed him.

Silky was stunned into silence but then on seeing Charlie's gaze fixed upon him brightened up. "At least we know who we're dealing with."

Charlie explained to Jobe and Silky that as well as setting up and running the book on the majority of bare knuckle boxing fights in the city the Dead Cormorants also ran a number of 'supper clubs'. Jobe and Silky both knew that 'supper club' was nothing more than the cover name for a brothel aimed at attracting a more discerning clientele.

Charlie assured the two that his wife was far too pretty to be a streetwalker and would definitely be ensconced in a supper club. His expression changed from anger and despair to a mooning simpleton as he described his Elizabeth. "Ah she's a looker alright, eyes as bright as the shining moon and a complexion to match."

"Well even better then, it's common enough knowledge who runs their best supper room in town," said Silky. Only receiving blank looks from his fellow plotters he continued. "The Widow Hudson isn't it! Why she hasn't stepped foot outside of The Regal up Lord Nelson Street for over twenty years. All the new girls are brought to her and such is the reputation of the place they only have a bully or two around to keep the peace."

"No need to give a thought to any of their bullies," growled Charlie raising his cannonball of a head from where it rested on the lip of the tin mug he had made his own.

"How old is your daughter, Charlie?" asked Silky.

Charlie sensing Silky's concern answered slowly. "She'll be eleven next birthday," he said. Neither he nor Jobe had mentioned his daughter. At ten years of age there was every possibility she would be utilised as a maid, neither of them had wanted to entertain any alternative.

"We may have a problem,' said Silky rubbing his chin with worry. "It's well known that the Widow runs a scene for those who have a tendency toward violating youngsters or ghouls with a taste for the occult." He paused looking perplexed. "And there's enough rumours that she takes littl'uns in with the aim of flogging them off to the Frogs and Turks," Silky stopped as Jobe muttered something to himself.

"What's that you're saying, Jobe," asked Charlie his confusion and incomprehension returning him to a state of fear.

""The Maiden Tribute of Modern Babylon! Do you remember the story I told the lads just before I got sent to the reform ship, Silks? The night the storm burst the canal bank and flooded Pumpfields?"

Silky looked at Jobe with a blank expression.

"The journalist who bought the young girl from her parents for a fiver," prompted Jobe.

"Oh yeah I remember! The newspaper fella who set up a sting to catch all them toffs up to no good with littl'uns. All them judges and aristo's snared, one of your best that was, Jobe," said Silky animatedly. He enjoyed Jobe's tales as much as the youngest of the boys and looked forward to them being reinstated. His animation or anticipation didn't last as Jobe's meaning struck home.

Jobe was also silent. He'd dramatised the events of his tale introducing the arrest and conviction of judges and MP's to entertain the listening boys, but the original investigative pieces written by, Jobe couldn't remember the newspaper owners name, had been sordid enough to create a moral panic among the ruling classes, forcing a hardcore of MP's, who up until the scandal, had been steadfast in their efforts to block any legislation that raised the age of consent, to vote and implement the Criminal Law Amendment

Act of 1885, raising the age of consent from thirteen to sixteen and making it illegal to procure girls for prostitution by administering drugs, intimidation or fraud.

The point wasn't wasted on Charlie either. He looked at Silky. "My apologies, Silky lad, I told you I wouldn't be asking for your help but happen I'm going to need it."

About The Author

I was Born in Liverpool, England in 1976. The year recently voted Britain's happiest, an indicator of things to come, I've always maintained the uncanny skill of arriving at the party just as everyone else is getting their coats!

I've loved books and reading them for as long as I can remember. As was the way back then I was always staying out in relatives houses whether it be my nans, aunties or uncles. None of them were big readers so after reading my nans dog-eared stack of Mills and Boons for the tenth time I decided to try and write a story of my own.

That path, following a few detours, finally led me to Ruskin College, Oxford where I studied Creative Writing. Through no fault of the tutors, one being the much missed Alistair Wisker a man who found time to encourage those who had not previously received encouragement, writing became like mathematics to me, full of rules and formulae. That and the glorious by-products of student life led me to forgo my studies altogether and following stints working on the railways and in factories, in schools and more recently children's homes I've decided to revisit my love of writing.

With the support of my wife, Natalie and my three kids, Joseph, John and Evie I've managed to turn out another novel. Hopefully it won't be the last and the writing will continue to keep me off the tracks and out of the classroom.

BY THE AUTHOR

The Book of Jobe –
A Tale of Victorian Liverpool

The Book of Jobe II

Dogs and Other Mammals

Printed in Great Britain
by Amazon

36984374R00182